HELL'S
HORIZON

D0202354

HELL'S HORIZON

The City: Book Two

DARREN SHAN

GRAND CENTRAL
PUBLISHING

NEW YORK   BOSTON

This book is a work of fiction. Names, characters, places, and incidents are the product of the author's imagination or are used fictitiously. Any resemblance to actual events, locales, or persons, living or dead, is coincidental.

Copyright © 2000 by Darren Shan

All rights reserved. Except as permitted under the U.S. Copyright Act of 1976, no part of this publication may be reproduced, distributed, or transmitted in any form or by any means, or stored in a database or retrieval system, without the prior written permission of the publisher.

Grand Central Publishing
Hachette Book Group
237 Park Avenue
New York, NY 10017

www.HachetteBookGroup.com

Printed in the United States of America

First U.S. Edition: January 2011
10 9 8 7 6 5 4 3 2 1

First published in Great Britain in 2000 under the name Darren O'Shaughnessy by Millennium, an imprint of Orion Books.

Grand Central Publishing is a division of Hachette Book Group, Inc.
The Grand Central Publishing name and logo is a trademark of Hachette Book Group, Inc.

Library of Congress Cataloging-in-Publication Data

Shan, Darren.
   Hell's horizon / Darren Shan.—1st ed.
      p. cm.—(City trilogy; II)
   ISBN 978-0-446-55173-1
   1. Gangsters—Fiction.   2. Magic realism (Literature)   I. Title.
   PR6119.H35H35   2010
   823'.92—dc22
                                                    2010015233

For:

Bas, Biddy & Liam—my personal chakana

OBE (Order of the Bloody Entrails) to:
Helen Johnstone—the Paucar Wami of publicists

Editors:
Sarah Hodgson—the Ford Tasso of the present
Simon Spanton—the Frank Weld of the past

And all the villacs *of the Christopher Little order*

HELL'S
HORIZON

prologue

"room service"

In Room 812 of the Skylight Hotel a woman lay close to death. She was sprawled facedown across the bed, naked and lacerated. Her back had been cut to fleshy shreds. Dark blood seeped from the wounds, trickled down her sides and gathered in the folds of the crumpled sheets beneath. A spider crept across her face, sensed death and scuttled away to safety.

A maid entered. A thick-limbed, middle-aged woman. She spotted the blood-drenched body instantly. Anyone else would have shrieked and bolted. But death was nothing new to this lady.

Closing the door gently behind her, she moved closer to the body. A dripping knife lay on the floor close by. She was wearing plastic gloves but didn't touch it. Instead she stood over the corpse, gazing down appraisingly.

Kneeling, she pressed two fingers against the victim's neck and checked for a pulse. Nothing. She was about to leave, when...

A slight vibration. She prized an eyelid open. The pupil dilated in the light and when she took her finger away the lid twitched and the woman's mouth moved a painful fraction.

The maid frowned, then picked up the knife and scanned the wounds. She settled on one near the heart. Leaning over, she prized the flesh apart with her fingers, inserted the tip of the blade and wriggled it around in gentle circles, holding the woman down with her other hand, until she felt the body shiver for the final time.

She checked the pulse, the eyes, the lips.

Dead.

The maid dropped the knife, went to the bathroom, rinsed the blood from her gloves, balled them up and pocketed them. She strolled to the door, opened it, mussed up her hair, took a deep breath, then let fly with a scream, bringing staff and guests running.

part one

"she's my girlfriend"

1

Bill reeled in his line and switched hooks. We'd been fishing since Friday and all we had to show for our efforts was an undernourished trout we'd have thrown back any other time.

"Reckon that'll change our luck?" I asked.

"Probably not," Bill sighed, tugging at the collar of his jacket. He wasn't enjoying himself. I was happy to sit and chill, but Bill was a demanding angler and grew impatient when things weren't going his way. "I told you it was the wrong time of year."

"Quit moaning," I retorted. "What else would you be doing? Reading or fiddling with fireworks in your cellar. At least here we can enjoy the fresh air."

"Long way to come for that," Bill grumbled.

"There's the view too," I noted, nodding downstream at the trees and fields. In the distance we could see the hump of the city's skyline, but it didn't distract too much from the beauty of the open countryside.

Bill's expression softened. "Know what we should do? Build a shack and move out. Fish from dusk till dawn."

"Sounds good to me, Huck Finn."

Bill smiled and jiggled his line. "We should do it."

"I'm with you all the way."

He sighed. "But we won't, will we?"

"Nope." He looked so miserable, I had to laugh. "We're city boys. We wouldn't last pissing time living wild."

"Speak for yourself," he snorted, but he knew I was right. Bill thrived on city life. Take him away from the metropolitan buzz and he'd shrivel up and die.

We were silent awhile, thinking about the lure of the simple country life. Then Bill spoiled it all. "How's The Cardinal?"

"You know I don't see much of him," I muttered.

"It's not too late to get out," he said. "There's plenty of security jobs going. A man with your experience could make a—"

"Bill, don't."

He cocked an eyebrow at me. "Conscience pricking you, Al?"

"We've been through this before. I like what I do. I'm not gonna quit."

"What if you're asked to kill a man one day?"

I sighed and stared into the cool night water.

"Maybe you've already been asked," Bill said softly.

I maintained my silence.

"Have you killed for that monster, Al?"

I looked over at him. "You really want to know?"

Bill chewed his lower lip, studied my face and shook his head. "No. Guess I don't."

Bill was a cop. I worked for a gangster. Our friendship eased along nicely so long as we didn't discuss work. He'd only raised the subject now because it had been a long weekend and he was irritable.

I checked my watch. "Monday morning beckons. We'll have to be on our way soon if you want to beat the rush."

"I should have taken the day off like you." Bill sounded regretful. He reeled in his line and began dismantling his rod. Stood and gazed off at the city, then said, "Fog's up."

I squinted and saw banks of thick green fog billowing over the roofs of the city like a dome. The city was famous for its mysterious green fog, which blew up at random and made a mockery of meteorology.

"Great," I groaned. "That adds a couple of hours to our journey."

"Roads are fairly quiet this time," Bill said. "Shouldn't delay us too long. Want me to drive?"

"You drove coming. My turn going back."

"I know, but it's my car—I don't want you wrapping it around a tree. I'll take the wheel if you'd prefer."

I shook my head. "I don't mind."

"In that case, I'll treat myself to another beer."

While Bill was cracking open a can, I began tidying everything away. It didn't take long. I asked if he wanted the trout but he said I could take it. I put it on ice and loaded it along with the gear.

I looked at the distant city again, which had all but disappeared under the fog. A stranger to these parts might have missed it altogether, mistaken it for a shrouded lake.

"Looks like it's down to stay," I noted.

"Yeah," Bill agreed, rolling up a sleeping bag and sticking it in the back of the car. "Could be a bad one."

I hit bed as soon as I got back. Since I'd booked the day off to make a long weekend of it, I left the alarm off and slept in late, a luxury I rarely enjoyed. I woke about twelve and spent the next hour propped up on the pillows, listening to the sounds of the street outside. It wasn't as busy as normal— the fog kept a lot of people inside.

I turned on the radio. A DJ was talking to a woman with piles. She was sick of the attached stigma. She wanted to build a society where people could discuss such matters openly, without fear of embarrassment. The DJ was on her side and invited listeners to call in with their own—as he elegantly put it—*piles files*.

I surfed the airwaves. Found a couple of politicians arguing about the fog. One wanted to know why more wasn't being done to make life easier for the citizens during times of siege. He wanted extra-strong streetlights, emergency buses and trains, home delivery services for the elderly and single mothers.

I didn't stick around for the counterargument. I'd heard it all before. You got these idiots on the radio every time the fog rolled in. If I kept on searching, I'd find a thin-voiced professor of whatever explaining how the fog formed, how long we could expect it to last, what the authorities should be doing to prevent future upsets.

I switched off and went to the bathroom. Drank some water, dug out a good book, switched on my reading lamp and sat down for a couple of hours of glamorous molls and steel-eyed heroes.

Early afternoon, I rang Ellen.

"What's up?" she asked.

"Just checking if tonight's still on." We'd made arrangements to go for dinner together. The Golden Moon—I'd blow most of the week's wages there, but Ellen was worth it.

"Why wouldn't it be?" she snapped.

"You've been busy lately. I thought you might want to beg off."

"I *have* been busy but I'm no slave. I'll make it. Meet you there at nine?"

"Nine," I agreed and she hung up.

I called Nic next. She'd wanted to come on the fishing trip. Got in a huff when I told her it was guys only. I wanted to make things right but there was no answer. I let it ring till her voice mail cut in, then severed the connection—I hate leaving messages.

I took the trout out of the fridge, stared at it and sighed. It seemed a waste of time, going to all the effort of cleaning and cooking a pissant fish like this. But I didn't want to throw it away—I wasn't raised to dump good food. So I set to work.

As I was cutting off its head, I realized there was something in the trout's mouth. Prying its jaws apart, I discovered a black ball. I dug it out, wiped it clean and held it up to the light. It was a pure black marble, with two golden worm-like squiggles down the sides. Puzzled—how had the trout taken the bait when its mouth was stuffed?—I laid it on a shelf over the bread bin and got on with the cooking.

A few hours later, in the smart-casual clothes I kept at the back of my tiny wardrobe for special occasions, I hailed a cab and went to meet Ellen, my recently decreed ex-wife.

The fog had started to clear, sooner than expected, so the cab made good time and I arrived early. I waited for Ellen in the lobby of the Golden Moon, which was a favorite restaurant of ours. The prices had escalated sharply since our courting days, but little else had changed. It was one of the few physical links we had to our happier past.

Ellen arrived promptly at nine, looking her elegant best. She kissed my cheeks and gave me a hug. The eyes of the other men in the lobby were tinged with green. That was the great thing about dining with her in places like this—I might be shabby as a sheep in the run-up to shearing, but I still had the most beautiful woman in the city clinging to my arm.

"You could have worn a suit," she said critically as she let go of me.

"If I wore a suit, next thing I'd have to start shaving regularly, washing daily and changing my underwear once a week."

"Horror of horrors." She smiled, straightening my tie. "Did *I* buy you that shirt?"

"Probably." It was a dark purple satin number. Of course she'd bought it—I despised the damn thing and wouldn't have worn it otherwise.

"Suits you," she murmured, then we headed up. A curt waiter directed us to our table. We ordered before sitting, without looking at the menu. In the old days there'd have been two or three bottles of wine to accompany the meal, but tonight we shared a bottle of mineral water instead.

"Any luck with the fishing?" she asked.

"Don't ask," I groaned.

We discussed work—mostly Ellen's, since she never enjoyed hearing about the Troops—and old friends. Not a word about my alcoholic past or all the times I'd let her down. Ellen wasn't bitter or vindictive that way.

It was my fault the marriage didn't work. I was an asshole. Got too involved with work. Spent endless nights out drinking with the boys. Slept around. Treated Ellen like a cheap accessory. She didn't need that shit. She was a beautiful, intelligent, career-minded woman who could have had her pick of men. She chose me when I was young and passionate, prepared to listen to what she was saying and be there for her. When I hit the bottle and acted like a prick, she dumped me, the way any sane woman would.

The food arrived and we tucked in. We'd always shared a healthy appetite, so neither of us said much till the plates had been cleared.

I glanced around the restaurant, noting how few of my own race were present. The city opens its doors to people of all colors and creeds, but if you don't think there's a wide dividing line between whites and blacks, you're living in a dream world. In the Golden Moon—a place of money and style—I stood out like a drag queen in a church choir.

"What's the special occasion?" Ellen asked, burping lightly.

"Nothing. Just fancied a night out with the woman of my dreams."

"Don't bullshit me, Jeery," she snorted. "I know how that mind of yours works—you don't do nothing without a reason." The double negative was an old joke between us. "Last time you invited me out on a date was the day our divorce went through. Need money? Representation?" She worked for a law firm, one of the best in the city.

"You know I wouldn't come to you for that," I said, upset that she'd think such a thing.

"I was joking," she said, covering my big black knuckles with her small white fingers. "Don't go getting precious on me, Al."

I smiled, turned my hands around and tickled her palms the way she liked. "Know what day it is?"

"Monday."

"Six months since the divorce was finalized."

She frowned and calculated. "That was a Friday, wasn't it?"

"Yeah, but the date's the same."

She shrugged. "If you say so. That makes this…what…a semi-anniversary?"

"Yeah. I tried not to dwell on it, but the date got stuck in my mind and I felt we should commemorate it."

"You're a strange guy, Jeery."

"Only figured that out now?"

"This isn't a ploy to win your way back into my good books, is it?" she asked suspiciously.

"You mean get you drunk, harp on about the good old days and hope it leads to your place and a roll in the hay?" She nodded. "Absolutely." I raised my glass of mineral water and clinked it against hers. "Drink up—a couple more of these and we'll be flying."

"To flying," she smirked.

We lingered over dessert, reviewing the past six months. We'd been separated nearly two years by the time of the divorce, so it wasn't as if we were raw from the rift. I'd straightened myself out and Ellen had forgiven me long before one of her colleagues drew the final legal line between us.

"Find a woman yet?" Ellen asked as the meal drew to a close.

"No one could replace you," I said, giving her the doe-eyed treatment. She tossed her napkin at me.

"Seriously."

I thought of Nic and smiled. "I've been getting some action. Nothing meaningful. You?"

She sighed. "The only men who chase me these days are married, middle-aged lawyers who think I'm easy because I'm a divorcée. It's becoming a struggle just to get laid."

The waiter brought the bill and I settled up, trying not to stare at the figure at the bottom. Ellen offered to go halves but I waved her money away. I hadn't treated her much the last few years of our marriage. I owed her a meal or two.

"Where are you off to now?" she asked.

"Back to the apartment."

"Ali still working downstairs?" I nodded. "Tell him I'll be by one of these days for a bagel." As newlyweds we'd lived in the apartment block that I'd returned to following the dissolution of our marriage. We'd shared some good times there, poor as we'd been.

"I'll pay for the cab," Ellen said as one pulled up in answer to her hail.

"That's OK," I told her. "I'm walking."

"You sure? The fog's still pretty strong in places. You might get mowed down."

"I'll take my chances." I kissed her cheeks. "See you, Ellen."

"Soon," she said. "You don't need to wait for special occasions to call. Get it?"

"Got it."

"Good."

We smiled, then parted. I watched the cab disappear into the fog, then went for a walk. Back home I collected the marble from the kitchen and took it to bed. I studied it for ages, running my fingers along the streaks of gold. I fell asleep with it in the palm of my left hand, but when I woke in the morning it was gone, and although I searched all over, I couldn't find it anywhere. It seemed as if it had been lost to the shades of the night.

2

Tuesday morning. Back to work.

I cycled to Shankar's for breakfast. One of the perks of working for The Cardinal—free meals at Shankar's. I wasn't a regular—most mornings I grabbed a bagel from Ali or a sandwich at work—but I liked to pop by a few times a week.

I parked out back. My bike was my only means of transport. I cycled everywhere, unless on a job with the Troops. I started using it when I got busted for drunk driving some years ago. Enjoyed it so much, I stuck with it even when I got my license back.

Shankar's was a huge, open-plan, two-story structure (the upper floor was made out of glass) but barrenly decorated. Leonora Shankar was a famed minimalist.

I spotted a flock of Troops gathered by a table near the door and slotted in. Jerry and Mike were the only ones from my shift but I knew the rest of them. Most members of The Cardinal's personal army got to know each other over the years. There weren't that many of us, and we were all bound to the city, so we were a close-knit group.

"Back from vacation," Jerry noted, welcoming me with a raise of his mug. That led to questions about where I'd been, and I spent a pleasant quarter of an hour describing my fishing trip.

"Wish I could get up there," a sad-eyed guy called Oisin remarked.

"I've been working weekends since New Year's. Going up midweek ain't the same."

"Switch shifts," somebody told him.

"No point. The wife works weekends too. If I took a weekend off without her, she'd think I was doing the dirty."

"Women don't understand fishing," Mike agreed. "I went when I was younger. Every time I came back, my girl went through my stuff, looking for evidence. Got sick of it in the end, gave up the fishing. Should have given up her."

We all muttered and spent a few silent seconds reflecting on the ways of women. My coffee and toast arrived and I tucked in. I always started the day on a light meal.

"Anything happen while I was away?" I asked.

"A couple of new boys started," Jerry informed me. "Been showing them the ropes."

"Tasso and Weld are at it again," Mike added. Ford Tasso was The Cardinal's right-hand man. Used to be commanding officer of the Troops. Frank Weld replaced him several years ago but Tasso continued to think of the Troops as "his men" and was constantly criticizing Frank's handling of them. I had sympathy for Frank but I liked Tasso and had to admit that life had been more interesting when he was head honcho.

"What's it this time?" I asked.

"Some broad was killed in the Skylight last Friday," Jerry told me. "Wasn't authorized. The Cardinal's furious. He chewed out Tasso, and Tasso chewed out Frank. The two have been screaming at each other all weekend. Tasso's saying nobody would have gotten past the Troops when *he* was in charge. Frank's going on again about the security arrangements at the Skylight."

Frank had been looking to upgrade security at the Skylight since he took over from Tasso. It was one of The Cardinal's key establishments, where many of his staff and clients stayed when in town. But unlike Party Central—which was pretty much impregnable—it was poorly guarded. The Cardinal liked it that way—it made his guests feel more relaxed—but Frank, who took the flak whenever anything went wrong, hated the setup.

"Guess he'll be bitching at us all week," I sighed.

"We've already had a day of it," Jerry said. "Yesterday will go down as one of the biggest pain-in-the-ass Mondays in history. You were lucky you missed it."

"Yeah," Mike said, checking his watch and drinking up, "but it'll be even worse if we're late today. Slightest excuse, he'll be on our case. Let's split."

"But we've half an hour yet," I protested.

"You think Frank will give a shit?" Mike replied. "I was ten minutes early yesterday and almost got my marching orders."

"Great to be back," I grumbled, finished my coffee and grabbed the last slice of toast. "OK if I stick my bike in the back of the van and come with you guys?"

Jerry's got a soft spot for his van and normally vetoes such requests. But he took pity on me this once and helped me load it in, making sure I didn't scratch the paint.

Frank spotted us entering and made a production of checking the clock in the downstairs locker room of Party Central. We were a good eighteen minutes ahead of schedule.

"Come in this time again," he growled, "and it'll be to pick up your personals."

While Frank stormed out to berate latecomers, we got into uniform. Dark blue pants and jacket, light blue shirt (a similarly shaded sweater for cooler seasons). Green-blue beret. Black shin-length boots. No tie, thank God. I had three uniforms, which I kept spotlessly clean. Ford Tasso hadn't paid much attention but Frank was big on presentation. Rightfully so. It was different in the old days, when the Troops were an illegal band of thugs. The Cardinal had grown in stature and we were a city-approved force now, with all the trappings of respectability. We even got the occasional tourist stopping by Party Central to check us out. We worked for a gangster, sure, but we were one of the public faces of his organization, and as such we had to present a smart, professional front.

Jerry studied the shine of his boots, shook his head and started working up a mouthful of spit. Mine were OK so I headed up a flight of stairs to one of the building's many conference rooms, where my duties for the day would be posted.

The room was half-full of soldiers, some coming on watch like me, some going off, some on their break. I found my name on the bulletin board and scanned to the right. Front door till lunch, yard patrol in the afternoon. That meant a rifle. Damn. I hated any weapon that required more than a single hand to operate.

I signed for the Kalashnikov—a throwback to Tasso's time—and a pretty young girl called Anra handed it over.

"Missed you yesterday," she said.

"Vacation," I explained.

"Anywhere exciting?"

"Upriver. Fishing."

"You on for some overtime this week?" she asked.

"Sure."

"What suits you?"

"Tonight and tomorrow. I'll see after that."

Overtime was never a problem in the Troops. I'd been putting in a lot of extra hours the last year or so. Nothing better to do with my time. Besides, keeping busy made it easier to stay off the bottle. Back when Ellen and I split, I hit it hard. Almost got drummed out of the Troops. Sunk about as low as you can get without going under, before Bill pulled me out of the slump.

I spent the early part of the day out front of Party Central with nine other Troops and a couple of red-suited doormen. We were the first line of defense. We looked pretty lifeless to the hordes of people passing in and out, as if we were only there for show, but we were on constant alert, observing all who entered, ready to open fire at the first sniff of a threat. We weren't on the lookout for weapons—the X-ray machines would pinpoint those—but telltale facial expressions and tics. Our job was to spot people who didn't belong.

Each of us had spent years studying the art of body language. You didn't simply join the Troops and go on watch at Party Central. There was a six-month induction period, followed by five years in various branches and posts. Only then, if deemed worthy, were you introduced to the Party Central setup. A couple of months patroling the middle floors of the building, where you couldn't do too much harm, then a gradual drift toward ground level. Several months pounding the beat in the rear yard, eventually moving out to guard the fences, and finally the front of the building and the lobby, where only the best were placed.

An unofficial extra requirement for front-line Troops was that they'd drawn blood during their tenure. All of the ten guards on duty had killed at least once in the name of The Cardinal.

I'd killed three times. The first was a butcher, after a mere eleven months in the service. He hadn't been scheduled for execution. I'd gone around to his shop with a couple of more experienced Troops to squeeze protection money out of him. He was a stubborn, foolish old man. Lost his head. Let swing with a thigh-length blade. My colleagues ducked. That left me with a clear shot. I drew, took aim and—as he raised the knife high and roared like a bull—put four bullets through the center of his forehead, neat as you please.

It was a month before they let me back into uniform. A month of psychiatric analysis. I didn't think that was necessary—as I kept telling them, I didn't enjoy killing but wasn't afraid of it—but this was back when The Cardinal was fighting to have the Troops legalized. We were in the public eye, a topic of hot debate, and a lot of people claimed we were no better than hired assassins. Tasso and his administrators had to play things cautiously. Hence the kid-glove treatment.

It was four years until I killed again, in a free-for-all shoot-'em-up with Russian mafia muscling in on The Cardinal's territory. A hundred of us against thirty Ivans. The fighting raged through an apartment block they'd annexed. I was part of the third phalanx of Troops sent in. Ran up against a teenager in a dark, smoky hallway. He had a sock filled with coins and stones. I had a dagger that could have slit a bear's chest open.

I started at Party Central a couple of weeks after that.

The third was three years ago. A crooked cop. It was the first time I'd been specifically sent to kill. I broke into his home while he was out. Gagged and tied up his wife and kid. Stood behind his bedroom door when I heard him entering downstairs. When he came in, I stepped out and put the lips of my gun to the back of his head.

Boom.

I nearly quit the Troops after that. It wasn't the killing that got to me, but his status. He could just as easily have been a straight cop. Could have been *Bill*. You don't make choices when you're in the Troops—you go where told, shoot when ordered. I'd always known I might one day cross swords with Bill, but I only seriously contemplated the possibility after my run-in with the cop.

I came close to packing it in. Life would have been so different if I had. I might have patched things up with Ellen. I won't say the job's what came between us, but it didn't help. If I'd found legitimate employment and spent more time working on my marriage than polishing my guns…

But past is past. No changing it. I dithered, drank, broke up with Ellen, drank some more. Bill finally weaned me off the bottle in his own inimitable way—he dragged me out of my apartment one drunken night and stuck a gun in my mouth. Told me his father drank himself to death. Said he wouldn't let it happen to me. He'd rather kill me himself. Quicker that way. I stared into his eyes, found not even the ghost of a bluff, and went cold turkey the next day.

I had a long talk with Tasso once I sobered up. Told him I was thinking of quitting. Spilled my fears. He listened silently. Doubtless he'd heard it all before. When I finished, he shrugged his impossibly broad shoulders and sighed.

"What do you want me to say? Promise not to send you out to kill one of your friends? I can't. Killing's what you've been trained for. It took a long time to make a Troop of you, Algiers. If you want out, fine, you're out. But if you stay, you carry on the same as before. You don't get to choose your targets. You kill who you're told, and if you don't, you'll be killed too."

Tasso always served it to you straight.

I thought it over, weighed up the options and decided I was better off here than anywhere else. At least in the Troops I knew the score. So I carried on as normal and prayed I'd never have to go face-to-face with Bill or any of my friends.

I spent lunch in an underground canteen watching sports on the TV. One of those world-sports programs, cutting from surf trials to beach buggies to cliff-diving. It was on most days around this time and was the only kind of regular show on my itinerary—I didn't have a TV at home.

Frank turned up toward the end of my break. Three-quarters of the people present sprang to their feet and started back to their posts, but he waved a hand at them and smiled ruefully. "It's OK. I'm back to normal. No need to rush off."

There were some cheers and everybody sat down again. That was the good thing about Frank—his moods passed quickly.

"Have a good weekend, Al?" he asked, taking the seat beside me.

"So-so."

"How's Bill?"

"Fine."

Lots of people knew Bill. He ran a lucrative sideline in fireworks and had staged many private displays for friends and associates of The Cardinal's. Bill was honest but realistic. If you were a cop in this city you could be straight but not antagonistic. It didn't pay to get on the wrong side of The Cardinal.

"Hear about the stairs?" Frank asked.

"What about them?"

"We're to keep off them, nights, till further notice."

"How come?"

Frank shrugged. "Orders from above. No patrols. No guards on the doors." He wasn't happy. "You use the stairs a lot, don't you?"

"Yeah. Keeps me in shape."

He glanced about to make sure no one was listening. "You working overtime this week?"

"Three or four nights, most likely."

"Mind if I assign you to the upper floors?"

I smiled. "I go where I'm told."

"Good. And, y'know, I might send word a few times a night that I need to see you down below, and, when you're coming—"

"—I'll take the stairs?"

"Right," he grinned. "Unofficially, of course. Just taking the opportunity to grab a spot of exercise." He stood, checked the TV—two bare-chested giants were using their teeth and lengths of rope to haul trucks in a race against each other—and shook his head. "Don't like leaving the stairs unguarded. The orders come from The Cardinal, but try reminding him of that if something goes wrong…"

Still shaking his head and muttering, he clapped me on the back and went about his rounds.

Cloak-and-dagger stuff like that was par for the course in Party Central. The Cardinal moved in mysterious ways. You often saw men and women of power roaming the corridors of Party Central, pulling their hair out by the roots. The braver ones—like Tasso and Frank—took matters into their own hands and plotted behind The Cardinal's back, doing their best to protect him from his crazy flights of whimsy. It was fine if he didn't find out, but if he did…

I wasn't looking forward to taking the upper-floors watch—not much happened up there at night—but it always paid to do a man like Frank Weld a favor. You never knew when you might need one in return.

I spent the afternoon in the massive rear yard of Party Central. This was my favorite spot. Business was brisk, as a result of which time—the foe of body-guards worldwide—flew by. Cars had to be checked and rechecked. The fence had to be probed hourly for weak points. Delivery teams, chauffeurs, executives—all were subjected to our scrutiny and tracked into the building if they looked in the least suspicious. The yard could have been Party Central's Achilles' heel if not properly policed. As it was, you had a better chance of blasting your way through the front than squeezing in by the back.

At the end of an uneventful shift I ducked out to grab a pizza. Shared it with a couple of guys in the canteen when I got back. Jerry was among them.

"Frank get onto you about the stairs?" he asked as we ate.

"Yeah."

Jerry made a face. "I hate the espionage shit. If The Cardinal says leave the stairs alone, we should leave 'em the hell alone. For all we know, he plans on running a team of cannibal ninja bastards up and down them all night long."

Cannibal ninja bastards. I had to smile. "You could have said no."

"To Frank?" Jerry snorted. "I also could have said, 'Here's my ass—ram a stick of dynamite up there and blow me to fuck.' It was different with Tasso—he didn't sulk if you turned him down. But Frank..."

I nodded. Frank did tend to take things personally.

"Wanna go out later?" Jerry asked. "I'm meeting a coupla guys in a club."

"I'll pass," I told him. "It's been a long day."

Pizza finished, we took the elevator up, Jerry to the sixteenth, me a couple of stories higher. Offices were few and far between up here. Most petered out at the fourteenth. The Cardinal occupied the fifteenth. Beyond that sprawled the legendary floors of files—room after room packed with newspapers, reports, data sheets, populace surveys, birth and death certificates, volumes of city history, housing plans, income tax returns. The myth ran that The Cardinal had a detailed dossier on every one of the city's millions. That couldn't be true, of course, but he probably had something on the majority of them.

I made the rounds of the mainly deserted rooms, breaking off two or three times an hour to meander down the stairs and back up again. I ran into other similarly deployed Troops a couple of times but we never acknowledged one another's presence.

I was on my way up from the third floor at about half past nine when Frank came storming down, his face a furious twist of lines.

"Jeery!" he snapped. "What are you doing on these stairs? Haven't you heard they're off-limits?"

I paused, wondering if he was joking or testing me. "You want me off the stairs?" I asked cautiously.

"Of course I want you off the fucking—," he started to roar, then caught himself and forced the bleakest of grins. "I know what I said earlier, but those orders are canceled, OK?"

"OK."

Frank studied my face, daring me to question him. When I didn't, he relaxed slightly and drew a long, disparaging breath. "Know what the crazy bastard's done now? Ripped three-quarters of the guard out of the yard. Told me it was an exercise."

"What do you reckon he's up to?" I asked.

"Fucked if I know," Frank replied. "Seems like he's clearing the way for an invasion. There's a gap out back that you could drive a fleet of tanks through. But what do *I* know? *I'm* just the head of this goddamn army. *I'm* a nobody."

He fumed for a few seconds, then grimaced. "Anyway, with this other shit going on, we may as well forget about the stairs. Let the lunatic have his way. Finish your shift, then do whatever the hell you want the rest of the week."

"Fair enough."

"And pass on the word, would you?"

"You're the boss, Frank."

"Ha!"

I saw the shift out, then took an elevator down to the basement and made for my locker. It had been a long night and I was looking forward to changing clothes and getting home. When I opened the door, something rolled out of the bottom and spun away down the floor. I thought it was a coin and I wasn't going to bother with it, but then I noticed the dark sheen of the rolling object and hurried after it. I stopped it with my foot, then picked it up and studied it with incredulous suspicion.

It was the small black marble I'd found in the trout's mouth and then lost. Only now the golden squiggles down its sides no longer reminded me of worms. They'd been broadened and touched up. Now they looked like *snakes.*

3

The marble bugged the hell out of me and I slept fitfully. By morning I knew I must have had it on me all along, and was only imagining the change in the squiggles, but part of me wasn't convinced. I laid it on a wad of cotton wool on the mantelpiece in my living room and kept a close eye on it for the next day or two, but when nothing further happened I forgot about it and concentrated on work.

Wednesday was another busy day. I didn't get home till two in the morning. Spent the last four hours covering for a sick colleague on the fifteenth floor, one of seven Troops guarding the elevator doors. A further ten soldiers would usually be on each of the three stairway openings, and more patrolling the corridors, but due to The Cardinal's recent instructions the floor was largely deserted.

It could be difficult staying alert in such conditions. The warm air, the peaceful corridors, the mostly inert elevator, the carpets tickling the soles of my feet. Party Central was layered with thick, expensive carpets from the second floor up. No shoes were allowed. Had to check them in downstairs, even if you were only running a quick errand. Most of the carpets were more comfortable than an average mattress. The temptation to lie down and snooze was overwhelming.

But I was paid to ignore such temptations, so I focused on the doors of the elevator, didn't let my mind wander, and kept my hand close to the butt of my gun. In the unlikely event that we ever came under attack, I'd be ready.

I meant to call Nic—I still hadn't spoken with her since I got back—but didn't get a chance. It was too late when I got home so I simply undressed and crawled into bed, same as the night before.

Thursday, the shit hit the fan.

I'd clocked on an hour before midday and was changing into my uniform in the basement when Vincent Carell stormed in. Vincent was one of Tasso's men. Thin, face like a ferret, not blessed in the brains department, quick to draw his dick and his gun. I never knew why Tasso placed so much faith in him.

A guy called Richey Harney was by my side, slipping off his boots. "Richey!" Vincent barked. "With me."

Richey glanced up, pained. "I was on my way home."

"*Was*," Vincent snickered.

"But Frank said I could leave early. He—"

"I don't give a fuck what Frank said!"

"It's my daughter's birthday," Richey moaned. "I missed her First Communion last month. If I miss this, my wife'll kill me."

"Do I look like I give a fuck?" Vincent snapped.

Richey lowered his head and muttered something, then started lacing up his boots again. Sap that I was, I took pity on him.

"Could you use me instead? I just arrived—I'm fresher than Richey."

Vincent rolled his eyes, then nodded. "Sure. One asshole's the same as another. Meet me out back three minutes from now."

"Thanks, man," Richey said softly as Vincent left.

"No problem. You'd do the same for me, right?"

"Sure." Richey laughed lamely.

Vincent had calmed down by the time I reported for duty. He tapped the dashboard of a glistening ambulance. "I love these," he said as I got in, then jammed his foot down. The Troops on the gate only just got it open in time. Their curses trailed us out of Party Central.

"Where are we headed?" I asked, raising my voice to be heard over the blaring sirens Vincent had activated.

"The Fridge," Vincent replied, taking a corner like a Keystone Kop. He always drove like this when Tasso wasn't around.

"Dropping someone off?"

"Picking someone up."

The Fridge was a privately owned morgue, sometimes referred to by brave—but foolish and short-lived—reporters as the Elephant's Graveyard of the city. It was where The Cardinal's employees took undesirable corpses, bodies they didn't want washing up, victims they wished to keep on ice. Sometimes his own men were stuck away there too, if they'd died in suspicious circumstances and required an autopsy. Apparently the best pathologists in the country plied their trade behind the camouflaged walls of the Fridge.

"What's the deal?" I asked.

Vincent swerved to avoid a necking couple who weren't paying attention to the road, pounded on the horn, gave them the finger, then looked at me and grinned. "You heard about the girl who got sliced at the Skylight?"

I recalled my conversation with Jerry and Mike. "Yeah."

"Nobody knows anything about her. She checked in under a pseudonym. Might have been a hooker but wasn't a regular. We brought her out here to let the experts at her. They haven't gotten around to her yet—there's always a backlog at the Fridge. She wasn't supposed to be a priority but now she is—word leaked and we've gotta take her back."

"Back?"

"To the Skylight. A cop phoned Tasso. Said someone told him what happened. We have till midnight to return her and report her murder or he sweeps in with his men. If she ain't there, he'll go to the press."

"So? Kill the cop, can the story. That's SOP, isn't it?"

"Yeah," Vincent said. "But it's simpler to let the cops have her now that they know about her."

"Won't the state pathologist figure out how long she's been dead?"

"That asshole drives a BMW," Vincent said with a wink. "Gets a new model every year on his birthday. Gratis. He sees what we tell him to see."

The Fridge looked innocuous from the outside. Set close to the docks, it was a huge dilapidated building, broken glass in the windows, a couple of lights shining to deter tramps, graffiti scrawled by design across the lower walls. We parked down a side alley and let ourselves in. A short stroll down a corridor, through a splintered door, and suddenly we were face-to-face with a vast, whitewashed, stone monstrosity.

The entire interior of the old building had been hollowed out and this enormous box had been constructed inside. Or else they'd built this first, then placed the frame of the older structure around it. I never did think to ask.

Vincent made his way to one of the entrances and tapped in the security code. The door hissed open and a cold blast of air swirled around us. Vincent shivered. "Should have brought my long johns," he grumbled.

We entered.

This section of the Fridge contained nothing but coffin cubicles. Cold, metal containers, inside which, on ice-cold slabs, rested the dead. They stood in rows of a hundred, five cubicles high, twenty long. There were six floors of scaffolding above this first level, all stacked similarly, staircases and catwalks running around them.

Most of the nearby containers were occupied, their doors tagged and hung with accompanying files. Alongside the usual statistics—gender, height, weight, address, next of kin—were details of how they died, when they were admitted and by whom, and what was to be done with the body. Very little of the information was censored since none but The Cardinal's own was ever admitted.

Vincent located an internal communicator and pressed a button.

"Dr. Sines will be with you presently, Mr. Carell," a woman informed him before he had a chance to speak. "Please remain where you are. Refreshments will be provided if requested."

Vincent looked at me and grinned. "Hungry, Algiers?"

"I couldn't eat in here if I was starving."

"Chickenshit," Vincent laughed, but he ordered nothing either.

I climbed up a couple of flights and went walkabout while we were waiting, checking the roll call of the dead, examining their testimonies. Men, women, children, cops, gangsters, priests—all were represented. Vincent joined me after a couple of impatient minutes and we padded along quietly, one after the other. It was supposed to be good luck to find the final resting place of someone you knew.

"This is where we'll wind up," Vincent said quietly. "A couple of coins over our eyes, jellylike blood, blue skin and a slab for a bed."

"I'd rather burn than freeze in here," I said.

"That's what hell's for, Algiers."

We moved up another flight and I finally stumbled upon a name I recognized.

"I remember this guy," I said. "I was there when we took him out."

"Theo Boratto." Vincent frowned. "That was the night we picked up Raimi."

"Who?"

"Capac Raimi. The guy we let walk."

I thought back. I'd been part of a support platoon sent to eliminate Boratto and his cohorts. Tasso had lined us up beforehand and described a young man who would be with Boratto. He wasn't to be harmed. If necessary, we were to sacrifice our own lives before jeopardizing his. No reason was given.

"He's working for The Cardinal now, isn't he?" I asked, recalling scraps of gossip I'd picked up in Shankar's.

"Sure as shit is," Vincent growled. "The Cardinal's pet monkey."

A tall man in a white uniform appeared beneath us and called up, "Mr. Carell?"

"Yeah?" Vincent replied, leaning over the bar.

"I'm Dr. Sines. You're here to pick up Miss Skylight?"

"Got it in one, Doc."

Sines didn't say much as he led the way through the arteries of the Fridge. Five minutes later we entered a large, spotlessly white operating room. Stiff corpses hung from the walls by steel hooks, entrails tumbling down their fronts. I'd been startled the first time I saw them. Thought they were real. It was only when I noticed the pathologist laughing that I realized they were fakes. Lab humor—go figure.

Other doctors and assistants circled the room, ignoring us, up to their elbows in blood and gore.

Our *cargo* was lying facedown on a slab, naked, whitish-blue.

"I've taken her prints, measurements, photographs," Dr. Sines said.

"Had to work quickly. Been examining her back while I was waiting. A clumsy piece of work."

The back in question had been carved to pieces. Long slashes, deep gouges, thin red cuts and violent purple punctures. An uneven circle had been etched between her shoulder blades, several straight lines radiating from it at tangents.

"What's that?" I asked.

"Maybe a sun symbol," the doctor replied.

"I didn't notice that when I brought her in," Vincent said.

"There was a lot more blood then. We've cleaned her up. Amazing what comes out in the wash." He smiled briefly but Vincent and I remained stony-faced. "How do you want her?"

"What do you mean?" Vincent asked.

"You want us to leave her like she is or should we bloody her up again, make it look like she's just been killed? She's to be returned to the scene of the crime as I understand things."

"Yeah." Vincent scratched his nose uncertainly. "Fuck it, I got my suit bloody bringing her here—no point ruining it again dragging her back. We'll take her clean."

"Shouldn't we get a bag or something?" I asked.

"Doc?" Vincent sniffed.

"I think some form of wrapping would be appropriate."

"Then step to it, man! We're working to a tight schedule." Vincent smiled at me as the doctor bristled and clicked his fingers at one of his assistants. "Pays to keep them on their toes," he whispered.

"I wouldn't pester them," I whispered back. "Never know how they might take it out on you if you turn up here dead."

Vincent shrugged. "Like it matters a fuck at that stage. C'mon—let's turn her, so we're ready to tip her in. You wanna take the left or right side?"

"I don't care."

"Then I'll take the right—don't want to be the first to hear her heart if it starts beating again." He laughed ghoulishly and grabbed her arm as the assistant arrived with the bag. I took the other arm. It was cold. Stiff. Clammy. "Ready?" he asked and I nodded. "One. Two. *Three*."

We flipped her onto her back. Vincent tugged her toward the edge of the slab. I started pushing but then my gaze fell on her face and I froze.

"At least look like you're trying," Vincent huffed. "Don't leave me to do it all by my—"

He caught sight of my face and stopped.

"Christ, Algiers, you look worse than the corpse. What's up?"

I shook my head numbly.

Vincent leaned over and slapped me. "Algiers! Snap out of it. Focus on my lips. What's. Wrong?" He spoke slowly, as if to a dim-witted child.

"The girl," I managed to sigh.

"Like you've never seen a corpse before. It ain't like you know her or anything." He started to laugh, then stopped, his eyes narrowing. "Or do you?"

I nodded wordlessly.

"Shit." He licked his lips. "Who is she?"

"Nuh-Nuh-Nuh-Nuh," I stuttered.

"You wanna sit down? Doc, you got a chair?"

"I might be able to rustle one up," came the dry reply.

"No. Don't need one," I gasped. "I'll be OK."

"You're sure?"

"Yeah."

"So who is she?"

"She's…"

"Here we go again. Take a deep breath, Algiers. Concentrate."

I looked him in the eye and said it. "Her name's Nic Hornyak." A moment's silent beat and I added the kicker. "She's my girlfriend."

4

Firrst things first—we had to take Nic's body back to the Skylight. Vincent offered me an out but I said I'd see the job through. I'd been trained not to let personal feelings get in the way of work.

We said nothing as we crossed the city. What was there to say?

I averted my eyes as we bundled the corpse into the elevator at the Skylight. The general manager was waiting on the eighth floor with four Troops, who silently accepted our consignment. Vincent accompanied them to 812, making sure everything was suitably arranged. I stayed by the elevator, rubbing my hands up and down the sides of my thighs, wondering if this could be a dream. Maybe it was still Friday and I was upriver with Bill, dozing on the damp grassy banks.

"C'mon," Vincent said, taking me by the elbow and guiding me into the elevator. "I phoned Tasso. He's busy but said he'd call Frank and have him meet us back at Party Central." I could tell Vincent was bursting with questions but he kept them to himself.

Frank was standing by the gate at Party Central when we arrived. He told Vincent to park the ambulance and beat it. For once Vincent didn't argue.

We sat in a downstairs office and I told Frank about me and Nic Hornyak. He listened sympathetically, phrasing his questions delicately. When I was through, he took me for lunch to Shankar's. We ate quietly, heads down. I went for a long walk after that, sticking to backstreets, oblivious to my surroundings, trying not to think about Nic.

When I got back to Party Central, The Cardinal wanted to see me.

I hadn't seen as much of The Cardinal as a neutral observer might have supposed. He was a reclusive, rarely glimpsed creature. The more his empire grew, the less he ventured from his base on the fifteenth floor of Party Central. He even dined and slept up there.

I thought about it while waiting to be admitted and could recall only eight or nine occasions when I'd come within touching distance of the city's infamous crime lord. I'd shared a car with him once, on his way to the airport. He was heading for Rome to pay his last respects to the recently deceased pope, an old friend of his.

He hadn't said anything to me during the ride. I was up front, he was in the back with Ford Tasso, issuing last-minute orders. He had to be blindfolded before getting on the plane—he was terrified of flying. On the way back, Tasso told me and the two other Troops that if word of The Cardinal's fear leaked the three of us would be taken out and shot, no questions asked.

Another time, I ran into him coming out of a bathroom on the ninth floor of Party Central. I held the door open and saluted as he tucked the hem of his shirt back inside his pants. "Thanks," he said.

"*Thanks.*" The only word he'd exchanged with me prior to that night.

I felt sick. The one thing they don't teach you in the Troops is how to converse with The Cardinal, since it's not something you have to do in the normal run of things. How was I to address him? What would he ask me? How should I respond? I wasn't even sure I could tell him the time—my teeth were chattering. I was still in shock at finding Nic in the Fridge. Now this.

His personal secretary—Mags—tapped me on the shoulder. "Mr. Jeery," she smiled. "I've called you three times. He's ready and waiting."

"Oh." I wiped sweat from my brow. "Thank you." I stood.

"Do you want a glass of water?" Mags asked.

My throat was dry but I shook my head. The last thing I wanted was my bladder acting up during my meeting with The Cardinal.

"Don't worry," Mags said. "He won't bite you."

I managed a weak smile. She squeezed my hand comfortingly, then led me to the door, knocked and gently shoved me in.

The first thing I noticed was the puppets. Dozens of them, hanging from the walls, draped across his huge desk, slumped over in corners. I'd heard about them, of course—everybody knew about The Cardinal's penchant for puppets—but hadn't been anticipating the display. For a moment I thought I'd wandered into a toy store by accident. Then I spotted The Cardinal in a monstrous chair behind the desk and everything snapped back into place.

"Al!" he greeted me like an old friend. "Take a seat. Make yourself at home. Get you anything? Coffee, a snack, a beer?"

"No. Thanks." I was dazed by the reception. It wasn't what I'd been expecting. I pulled up a plastic chair and sat opposite The Cardinal. Out of habit my fingers strayed to my beret and I began to straighten it. The Cardinal watched, amused.

"You can take it off if you want," he said. "Never did like those damned berets. They were Mr. Tasso's idea."

I smiled gratefully and removed it.

The Cardinal wasn't handsome. Nearly six and a half feet, though you couldn't tell when he was sitting down. Too thin for such a big man. A crooked nose. Cropped hair. An Adam's apple that looked like a golf ball stuck in the middle of his throat. Gray skin. A leering gap in his lower face for a mouth. His dress sense wasn't the keenest either—a baggy blue tracksuit and sneakers. No jewelry. A cheap digital watch. If I dressed like that, I wouldn't make it past the rear gate of Party Central.

"Let's get down to business," he said. "You knew Nicola Hornyak?" I nodded. A file nestled snugly on his lap. I'd have loved to see what was in it. "Knew her long?"

"About a month."

"You were screwing her?"

"Yes," I answered calmly, overlooking his bluntness.

His eyes flicked down to the notes. "But you told Mr. Weld it wasn't serious."

"We'd meet a few times a week, maybe have a drink or something to eat, head home or to a hotel. Nothing more than that."

"Hmm." He studied his notes again. "You went out drinking together. I thought you were a teetotaler."

"I am. Nic ordered wine, I stuck to minerals."

"What about drugs?"

"No."

"Neither of you?"

"No."

"Nicola Hornyak never did drugs?"

"Not with me."

Again the "Hmm." Then he changed tack. "You've been with us quite a while. Respected by your superiors, admired by your colleagues. Brains. Talent. A hard worker. Haven't made much headway, though, have you?"

I shrugged, smiling uncertainly. "I get by."

"But you don't move up. A man of your ability and experience should have been promoted by now. I know you've been approached, by both Mr. Tasso and Mr. Weld, but each time they've offered you more responsibility you've turned them down."

"I'm happy as I am."

"Or afraid to advance?"

"I've seen what happens to those who slip while scaling the corporate ladder. Cleaned up after a few of them. Never seemed worth it to me."

"What if I handed you a promotion on a plate, if I said I was getting rid of Frank Weld and wanted you to take his place?"

I stared at him.

"I'm serious," he said. "Not about getting rid of Mr. Weld—I have no intention of dismissing such a valued employee—but maybe moving him to some other branch of the organization, where he won't clash with Mr. Tasso all the time. I've been working on a list of possible replacements. Would you care to be added to it?"

"I couldn't fill Frank's shoes," I mumbled. "I know nothing about management or leadership."

"Mr. Weld didn't either when he started. Few men do. Leaders aren't born—they grow."

"I don't know what to say. I thought you wanted to talk about Nic. This is…" I searched in vain for the words.

"I've had my eye on you for some time," The Cardinal said.

"On *me*?"

"Did you never wonder why Mr. Tasso spent so much time on you when you joined the Troops? Why he took you under his wing?"

"I thought he liked me."

The Cardinal laughed. "Mr. Tasso's interests and friendships are mine. I asked him to keep an eye on you."

"Why?" I was dumbfounded.

"Because I knew your father."

"Tom Jeery?" I gaped.

He nodded. "A fine man. Someone I was able to rely upon. I thought if the son turned out to be half as valuable, he'd be a good man to have on the books."

"I barely knew my father," I said. "He wasn't around much when I was growing up. Disappeared for good when I was seven. I had no idea he was involved with you."

"He asked me not to mention it. Didn't want his image tarnished." The Cardinal turned over a sheet of paper. "Did you kill Nicola Hornyak?" he asked, as if still discussing old friends and family.

"No!" I shouted, bewildered by his change of pace, momentarily losing my cool. "I wasn't even here. I was out of town. On a—"

"—Fishing trip. Yes, Mr. Weld told me. But that may have been a clever piece of subterfuge. It's convenient that your girlfriend's brutal murder coincided with your absence."

"I was with a friend," I growled. "Bill Casey. He'll vouch for me. He was with me the entire time. We even shared the same tent."

"I know." The Cardinal smiled. "I just wanted to see how you react when riled. You can learn a lot about a man by the way he responds when subjected to slanderous accusations."

There was a knock on the door and Ford Tasso entered. "Algiers," he greeted me. "Heard about the mess. How you holding up?"

"Quite remarkably," The Cardinal answered for me. "He takes loss firmly on the chin. Barely fazed by it."

"I'm fazed," I said sourly. I didn't like what he was doing. I hadn't been especially close to Nic but I was hurting from what had happened. The Cardinal was acting like it was some big joke. That pissed me off.

"Look at his face," The Cardinal chortled. "He'd love to throttle me."

"Go easy on him," Tasso said. "Finding a partner in the Fridge would have knocked the wind out of the most seasoned of us. Frank told me he didn't even know she was missing."

"You two are back on speaking terms?"

"For the time being." Tasso joined The Cardinal on the other side of the desk and glanced at the notes in his employer's lap. "The cops don't know about Al," he said. "Want us to keep him under wraps?"

The Cardinal sniffed. "Makes no difference whether they know or not."

"How about you, Algiers? Want us to hush things up?"

"Bill knew I was seeing her," I said.

"Bill?"

"Bill Casey," The Cardinal explained. "The pair were away fishing when the incident occurred."

"And he knows about you two?" Tasso frowned. "Then we can't keep it to ourselves. Howard Kett's handling the case." Kett was Bill's superior officer. Bill didn't have much time for him—Kett was a grade-A prick—but would feel compelled to reveal information as important as this.

Tasso and The Cardinal discussed other business for a couple of minutes, while I sat there like a stuffed squirrel. When their discussion came to an end, Tasso departed. He offered his condolences one final time and slipped out.

"You weren't listening, were you?" The Cardinal challenged me as soon as his right-hand man was out of earshot.

"What?"

"While I was chewing the cud with Mr. Tasso, I kept an eye on you. You tuned us out." He tutted. "You shouldn't be so courteous, Al. Have you any idea what certain people would pay to be where you are, to have been present while I was in congress with my number one aide? These are the types of opportunities one should seize, not turn one's nose up at."

"I'm not interested in seizing," I responded. "That's why I'd be no good as a replacement for Frank. I'm not an organizer."

"A pity. I had high hopes for you. Your father was far more ambitious."

I shifted my chair a couple of inches closer to the desk. "What did my father do for you, exactly?"

"Collected debts. Encouraged stubborn shopkeepers to see things my way. This was thirty, thirty-five years ago. We were still quite primitive back then."

"Do you know what happened to him?" I asked. "Why he vanished?"

"Your mother never told you?"

I shook my head. "She never spoke about my father. I think she was afraid of him. Whenever I asked, she said he was a bad man and I was to forget him. She died when I was a teenager, before I could make more mature inquiries."

"You never tried tracking him down?"

"I asked about him but nobody knew anything. Bill did some checking for me but came up blank. I always assumed he ran off with another woman."

The Cardinal rose and crossed the room to the huge window that afforded him a bird's-eye view of the city. He stood looking down in silence. I stared at his chair and waited for him to speak. I had a good idea what he was preparing himself to say.

"Tom Jeery was killed in the line of duty." He glanced over his shoulder to check how I'd taken that, noted my neutral expression and continued. "One of those stubborn shopkeepers pulled a knife on him. Cut deeper than he intended. Severed an artery."

"So he's dead." I'd thought, over the years, that he must be, but had always held out hope that one day he'd walk back into my life, even if it was just so I could deck him for cutting out on me and my mother.

"Your mother knew," The Cardinal said. "I informed her personally, as I did in those days, before I started delegating. A hard, cold woman, if you'll allow me to say so. Kept her emotions to herself. Refused my offer of financial assistance. Wouldn't even let me pay for a decent burial."

"Where *was* he buried?" I asked, head spinning.

"He wasn't."

"Then where…?" I winced. "The Fridge."

"He was one of the first occupants. You can retrieve the body if you wish to lay it to rest. I only held on to it because your mother showed no interest."

"After all these years, what would be the point?"

The Cardinal smiled. "My thoughts exactly." He beckoned me over to the window. "See those cranes off to the right?" I pressed against the glass and searched the horizon until I found the cranes in question. "That's where they're building the Manco Capac statue."

"The what?"

"Manco Capac was an Incan god. After hundreds of years, somebody's decided to raise an effigy of him. It's going to be one of the most incredible monuments ever constructed. It will put this city on the architectural map. You must have heard about it—reporters have been discussing little else since it was commissioned."

"I don't pay much attention to the news."

"No matter. I only pointed it out to show what a *real* mark of respect for the dead is like. Sticking people in the ground or running them through a furnace...I'd rather be jammed away in a dark corner of the Fridge or left outside to rot.

"Come," he said. "This conversation is veering toward morbidity. Tom Jeery has been dead far too long to shed any tears over. Let's return to the corpse in question—Miss Hornyak. I don't like it when people use my facilities for their own ends. Her murderer made a fatal mistake when choosing the Skylight."

He returned to his chair and picked up the file he'd been studying earlier. I took my seat again and concentrated on what he was saying. I'd think about my father later, on my own time.

"Any idea who killed her?" he asked.

"No."

"No enemies? Jealous ex-boyfriends? Business rivals?"

"She wasn't in business. She comes—came—from a wealthy family. Lived off inherited income. No enemies that I was aware of. Old boyfriends..." I shrugged. "She was beautiful. Rich. Exciting. Something of a tease. I guess there's lots of disgruntled exes hanging around, but none that I'm aware of."

"How did you meet? Miss Hornyak was a woman of means. Elegant. Sought after. You're not what I would consider a catch."

"We met at AA."

"She was an alcoholic?"

"Not really. She didn't talk much about it, but from what I picked up, her brother controlled the purse strings—her parents died when she was young, which was one of the things we had in common—and he felt she'd been drinking too heavily. He made her go. Threatened to cut her off if she didn't."

"So you got talking, one thing led to another, you realized you were two of a kind..."

"I wouldn't say that. Nic was in a different class. I knew nothing would come of our fling. We just fell into each other's lives for a while. It was a complication-free relationship—my favorite kind."

"Did you tell her what you did for a living?"

"Sure."

"Before you started dating or after?"

I thought back. "Before, I guess."

"You told her you were a Troop?"

"Yeah."

"Hmm. Ever consider the possibility that she was after more than sex?"

"I don't follow."

He tossed a large photograph across the table. It was of Nic's carved back. There was a lot of blood, so it must have been taken in the Skylight or just after she'd been delivered to the Fridge. I didn't touch it.

"Not very pretty," The Cardinal said. "You noted the design in the center?" I nodded. He fished something out of the file and threw it on top of the photograph. It was a golden brooch. I'd seen it on Nic a couple of times. At its center was a symbol of the sun.

"Recognize it?"

"Yes."

"She was wearing it the night of her murder. I don't think it's coincidence. Nicola Hornyak moved in dangerous circles. She became involved with men of violence. Perhaps she anticipated an attack of this nature. If so, would she not have sought protection? Found a strong boyfriend adept in the ways of death? A solider maybe...or a Troop?"

"She never mentioned any of this to me. We spent very little time together. It's possible..." But I wasn't convinced.

"I want to know who killed her," The Cardinal said.

"I do too," I breathed softly.

"Excellent!" he boomed, startling me. "That's what I hoped to hear. When can you start?"

"Start what?" I asked.

"The investigation. I want you to track down her killer. Find him, kill him, bring me his bones to pick my teeth with."

"But I'm not a detective."

"You are now," he grinned, eyes twinkling, "*shamus.*"

I spent twenty minutes trying to convince him I was the wrong man for the job.

"I know nothing about that line of work," I insisted. "I've been trained as a guard, to function as part of a unit. I know about lines of fire and body searches, how to spot trouble and deal with it. I don't know shit about trailing people, planting bugs or research."

"That's irrelevant," The Cardinal said. "I've had experts on the case since Saturday and they've uncovered nothing. You know the time frame for catching a murderer in circumstances such as these? Seventy-two hours. Three days to extrapolate from clues, interview witnesses and crack suspects. If you've turned up nothing by then, chances are you never will. That's what my experts tell me."

"Then why set *me* on it? If the case is dead, what's the point?"

"A case never dies, Al. People die. Empires die. Never mysteries. I want to find Nicola Hornyak's killer. It's not a major thorn in my side but it irritates me. The experts had their crack at it. Now it's time to do things another way.

"Do you know what Frank Weld did before starting work for me?"

"He was in the army."

"No. That's a misleading rumor I circulated. He executed pigs."

I couldn't prevent a skeptical smile.

"I'm not bullshitting you. He worked in an abattoir. Put a stun gun to their heads and fried their brains. Lost his job when he was found *interfering* with the livestock."

"Get the fuck out of here," I laughed.

"All right," The Cardinal smirked. "That last bit was a joke. But he did work in an abattoir. Before that he worked in a fish factory. Before that he was a bouncer in a club. Before that he served nine years for killing a man in a brawl over a prostitute."

"Is this on the level?" I asked, sobering up.

He nodded. "Not the stuff generals are generally made of, wouldn't you say?"

"So how'd he end up head of the Troops?" It was the question he'd been angling for.

"You're aware of my nocturnal informants?"

"Sure."

The Cardinal had a personal herd of gossipmongers. They came every night from various sectors of the city, men and women with secrets to impart. What they told him and what he did with that information, only he could say.

"Mr. Weld was one of them. He told me he'd caught his boss in the clutches of a young migrant worker. A juicy piece of trivia I'd normally have filed away and left to simmer. But there was something about Mr. Weld. Behind the shabby clothes, unkempt hair and bloodstained hands I saw a man of means struggling to emerge. So I took him into the fold, set my best groomers on him, and within months he was up and running.

"I work on hunches. I place little faith in systems or rules. I build on people. It's why I've flourished while so many others have fallen. The ability to see inside a man, to know what he's capable of, even if he doesn't know it himself... therein lies my secret.

"Do you know what true power is? It's the ability to manipulate other people and bend them to your way of thinking. To do that, you must first understand them. I understand people. I understand *you*. You don't seek responsibility because you know what you could do with it. You're afraid of who you could be. You don't mind getting your hands dirty as long as you're not making the decisions, because you believe that leaves your soul clean of blemish."

He paused a moment, allowing me time to challenge him. Shaking my head and lowering my gaze, I didn't.

"I've let you ride along anonymously. I haven't pushed you or strewn obstacles in your path or pleaded with you to get off your lazy ass and disturb the world. I'm not usually so lenient but I figured it would be better to let you grow a pair of balls in your own good time.

"You didn't, and events have conspired against you, so time's up. The days of blind obedience and moral *carte blanche* have come to an end. You have to show your true colors now. Put that brain of yours in gear. Contribute more than just footwork. If you can't or won't, I want nothing more to do with you. Take this case and prove yourself, or start looking for alternative employment.

"You have two minutes to decide."

Not wishing to appear a pushover, I spent ninety seconds pretending to struggle with my options, but in truth there was never a choice. To defy The Cardinal would have been suicide.

"OK," I sighed. "Tell me what you want me to do." Grinning, he leaned forward to explain, and the impression I had was of a vulture swooping in to feast on a kill.

5

I'd switched my cell phone off while in conference with The Cardinal.
As I changed clothes in the basement, I turned it back on. It rang before
I made the door.

"Al? This is Bill. I've got some bad—"

"I know," I interrupted.

"You do?" He sounded relieved.

"Can I ring you later, Bill? I'm kind of—"

"Sure. Whenever you want. I'll be here."

"Thanks."

I cycled home with The Cardinal's file under one arm, coming to
terms with all that had happened. Finding Nic... meeting The Cardinal...
learning of my father's death...a forced career change.

He'd put all my other duties on hold. I was an independent agent now.
Free to operate as I pleased. Answerable to no one bar himself. I was to
request assistance if I needed it. Frank, Tasso, the Troops, his lawyers—all
would be made available should I ask.

But where to start?

I hurried up the stairs, let myself in, switched on the lights and opened
the file. If I was lucky, The Cardinal's *experts* would have made my beginning for me, and I could simply follow their directions, tidy up after them,
make a few inquiries, chase a few red herrings, declare my investigation a

failure and get back to where I belonged. If I worked quickly it might be over by the weekend.

It didn't take me long to realize that wasn't in the cards.

The file was mind-boggling. Sheet after sheet of facts—where Nic went to school, her grades, her sources of income, friends, associates, names of those who'd made deliveries to her home, a seemingly complete list of shops she'd favored with her custom, clubs she'd frequented, vacations she'd enjoyed.

After an hour of scanning doggedly through the statistics, I threw the file away, stripped and had a shower. Turned it up hot, then down cold. Came out shivering but sharp. Dried myself, wrapped a towel around my middle and returned to the discarded papers.

A few minutes later I closed the file and laid it aside. The only way to approach something like this was with a purpose. What did I want? What did I *need*?

Drawing up a sheet of paper, I jotted down a few thoughts.

The names of those closest to her would be essential. I knew she had a brother but what about other relatives? Maybe someone stood to gain financially from her death.

Old boyfriends. Could be a jealous ex-lover among them.

Her sun brooch and the carving on her back. I'd have to check on those. Find out where she got the brooch. Go through the list of organizations she was a member of—perhaps one of them boasted a sun symbol for an insignia.

What else...?

The night in question. Last Friday. I'd have to know where she'd been, whom she'd been with, what she'd been doing. That would be the best place to start—I might pick up a name or two that would make my other inquiries less complicated.

Laying down my pen, I turned aside from Nic for a while to ponder the death of my father. I wasn't sure what I should feel. Even though I hadn't known Nic very well, I knew more about her than about Tom Jeery. He'd been a vague figure in my life, hardly ever home when I was a child, turning up out of the blue every so often, disturbing my mother, disrupting our daily routine. I had very few clear memories of him. A couple of trips to the movies. An afternoon spent together in a park. Playing soccer on the road behind my house. I'd always thought he was a salesman, never felt close to him, never thought we had anything in common. And now...

Now I'd learned we were both in the pay of the same master, that years before I made any move to join the ranks of The Cardinal, he'd been there, testing the waters, preparing the way. I felt cheated. Many of my childhood friends had turned to criminal pursuits, but I was the only one from the old neighborhood to serve with the Troops. I'd thought I was something hot when Ford Tasso singled me out for special treatment. Now I realized he'd only done it because of my father. That bugged the hell out of me.

I'd have to think on it some more one day. Make inquiries, find out what sort of a man he'd been, what kind of impact I should allow his death to have on me. But not now. I'd deal with Nic first and get The Cardinal off my back. Playing detective was going to take up a lot of my time. I couldn't afford distractions.

I passed a couple more hours scouring the file, digging out names and relevant details. There was more to Nic Hornyak than I'd imagined. I'd never pegged her for a virgin, but according to these reports she'd been with everything on two legs in the city. If I had to search among the ranks of ex-lovers for her killer, it would be a long, arduous task.

I'd had enough for one night, so I laid the file aside and prepared for bed. I'd go over it thoroughly in the morning. Hopefully sleep would clear my head and I'd be able to think directly.

It was while I was brushing my teeth that it hit me.

I wiped around my mouth and returned to the file. Picking it up, I leafed through, counting pages. Forty-three, excluding photos, of which there were plenty.

I checked some of the entries. Many of the sheets were photocopies with dates going back to Tuesday, Monday, Sunday. Interviews had been conducted with friends and relations. A lot of man-hours had gone into this. The investigation seemed to have been launched early Saturday.

But Vincent hadn't known the corpse's identity. Nor had Dr. Sines. The official line was, nobody did. She'd died a Jane Doe and lain in the Fridge, unidentified, until I turned up.

So how the hell had this dossier been compiled?

Frank wanted to see me the next morning, so I made Party Central my first port of call. He was in his office, catching up on a frightening tower of paperwork. He signed his name to stray pieces of paper while we talked.

"Heard about your promotion," he grunted. "Congratulations."

"Thanks."

"The Cardinal's told me I'm to put myself at your beck and call."

"Yeah?" I grinned. "Like a personal assistant?"

"Fuck you."

I laughed and handed him a stack of papers.

"Any idea what it's all about?" I asked. "Why he picked me and what he expects?"

"Didn't he tell you?"

"He did and he didn't. Said I should be setting my sights higher. Told me I was wasting my time where I was. I get the impression this is a test of some sort but I haven't a clue what I'll win if I pass."

"The Cardinal's a queer fish," Frank said. "Sometimes he seems to do shit just for the fun of it. And maybe he does. Many think so. But I beg to differ. I don't think he spits without evaluating every angle."

"How should I proceed?" I asked.

"Why ask me? I'm no detective."

"But you've had dealings with them. You know more about it than me. Do I need cameras, recorders, bugs? Approaching people—do I pretend I'm a real detective? What about the cops? And how do I recognize a clue from a lump of dog shit?"

Frank laughed and pointed at the space above the door behind my head. I turned and looked up. A sign hung there. WHEN IN DOUBT, DECIDE!

"Ford Tasso said that to me the day I started. When life got me down, I had one of the girls print it up. I glance at it twenty times a day, more if I have to."

"If I'd wanted dry old proverbs I'd have bought a fortune cookie."

Frank shrugged. "You asked for my advice—that's it. There's a thousand ways you could investigate. Sitting around thinking won't get you anywhere. Nor will doing things the ordinary way—The Cardinal doesn't want that. When I started, I made some lousy calls, but they were *my* decisions. The Cardinal respected that and left me to work things out. You've gotta do the same. Go out on a limb and hope you don't fail."

"I was looking for more practical advice," I grumbled.

"Then look elsewhere," Frank told me, and that was the end of our discussion.

I met Bill next, in a bar close to Party Central. We ordered sandwiches and sat in a quiet corner, away from the crowd, discussing Nic and what had happened.

"How are you holding up?" he asked.

"Pretty well, considering."

"I damn near fainted when Kett told me. We were joking about her Friday, on the way up, remember?"

"You said if the fish didn't bite, we should invite her up and tell her to bring a friend."

"I'm sorry, Al."

"Don't be. You didn't know her. I barely knew her myself." I took a bite out of the sandwich—the bread was stale—and chewed mechanically. "Who told Kett about her?"

"He won't say. All I know is, he got a call at home, Thursday. Somebody told him there'd been a murder at the Skylight and the body had been removed. Gave him the room number, date and time, a description of the victim."

"Her name too?"

"Yes."

"Any idea who the caller might have been?"

"If it had been any other hotel, I'd have said a maid or bellboy. But employees are more tight-lipped at the Skylight. My guess is it was another guest, somebody with a conscience. Or it could have been the killer."

"You reckon?"

"The symbol gouged into her back—he didn't do that for fun. When someone goes to that much trouble, he's looking to be noticed. He might have wanted the case dragged through the media. Maybe he's planning to strike again and wants to be recognized when he does."

"A serial killer?"

"Possibly. But from what I've gathered it was a clumsy kill. Slow and messy. So we've either got a beginner on our hands or somebody who wants us to *think* he's a beginner."

"Any clues?" I asked. "Any leads?"

"Not by the time *we* arrived, but the better part of a week had passed before we were called onto the scene. Whoever brought her back might as well have dropped her off at the station."

I hadn't told Bill that I'd collected Nic's body from the Fridge. Didn't intend to. Those were the kinds of details you learned to withhold from friends. Nor did I plan to tell him about my meeting with The Cardinal.

"What are your chances of catching him?" I asked.

"Slim to none. If we'd been informed as soon as she was discovered..." He sighed. "The pathologist will do his best, but I doubt he'll discover anything useful. We've questioned the staff—nothing. There's a few to go but we won't get anything out of them. Unless he strikes again or Kett receives another phone call... *nada.*"

I nodded slowly. I'd figured as much.

"What about a private investigation? Any point?"

"You could hire someone," Bill said. "Costly. Probably wouldn't achieve anything. But it couldn't do any harm."

"What if *I* was to investigate?"

He frowned. "Don't be crazy. What do you know about detective work? It's not as easy as it looks in the movies."

"I know. But how would I go about it?"

He studied me silently for all of a minute.

"You're not asking my opinion, are you, Al? You're committed to this already. Right?"

"Right."

"Jesus." He pushed the remains of his sandwich away. "How far are you into this?"

"I've got some names. Background information."

"Any angles?"

"I was hoping you'd provide me with a few. Old enemies, a family feud—something like that."

He smiled wryly. "I told you, it's not like in the movies. Motives and deaths of this nature rarely go together. Nic checked in under a transparent pseudonym—Jane Dowe. Why do people normally give false names in hotels?"

"Because they're there to fuck?"

"Crude but precise. Chances are she picked up a guy, took him back to the Skylight, he turned psycho, end of story."

"Did anybody see the two of them together?"

"The receptionist remembers Nic but insists there was no one with her in the lobby. The room to the right of hers was unoccupied. The old couple in the room to the left went to bed early and slept the night through."

"If I investigate," I said slowly, "where should I start?"

He sighed and rubbed the back of his neck. He looked old and tired in the dim light. Bill had been talking about taking early retirement for a couple of years—looking at him now, I began to think maybe he should pack it in, before the job made a premature end of him.

"You might glean something from the staff at the Skylight," he said reluctantly. "They weren't anxious to talk to us. Given your connections, there's a chance they'd be more open, assuming they know anything. But leave it for a couple of days. You don't want to run into Kett. Let us complete our investigation and move on before you poke your nose in."

The previous detectives had already interviewed the staff and come up blank, but I'd have a crack myself, as Bill suggested, though I wasn't sure I could wait until the dust settled.

"What about friends and family?" I asked. "Anybody suspicious?"

"None that we know of, though we've only been on the case twenty-four hours and those are the kind of details you don't unearth immediately. Her closest friend was Priscilla Perdue. Know her?" I nodded. The name was in the file and Nic had spoken of her a few times. "And there's her brother. We couldn't get anything out of him. He didn't bat an eyelid when we called him in to tell him about the death and ask him to identify the body."

"That's peculiar, isn't it?"

"Not really. People react to death in all sorts of ways. Very few weep openly in front of the police.

"Apart from those two, I can't help you. I might know more in a day or two but right now we're struggling to get inside her head. Nic kept her personal life to herself. In fact, if you haven't any objections, I'd like to hear what *you* have to say about her."

We ordered another round of orange juices and I ran Bill through my time with Nic. Toward the end of our talk he returned to the topic of detective work and honored me with some much-needed advice.

I shouldn't bother with bugs—such technology was for the professionals. He told me to be honest when interviewing people, tell them who I was and why I was interested in Nicola. "That way they'll have sympathy for you and may be more inclined to talk. If you pretend to be a real detective, they'll see through you and close up shop."

He stressed the importance of keeping things simple. "Don't weave webs of intrigue. Murder's not a complicated business. If you start building up networks of suspects and theories, you'll chase your tail into madness. Take people at their word. Turn a blind eye to conspiracies. Look to narrow your options. Jump to no conclusions, especially dire ones."

I listened intently, filing his words away.

We parted with a handshake and a smile. If Bill had grave misgivings about my getting involved, he kept them to himself. Told me to call if I needed help or ran into a blank wall. I promised to let him know if I discovered anything.

I cycled back to Party Central and flicked through the file one more time. The moment had come to take my first step. I probably should have heeded Bill's advice and waited a few days before interviewing those close to Nic. But, keeping Frank's motto in mind, I decided to strike fast, figuring people in mourning might reveal more than they would when composed. I grabbed my bike, tucked my pen and notebook away and set off for the twisting maze of city streets beyond the gate. As I cycled into the wind, a cliché whistled through my thoughts, and I grinned—Al Jeery was on the case!

part two

"i'm your man"

6

I called on her brother first. Nic had never told me much about him, apart from his name, Nick, which was confusingly similar to her own. Nicholas and Nicola, but both had used the abbreviations since childhood, prompted by their father, who had a peculiar sense of humor. I'd asked why they let the arrangement stand now that he was dead. She said neither wanted to change. She liked Nic and he liked Nick. Besides, they didn't see a lot of each other, so it wasn't that big an issue.

He was twenty-nine, three years older than Nic. He had inherited the bulk of the estate when their parents died and was to have been Nic's financial guardian until she turned thirty, whereupon she could have drawn from her share of the funds as she pleased. He had no head for business but he spent conservatively—he hadn't frittered the family fortune away and there was a sizable amount left in the kitty.

The two weren't close, but there didn't seem to be any bad blood between them. They just didn't have much in common. Or, to put it another way, they had *too much* in common—as well as sharing names, they also shared a taste in men. Nick Hornyak was, as the file succinctly phrased it, "bent as a eunuch."

Nick lived in the family mansion in the suburbs. An architectural monstrosity, oozing old money. It had been Nic's home too, though she'd hardly spent more than a few months there in the last several years of her life.

The butler wasn't impressed when he saw my bike leaning against one of the pillars. "Deliveries to the rear," he said snootily, and I had to jam my foot in the door to buy the time necessary to explain who I was and why I was there.

Master Nick, he informed me, was not at home and not expected back any time soon. He didn't answer when I asked where I could find the absent master, so I said I had some personal belongings of Nic's I wanted to pass on. He deliberated for a couple of grudging seconds, then told me I'd probably find Nick at a club called the Red Throat.

I'd meant to ask the butler about Nic—household staff are supposed to know all the secrets of their lords and ladies—but his cool manner threw me. I'd felt like a fish out of water to begin with—the last thing I needed was to be taken down a peg by a gentleman's gentleman.

The Red Throat used to be called the Nag's Ass. It had been a real dive until a decade ago. I'd come here a couple of times during my early tenure with the Troops, hunting scum. The neighborhood had improved since then and the Nag's Ass had come up in the world. The name wasn't the only change—it had undergone a complete renovation, an extra floor had been added, the front had been adorned with blushing red bricks, stained-glass windows of various designs dotted the walls. I wouldn't have recognized the place if I'd been passing.

Bouncers guarded the door, even though it was early in the day and there was no obvious call for them. They stared neutrally at me as I passed, eyes sloppily scanning my body for revealing bulges. Real amateurs. They wouldn't be joining the Troops any time soon.

The red walls inside were draped with pink banners and sensuous photos of James Dean, Brad Pitt, Leonardo DiCaprio and hordes more pinup boys. Low, throbbing music spilled from the many speakers. A "wet jockstrap" DVD played on the TV sets.

I wandered to the bar and waited patiently while the barkeep—female in appearance, though I had my doubts—polished glasses. I was casing the joint (I had the detective lingo down pat!) when the barman—his voice ruined the illusion—cut in. "Hi. New in town?"

"What makes you ask?"

"Don't recall seeing you before."

"You've got a memory for faces?"

"No. We're packed wall-to-wall most nights and I don't even notice the regulars in the crush. But days are quieter. The usual crowd. You get to know them." He went on polishing.

"Do you know a guy called Nick Hornyak?" I asked.

"Maybe." He grew wary. The hand polishing the glass slowed. He was getting ready to call a bouncer.

"A friend of mine told me to look him up," I lied, upping my voice an octave. "Said he might show me around the city and set me up with a place to stay."

The barman resumed polishing, doubts vanishing with the smudges on the glass. "He's shooting pool." He nodded toward one of the tables in an alcove to the left. "Alone. Likes to work on his technique." Eyes twinkling, he took my order—lemon juice—and put one of the spotless glasses to use.

I walked over slowly, studying Nic's brother. He looked younger than his years, tall, handsome, expensive silk shirt, a gold St. Christopher medallion dangling from his neck, long hair gelled back. He'd have to watch that hair—dangerously thin. By the time he was thirty-five he'd be sticking chunks back on with glue. I knew about hair. Used to date a hairdresser.

He strolled around to my side of the table and I saw he was wearing a miniskirt. He flicked me the eye, grinned, bent to make his shot. I traced the hem of his blue tights up his long, shapely legs. From this angle he would have excited any guy who didn't know better. He even had the roll of the hips pegged.

He sank a ball, turned, leaned against the table and smiled. "I love playing with balls and forcing my way down dark, tight holes. How about you?" I'd watched a lot of noir flicks in my time, but I'd never seen Bogey come out with an innuendo as blatant as that!

"I'm more into chess," I replied drily. When he pouted, I added, "But I like your dress."

"Silly, isn't it?" he simpered, lighting a cigarette. He offered one but I shook my head. "I only wear it when I'm hanging around. I would have made more of an effort if I'd been expecting company."

"My name's Al Jeery," I said. "You may have heard of me?"

"Should I have?"

"I was a friend of your sister's."

His guard came up instantly. "She had a lot of friends. They've been coming in droves to share their condolences. You'd be amazed how many are reporters."

"I'm not a reporter, Mr. Hornyak. I'd been seeing Nic for a month before she died. We were close."

"Lots of people were *close* to Nicola. How do I know you're telling the truth? I had one esteemed member of the press pretend to be a long-lost cousin last night."

"I met her at AA. We were—"

"AA? What was Nic doing there, for God's sake?"

I frowned. "You didn't know she was attending?"

"My sister and I rarely discussed matters other than those of a sexual nature."

"But she told me she was there because of *you*. That you threatened to cancel her allowance if she didn't sort herself out."

"I made no demands of Nicola. She took what she liked. I never said boo." I was confused. He noted it and smiled. "Nicola was a complicated woman. I knew her twenty-six years and she still had the capacity to startle me. Don't let it worry you—she often spun lies and fairy tales." An eyelid raised slyly on "fairy."

"Why are you here?" he asked.

"I want to know why she was killed and who did it. The police are writing her off as a statistic. I think she deserves better. I think she deserves the truth."

"A crusader." He whistled. "Are you a detective, Al?"

"No. But I've got time. Resources are available to me. I'd like to talk with you about her and ask some questions. You don't mind?"

He thought it over, then shrugged. "It's a slow afternoon. How can I help?"

I opened my notebook, hoping I looked as if I knew what I was doing. "Let's begin with the basics. Did you see Nic the day of her death?"

"No."

"When did you last see her?"

He scratched his chin. "About two weeks before. We ran into each other in a club. We exchanged some comments about the atmosphere, the fashion, the music. Parted after a couple of minutes and went our separate ways."

"You didn't see her again?"

"No."

"Did you talk with her on the phone?"

"No. I didn't e-mail or text her either, write a letter or waft smoke signals her way. As I said, we weren't close. We'd gang up occasionally for a night on the town, but only three, maybe four times a year." He stubbed out his barely smoked cigarette, turned and shot pool again. "I don't have much time for women, and Nic didn't have much time for my kind of man."

"Who was she with when you last saw her?" I asked.

"Some black guy with a bald head. He was sitting by himself at a table, looking standoffish."

"Notice anything about him? Any distinguishing features?"

"I think he was tall. Thin. Black as sin." Nick smiled. "That was quite poetical, wasn't it?"

"You should publish. Anything else?"

"I really didn't get a good look."

I made a note of the bald, thin, black man and moved on.

"Did anyone have the knives out for Nic?"

"If they did, and I knew, I'd have told the police and they'd have questioned the guilty party."

"People don't always tell the cops everything."

"But I did. I like the police. We get lots of officers here. I've always found them most obliging."

"You really don't know anything about her death?"

"No. There's nothing I can tell you that I didn't..." He paused.

"Yes?" I prompted him.

"She was wearing a brooch when she was killed."

"With a symbol of the sun. I know."

"The police asked me if I knew about it. I didn't. But a few of her friends who called me since the news broke told me it had been a present from some mystic guy she used to see."

Her file had mentioned an interest in the occult. I flipped my notebook over and scanned down some of the peripheral names I'd scribbled in the back. "It wasn't Rudi Ziegler, was it?"

"The very one. Nic was into contacting the dead, fortune-telling, crackpot stuff like that."

"And Ziegler gave her the brooch?"

"According to those in the know. I was going to contact the police about it. Do you think I should?"

"I doubt it'll matter. They'll find out from the same sources as you." I made a big ring around Ziegler's name and stared at it. "Do you know Rudi Ziegler?"

"Heavens no! I wouldn't be seen dead in the company of witch doctors."

"You know nothing about him?"

"Only what I heard from Nic's friends. As far as I can make out, he's a hole-in-the-wall Houdini—mirrors, hidden speakers and flashes of light."

"Anything else you can tell me?"

He thought for a minute. "Nothing springs to mind."

"You don't seem too cut up about her death," I commented.

He sniffed. "What can I do about it? She's dead. I'm not into grief trips. It's a harsh world. Nic knew that. She ran into the wrong guy at the wrong time. Could happen to any of us. Those are the risks we take."

"What if it wasn't random? She may have been targeted. What if you're next on the list? A distant relative looking to get his hands on the Hornyak estate or someone your father destroyed in business years ago?"

"No." He sank the eight ball, lit another cigarette, racked the balls up and started a new frame. "Nic got unlucky. The perils of fucking anything that moves."

"You're the soul of compassion," I said bitterly.

"Screw compassion. Death's nothing new to me. I've watched friends die slowly from AIDS. Seen guys stabbed outside clubs, purely because of where they stick their dicks. You live with the losses or go nuts. Besides, I wouldn't have wished death on Nic, but it could have happened to nicer people, know what I mean?"

"Not really."

He fixed his gaze on me. "Nic was my sister and I loved her. But she was no angel. You knew her a month. From what you say, you only saw the best of her."

"You reckon?"

"That bald guy in the club I was telling you about—that was two weeks ago. Were you still *close* with Nicola then, Al?"

I stiffened, preparing a retort, then realized he wasn't insulting me, merely opening my eyes to the truth. I relaxed and nodded slowly.

"You weren't the first she did the dirty on. You don't even make the first few dozen. If you think she was an unsullied innocent and it's your duty to avenge her, you're a fool. My advice—let it lie. She wasn't worth such devotion."

His cruel honesty unsettled me and I realized, as I had when studying her file, how little I'd known about her.

"I'll leave you to your game," I said.

"So soon? Stay awhile. Go a few frames with me. You never know where it might lead. I've a wardrobe full of Nic's old clothes and I can fit into most of them."

"Tempting," I grinned, "but no thanks."

"Your loss," he pouted, then winked. "Bye, Al. Call again someday. Catch me in something *hot*."

I smiled, shook my head and left.

I felt reasonably good as I cycled back to Party Central. I'd made a start, and while I hadn't cracked the case, I hadn't collapsed at the first hurdle. I was pleased with the way the questioning had gone. I'd handled myself professionally. And I'd stumbled onto a possible clue in the process—Rudi Ziegler. Maybe I was cut out for this detective business after all.

I jotted down a few thoughts after my meeting with Nick. Apart from the Ziegler connection, there was the AA discrepancy to ponder. Why did Nic lie to me? Most probably she just didn't want to admit she had a problem.

A lot of people at AA meetings started out "without a problem" and were only there "at the insistence of…" (fill in the blank).

I made a note all the same—I'd need a new notebook soon if this kept up—then put it to one side and called Priscilla Perdue. No answer at home or on her cell phone, so I tried the beauty salon where she was an assistant manager. I had to brave the suspicion of a cautious secretary but finally I was put through.

"Priscilla. Sorry about the delay—journalists have been on my tail all day. How may I help?" She had a cute, squeaky voice.

"My name's Al Jeery, Miss Perdue. I was a friend of Nic Hornyak's. I was—"

"Al Jeery," she interrupted, and I heard her tapping the back of her teeth with her tongue. "You were Nic's little brown soldier."

"Excuse me?"

She giggled. "Please don't be offended. That's how Nic described you. She said she was dating a big, brown, bulky soldier, with thick stubble for hair and the physique of an action doll. I was jealous."

I didn't know what to think about that, so I cleared my throat and said, "Miss Perdue, I'd like to discuss Nic with you. I'm running a private investigation into her—"

"Do you mind if we do this some other time?" she interrupted. "I'd rather talk about Nic outside of working hours. Doesn't do to cry in front of the customers."

"Of course. I'll call after the funeral and—"

"You needn't wait that long. I've been surrounded by well-wishers since news of the murder broke, but they're all old friends and have nothing new to say. Are you free tonight?"

"Sure."

"You have my address?" I had. "Pick me up, ten o'clock?"

"I don't have a car," I told her.

"That's all right. We can use mine."

I spent the intervening hours reading about Priscilla, preparing for our meeting. She came from a well-off family. Twenty-seven. Married for a couple of years when she was nineteen. Husband owned a chain of clothes boutiques. He was shot dead during a robbery. She got involved with his attorney, who ran off with most of her money, never to be seen again. No serious relationships since, but many short-term affairs.

The photos were few and poor, the most recent from the days of her marriage. I reported the lack of up-to-date material when handing the file back to the secretary on the seventeenth floor, from where it had come, as we were always meant to when encountering substandard data. My comments would be passed on and, within days, a team of operatives would be scanning newspapers and records, gathering photos, business transcripts, gossip tidbits, etc., updating and fleshing out her profile.

I went home to change. I hadn't asked where we'd be going, so I didn't know whether to dress formally. I played it safe and dressed smart-casual, tucking a tie into my pocket in case it was required.

She lived in an apartment block that put mine to shame. Couldn't be doing too badly if she was able to maintain payments on a pad in a place like this.

I was about to buzz for her when she appeared, clad in blue, keys in her left hand. She was on the short side but otherwise as close to perfect as I'd seen in a long while. A model's curves, wide blue eyes, round red lips, delicate cheekbones, and long blond hair that would have been any stylist's delight.

"Al Jeery, I presume," she said, eyes flicking over me.

"Miss Perdue."

"Call me Priscilla. And I'll call you Al." She jangled the keys and smiled. "Race you to the car." She sprinted past me, a strong stride. I had no option but to run to keep up.

She was slightly out of breath when we reached her car, an old BMW. I wasn't.

"You're in good shape," she complimented me.

"For my age," I modestly agreed.

We got in. She noticed my critical eye—the car was in poor shape.

"It's a car like this or a cheaper apartment," she explained.

"I thought you managed the salon." Flattering her.

"Assistant manager. I do most of the work but my boss claims the profits. I make enough to keep me in style if I spend wisely. Unfortunately I've never had a head for money. It comes, it goes, and hardly any seems to be left over at the close of the weekend."

She drove carefully, eyes glued to the road, not talking.

When she pulled up and I saw where we were—the Kool Kats Klub—I stiffened and a lot of the joy seeped out of the evening. Priscilla noted this and frowned. "What's wrong?"

I subjected her to a level gaze. "Nice choice of venue," I said sarcastically.

"The Kool Kats?" she laughed. "I come here all the time. What do you have against...?" She slapped her forehead and groaned. "How much dumber can I get? I'm sorry, Al. I didn't think. We'll leave."

"No." I forced a smile. She was testing me—she knew exactly what she was doing when she picked this place. "I'm fine."

The Kool Kats Klub was better known as the Ku Klux Klub, the name it had originally opened under, until the clamoring of irate citizens forced the change. It was a nest for the racist rich. I'd been inside once with the Troops to apprehend a pedophile. The sympathy of the clientele, as I dragged the son of a bitch out, was firmly on the abuser's side, even though they knew him for what he was.

It hadn't changed much. All the walls painted white. White customers, white staff, even a couple of pure white cats that roamed the halls imperiously.

The receptionist's nostrils flared when he spotted my black face bobbing into the lobby, and when he smiled it looked as if he were passing a kidney stone. "May I help you, *sir*?" he asked icily, hands fidgeting at the buttons of his waistcoat.

"I'm collecting for disabled Negro war veterans," I said, just for his reaction. If his jaw had been detachable it would have dropped to the floor, sprouted legs and scuttled away in shock.

"Ignore him, Martin," Priscilla said, taking my arm and giggling. "Mr. Jeery is my guest for the night. I trust he will be treated with respect."

The receptionist focused on Priscilla and smiled shakily. "Miss Perdue. Of course. Any guest of yours is a guest of ours." His eyes flared beadily over me. "Would you care to be seated anywhere in particular?"

"My usual table."

He coughed, nodded sharply and led us to Priscilla's "usual table," which was situated in the center of the dining room.

"Miss Perdue," the receptionist said once he'd seated us. He faced me and blanched. "*Sir*," he added with a curt nod and hurried away.

"Thanks, Martin." I tossed the smallest coin I could find after him. The clink as it hit the marble floor was the loudest sound in the restaurant.

Faces darkened as I was ogled by incredulous diners. Angry women whispered to their partners, who shook their heads, sneered, then deliberately turned their backs on me. A couple of boys shouted, "Look at the nigger!" and were quickly shushed by their mothers, who then quietly applauded them.

Priscilla acted as if nothing were wrong and I went along with the game, smiling vacuously, idly examining the decor, pretending to be one of the gang, perfectly at home, unaware of the arctic atmosphere.

"We seem to be creating something of a scandal," Priscilla said as we were handed wine menus by a silently outraged waiter.

"That's what we came for, wasn't it?"

"Why, Al," she gasped, eyes widening innocently. "Whatever do you mean?"

"You wanted to see what would happen when you threw Nic's little brown soldier to the lions."

"Al! I never—"

"Stick it up your ass," I said pleasantly. "Let's talk about Nic."

"You may leave if you wish," she said, eyes downcast.

"And miss a great meal? I wouldn't dream of it."

She squinted at me, then nodded. "Tell me what you want to know."

I asked about her friendship with Nic, how long they'd known each other, what sort of a life Nic had led, the men she'd dated, if she'd been in trouble lately.

They'd been best friends for years. Nic had led a full life. She'd lived fast and partied hard. There were lots of men, more than Priscilla had been able to keep up with. No trouble—everyone liked Nic.

"Is it possible one of her boyfriends grew jealous?" I asked.

"Maybe. She sometimes strung the poor dears along. I told her she shouldn't, but Nic found it hard to let go of men. She was peculiar that way. But none of the boyfriends I knew would have done something like that."

"Could you give me a few names?"

"I'd rather not," she said plainly. "I told the police—I had to—but now my lips are sealed." She leaned forward. "I thought you simply wanted to know more about Nic, because you were curious. But that isn't it, is it?"

"I want to know who killed her."

"We all *want* to know. But you plan to find out, right?" I made no reply but she read the answer in my face. "So you're a detective too. A man of many talents."

"I just want to make a few inquiries, help the cops if I can. A case like Nic's is likely to slip between the cracks and never be solved. If I can uncover a suspect or some clues, I'll pass them on to those in the know and maybe something will come of it."

"Why not hire a real detective?"

A good question. I couldn't tell Priscilla it was to appease The Cardinal, so I rubbed my fingers together and said, "Moola."

"God, I know about that. So you've taken the task upon yourself. You're either very brave or very stupid."

"A bit of both. How about it, Priscilla? Will you give me a list of Nic's old boyfriends?"

She shook her head. "I'm even less inclined to reveal their identities now that I know what you're up to. I don't like the idea of an amateur sleuth hounding my friends. No offense intended."

"None taken." Our drinks arrived, wine for Priscilla, a nonalcoholic cocktail for me. Mine had probably been spat in by every waiter in the building—twice by good old Martin—but I drank it anyway and made a show of enjoying it.

"How about a guy called Rudi Ziegler?" I asked, wiping around my lips with a napkin. "Know him?"

Priscilla hesitated, then, since I knew the name anyway, nodded. "A fortune-teller. Nic thought he was marvelous. She used to plead with me to accompany her to his séances or tarot readings or whatever it is he does."

"You never went?"

"No. I don't believe in such nonsense."

"Nic did?"

"Absolutely. If it wasn't Ziegler, it was Madam Ouspenkaya or Mister Merlin. Remember when *Time* ran an article about this city's supernatural underbelly, how we have a higher proportion of mystics and crackpots than anywhere else?"

"I remember people talking about it, yeah."

"They ran a list of names—hundreds—and Nic told me she knew practically seven out of every ten."

"But Ziegler was special?" I asked hopefully.

She shrugged. "He was flavor of the month. She'd been hung up on others before him and there would have been others after."

Priscilla was playing with her glass. Most of her fingers were adorned with rings, two or three to a finger. One on her left hand had a flat, round top, out of which jutted a diagram of the sun.

"Do you know anything about a brooch of Nic's?" I asked, eyes on the ring. "There was a picture of the sun on it. She was wearing—"

"—It when she died," Priscilla finished. "Yes. I heard. It was a present from Ziegler. I told Nick—her brother—about it when he called. And the police."

"Think it means anything?"

"No. It was a worthless trinket. Apparently Ziegler hands out lots of similar jewelry to his clients." She raised the hand with the sun ring and flashed it at me. "Nic got this from him too. She gave it to me because I said I liked it. I only started wearing it this morning. It reminds me of her."

She lapsed into silence and twisted the ring a few times with the fingers of her other hand.

"Generosity was always one of Nic's failings." Her voice was close to breaking. "This ring's a cheap bauble but she'd have given it to me even if it had been worth a king's ransom."

Another indignant waiter arrived to take our order. I'd meant to pick the most expensive dishes on the menu, but Priscilla's sudden slide into sentiment had softened me. There was a cold edge to Priscilla Perdue—bringing me to the KKK had been a calculated act of provocation—but I had a feeling that she was warmer than she pretended. So I ordered a plain fish dish that wouldn't leave her penniless.

We chatted about Nic some more. Priscilla had last seen her four days before the murder. Nic had been acting strangely all week, distant.

"You think she sensed what was coming?" I asked.

"Possibly. Or it may just have been one of her moods. She often fell into lengthy periods of sullen silence and went off by herself."

"I know you don't want to discuss her boyfriends," I said, "but there's one I was hoping to check on. A tall, bald, black man. Do you know if she was seeing anyone like that?"

"You mean the guy with the snakes."

"Snakes?"

"I saw them together a couple of times. She never introduced us. Only laughed when I asked his name and said he was her snake-boy."

"What's the deal with the snakes? Did he own one?"

"He had two. Carried them with him everywhere." She laughed at my confusion. "Not real snakes," she explained. "Tattoos. On his cheeks."

I froze.

"Are you all right?" Priscilla asked. "You look like you've swallowed a rotten egg."

I counted to ten inside my head and when I spoke it was with only the vaguest hint of a stutter. "Nic was seeing a bald, black man with snakes tattooed on his face?"

"Yes."

"Down his cheeks, one on either side, multicolored?"

She smiled uncertainly. "You know him?"

"I know of him."

I placed my napkin on the table and stood. "I have to leave now."

She got up as I stepped away from the table. "What's going on, Al? Did I say something wrong?"

"No. I just have to go."

"But the meal is on its way."

"I've lost my appetite."

"But...Al!"

I was gone before she could say any more.

Outside I walked fast, away from the Ku Klux Klub and its exclusive band of patrons, ignoring the hisses, catcalls and slow handclaps that accompanied my departure. I walked until my lungs pained me, then paused, doubled over, took several deep breaths, and walked some more. Finally I stopped by a deserted bus shelter and perched on one of the folding plastic chairs.

Black. Tall. Bald. Snakes tattooed on his cheeks. Only one man in the city answered that description—*Paucar Wami*. The city's deadliest, most feared assassin. If Paucar Wami was involved, that was it for me. I didn't care what The Cardinal threatened to do. I'd make an appointment, tell him what I knew, then hand in my resignation. I'd rather face the wrath of The Cardinal than the prospect of a showdown with Paucar Wami. Any day.

7

By the time I arrived home I was dying for a drink. Nights are the worst time for a reformed alcoholic, especially one living alone. The long hours of dark loneliness and need, the nocturnal thirst, memories of past, brighter, livelier nights when the bottle was your ally and the world was your friend.

I usually fought the craving with food. I'd tuck into a burger, Chinese or fried chicken, read a trashy novel and do my best to tune out the real world and its many liquid pitfalls. Tonight it was extra-important to divert my thoughts, and quickly, before fear pushed me over the edge of sobriety.

Pulling up to the curb outside my apartment, I hurried into the bagel shop. Ali was inside. I don't think that was his real name but it's what everyone called him.

"Hello, my friend," he greeted me.

"Hi, Ali," I smiled back.

"Dining at home tonight?" he asked.

"It's cheap and the company's good."

He laughed. "You will not get fat this way, my friend. You need a new wife. A woman would fatten you up."

"Then nag me about my love handles. I'd have to exercise to work the weight off. Then I'd be thin again."

"There is wisdom in your words," he chuckled, then turned to the bagels. "Salmon and cream cheese?"

"Four times over," I said, licking my lips.

"Four?" he blinked.

"You said I needed fattening up."

Ali stuck the wrapped bagels into the microwave and adjusted the setting.

"How is our friend The Cardinal today?" he asked as he handed over the bagels. According to him, The Cardinal used to go to a shop he ran uptown many years ago. I used to tell him I never saw The Cardinal but he didn't believe me, so I'd taken to acting as if the two of us were best buddies.

"He's fine. Asked after you the other day."

"Did he?"

"Said you should come by some night, chat about old times."

"I may just do that," he said, grinning from ear to ear.

I shook the bag of bagels. "I'm off before these get cold. See you, Ali."

"Soon, my friend."

I unwrapped one of the bagels and chewed it as I made my way up the stairs. I'd finished it by the time I let myself in and the other three didn't last much longer. I realized I needed more food, so I hurried back downstairs to the nearby 7-Eleven and loaded up on chocolate. I spent a few hours nibbling and trying to concentrate on a biography of Ian Fleming, the guy who invented James Bond. But it was hard. Thoughts of Paucar Wami were impossible to escape from. And if I managed to momentarily forget about him, my eyes would flick to the dark marble with the gold squiggles on the mantelpiece and the worry would flood back. The marble and Wami couldn't be connected, but it now seemed to serve as some kind of omen and looking at it filled me with unease.

Priscilla rang close to midnight, a welcome distraction. She apologized for taking me to the Kool Kats Klub and suggested another rendezvous, this time at a place of my choosing. I said maybe. She urged me to think about it—she really wanted to see me again. Also, if I was serious about investigating Nic's murder, she'd like to help, short of giving me the names of Nic's old boyfriends. We discussed her some more, then she hung up.

I returned to the Fleming biography but couldn't focus. My mind kept fixing on the image of Paucar Wami with Nic. I'd never met the notorious killer but I was able to picture him—tall, dark, sinister, arms wrapped around Nic in Room 812 of the Skylight, fingers working at her back, sucking the life from her pain-contorted lips.

I put the book to one side, undressed and readied myself for bed. But sleep was harder to slip into than the biography and I spent most of the night chasing it in vain. On the few occasions I dozed off, I slept fitfully and dreamed of long, undulating snakes with forked, flicking tongues.

I got up at six, ate a slow breakfast, then cycled to Party Central to book an audience with The Cardinal. I was told he wouldn't be available until late evening, unless it was an emergency. I said I'd wait, then headed down to a cafeteria to brood about Nic and Paucar Wami.

I'd calmed down since the night before. Though my fear of Wami persisted, I couldn't simply march into The Cardinal's office and tell him I was through. The Cardinal had a quick temper. I'd have to be diplomatic. I'd tell him about Wami and state my reluctance to continue. Hopefully he'd show mercy and let me off the hook.

In the meantime I decided to set up an interview with Rudi Ziegler. That way I could face The Cardinal with proof that I hadn't been sitting around idle.

I requested Ziegler's file, expecting a slim volume like Nic's, only for a thick ledger to arrive. I took it to a private reading room and pored over it. It was mostly lists of his clients and the details—where known—of what he'd been up to with them, how much he was milking them for. I skipped the bulk of it and focused on his background info.

Rudi Ziegler was his real name. Fifty-one, of Eastern European stock. A bachelor. No close family. No clashes with the law. Declared about ninety thousand annually but drew in the region of one-fifty to two hundred. Had a good reputation but wasn't above ripping off wealthy old women. Went abroad every year for a month's vacation. Didn't own much in the way of property apart from a moderate villa on a Caribbean island. No business interests outside of his own.

He specialized in Incan guides. From what I could gather, every medium has a spirit guide who helps put him in contact with the dear departed. Usually it's an Indian or a little girl, but Ziegler preferred Incas. And—this caught my attention—the Incas used to worship the sun.

I scribbled swiftly. "Incas—sun worshippers—Nic's brooch—Priscilla's ring—carving on Nic's back—*connection???*"

I was hoping there'd be dirt on him—clients who had mysteriously vanished, contacts of his who'd met with nasty ends—but I couldn't find any. If The Cardinal didn't yank me off the case I'd return to this file, but the day was wearing on and I wanted to be back in time for my big meeting. I returned the file, then called Ziegler—an answering machine. His cell phone cut directly to voice mail. I pondered my next move. I could wait and call again, or I could head over and try catching him at home.

I was in no mood for waiting, so I tucked Ziegler's address away in a pocket, fetched my bike and went searching.

Rudi Ziegler lived above a butcher's shop in a run-down part of the city. I parked out front and chained my back wheel to a fire hydrant. The lower hall door was open, so I entered. The smell of blood tracked me up the stairs like a dog. I found his door and knocked.

A sleepy Ziegler answered. He was overweight, flesh hanging off him like warm wax. Quivering gray lips, red spiderwebs for eyes, purple, vein-shot cheeks. There was a half-empty bottle of vodka in his hand. He was dressed in a shabby robe and moth-eaten slippers. Hard to believe this wreck of a man drew a couple of hundred grand a year.

"May I help you?" he asked in an oddly lyrical voice. I took another look at him, surprised the throat had survived the ravages of drink when all else hadn't.

"Rudi Ziegler?"

"None other. Come in, please." I followed him in and he shut the door. "Do you drink?" he asked, offering me a swig. I shook my head. "Wise man. Demons dwell within." He blew his nose into a satin handkerchief and studied me. "You're here about Nicola, aren't you?"

I twitched. "How did you know?"

"I have my ways," he said, lowering his face so that it darkened and split into a wizardish smile. "She came to me in a vision last night and said I could expect a stranger to call and ask intrusive questions. She told me not to cooperate." I stared, edgy, until his laughter took the spine-tingling sting out of the moment.

"A joke," he sighed. "The dead don't talk to me, despite what my business card says. I've just had so many people here this last week, first detectives, then the police, that I've grown accustomed to their inquisitive appearance. Besides, my clients don't turn up uninvited."

"What detectives?" I asked curiously.

"They didn't leave names. Nor did they tell me what they wanted. It was only when I heard about her death that I figured it out."

They must have been The Cardinal's men, the ones who put the file on Nic together.

"May *I* ask some questions, Mr. Ziegler?"

"By all means. Follow, dear boy, follow." He led the way through to a large room that served as his work chamber. The walls were covered with billowing curtains and the scent of incense hung heavily in the air. A large table dominated the center of the room. Clothes and bric-a-brac were scattered untidily everywhere I looked. A huge sun medallion was pinned to the ceiling.

When we were seated I told him who I was, explained how I wasn't a detective, just a concerned friend. He said it didn't matter, he'd talk to me anyway. I started off by asking about his profession. "Is this where you work?"

"It is." He cast an eye over the room. "Though it's usually not in such a state. Nicola's death left its mark." He shook the bottle of vodka. "You wouldn't see this out so early on a normal day."

"Can you tell me more about what you do? Do you tell fortunes, locate missing people, speak with the dead?"

"A bit of everything. I'm a dabbler." He stood and tidied some magazines away. "I provide whatever my clients wish. If they want their fortune read, I put the crystal ball or tarot to good use. If they want to speak to the dead, I oblige—I'm quite good at throwing my voice. If they want to *see* the dead, I do that too. Mirrors and smoke. Projected images."

"You're very open about your deception."

"I have nothing to hide from those who are not interested in hiring me."

"How about dark magic?"

"I don't believe in magic," he snapped. "I trade in tricks, shadows, illusions. Nothing else."

"But if your client believes, and wants to see demons and devils, what then?"

"I turn them away. Illusions stretch so far but no further. I'm good, Mr. Jeery, a professional. But I have my limits."

"You don't dabble in the dark arts at all?"

"Never. I use Ouija boards and cards, but never in the right way, never—"

"The *right* way?" I was on him in a flash.

"The correct way. The actual—"

"You just said you didn't believe in any of that."

"I don't, but—"

"Then surely *any* way's the *right* way."

He dabbed at his forehead with his handkerchief and downed another shot of vodka. "I don't *believe*," he said softly, "but one encounters things in my line which cannot be explained, apparitions which cannot be accounted for. Are they demons? Souls of the dead made visible? I don't know. I simply play games with the forces of the arcane. Games are all I'm interested in."

"Was Nicola Hornyak only interested in games?" I asked.

"No. At first she was happy with what I had to offer—my bag of voices, Incan spirits, clouds of fog and changes in temperature. But she soon wanted to take it further."

"How far?"

"She wanted…" He laughed. "She wanted a lover. A spirit lover. She wanted to screw a demon."

"Christ."

"I fobbed her off for a time with vague promises—I claimed to be privy to certain ancient rites—but eventually, when pressed, had to say that I was afraid of opening up dark portals which were best kept closed. That sort of garbage."

"Why not tell her the truth?"

"And put myself out of business? I never tell my clients they're barking up banana trees. You don't get rich that way."

I mused on his words, then asked what happened next.

"She moved on."

"To another mystic?"

"I'm not sure. She came a few more times, but not as regularly as before."

"When did you last see her?"

"About a month before her death. Maybe three weeks."

"Why did she come?"

"To show me her demon lover."

I frowned. "What are you talking about?"

"She came with a menacing-looking black man. According to her, he was her lover from beyond. She wouldn't tell me how she'd contacted him, but said he was everything she'd ever wanted, and more." He giggled into a fist. "I'd love to know what he did to convince her of his credentials."

"What did he look like?" I asked, though I already knew.

"Very dark-skinned. Tall. Bald. Tattoos of snakes on both cheeks."

"Did he speak while he was here?"

"No. He remained in the background. She was only here a few minutes. Popped in to show him off and then she was on her merry way. Off to make whoopee with Beelzebub."

That clinched it for me. Nic ran into Paucar Wami while playing games, he toyed with her until she ceased to amuse him, then killed her. But I decided to press ahead with a few more questions—if, as I hoped, this interview marked the end of my career as a private detective, I wanted to go out on a high note.

"You know Nic was wearing a brooch when she was found?"

"One of mine. Yes. And an image of the sun had been carved into her back."

I nodded at the sun symbol attached to the ceiling. "You use Incan spirit guides, don't you?"

"Yes. They add an exotic touch."

"Could Nic's death tie in with any of that? Might the killer have been one of your other clients, somebody—"

"I doubt it," he interrupted. "The Incas were as brutal as any other conquering nation, but they weren't savages. Besides, they worshipped the sun. If Nic was intended as a sacrifice to Incan gods—which is what you seem to be suggesting—she'd have been murdered during the day, for the sun god to see. And why murder her at the Skylight? You've heard of the Manco Capac statue?"

I was about to say I hadn't when I recalled The Cardinal pointing out some cranes to me. "Yes."

"That would be the perfect location for a sacrifice. If Nic had been killed there, I'd say pursue the angle. As things stand, a much likelier explanation is that her killer noticed the brooch and copied its design, perhaps to throw a red herring into the works."

That made sense, though I didn't admit it out loud.

"Did she ever bring anybody else here?"

"No. I prefer to meet clients on a one-to-one basis."

"Who introduced her to you?"

He hesitated. "One of her friends. I forget her name. She attended a few sessions, then quit not long after persuading Nicola to come. Hasn't been back. I've never had a good memory for names."

On impulse, I produced one of the photos of Priscilla I'd taken from her file, the best of a bad lot. "This her?"

He masked his look of recognition quickly—barely more than a slight lift of his eyebrows—but I'd been trained to notice the most minor body tic. "I'm not sure," he said. "The face looks familiar but I really couldn't say."

He was lying. Priscilla had lied too—she'd told me she'd never been here.

I pocketed the photo and stood. "Thanks for seeing me, Mr. Ziegler." He rose, smiling. "You don't have any names you could pass on? Other mystics she'd have been likely to visit?"

He lifted his hands helplessly. "I could give you a dozen. But I'm not part of a network—I rarely make referrals. I have no idea who she may or may not have seen. You can try calling around but I doubt you'll get very far. Only a two-bit operator would reveal a client's name, and Nicola was not the sort to get involved with merchants like that. She was cautious. Lighthearted but not light-headed."

"Well, thanks again." I shook his hand.

"Glad to be of assistance," he said. "She was a lovely lady. She did not deserve to meet with such a horrible end."

"If I need to contact you again?" I asked.

"Any time. Mornings are best, when I'm at my quietest. But if it's urgent, any time."

"Great."

"Take care, Mr. Jeery," he said and closed the door.

I hurried down the stairs, the smell of blood rising from the shop below, sticking in my nostrils, to my clothes, my hair. I'd need a shower when I got home—wouldn't do to visit The Cardinal stinking like a gutted pig.

The mystic knew Priscilla. And she knew him. I could understand Ziegler's covering up—client confidentiality—but why would Priscilla lie about something so trivial?

I waited two hours to see The Cardinal, at the end of which I was told he would be unavailable for the remainder of the night. Cancellations weren't rare—his time was at a premium. Members of government and foreign dignitaries had been stood up many times before me, so I didn't take it personally. I rescheduled for three o'clock Sunday afternoon and took the elevator down to the basement, where I changed out of my uniform again.

A light breeze was blowing at my back most of the way home and I coasted along with it. As I pulled up outside my apartment block a light went on in a car parked several feet farther up. I glanced over and saw Howard Kett hunched behind the wheel, eyeing me coldly. The light went off and I knew he wanted to see me.

Leaving my bike, I went to see what Kett was after. I let myself in the passenger door. We sat in darkness for all of a minute, saying nothing, Kett staring directly ahead. He was an old-fashioned cop. Big heart, big hands, big, thick head, of Irish descent. Did a lot of community work in his spare time. Solid gold if you were a law-abiding citizen, one of hell's demons if you weren't. He had a special loathing for The Cardinal and those who served him.

"You're an arrogant son of a bitch," he finally growled.

"You came all this way just to tell me that, Howie?" He hated the nickname. "You should have phoned."

"I came this morning but you were gone. Been sitting here more than an hour."

"Again—the phone."

"You were banging that Hornyak kid." No beating around the bush. The insolence would have startled me if it had been anybody else. With Kett, I expected it.

"So what?" I said as evenly as I could.

"Why didn't you come forward when you heard what happened?"

"No point. I was out of town when she was killed. Nothing to tell. I figured, if you wanted to question me, you'd come. And here you are."

"Did Casey know you were seeing her?"

"No," I lied.

"Bullshit," Kett snarled. "I always said his friendship with you would be his downfall. If I find out he knew you were involved with her and deliberately suppressed the information, he's finished. I'll drum him out myself."

"Bill's my friend, not my confessor." I leaned back in the seat and flicked on the overhead light. Kett immediately quenched it—he didn't want to be seen. "What's up, Howie? Planning to beat a confession out of me?"

"Like you wouldn't have a team of The Cardinal's finest lawyers on me in ten seconds flat if I did." He prodded me in the chest. "But I'll tell you this, Jeery, if you bother Nicholas Hornyak again, I'll do more than slap you around."

"What's Nick Hornyak got to do with anything?" I asked quietly.

"I know you were pestering him."

"How?"

"I have my sources," he said smugly.

"All I did was ask some questions. He didn't—"

"You don't have the right to ask shit!" Kett roared, then lowered his voice. "You were humping the broad—so what? So was every leprous son of a whore with a one-inch excuse for a dick. Don't interfere, Jeery. This isn't your business."

"Whose is it? Yours?" I laughed. "You don't have a hope in hell of finding her killer."

"That ain't here and that ain't there. I'm paid to check on dumb bitches who go and get themselves fucked over. You aren't. I don't want you sniffing around."

"You can't stop me."

"No?"

I smiled in the darkness. "No."

Kett cursed quietly. "Let's talk about this reasonably. We don't have to be at each other's throats. You were right when you said we probably won't find her killer, and if you want to waste your time chasing him, I won't try blocking you—though I could if I wanted," he insisted. "But I'll leave you be as long as you don't go meddling where you shouldn't."

"I'm listening, Howie."

"Nicholas Hornyak didn't kill her."

"I never said he did."

"So why question him?"

"That's a dumb question for a cop to ask," I chided him.

"OK," he bristled. "You wanted to learn more about her, where she came from, what sort of a life she led. You wanted to rub him up for clues and contacts. I get it. But that's where it ends. Don't go near him again."

"Why? Has he got something to hide?"

"No. But he likes his privacy."

"Don't we all?"

"Sure, but Hornyak's got the money to protect it. He has friends in high places, who know people like me, who don't like it when he runs to them with tales of being manhandled by some punk ex-humper-of-his-sister."

"I didn't manhandle him. I asked some questions. He answered politely. We parted on good terms. I don't see what the problem is."

"I don't care what you see or what you think," Kett sneered. "I've warned you nicely—stay away from Nicholas Hornyak. Next time it might not be a cop that's sent. And it might be more than a verbal warning."

"You threatening me, Howie?"

He laughed. "Now who's asking the dumb questions?"

"These *friends* of Nick's," I said slowly. "Don't suppose you'd care to pass their names on to me, so I could drop them a line and let them know—"

"Out," he snapped, reaching over and opening the door. I swung my legs out and stepped onto the pavement. "This conversation never happened," he hissed. I smiled at him in answer and slammed the door in his face.

Upstairs I dug out my notebook and jotted down a brief transcription of my encounter with Kett. When I was done I read over what I'd written, scratched behind my ears with the tip of my pen and wondered what it added up to. I'd said nothing to Nick to warrant such treatment. I'd had no reason to suspect him of any involvement with the murder. Until this.

It didn't make sense. Sending Kett after me had only raised my suspicions. I found it hard to believe the sharp guy I'd found playing pool in the Red Throat would make such a clumsy move, implicating himself when there was no need. He might be toying with me—using the ever-serious Kett to mess with my head—but so soon after his sister's death?

Something was foul. Howie or Nick had made a dumb move by coming down on me. But the fact that I couldn't figure out which it was, or why they'd done it, hinted that I was dumber than both of them. The sooner The Cardinal pulled me off this crazy case and put me back on patrol at Party Central, the better.

8

I was passing a peaceful Sunday morning in bed, enjoying the lazy silence, when someone knocked on the door. I groaned, shrugged off the covers, pulled on a pair of shorts and a shirt, and went to see who it was. I discovered a skinny mulatto kid on the landing, leaning on a skateboard almost as big as himself.

"Help you, son?" I said as pleasantly as I could.

"Al Jeery?"

"Yeah."

"Fabio asked me to fetch you. Says he needs your hands."

It had been a couple of years since Fabio last called but I knew instantly what he wanted. "Give me a few minutes to change," I said, and slipped back inside.

I asked the kid where we were going when I was dressed but he wouldn't tell me—insisted on leading the way. He hopped on his board, waited for me to mount my bike, then set off, cutting a fair pace through the quiet streets. I had to be sharp to keep up, especially when he turned corners in a screech of dust and vanished halfway down dark alleys while I was struggling to brake and correct my course.

It was a muggy day and I soon began to wish I'd stuck with the shorts, but it was too late to turn back. I just had to sweat and bear it.

My guide led me deep into the south of the city, its literal heart of darkness, where members of the Kool Kats Klub feared to tread. It was familiar territory—I'd grown up here—but I hadn't been back much since marrying Ellen and moving out.

The skater stopped outside a six-story building of sorry-ass apartments, most of which were occupied by squatters or those existing just above the poverty line. "He's in 4B," the kid sniffed.

"Thanks." I started up.

"Hey! He said you'd tip."

I eyed the grifter suspiciously. I doubted he'd have skated all the way over and back unless he'd been paid in advance. But I have a soft spot for cocky runts, having been one myself. I tossed a balled-up note that he caught in midair. Leaped back on his board and disappeared. Didn't occur to him to thank me.

I climbed the creaking stairs to the fourth and found Fabio in a chair outside the apartment, sipping a beer, waiting patiently. Fabio was the city's oldest pimp, a hundred and three if rumors were to be believed. He'd been a big shot once, long before The Cardinal came to power, but these days he eked out a meager living from a handful of aging ladies of the night. He called them his retirement posse.

"Morning, Algeria," he greeted me in his slow drawl.

I took his wrinkly, age-spotted hand and shook it gently. He'd been good to me when I was growing up. Running errands for him had kept me in pocket money and he'd watched out for me when my mother died.

"How're the hands?" he asked, turning them over to examine my palms.

"Haven't used them a lot lately," I sighed. "Not since you last called me out. The drink put paid to that."

"You're off it now though, ain't you?"

"Trying."

Fabio stroked the smooth palms. "Reckon you can still work the magic?"

"I'll try," I said, "but I can't promise."

"That'll do for me." He stood and pushed through the open door. A large black woman was on the floor of the tiny but tidy living room, playing with a boy no more than six or seven years old. She looked up at me and smiled.

"Algeria, this is Florence," Fabio introduced us. "Flo, this is Al Jeery, the guy I was telling you about."

"I'm pleased to meet you, Mr. Jeery." She had a warm voice.

"Same here, ma'am," I replied, then cocked an eyebrow at Fabio. "Her or the kid?"

"The kid. Father's doing fifteen—killed a guy in a brawl. Used to be pretty free with his belt when he was around. Maybe worse, but we ain't sure about that. Kid's been having nightmares for months. Flo's tried explaining that he don't have nothing to fear, the bastard's locked up and won't be coming back, but it ain't helped. He's a bright kid but falling to pieces. Barely sleeps, tired all day, gets into fights. She had to take him out of school."

"He should see a psychiatrist," I said.

"Look around," Fabio snapped. "This look like the Skylight? Flo's one of my girls but she's barely working—spends all her time fussing over the kid. She can't afford no goddamn psychiatrist."

"Is that why you're helping her, because she's not earning for you?"

He snickered. "You know me inside out, Algeria. But that don't change the facts—this kid needs help, and it's you or it's nothing."

Fabio knew I was a sucker for a lost cause. This wasn't the first time he'd tugged at my heartstrings to manipulate me, but I never could bring myself to hate him for it.

"I'll give it a go," I sighed, removing my jacket. "But if he resists, or it doesn't work first time, I won't push."

"It'll work," Fabio assured me, then nodded at Flo to stand.

"What's your son's name?" I asked.

"Drake." She was nervous. "You won't hurt him, will you?"

I smiled at her. "No. Fabio's explained what I do?"

"Kind of."

"There's no risk involved. It works or it doesn't. Worst case, Drake goes on like he is. Do you have a pack of cards?" She handed them over. She'd been holding them since before I came and they were warm from the heat of her hands.

I knelt and waited for the kid to look up and catch my eye. When he did I smiled. "Hi, Drake. My name's Al. I'm a friend of your mother's."

He studied me suspiciously. "Are you gonna take me away?" He had a thin, reedy voice.

"Why do you think that?"

"My daddy said if I wasn't good, a man would come and take me away."

"But you've been good, haven't you?"

"I been kicked out of school," he said, half-ashamed, half-proud.

"That's nothing. I got kicked out of four schools when I was a kid." It was the truth. "Does you good to have a break from all that teaching."

"What were you kicked out for?" Drake asked.

"Can't say. Not in front of a lady." I winked at Flo. "Want to see a card trick?"

He perked up. "Is it a good one?"

"Best around."

"My friend Spike does tricks. He taught me a few."

"I bet he's never shown you one like this." I started shuffling slowly. "Keep your eyes on the cards." I shuffled for a minute, then slapped four cards down on the floor. "Pick one but don't tell me." He ran his eyes over the cards. "Picked?" He nodded. I gathered the cards and shuffled again. "Watch the deck. Don't look away even for a second. Trick won't work if you do."

I speeded up the shuffle, speaking softly, telling him to keep watching. I flipped the deck over, so he could see the faces of the cards, and moved up another few notches, telling him to watch the colors, focus on the numbers, concentrate.

After a couple of minutes I laid down another four cards. "Is one of them the card you picked?" He gazed in silence, as if he wasn't sure, then slowly shook his head. I picked them up and shuffled again. This time I didn't have to tell him to watch the cards—his eyes followed of their own accord.

Three or four minutes later I laid the cards aside and waved a hand in front of Drake's wide-open eyes—no reaction. I smiled tightly at Fabio and Flo. "It's working. Have a pillow ready for when I'm through."

I placed the index and middle fingers of both hands on either side of Drake's head and softly massaged his temples. I crossed my legs and sat opposite the boy, hunched over so our heads were level.

"Look into my eyes, Drake," I whispered. "Focus on my pupils. Do you see cards in them? Colors?" He nodded. "Concentrate on the colors and count to fifty inside your head. Can you count that high?" He shook his head. "Then count to ten, five times. Can you do that?" A nod. "Good boy. When you're done, close your eyes and sleep. But carry on listening to what I'm saying, OK?"

I continued rubbing his temples while our gazes were locked. I tried not to blink. I spoke as he counted, commenting on the colors, the blood-red hearts, the night-black clubs, the sparkling diamonds, the plain spades. When he closed his eyes I took a deep breath, let my lids shut and pressed my forehead to his.

"Breathe slowly," I said. "Take a breath, hold it for five seconds, let it out, then breathe again." I breathed the same way and within a minute we were coordinated, lungs working in harmony, as if connected. My fingers never stopped at his temples, neither slowing nor quickening.

"I want you to think about your nightmares, Drake. Who appears in them?" I felt his frown and his head shook slightly. "It's all right. You can tell me. Nobody can hurt you while I'm here. Who appears in your dreams?"

"Daddy," he said quietly.

"Think about your dad. Focus on him and the way he looks when you sleep at night, the things he does. Are you doing it, Drake?"

"Yes." He was frightened but he trusted me.

"Now I'm gonna help you push the nightmares away. You feel my head against yours?" A nod. "Imagine there's a tunnel between them, linking us. It's wide, as wide as it needs to be. You see it, Drake?"

"Black," he whispered.

"Yes. But you needn't be afraid. It's only a tunnel. There's red in it too, if you look closely. Can you see the red?"

A pause, then, with excitement, "Yes! Red. Like the cards."

"Exactly. That's all it is, Drake, a tunnel of cards. Are you afraid of it?"

"No." Positive this time.

"Good. Now take those nightmares, all the pictures of your father, and push them down the tunnel. It's easy. They'll slide along like ice cream through a cone on a really hot day. Are you pushing?"

"Yes."

"Push steadily, until they're gone from your head, every one of them, so that they come out the other end of the tunnel, on *my* side."

"They're bad dreams. I don't want to give them to you."

"It's OK," I said, touched by his concern. "They can't hurt me. I know how to deal with them."

A long silence followed. I felt Drake pushing as told, his tiny muscles quivering as he thrust. I pictured his bad thoughts spilling into my mind and mentally slid them to the rear of my brain as they gushed in, rendering them harmless.

Eventually he went limp and started to fall away from me. I held him in place with my fingers and said, "Don't move, Drake, not yet. We aren't finished."

"I'm tired," he moaned.

"Me too. But it won't be much longer." When he was straight, I rubbed the sides of his head again. "Are all the nightmares gone?"

"Yes," he whispered.

"Good. Now I want you to close the tunnel. Just pull at a few of the cards and the whole lot will come tumbling down. Are you pulling, Drake?"

"Yes."

"Are the cards collapsing?"

"No, they're ... Yes! Now they are. Falling everywhere."

"Is the tunnel gone?"

"Almost. It's going ... it's ... gone."

I sighed deeply and peeled my head away from the boy's. I left my fingers where they were and kept my eyes shut. "When I remove my hands, I want you to lie down and rest. You've done a lot of good work today. Don't fight sleep when it comes—you've got nothing to be scared of anymore. The nightmares are gone. You got rid of them; they won't ever come back."

"Are you sure?" he asked.

"Yes. You pushed them down the tunnel, then tore it apart. There's no way back for them. Understand?"

A pause, then, "No way back."

"Gone for good?"

He nodded.

"Count to ten now, Drake, and when you get to the end, I'll let go and you can sleep. Do you want to sleep?"

"Uh-huh," he yawned.

"Start counting."

When he reached ten he toppled. I caught him by the shoulders, then opened my eyes and called for the pillow. Fabio laid it on the floor and I leaned the boy down, positioning his head so it rested on the soft material, then tucking his arms in and straightening his legs.

"There," I said, sitting up, exhausted. "He should be all right now. He might be a little confused when he wakes. Treat him carefully for a day or two, give him plenty to eat, keep him inside. If he seems OK after that, let him out to play, then try him at school when they let him back in."

"Will the dreams return?" Flo asked, standing over the sleeping boy, a look of uncertain hope etched into her features.

"I doubt it. If they do, send for me and I'll try again. But he should be fine." I told Fabio I'd only give it one shot, but that was before meeting the boy. It's never easy to be clinical once you become personally involved.

"You want something to eat or drink, Algeria?" Fabio asked.

"A glass of water and some fresh air."

"Coming right up."

Flo coughed and looked sheepish. "I can't pay you, but in a month or two—"

I raised a hand. "Send me a card next Christmas, tell me how he's doing and we'll call it quits."

"Thank you, Mr. Jeery," she sobbed, taking my hands and squeezing hard.

"Thank *you*, ma'am," I replied, "for trusting me."

Fabio handed me the water, I gulped it, then he led me downstairs, into the open, to recover.

I'd been *curing* people since I was a kid, guided by Fabio, who'd been the first to note my calming influence. He'd spotted me hanging around, befriending wild cats and dogs. I used to slide up to them, ignoring their growls and raised hackles, talking softly, extending my fingers. Within minutes they'd be flopping over onto their backs, offering me their stomachs to rub, letting me play with their ears and feed them scraps.

Fabio initially tested me on a scattering of people plagued with migraines. He found that by talking to and touching them I was able to bring measures of relief to their lives. After that it was troubled friends of his, old men and women who sat around mumbling to themselves, tormented by visions of the past. I'd hold their hands and talk, and they seemed lighter of spirit when we departed. One old dear said she'd had her first full night of sleep in twenty years after my visit.

Fabio helped me develop my skills, modeling my techniques on those of other healers. We tried various methods before settling on the cards, which suited me best. Fabio hoped to make a killing, bring me along slowly, keep it low-key so I didn't attract the attention of sharper operators. Then he planned to launch me on a wealthier clientele and make them pay through the nose.

Things didn't work out that way. My mother was proud of my healing abilities but believed it would be immoral to profit from them. She blocked Fabio's efforts to turn me into a cash cow, coming down hard when she caught him pulling a sly one behind her back, terminating contact between us for months at a stretch.

He tried convincing me to go on the road with him when she was gone but she'd died slowly, horribly, and for a couple of years I wanted nothing to do with sick people. I turned my back on my powers, on the ill, on Fabio. He remained a friend—maybe because he liked me, maybe because he thought I'd come around in the end—but by the time I got my life back on track I was part of the Troops. The lure of the healing profession had passed me by.

Resigning himself, Fabio settled on asking for occasional favors, only calling me when he was in a fix. Nobody other than Fabio and those I helped knew of my powers. I never advertised. I didn't want hordes of miracle-worshippers camping out on my doorstep.

I'd no idea where the power stemmed from. I didn't believe in God; I hadn't made a study of the phenomenon; it wasn't something I sought or cherished. It was just a talent I'd been born with. Maybe it was the city—as *Time* had attested, these streets were paved with supernatural wonders. Perhaps some of the wonder had rubbed off on me.

I'd almost forgotten about the power these last few years. Alcohol had screwed up my head. I could hardly help others when I was in dire need of aid myself. And since sobering up I'd had more pressing matters on my mind—divorce, staying sober, work, piecing together a new life.

I thought about it while sitting in the wreck of a burned-out car with Fabio at the foot of the block. I brooded upon the old questions: How do I do it? Can any harm come of it? Is it spiritual, physical, psychological? Did I really help Drake or had I just driven the demons deep for a while?

Fabio sighed and patted me on the back. "You ain't lost your touch, Algeria. You were smooth. Way quicker than you were last time I called you out."

I grunted, recalling the hours I'd spent on his last "customer," another of his street maidens, a young woman who'd been in and out of mental hospitals her entire life. I was still drinking at the time. I seemed to help her, but a few months later she plunged to her death in the river.

"Thinking about Cassie?" he asked. "That wasn't your fault. She was messed up bad. If anybody was in the wrong, it was me, for letting you at her in the state you was in."

"Think I could have saved her today?" I asked.

He shrugged. "Who knows? A kid like Drake hasn't had time to let the pain sink deep. Different when a sufferer's older and the trouble ain't so easily identifiable. You tried. That's the most any of us can do."

I stared up through the fire-eroded roof, letting the sun warm me.

"Feel good?" Fabio asked.

"Yeah."

"You should do it more often."

I smiled. "Hire a tent? Preach the Bible? Go out into the world and cure the masses? Earn a fortune?"

"That ain't what I'm talking about. You got a God-given talent, no matter what you believe. It's a sin to waste it, working for The Cardinal, staining your hands with blood when you could be using them to heal. It ain't right."

"I couldn't do this full-time, Fabio. It's nice to come here every so often, do a good deed and go back feeling like the man who broke the bank at Monte Carlo. But the Troops are my life. Party Central's where I belong."

"A man of healing don't belong nowhere but among those who need him." Fabio sniffed righteously. "You should be helping people live, not killing them."

"I don't kill many," I replied, low-voiced.

"Makes no difference. You got a calling. I'm no holier-than-thou missionary—I've killed in my time, yes I have, and I'd do it again if I had to. But you..." He scowled. "I'm wasting my breath, ain't I?"

I sighed. "This is the path I've chosen."

"OK. I'll shut up." He turned and smiled. "How's life otherwise? Get over the shock of finding your woman in the Fridge yet?"

I shook my head, bemused. "How'd you know about that?"

"I pick things up." He wasn't boasting. Fabio was as close to the heartbeat of this city as anyone I knew. I decided, since he'd brought it up, to ask a few questions. There was no telling what I might learn from an old gossipmonger like Fabio.

"Any idea who killed her?"

"Nope. Word is it was a crazy, maybe from out of town. A john she picked up somewhere and—"

"A *john*? She was a pro?"

"You didn't know?"

I shook my head, stunned.

"She wasn't a regular. And she kept it quiet. Nobody would have known, except sometimes she'd ball a guy in an alley or take him back to her apartment or a fancy hotel, and he'd talk, bragging the way you do when you're young."

"Nic was a *hooker*?"

"An amateur. That could be another angle—she might have tricked where she shouldn't, or rubbed a pimp up the wrong way. But word of that would've spread. My money's on the john."

Nic's being a pro changed everything. I'd been looking for boyfriends when it seemed I should have been scouring the streets for *clients*.

"Did you know any of her customers?" I asked.

"A couple, but they're both in the clear—I did a bit of checking. As for the rest, I haven't a clue. I never heard of her going with the same guy twice. You can ask around but I doubt you'll unearth anything. Your best bet is to have a chat with a bitch called Priscilla Perdue. They used to—"

He stopped when he saw my face falling.

"Know her?"

"I had a drink with her last night."

"How come?"

"I didn't know much about Nic. I've been trying to put together a clearer picture. It seems important now that she's gone."

"Uh-huh." If he guessed I was lying, he kept his suspicions under wraps. "That Perdue's a nasty piece of work, ain't she?"

"She seemed sweet enough," I hastened to her defense. Then I remembered the Ku Klux Klub. "A little rough around the edges."

"She got no edges," Fabio chuckled. "She's sharp all over, like a porcupine."

"She said nothing to me about Nic being a hooker. Is she one too?"

Fabio shrugged. "She sleeps around like a whore, but I don't think she does it for money. She's a strange bitch. Used to dress all in black a few years back, holes in the skirts around her bush, so everyone could see. Walked around with her tail in the air, like those posh-ass cats in the Pepé Le Pew cartoons."

"Think she had anything to do with the murder?"

"It wouldn't surprise me, but it's not something I'd assume. As far as I know she's never been into anything other than old-fashioned sleaze."

We chatted a bit more about the two girls—he had no further revelations—then life in general. He asked how I was getting on at Party Central. Since he didn't seem to know I'd been reassigned, I said everything was fine. I started to ask after old friends but then noticed the time and said I had to run.

Fabio told me not to be such a stranger, to call again soon. I said I would but we both knew it was an idle promise. I asked him to keep me apprised of Drake's progress and let me know if the nightmares returned. We parted with a handshake and a few words of farewell, then I was on my way to Party Central for my meeting with The Cardinal.

He was seated by the window when I entered, playing with a puppet, looking pensive. When he spotted my reflection in the glass he turned and brightened.

"Al!" he boomed. "If you've cracked the case already, I'll be impressed."

"Afraid not," I grinned ruefully. "I've made some inroads but that's not why I'm here. There's a problem…"

I told him about my meetings with Nick, Ziegler and Priscilla, the descriptions of Nic's companion each had presented me with and my belief that the man was Paucar Wami. He listened silently, his face a blank.

"You've been busy," he grunted when I finished, laying aside the puppet.

"I thought I should tell you about him before I went any further."

"You did right." He began biting the nails of his right hand. "Tell me what else you've discovered about her."

I went through the past three days as fully as possible. I told him about Nic's secret sex life and her connection with Priscilla Perdue, about Ziegler, his sun symbols and pretending not to know Priscilla. He said nothing, letting me tell it my own way.

"You think she may have been a sacrificial lamb to the god of the sun?" he asked at the end.

"Probably not. She introduced Wami to Ziegler. If Wami killed her, he might have carved the sun symbol into her back to point the finger of guilt at the medium."

"You believe Ziegler's innocent?"

"He knows more than he's admitting, but I don't think he killed her."

"You think it was Paucar Wami."

"Yeah."

"And if it wasn't?"

I shrugged. "A john who did it for kicks."

He nodded slowly, then said, "It *wasn't* Wami."

"Oh?" I didn't dare say more.

"You're forgetting the way she was killed, the messy slashes. The experts say it was the work of an amateur."

"That could have been intentional," I suggested. "He might not have wanted to be linked to the death. It may have been done to throw us off the scent."

The Cardinal smiled. "You know nothing about Paucar Wami. He's killed under many guises in his time, but never pretended to be anything other than a professional. He takes pride in his work and fears no one. He would never spoil the beauty of a kill."

"You think killing's beautiful?" I kept a neutral tone.

"I can take or leave it. But to Wami it's an art form. He has made death his life's study. It's all that interests him. Murdering in this fashion would be entirely out of character."

I shifted on my feet—he hadn't asked me to sit—and cleared my throat. "Sir, you're correct when you say I don't know anything about Paucar Wami. But he's a killer. And I know he—or somebody fitting his description—was seen with Nic in the weeks prior to her death. In the absence of other concrete suspects, I think it would be lunacy to—"

"Are you calling me a lunatic?" The Cardinal asked. He didn't seem insulted, merely curious.

"No, sir," I checked myself. "Of course not. But I think we should explore this. If he's out of town, we can cross him off our list. But if he's here and he *was* the one she was seen with…"

The Cardinal was silent awhile. When he spoke, it was over his fingernails, and only barely audible. "Wami *is* here. He took out Johnny Grace a couple of days ago."

I rolled onto the balls of my feet as though to breathe in the fumes of proof. I wanted to shout, "There! You see!" but didn't. Instead I held my tongue and let The Cardinal draw the conclusions himself. After a long pause, he spoke.

"If Wami is the killer—and I still harbor strenuous doubts—we must tread carefully. He's not a man to cross lightly. I'd like to know his reasons for killing Nicola Hornyak, and why he chose the Skylight, but I won't push. Knowing it was him would be answer enough."

I phrased my next question as cautiously as possible. "Do you need *me* to ask him? I believe you've had dealings with Paucar Wami in the past. Couldn't you get in contact and…?"

The Cardinal's face darkened. "Are you telling me how to run my investigation?" he snapped.

"No, sir, I was just—"

"Just nothing!" he roared. "If I wanted to call Wami, I'd call him. I don't need a flunky like you telling me—"

He cut himself short. I stood quivering, fearing for my future. After a few seconds of seething silence, he grinned wickedly. "Stop shaking. I'm not going to eat you."

"Could I have that in writing, sir?"

His grin spread. "I like you, Al. We'll get along fine if you don't tell me what to do. I've never been one for taking orders, even in the form of polite suggestions. I *could* contact Paucar Wami and put the question to him myself. But I won't. That would be cheating."

"Cheating who, sir, if you don't mind my asking?"

"Thee and me, Al. I promised you a chance to make a name for yourself. It wouldn't be fair to deny you after you've made such an impressive start."

"I wouldn't mind," I hastily interjected.

He laughed throatily. "I'd also be cheating myself out of a good show. It's drama of this nature which renews my faith in life. Ordinary diversions bore me. Alcohol, drugs, books, gambling, women—all are wasted on me. Do you know what keeps me going, Al? People out of their depth. I thrive on it."

"Some call that sadism."

A potentially perilous answer but he dismissed the notion with a snort. "Sadists enjoy watching people suffer. I prefer to see people triumph, or at least put up a good fight as they go down. The thought of a confrontation between you and Paucar Wami fascinates me. If he threatens your life, will you run or stand up to him?"

"No doubt about it," I said. "I'll run."

"I don't think so," The Cardinal smiled. "That's why I chose you for this. Not because I knew about Wami's possible involvement but because I sensed situations of this nature might develop, situations which would exhaust a normal man but which one of your resolve and resources might endeavor to surmount."

"What resolve and resources? I don't have any."

"You sell yourself short," he contradicted me.

He could be an infuriating son of a bitch when he wanted. How can you argue with a man who's full of praise for you?

"What happens now?" I asked. "I go after Wami, he kills me, you look for a new source of entertainment?"

"Possibly," The Cardinal nodded. "Though it needn't pan out that way.

I think we should grant Wami the benefit of the doubt. If you approach him diplomatically, you might emerge from the encounter unscathed. Plus, if he is the killer, I won't demand his head, just proof. If you can pin him to the scene of the crime without confronting him, all the better."

"If I made a formal request to be transferred—"

"—I'd turn it down."

I put on a brave front. "And if I quit?"

"Resign from the Troops?" The Cardinal stroked his nose. "That would be...disappointing."

"Would you punish me?"

"No. I'd wonder how I'd misjudged a man so badly, then dismiss you from my thoughts and leave you to eke out a worthless, shameful excuse of a life."

"Who gave you the right to pass judgment on me?" I snapped.

"Nobody," he replied coolly. "I took it." When I looked away, disgusted, he slid into sympathetic mode. "It's not me you stand to fail—it's yourself. Be honest, hasn't it felt good to be out on your own, following your instincts, homing in on the truth?"

I nodded slowly. "I've enjoyed it more than I thought I would."

"Because this is what you were meant for. Not so much the investigating, rather the use of your mind. You're one of those rare beings with the power to create your own destiny. I'm trying to free you. That's not my main motive—the game appeals to me the most—but that's the true prize for you. All I get out of this is amusement. You can gain *freedom*."

"You're the original Good Samaritan, aren't you?" I chuckled.

"More the genie of the lamp," he answered earnestly. "I can make dreams come true, but at a price."

"What's my price?" I asked.

He shrugged. "That's the thing—you never know until you wish."

"If I stick with it," I spoke my thoughts aloud, "what's the next step?"

"Locate Paucar Wami. Reconstruct his movements on the night of the murder. Explore his relationship with Miss Hornyak. If you can arrange an audience, it will be easy to ascertain whether he's guilty or not—Wami does not lie."

"Never?"

"Not about killing."

"A killer with an ethical code. Cute."

"It's ego, not ethics. He can afford honesty since he lacks fear. He speaks the truth because it can't hurt him. Those who would seek to use his words against him are easily eliminated."

"If he killed Nic, and tells me, will he kill me too?"

"If he thinks you'll become a nuisance . . . maybe."

The Cardinal's honesty was refreshing but unsettling. I decided to meet it with some of my own. "How much cooperation can I expect if I go after him? You've been protecting Paucar Wami for decades, keeping his name out of the media, quashing reports, quelling gossip. Are there files on him?"

"None that I care to share. We have an understanding—I keep tabs on him but keep them to myself. In return, he doesn't kill me."

"Wami couldn't get to *you*," I said.

"Paucar Wami can get to anyone he likes," The Cardinal replied. "Only the dead are beyond his reach. Any man who thinks differently is a fool, and Mama Dorak raised no fools." The Cardinal's real name was Ferdinand Dorak, though he rarely used it.

I hesitated, not wishing to capitulate without the semblance of a struggle. I asked more questions about Wami, which he deflected. He even refused to give me a full description, revealing no more than what I already knew, that Wami was tall, dark, bald and tattooed. I requested photographs, fingerprints, contact names, past addresses—all denied.

Eventually he checked the time and said I had to leave—business couldn't grind to a halt on my account. He needed a decision. Was I on the case or not?

I should have backed out. I could sense the stakes mounting. Paucar Wami wouldn't be easy to find or talk to. This was my chance to cut my losses and run. Tuck my tail between my legs and slink out like a skunk.

And I would have, pride be damned, if not for The Cardinal's raised eyebrows. He *expected* me to quit. Provoked by that look, determined not to gratify the smug son of a bitch, I stuck out my hand, took The Cardinal's, looked him in the eye and said as pompously as possible, "Mr. Dorak, I'm your man."

9

I reported to Party Central first thing Monday morning and spent hours locked away in the vaults of the upper floors, trying to make sense of the phenomenon of Paucar Wami.

He was one of the city's most vivid yet mysterious legends. I'd heard rumors of his monstrous deeds while growing up and, for a long time, I thought he was a fairy-tale monster. I didn't believe such an assassin could exist outside of fiction. I wrote him off as a bogeyman and it wasn't until I joined the Troops that I realized the stories were true—and that I'd only been exposed to a selection of them.

Yet even to the Troops he was a mythical shadow, rarely seen, never openly discussed. New recruits learned by word of mouth never to mess with Wami. If you spotted him lurking around Party Central, you let him pass. If you encountered him on duty, you turned a blind eye. He was the invisible man.

Yet it was only when I went searching for him in the files that I began to understand how low-profile he actually was. He'd been around since the tail end of the seventies, murdering freely. The records should have been bulging with mentions of his name. But there was no trace of him. His name was absent from all the newspapers and police reports that I had access to. No birth certificate. No school statistics. He'd never paid taxes. Wasn't listed on medical forms. Owned no property. No cars or guns registered to him.

In the course of my investigation I noticed entries that had been tampered with. It wasn't the first time I'd encountered such reappraisal. The Cardinal liked to write the history of the city his way, regardless of the facts. If that meant altering headlines and articles in the newspaper archives, so be it. If fresh film footage was required to replace clips that contradicted his version of the truth, his technicians—first-class graduates of the film industry—digitally tampered with the originals.

The Cardinal refused to share his personal files on Wami, and as far as the accessible data went, the man was a ghost. After several frustrating hours I abandoned the computers and dusty old files, and went looking for the truth on the streets.

As a Troop, I had all sorts of dubious contacts. I was sure I'd find lots of snitches who'd talk. And I did, but only to a point. Plenty of people were willing to swap Wami tales with me, usually in return for nothing more than a drink. The difficulty was separating reality from invention. Wami had pulled off so many incredible stunts, it was possible to believe anything about him. Normally, if someone spun a yarn about a lone assassin wiping out a twelve-strong Triad faction with his bare hands, I'd dismiss it. But I knew the Triad story was true because I'd been on mopping-up duty that night.

Some of the tales were ludicrous bullshit, those that claimed he moved at superhuman speeds, lifted cars above his head and scaled walls like a spider, breathed fire and disappeared into clouds of smoke, didn't bleed when cut. But most, far-fetched as they might seem, were plausible.

For all the larger-than-life accounts, I was no wiser at the end of the evening than at the start. I'd learned much about his methods, targets and aliases—he was known by many names, some of which I jotted down to check on later—but nothing about where he came from, what motivated him or how one tracked him down. He had no accomplices. There was no procedure for hiring him. Nobody had a photo of him, an address or a phone number. He seemed to be without relatives, friends or a past.

I put out a few feelers, asking to be notified if he was spotted or if anybody could tell me about his history. Then, having taken the first steps toward locating the famed killer, I decided I'd had enough of Paucar Wami

Darren Shan

for one day. It was time to explore other angles. Time to talk to the staff at the Skylight.

The manager was out when I arrived but the assistant manager recognized my name from a memo that had been doing the rounds. He placed himself at my disposal and said I'd been cleared to speak to whomever I wished. If anyone refused to cooperate, I was to refer that person to him and he'd sort things out.

I spent the afternoon talking to all the staff I could find. I learned nothing. They hadn't seen anyone suspicious lurking in the corridors of the eighth floor, and only a lone receptionist remembered seeing Nic the night of her death. Even the Troops who guarded the doors and fire escapes were no help. I hadn't expected them to be—the brief was different for Troops assigned to the Skylight. At Party Central we were told to suspect everyone and make our suspicions known. Here the Troops were under orders to look away. The Skylight wasn't a fortress. Guests were supposed to feel at ease.

One person objected to my questioning—Valerie Thomas, the maid who had discovered Nic's body. She was a big woman, ugly, with a disdainful streak the width of a river. She was doing her chores when I caught up with her and refused to pause. I had to chase her around from room to room while we talked.

"She was dead when you found her?" I asked.

"She wasn't doing no dancing," Valerie snorted.

"The coroner put the time of death very close to when the body was found. It's possible she might have been alive when you entered. Did you check?"

"You know what I did," she said. "I saw the body and screamed. I didn't go anywhere near it."

She didn't strike me as the screaming kind.

"You're sure? A lot of people would check for a pulse, or just hang around and stare for a while. If you *did* look at her or touch her, it's nothing to be ashamed of."

"I opened the door," she said. "I saw the body. I screamed. I didn't go near it."

She could have sung her testimony.

"You saw nothing on the floor or bed?"

"Just the knife."

"Nothing else?"

"No."

"No jewelry, money, anything like that?"

She stopped and stared at me. "Are you accusing me of theft?"

"I didn't mean to offend you," I hastily assured her. "It's just, if *I* saw something on the floor, a diamond necklace or a roll of money, and it was lying there, easy pickings, nobody around, I'd—"

"I *saw* nothing," she snapped. "I *picked up* nothing. I'm clean. Ask the boss. I haven't stolen a thing, ever, even if a guest has checked out and left it behind. I hand in lost property. You ask. I saw and took *nothing*. You accuse me of theft again, I'll throw this bucket of water in your face."

"Ma'am, I'm sorry. But there's a dead girl involved."

"I know. I found her."

I took a deep breath. "Good day, Miss Thomas," I said, offering my hand, which she ignored. "Thanks for your time."

"Piss off," she replied curtly. So I did.

I dropped in to 812 in the course of my rounds. The room where Nic had been butchered was no different from any of the other rooms but it felt colder, emptier. I circled the neatly made bed, imagining Nic bound to it, gagged, struggling, screaming silently as her life was cut out of her. It had been slow, painful, clumsy. It must have been awful.

Could I have saved her if I'd been in town? Had she favored me with her company in return for protection? Did she die cursing me for letting her down? Or was I the furthest thing from her mind, a guy she'd just picked up for sex? I'd probably never know. She was gone now, and all her reasons and answers had gone with her.

The manager, Terry Archer, turned up before I left. I mentioned Valerie Thomas to him and asked if there was anything suspicious about her. He shook his head. "She's been a foul-tempered bitch since the day she started.

Even speaks to *me* that way. But she's a hard worker. I'll take a rude work-horse over a polite layabout any day."

"Might she have taken something from the room?"

"It would be out of character if she did." We were in Terry's office. He leaned back in a leather chair and yawned. "Sorry. This murder's played havoc with my schedule. I spent the weekend shacked up here, dealing with irate policemen, trying to keep the peace between them and the Troops."

I smiled. We were forever in conflict with the cops. They hated having to play second fiddle to a band of mercenaries. They loved any excuse to barge in and read the riot act.

"Find out anything?" Terry asked.

"No. I thought somebody might have recognized her but…"

"Thousands of customers pass through the Skylight every day," he sympathized, "and those are only the official guests. More use the restaurant, bars and function rooms. If somebody doesn't want to be noticed, they aren't."

"What did the police make of it?"

"At first they reckoned she'd tagged along with a one-night stand. Then they discovered she was a sometime prostitute. They decided it was a client she'd brought back or met in the hotel." He didn't seem too sold on the theory.

"You don't agree?"

"The Skylight has its share of nightwalkers, like hotels the world over. But it's a closed shop. Unwanted competition is harshly dealt with. Even an amateur hooker knows better than to bring a trick here."

"Maybe one of the regular girls took offense and…" He was shaking his head before I finished.

"Some of them are vicious enough, but they wouldn't do it here. They know better than that. They'd have taken her elsewhere."

"Perhaps she *was* a regular," I suggested. "Maybe this wasn't the first time she used the Skylight. Have you any way of checking?"

Terry reached into a drawer, produced a slim purple file and tossed it across. I opened it to discover a long list of names, both male and female.

"Every hooker's name is registered," Terry said. "Even those who only use our rooms once in a blue moon."

"They let you tag them?" I asked, scanning the names.

"It works to their advantage. Those on the list aren't troubled by security. Room discounts. The first to be called when a guest requests company."

"What if one of them—"

I stopped. The file contained close to twenty sheets, not just names, but phone numbers, contacts, sexual specialities, background details, medical histories, even photos. Near the bottom of the sixth sheet, a name jumped out at me. *Priscilla Perdue.*

Terry noticed my pause and leaned over the table, craning his neck. "Priscilla Perdue," he muttered. "Blond. Very upmarket. Has a thing for women."

"A thing for women?" I repeated.

"I believe so. It doesn't say here but I think it's mostly those of the fairer sex she swings for."

"Does she use the Skylight often?" I asked.

"Once or twice a month. You always know when she's around. She blazes in, customer in tow, acting like a movie queen. In fact we're not sure if she's a pro or not—word is she doesn't charge—but we put her on the list all the same."

"Do you have a photo of her?"

"No, but I can get one."

"Please."

I read the profile while Terry had a photo e-mailed across. There was nothing I didn't already know—height, weight, measurements, place of work. Even the photo, when it came, was familiar, one of the shots from the file in Party Central.

"Mind if I quiz some of your staff again?" I asked.

"Quiz away," Terry said.

An hour later I left the Skylight in a daze. Plenty of the staff recognized Priscilla from the photo but it was the response of three in particular—a receptionist, a barman and a waitress in the ground-floor bar—that set my head spinning. All ID'd her and then, in answer to my second question, "When did you last see her?" replied—

"Friday before last. She checked in by herself."

"Friday last week. Ordered a piña colada. Took it to a table in a corner. Nobody with her that I saw."

"Friday, I think. Not this one—a week further back. I collected her glass after she left. She barely touched it. She was on her own, but I think I recall seeing somebody drop by her table not long before she left."

Priscilla had been in the Skylight when Nic was killed.

10

Nic's funeral was the next day. I'd been of two minds about whether or not I should go but on the morning I decided I couldn't miss it. I wasn't a funeral connoisseur—hadn't been to any since my mother's—but this was different. It was business.

There was a police cordon outside the crematorium to keep back the press and spectators. Only her closest relatives and friends were being admitted. My name wasn't on the list and the cop on duty refused to admit me. A quick call to Bill fixed that and I was soon being waved through.

The small funeral parlor was nowhere near capacity. It was almost time for the ceremony yet I counted only fourteen heads. Nick was up front, dressed soberly. Priscilla was beside him, weeping into a handkerchief, clutching the hand of a woman I didn't recognize.

Rudi Ziegler was seated near the rear of the room. He was weeping loudly, letting the tears course down his face unchecked. Nearly everybody was sobbing, except me and Nick. I didn't cry because it would have been hypocritical—I hadn't known her that well. What was Nick's excuse?

Nic rested in a rainbow-hued coffin molded out of some kind of plastic. The top quarter was transparent, so we could see Nic's head and shoulders. She was a beautiful corpse, serene as only the dead can be. Her face had been left unmarked by her assailant and I couldn't stare at it for long without getting a lump in my cynical throat.

I got a shock when the priest emerged—it was Elvis Presley! Forelock and sideburns, wiggling hips, flares, white suit with sequins. The mourners burst into smiles when they saw him striding to the head of the coffin. Obviously this was an in-joke I wasn't privy to.

He gave a nice speech. Said Nic had been a life-loving woman, deep, honest, thoughtful, with far more to her character than the frivolous front she showed to the world at large. He said this was how Nic had wanted to go, with lots of color and a touch of merry madness. If she was looking on, he hoped she was enjoying the show. "This one's for you, Nic," he mumbled in his best Elvis impersonation, then launched into "Heartbreak Hotel," a cruel choice in my opinion.

As he gyrated, two of his assistants—both dressed as glam rockers— emerged from the sides and loaded the coffin onto a conveyor belt. Elvis stood to attention and crooned "Glory, Glory, Hallelujah," slipping off into the shadows as he sang. Somebody threw a lever and the coffin glided backward, Nic's final journey.

Rudi Ziegler howled at that point, stumbled to his feet and brushed past me, lurching for the exit, sobbing pitifully like an old drama queen.

A few of the mourners glanced over their shoulders. Priscilla was one of the curious. She spotted me and frowned, then smiled weakly and mouthed the words, "See you after?" I nodded. The coffin began to disappear through the curtains and she diverted her gaze, took Nick's hand and squeezed. He still hadn't shed any tears, though he looked shakier than before.

I ducked out. I'd seen enough. I knew what would happen behind the curtains—the body would be taken, incinerated, the bones fed into a machine to be ground into ash—but what would they do with the coffin? Respray and use it again? Give it to Nick to take home? I could have asked one of Elvis's assistants, who'd come out and was scattering large, scented flowers along the hall floor, but I wasn't that desperate to know.

The mourners filed out, turning left as they came, following the path of flowers. I stood to the right of the door, military stance, hands crossed in front of my abdomen, head bowed as a mark of respect. Most of the guests ignored me but one old man paused and half turned. I started to raise a hand and smile, then saw his blank white eyes. I lowered the hand and coughed politely instead of smiling. His head twitched, then he nodded to acknowledge my presence, listened for the footsteps of the others and strolled after them.

Nick and Priscilla came last. I was about to step forward to offer my condolences but she spotted me and shook her head. She led Nick along—he was walking mechanically—handed him over to one of his friends, then backtracked.

"Thank you for coming," she said, kissing my cheeks. "Nic would have liked that." Her eyes were red. She was clad in a dark dress that sexily accentuated her curves. I tried not to focus on it—I didn't want to get a hard-on in a crematorium. It would have seemed disrespectful.

"I wasn't sure I'd be welcome," I muttered.

"Of course you are." She dabbed at her eyes with the handkerchief. "I just didn't want Nick to see you. He's been bottling his emotions in and I think he's looking for an excuse to explode. You might have been it."

"What was with the Elvis routine?" I asked.

Priscilla smiled. "Nic loved Elvis. This was what she would have wanted."

"Who chose the song?"

She winced. "I did. It was Nic's favorite. I only realized how inappropriate it was when he started singing. I could have sunk through the floor."

She glanced up the corridor. Nick had disappeared from sight. "I'd better head after him. He's arranged a wake at the family home. Invited a load of friends, most of whom hardly knew Nic. It'll develop into an orgy if there's nobody sensible to control things."

She started away.

"Could we get together sometime?" I asked. "Dinner? A drink? There are some questions I'd like to ask."

"Of course. Not tonight, though. How about tomorrow?"

"Great." I hesitated. "You're not thinking of taking me to the Kool Kats Klub again, are you?"

She had the good grace to blush. "I apologized for that already. How about Cafran's? Know it?"

"I can find it. Seven?"

"Fine."

She departed.

I stood there a few minutes, letting her coast out of sight, then slowly followed. Outside the mourners were getting into their cars. I looked around for the blind man, wondering whom he was leaving with, but couldn't locate him. A journalist moved in to take a photo of me but the cop who'd barred my way earlier stepped in front of him and sent him on his way.

"Didn't think you'd want your picture in the papers," he said.

"Thanks."

"Don't mention it." His eyebrows lifted. Looking over my shoulder, I saw Elvis emerging, peeling off his sideburns. "One of the mourners?" the cop asked.

"No. The priest." He checked to see if I was pulling his leg. Chuckled when he realized I was serious.

"Wish I could have been there. Did he sing?"

"Like a bird." I asked to see the list of mourners and jotted down the names for future reference. Looking through them, I frowned and re-counted. "There's only thirteen."

"That's right."

"But there were fourteen at the service."

"Including you, yes."

"I mean without me." I thought about the blind man and asked if the cop had noticed him.

"No. And I checked everyone through."

"Could he have entered another way?"

"I can check with the guys on the other doors. Most likely he was from another party and got lost, or else he's a professional mourner who squeezed in before we came."

"A professional?"

"There's always a few hanging around. They drift from funeral to funeral. Want me to look into it?"

"Don't bother. It's not important." I tucked my notebook away, thanked him for his help and took one last look at the palace of the dead.

I shivered as I spotted a stream of smoke rising in the air, then turned my back on the crematorium and hurried away.

I couldn't rid myself of the image of Nic writhing inside the oven—or whatever it is they use to burn the bodies—flames creeping over her flesh, consuming her whole. I knew I wouldn't be able to keep my mind on work, so I put the case to one side for the rest of the day and headed over to the Fridge to pay a belated call on another member of the unto-infinity club.

A girl called Velouria noted my request, checked my credentials, then tapped the name "Tom Jeery" into a computer. It came up blank. "When was he left here?" she asked.

"I don't know the exact date. Early to mid-eighties."

"Then he probably won't be on the database." She keyed out of the screen and rose. "We can't transfer names without permission—the system's too easy to hack into. We only started putting them on disc in the late nineties, checking whether we should or not as each new inhabitant was brought in. Never bothered backdating—too much hassle trying to track down relatives or connected personnel."

"You're saying you can't find him?"

"Of course we can," she sniffed, "unless he was entered as a John Doe. But it'll take a while. Without a precise date I'll have to go through the entry books. Do you want to leave it with me and come back?"

"I'll wait," I told her and settled into one of the uncomfortable plastic chairs.

I wasn't sure what I hoped to gain by the visit. I'd hardly ever dropped by my mother's grave, and I'd loved her. Maybe I hoped to unleash a flood of memories when faced with his tomb. Though my father hadn't spent much time around the house when I was growing up, I was sure I must be harboring more memories of him than the meager few I was currently aware of.

Several doctors and assistants passed by as I was waiting, barely glancing at me. I was surprised when one stopped and addressed me warmly.

"Lost another girlfriend?"

I didn't recognize the grinning doctor when I looked up, but placed him within the few seconds it took to rise and take his hand. "Dr. Sines."

"Bit of a shock last time you were here," he chuckled. "Recover yet?"

"Just about. They buried her today."

"Oh?" He didn't seem overly interested. "They normally hold on to the body for longer in cases such as these. She must have had relatives with connections."

An impatient colleague of the doctor's, who'd been marching with him, asked Sines if he was coming. Snappy, as if he had no intention of waiting around.

"In a minute," Sines snapped back. "So, find out where she was murdered yet?"

"Excuse me?"

"Nicola Hornyak. I heard you were handling the investigation. Have you located the scene of the crime or are you still searching?"

"I don't understand. Nic was killed at the Skylight."

He laughed humorlessly. "You haven't been keeping up to date. From the subcutaneous particles we discovered—the dirt in her cuts—she wasn't attacked in the hotel. She died there, but the wounds were inflicted earlier, possibly on a building site, judging by the sand and industrial dust."

I stared, boggle-eyed. "Why the hell wasn't I informed?" I roared.

"Don't ask me. I passed on our findings, first thing Saturday. The state coroner reached the same conclusion, I hear, although he's been *persuaded* not to go public with the news."

"Who did you tell?" I growled.

"It was FMEO."

"What the fuck does that mean?"

"For My Eyes Only. *My* being The Cardinal."

"You told The Cardinal?"

"Yes. He mentioned your name and said he'd pass it along. Thanked me and asked me to keep it quiet. Which I have." He frowned. "Until now. I assumed you knew. He said he was going to... You won't tell him I let it slip, will you?"

I shook my head slowly. "Not if you'll keep me informed of any subsequent developments. Let me give you my number." I texted it across to him.

"There's nothing else to tell," he said. "I e-mailed my report to The

Cardinal, but it was a long-winded version of what I'd told him already. The assault took place somewhere other than the hotel. Her assailant may have thought she was dead when he took her there—she can't have been too lively when she was dropped off. She died a few hours later, around the time her body was discovered."

"And you think she was tortured on a building site?"

"It's a strong possibility. Or it may have been in a garage or somebody's backyard—the materials could have been present there too."

Velouria returned, smiling, holding a file to her chest. "When you're ready, Mr. Jeery."

"I have to go," I told Sines.

"You're not the only one."

"You'll call me if anything new crops up?"

"It won't, but if it does, I will."

"Thanks."

The news had knocked me soaring out of bounds. Nic hadn't been murdered in the Skylight. What bearing did that have on the case? For starters it seemed to rule out the single-killer theory. The Troops guarding the hotel weren't the most alert but they wouldn't fail to spot somebody dragging in a corpse, not unless someone else distracted them. Perhaps one of *them* had been in league with the killer. And what of Priscilla? I knew she'd been in the lobby and restaurant the night of the murder, which had seemed to implicate her. But if Nic had been killed elsewhere…

I'd have to spend more time on this. I wasn't thinking clearly at the moment, so I pushed it to the back of my mind and left it there. I'd return to it later, in my apartment, after a good meal and a long shower.

I followed Velouria through the maze of cubicle-lined corridors. My brain kept throwing Sines's words back at me but I refused to be drawn into the marsh of possibilities. I was here to pay my respects to my father. Nic could wait.

The geology of the maze shifted subtly the farther we progressed. The style of the containers changed—they were larger, rounded at the edges, some decorated with brass or gold fixings. There were fewer per row—some even stood by themselves—and flower-basket frames hung from hooks on the doors (though bouquets were scarce). Velouria noticed my interest and explained that this was an older section of the Fridge. The original designers had tried to inject a modicum of warmth, unaware of its true purpose. The current administrative team was planning to renovate in the near future—they could fit twenty percent more bodies in once the coffins were streamlined—but that would be a monster of a job, which nobody was looking forward to.

Velouria stopped at the second cubicle in a row of six. They were stacked two high. My father's was on the lower bunk. I stared at his name, embossed on a thin strip of metal. No file was attached. I inquired about that and Velouria checked her notes. "The information on these older inmates is often sketchy. Most were simply dumped here. In some cases they didn't even give us a name. We might have a file on him somewhere. I can look it up if you want."

"No need." I read the name again and cleared my throat. "I'd like to be alone."

"Sure. Want me to wait nearby or can you find your own way out?"

"I've got a good sense of direction. You can leave."

"If you get lost—and, trust me, it's easier than you'd think—buzz for help and we'll send someone to find you."

She left and I was alone. With my father.

I ran my fingers over the name and shivered as I realized that this could be me one day, locked away in one of these cramped cubicles, never visited or disturbed. If I had children—not that I had any current plans— would they wind up standing here as I was, tracing my name with their fingers, wondering what their old man had been like?

I stood around for a couple of minutes, waiting for memories to flood back, but they didn't. I resurrected my old snapshots of him but found nothing new. Maybe if I saw the body...

I didn't act on the thought straightaway. He'd been here a long time. The refrigeration process couldn't be relied upon. The body might have decayed. I could find myself face-to-face with a rotting-flesh zombie like those moviemakers are so fond of. The picture I had of Tom Jeery was of a tall, strong, healthy man. Did I want to risk replacing that with an image of a time-eaten corpse, sunken cheeks, exposed bones and a fetid stench?

I decided to peek. Though it hadn't been easy to look at Nic in the crematorium, I was glad I had. I had a final image of her to cling to, which drew a line between the live and dead Nic. It was good to look upon the faces of the dead.

I considered checking with Velouria before proceeding, but he was *my* father—if anyone had the right to violate his final slumber, it was me. I studied the door. Some of the newer models came equipped with computerized locks but this was a plain old spin-lock, no keys or codes required. I spun the wheel slowly. There was a crackle when the door opened, a hiss of cold air, then I felt the slab slide forward a few inches of its own accord before shuddering to a halt.

I wiped around my brow, took firm hold of the door, swung it back, grabbed the slab and tugged. It resisted, then slid out smoothly, a wave of white icy gas rising from it, causing me to cough and avert my eyes. When I'd recovered, I leaned into the misty fog, waving my hands, dispersing it. The slab came into focus and I held my breath, searching for my father's face.

The mist lifted. Only wispy tendrils remained. And when they cleared…

Nothing. The cubicle was empty.

I remained rooted to the spot, wondering if the body had slipped to the floor or remained jammed inside. I bent over and peered in—nothing. The floor was clear too. I checked the sides of the container, but it was solid.

As I withdrew, a small object caught my eye. A piece of paper lay in the space where my father should have been, neatly folded in half and resting on its edges. I picked it up and stepped back, mind going in a thousand different directions all at once. I checked one more time for a corpse—as if I could have missed it!—then unfolded the paper with trembling fingers and read the three short words printed in black across it—OUT TO LUNCH.

part three

"a severed human head"

11

I spent the next few hours raising unholy hell. I summoned Velouria and her superiors, along with one of the managing directors who happened to be present. I ranted and raved. Made threats. Took out my gun at one stage and waved it over my head like an Indian shaking a tomahawk. Eventually they sent along my good buddy Dr. Sines to calm me down. He tried leading me away to a quiet anteroom but I stood my ground—I had crazy thoughts of the body's being replaced while I was absent.

"Bodies go missing all the time," he sighed, offering a cigarette—which I refused—and lighting up. The posse of doctors and nurses who'd gathered to watch the sparks fly was dispersing. "It's no big deal."

"He was my father!"

"A father," Sines noted, flicking through the file, "you never visited or checked on until today."

"I didn't know he was here," I growled.

Sines couldn't have looked less sympathetic. "If his own son wasn't interested in his whereabouts, you can't be too surprised that we weren't either."

"You're paid to take an interest!"

"No," he corrected me. "We're paid to check bodies in and stack them away. If we're told to care for a body, we do. Otherwise it's fair game."

"Fair game for *who*?"

Sines asked if he could push in the slab and close the door of my father's tomb. I took one final look, put the note back and said he could. Then he continued in a lower tone. "Any number of people could have made off with it. Your lot for starters. The Troops come here every so often and cart a corpse or two away."

"What for?"

"The mind boggles—you can do a lot of things with a body. They're your people, not mine. You figure them out.

"Then there are certain doctors—this is something I'd never admit in public—who act rather more freely with the bodies than they should. Corpses are hard to come by on the outside. If one of my colleagues needs a cadaver to experiment on, he takes one. No forms to fill in and no questions asked unless the body has been tagged for sanctuary, and those are never interfered with."

"That's sick," I muttered.

"What if one of them finds the cure for cancer?" He smiled. "But let's not get into that argument. Besides, I think the presence of the note precludes professional involvement—pathologists aren't noted for their subtle sense of humor. My guess is it's the Troops or one of the Fridge's underlings."

"A nurse?"

"Nurses, porters, watchmen, maintenance, canteen staff…take your pick."

"What would they want with the body?"

"Use your imagination," he chuckled. "Somebody wants to be the talk of a party, or wants to scare the wits out of his dear old grandmother, or wants to cut a head off and use it as a bowling ball. I could go on all night."

"How do we narrow down the list of suspects?" I asked.

"We don't," Sines sighed. "Your father's body has been here a long time. It could have been taken a week after his arrival or yesterday—there's no way of knowing. An investigation can be instigated if you insist, but I'd advise against it, as the odds of revealing the culprit are slim at best."

I'd calmed down—Sines had a soothing influence—and, thinking it over, I knew he was right. Raising a stink would be counterproductive. It would only draw attention to me. Plus it would eat into my time and distract me. This was a mystery for another day, when I didn't have The Cardinal riding on my back.

"I'll leave it," I said, "but not indefinitely. That's my *father* somebody's fucked with. How would you feel if it was your old man?"

"Peeved," he smirked. "Because I like you, I'll ask around on the quiet. Pretend I'm fishing for anecdotes. Might learn more that way—a practical joker is usually incapable of keeping his lip zipped if he thinks he's bragging to a fellow clown."

"Thanks, Sines." I hadn't expected the offer.

"But on one condition," he added.

"Name it."

He shook his ID badge at me. "Would you please call me *Dr.* Sines?"

As I was making notes of my meeting with Sines back home I remembered something Rudi Ziegler had said. Flipping back a few pages I found my minutes. When I'd asked Ziegler if he thought the carving on Nic's back had anything to do with the Incan brooch she was wearing, he said he doubted it. The Incas were sun worshippers and she had been killed at night. Besides, why kill her at the Skylight? If it had been Incas, a more suitable venue would have been the site of the Manco Capac statue.

I jotted down in capitals, "MANCO CAPAC STATUE—INVESTIGATE" and circled them with my pen. It was too late to go there now—they'd be closing down for the day—but first thing tomorrow…

I felt too agitated to stay indoors. If I sat around brooding, my thoughts would return to the bare slab, the hiss of gas and my father's absent corpse. I needed to be active.

I took to the streets and asked after Paucar Wami again. Word of my interest had spread and many knew why—they'd heard about Nic and my connection to her. The rumor doing the rounds was that I loved her and had sworn a blood oath over her dead body to get even with her killer. I didn't bother denying it.

I learned nothing new, though there was a lot more talk about Wami tonight. There'd been a few sightings of the killer and these, coupled with the questions I'd been asking, had convinced many people of his involvement. Several claimed to have seen Wami kill her, and a few poor souls swore blind they'd helped him, but when pushed, none could produce the slightest shred of evidence.

I rolled home late, legs stiff, notebook full of names, half leads and theories. Several people had mentioned Fabio—he allegedly knew more about Wami than most—but I didn't want to call around so soon after our last meeting, making it look as if I were asking for a favor in return for my curative turn. I'd give it a couple of days and only try the centenarian pimp if all else failed.

I cleaned the apartment, hoping to tire myself out so I'd fall asleep quickly and not lie awake, tossing and turning, thinking about my father.

It didn't work. Exhausted as I was, sleep proved elusive, and when I managed to drop off for a few minutes my dreams were filled with empty coffins, laughing skeletons and screaming, dislocated ghosts.

The building site was a hive of activity. Men popped in and out of portable sheds like ants. Foremen with megaphones coordinated their troops with tinny bellows. Overhead cranes shifted huge weights from one end of the site to the other. Most attention focused on the center of the industrial wasteland, where scaffolding circled two similar structures standing side by side—a huge pair of legs, I assumed.

I wandered around the site without being questioned, observing the bustle with interest. Judging by the size of the legs, the completed statue would be monstrous. I wondered who was financing its construction. I checked some vans and cabins for names, but there were several companies involved, all of whom had probably been subcontracted. The laborers were reluctant to be drawn into conversation—they were behind schedule, I learned, and would miss out on bonuses if they didn't finish on time.

The guy must have been incredibly influential, whoever he was. This was a busy part of the city. Construction was interfering with traffic, and I'm sure the dust and noise weren't welcomed by those in the neighboring buildings. You'd need friends in high places to nudge something like this along. I wondered if one of those *friends* was also a friend of Nick Hornyak's, maybe the one who sicced Howard Kett on me.

I was wandering around, exchanging pleasantries with the natives, when I spotted a familiar figure near the scaffolding, talking to a foreman.

I waited until he was alone, then sneaked up behind him and murmured in his ear, "Are you following me, Mr. Ziegler?"

Rudi Ziegler spun on his heels, blinking anxiously. He was dressed in a heavy plastic coat, industrial green overalls and rubber boots, and goggles to protect his eyes. When he saw me, he relaxed and raised the goggles.

"Al Jeery," he smiled, fanning his face with his pudgy hands. "You gave me a start." He frowned. "Why ask if I'm following you?"

"You were at the funeral yesterday—so was I. And now we're both here."

"You were at the funeral? I didn't see you." He exhaled heavily through his nostrils. "Then again, I didn't notice much. I thought it was barbaric of them to have that transparent lid on the coffin. Her brother's idea.

"As for being here, I've been coming three or four days a week for the last fortnight. I petitioned for a statue to be erected in memory of our Incan forebears some years ago, but it came to nothing. Now this." He beamed like a child.

"That's going to be Manco Capac?" I asked. "The sun god?"

"The *son* of the sun god," Ziegler corrected me. "Manco Capac was the founding father of the Incan empire. His followers believed he was a direct descendant of the sun deity."

I nodded studiously. "When and where did this guy live, exactly?"

"About 1200 AD, along the western coast of South America."

"Mind telling me what we're doing building a monument to him here, today?"

"This city has strong Incan roots. Didn't you know?" From my blank expression he gathered I didn't. "This was an Indian village in earlier times. A small winter settlement. In the sixteenth century—just before the Spanish invaded—a band of Incas arrived, settled and made it home."

"How'd they get here?" I asked curiously.

Ziegler shrugged. "Nobody knows. It's puzzled archaeologists for decades. When the signs were first unearthed, many thought it was a practical joke, that old Incan artifacts had been buried by pranksters. Further investigation proved that wasn't so. Incas *were* here. Not only that—they made this city what it is, laying the foundations upon which the modern version was built."

"That mean we're a bunch of Incan offspring?" I asked.

"Our bloodlines are intriguingly mixed," Ziegler said, readjusting his goggles as a dust cloud swept over us. "Many races have found their way here over the centuries. But those whose roots stretch back more than a couple of generations are almost surely linked—however tenuously—to the Incas."

"And one of them's decided to pay tribute at last." I smiled. "Was it you?"

Ziegler smiled with me. "I wish. Actually, I'm not sure who the bene-factor is. But yes, it *is* nice to see. For someone who's spent his life dabbling with all things Incan, it's a tremendously exciting development. They're not just building a statue but a museum. They'll be shipping in ornaments, manufacturing replicas, hosting wild Inca-style parties."

"That won't do your business any harm," I noted.

"True—and don't think I'm not making plans to cash in—but that's not why I'm here. The financial aspects pale in the face of the staggering aesthetic majesty of the project."

Ziegler stared lovingly up at the legs. I didn't like to break into his reverie, so I studied them with him, watching as the cranes added to the lower sections, thickening them—I guessed—to support what would surely be a massive upper body.

"This Manco Capac," I said. "How do they know what he looks like? I mean, 1200 AD...that's a while ago."

"It is indeed," Ziegler agreed. "But even primitive cavemen boasted art-ists. I'm not sure which source the designers have gone with for the statue, but there are several possible portraits to choose from. The result may not be entirely accurate, but it's the symbolism which counts."

Symbolism. Symbols...

"Didn't you tell me the Incas had a thing for human sacrifice?" I asked.

Ziegler nodded. "Almost every society has a history of offering its own kind to the gods. The Incas were no different, although they were more subtle about it than most."

"How can you have a subtle sacrifice?" I laughed.

His face misted over. "They would pick the most desirable of their virgins—male and female—and deck them out in fine robes, adorn them with flowers, feed them exotic fruits and parade them around like celebrities. Then they'd slip them drugs to dull their senses, haul them up a mountain and leave them in an exposed place to freeze. There wasn't much pain, just a gentle drifting off and a glorious union with the gods." He sighed happily. "It must have been beautiful."

I decided not to comment on that.

"Was that how they killed all their victims? They never varied the routine, used, for instance, *knives*?"

He cocked an eyebrow. "The Incas reserved the holy sacrifices for special occasions. I'm sure there were plenty of other, smaller, messier sacrifices. But not with knives—the Incas weren't metallurgists."

"They must have had cutting implements of one kind or another," I said.

"Of course. Jagged rocks, crystals, sharpened bones."

"So they had knives of a sort."

Ziegler smiled thinly. "Of a sort."

"The sort that could have been used to carve a sun symbol on Nic's back?"

"I very much doubt it," he sniffed.

"Remember what you told me about that when I came to visit?"

"Refresh my memory."

"You said, if it had been Inca-related, they wouldn't have killed her in the Skylight—they'd have done it out here. You still stand by that?"

He looked puzzled. "I think this would be a good place for a sacrifice to the sun to be made, yes, but she wasn't killed here. She was killed at the hotel."

I said nothing, but coughed discreetly and glanced away.

Ziegler stared hard. "Are you implying she wasn't?"

I hesitated, pondering whether to play my ace, then opted against it—better to keep it quiet for the time being. "Of course she was killed at the hotel," I said. "But maybe she'd been here beforehand. Did you ever discuss this place with her?"

"I might have mentioned it, but only in passing. She'd moved on from Incas and the sun by our last few sessions. Demons were more her style."

A truck approached and we had to get out of the way. Ziegler led me clear, treading confidently, at home here. I spotted a tall man in robes standing not far from us. He seemed to be gazing at the statue but he couldn't have been, because when he turned I saw that his eyes were white. They stared blindly in my direction, as the eyes of the man in the funeral parlor had. At first I thought it was the same guy but that was ridiculous— a man without the use of his eyes was hardly likely to be trailing me around the city.

"How big's this thing going to be?" I asked, keeping an eye on the man in the robes, wondering what he was doing on the building site.

"About nine hundred feet," Ziegler replied.

I gawped at him. "Christ! Why the hell are they building it so big?"

"It'll be hollow inside," Ziegler told me. "The museum artifacts will be housed in the body, for viewing on the way up. It's also been designed to receive the fullest effects of the sun. The head's going to be packed with mirrors, which will turn it into a giant sphere of light. You'll be able to climb to the top when it's finished and bask in a room so bright, it'll be like sitting inside the sun."

"Sounds dangerous. Light that bright could"—I looked around for the man in the robes, but he was gone—"blind you." I frowned, shook my head, then pointed at the cranes. "How do they set those things up?"

Ziegler shrugged. "I haven't the foggiest."

"Puzzles the shit out of me whenever I think about it."

"Why don't you check with somebody who knows?"

"Each time it pops into my head, I mean to, but then I forget about it again."

We didn't say much for a few minutes. Just stood and stared at the towering cranes, immersed in our thoughts. Ziegler was probably dreaming about Incas. I was thinking about the symbol carved into Nic's back.

Finally the mystic stirred. "I must be leaving. I'm seeing a client in an hour. By the time I get home, wash and change, it'll be—"

He stopped and stared off into the distance. It took me a few seconds to spot what he was focused on, then I saw it, a fall of rain that looked like a vertical column to the heavens, a hundred feet beyond the statue.

Ziegler hurried toward it and I moved quickly to keep up. "What is it?" I asked as we ran.

"The rain of the gods," he gasped, flushed with excitement. "Have you never seen it?"

"No."

"It isn't common. This is only my third sighting."

We stopped short of the extraordinary fall of rain, which was hitting the ground in a fenced-off area. No guards or workmen were nearby. Ziegler was wringing his hands so much, it's a wonder he didn't squeeze them to pulp.

"Incredible," he sighed. "I've never been this close."

"It's odd," I agreed. The rain fell in a perfect rectangle, maybe six feet wide by a foot deep. The surrounding area was bone-dry, apart from some splashing at the edges.

"The *villacs* believed this was the voice of the sun god," Ziegler informed me. "This was how they communicated with him."

"*Villacs?*"

"Ancient Incan priests."

While we were studying the shower, the blind man I'd noticed earlier emerged from the far side. He was closer to the rain than we were and his white robes were specked with wet spots. He was old, with short, white hair. A mole sprouted from the left side of his chin. His head bobbed forward and backward lightly, and he seemed oblivious to our presence.

I turned to ask Ziegler more about the *villacs*, when the blind man darted toward me, grabbed my left arm and spun me into the rectangle of rain. I opened my mouth to roar, but before I could utter a syllable the world disintegrated into shards of light and I had to cover my eyes with my hands.

When I removed my fingers after a couple of wary seconds, I was no longer in the yard. I wasn't even in the city. I was standing on a rock at the edge of a cliff, gazing down on a fertile valley.

"It's beautiful, isn't it?" someone asked. Turning, I saw the blind man.

"Yes," I answered peacefully. Part of me knew this couldn't be happening, but I'd fallen prey to the mesmerizing vision.

"We must leave soon," the blind man said, and I nodded in reply. "We can never return."

"Never," I echoed.

"But we will build anew. And this time we will build forever. See the rivers?" He pointed to three tributaries that trickled down from the mountains to meet in the valley and form a large snake of a river. "Those are the rivers of blood. The Blood of Flesh." He pointed to the river furthest left. "Dreams made Flesh." This time he pointed to the river to the far right.

"And Flesh of Dreams," I said, nodding at the middle line of red.

"Yes. And the place where they meet, do you know what that is called?" I thought for a moment but came up blank. "It is the future. And it's ours."

The blind man moved behind me and placed his fingers on my shoulders. I made no move to stop him as he gently pushed me. Nor did I scream or feel the slightest sense of fear as I fell. Instead I spread my arms, raised my chin and flew. I glided like a bird over the middle river of blood, close enough to touch it. When I reached the spot where it joined with the others, I hovered and stared down into the churning pool of blood at the intersection.

There were faces in the red pool, none of which I recognized. Old and young, male and female, black and white. They eddied around in the pool like fish caught between conflicting currents. After a while I realized there was a face beneath the others, far bigger than the rest. At first I thought it was my own face, but then the blood lightened a shade and I noticed murky snakes writhing down the specter's cheeks. I knew it must be Paucar Wami. The thought didn't frighten me. Nothing in this world of visions scared me.

While I watched, the vision of Paucar Wami opened its eyes—dark green slits—and smiled. Its lips mouthed the word, "*Come!*" I dived into the pool in response. As soon as I parted the surface of the bloody waters, a red gauze dropped over my eyes. The red swiftly turned to black, then I was slipping out of the vision, out of the pool, back into the real world and...

...Rain.

I opened my eyes and gazed upward as the rain cascaded down. Then arms yanked at me. I was expecting the blind man who'd propelled me into the shower, but it was the less mysterious Rudi Ziegler who had hold of me.

"You're drenched," he tutted, tugging at the sleeves of my jacket.

"What happened?" I asked numbly. I took a step forward, lost control of my legs and slumped to the ground.

"Some crazy blind man in robes thrust you into the rain," Ziegler said. "I've spent the last minute trying to drag you out. You seemed oblivious to me."

"My mind was...elsewhere." Then, as my senses returned, I glanced around. "Where'd the blind guy go?"

"Heaven knows," Ziegler sighed.

"A pity," I muttered, and stood. Ziegler helped me.

"Will you be all right?" he asked as I wobbled uncertainly.

"I'll be fine," I said, taking a couple of half steps. I felt more confident after that. My strength was returning. "Fine," I repeated and smiled to show I meant it.

"The rain's stopping," Ziegler said. Glancing up, I saw the last drops fall. There were no clouds overhead.

"If you're sure you'll be OK, I really must be going," Ziegler said. "My client won't wait."

"That's fine. Go."

Ziegler still looked concerned, but he nodded. "Are you coming?" he asked.

"In a while," I said. "I want to rest a bit first. Dry off in the sun."

"I can send someone to check on you."

"That won't be necessary."

He paused and I flashed him a grin. He smiled in return, bade me farewell and left. Once he was gone I sat again, stared at the spot where the fallen rain was seeping into the ground and pondered the meaning of my vision, in particular the face I'd half-glimpsed at the bottom of the pool of blood.

I changed into dry clothes back home. I couldn't get the vision out of my mind. I'd never experienced anything like that. What brought it on? The blind man? The rain? Had somebody slipped me some LSD on the sly?

Since the questions were unanswerable, I put them to one side and went in search of Paucar Wami again. After the vision it seemed more important than ever to find the fabled killer.

It was a vain search. Rumors were rife—he'd been seen in the north of the city, he'd murdered a priest in Swiss Square, he was holed up on the fifteenth floor of Party Central with The Cardinal—but none could be verified. Nobody knew where he was, what he was here for or how long he intended to stay.

Hard as it was to not focus on the vision, in the evening I let my thoughts turn toward Rudi Ziegler. If he was Nic's killer I'd eat my beret, but I couldn't shake the feeling that he was tied in with it somehow. Maybe he had referred Nic to some other mystic when she spoke of wanting to take a demon lover. I needed to find out how he dealt with clients who wanted to go a stage further, whom he sent them to.

I could have sicced one of The Cardinal's goons on him but The Cardinal hadn't told me the truth about where Nic was killed. I couldn't rely on him or those who answered to him. I'd have to use my own person, someone I could trust implicitly. My options were narrow. I didn't want to involve Bill. That left Ellen.

She was suspicious when I asked her to meet me at Cafran's for supper. She wanted to know what I was after. I wouldn't say. That fueled her curiosity, so she agreed to meet me at nine, which gave me two hours to talk matters over with Priscilla and get rid of her.

I dropped a progress report off at Party Central—The Cardinal hadn't asked for regular updates but I figured it was best to keep him informed—then headed home for another change of clothes.

As before, I didn't know how to dress for my date with Miss Perdue, but decided to play it safe—smartest suit, shoes polished until I could see the cracks in the ceiling in them, cuff links, a snazzy tie. I even ran a comb through my hair—it doesn't take much combing—and flossed my teeth. I wouldn't be shown up by her, no matter where she took me.

I arrived a quarter of an hour early and wished I hadn't, as it meant fifteen extra minutes of looking like a fool. Cafran's was a nice place but it wasn't a suit-and-tie job. Most of its customers were older than me, dressed casually, regulars who fitted in like the rubber plants. I stuck out like a sore thumb—King Kong's.

Priscilla was twenty minutes late but didn't apologize. She was dressed in the skimpiest of materials, a length of green rope around her torso—barely enough to cover her breasts—and a skirt so short it was little more than a glorified belt.

"My, my," she smiled, "look at Mr. Penguin."

"One insult and I'm out of here," I replied gruffly. "Let's just get to our table."

"The night's young, Al."

"But I'm not. I have business after this. I'm in a hurry."

"Very well." She laughed and took my arm.

We sat by the front window, where everybody could gawp at me. I settled into my chair, trying not to twitch in the stifling suit, and picked up the menu.

"You should have told me this was…" I stopped talking and listened to the music. "Is that 'Yellow Submarine'?"

"They play all those corny old songs here," she said. "That's why I like it."

"Great," I groaned. "Makes my suit all the damn dumber."

"Cheer up," she giggled. "You're distinctive. And don't bother with the menu—since you're in a hurry, we'll do without the meal. A quick drink and I'm gone." A short waiter in red suspenders, with an I LOVE CAFRAN'S badge pinned to his breast, approached. "A piña colada," Priscilla said promptly. "Al?"

"Mineral water, please." The waiter nodded dutifully and went to fetch the drinks. We talked about the funeral and the mourners. Priscilla hadn't noticed the blind man but knew most of the others and filled me in on their relationships with Nicola. I'd only meant to dwell on the preliminaries for a couple of minutes but one anecdote led to another and soon the time was flying by. When I found myself reminiscing about my nights of passion with Nic, I halted in mid-sentence, glanced at my watch, realized eight o'clock—and two more drinks—had come and gone and knuckled down to business.

I steepled my hands, cleared my throat and crab-talked up to the big questions. "You remember you told me you wanted to help find out who killed Nic?" She nodded. "You know I've been making investigations?" She nodded again. "Well, there's a few…That is, if you don't mind, I'd like to…"

She laughed. "Spit it out. I won't take offense, whatever it is."

"It gets pretty personal," I warned her.

She tipped her glass at me and lowered her lids. "Here's to getting personal."

I stared at the table, even though I should have been watching her face to gauge whether she was answering truthfully or not. "You lied about not knowing Rudi Ziegler."

A brief pause, then, "Yes. I go a couple of times a month. It amuses me. I let him play with his mirrors and summon fake spirits. I gasp, clap my hands and shake in my chair, like on a ghost train, then pay up and trot along home. He's a fabulous entertainer."

"Have you seen him since Nic's death, apart from at the funeral?"

"Yes. I introduced Nic to him. If he was involved in her murder, I would have felt partly to blame. I asked if he knew anything about it. He told me he didn't. I believed him."

"Why did you lie to me?"

"I don't know." She tossed her hair. "Maybe I didn't want to seem like a silly girl who throws her money away on cheap spooks."

"Maybe there were other reasons."

"Maybe," she admitted coolly.

I waited for her to break the silence. I didn't want to push any more than I had to. Finally she sighed and took a drink.

"OK. There were things I didn't want you finding out. *Seeeecrets.*" She made a big production of the word. "I thought if you knew about Rudi, you might worm them out of him."

"Why mention him at all if that was the case?"

"I figured you'd know about him anyway and it would look suspicious if I played dumb."

"These secrets," I said, watching my fingers curl into involuntary fists. "Was one of them about you and Nic? What you did in your spare time?"

A long silence. Then, "Don't play it coy, Al. What exactly are you asking?"

I blurted it out. "Were you and Nic hookers?"

She reacted calmly. "Yes. I introduced her to *that* as well." A slow, measured drink. "Some friend, huh?"

"Tell me about it," I said.

She finished her drink and crooked a finger at the waiter. I left my glass where it was. She didn't say anything until the next piña colada arrived.

"It wasn't about money. Not for Nic anyway—she was loaded. I did it for the cash occasionally, but most of the time for fun. Picking up rich guys and taking them to slums. Latching on to a bum and treating him to a night at the Skylight. Doing things we could never ask our boyfriends to do."

"How long had this been going on?"

"I'd been doing it since my late teens. Nic only started a year or so ago."

"Was she doing it while dating me?" I asked, thinking of the times I'd made love to her without a condom.

"Not often—the game had lost a lot of its appeal—but yes. The night of her murder..." She stalled.

"Go on," I prompted her.

She shook her head and gasped, "I can't."

When a long silence followed, a silence she showed no sign of breaking, I prodded her back into life. "I know you were at the Skylight."

Her head shot up. She'd been on the verge of tears but the shock froze them at the corners of her eyes. "How?"

"I told you I've been investigating." A smug grin almost made it to my lips but I thrust it back just in time.

Priscilla slowly twisted her glass, first to the left, then to the right, eyes on the drops of condensation as they slid toward the base. She started talking and didn't look up until she was finished unburdening herself.

"Nic set up a trick. We were meant to do him together—she liked three-way action. I arrived in advance and booked the room. Eight-one-two. Signed in as Jane Dowe, as I always did in hotels. Headed for the bar. On the way I ran into an old customer. I don't have regulars, but this was a Chinese businessman I'd been with several times. He asked me up to his room. I said I had a prior engagement. He told me to name my price."

"What's this guy's name?"

"None of your business," she responded sharply. "Besides, he was only here for a couple of days. He's back in Hong Kong now."

"Hard to check on," I commented.

"If I'd known what was going to happen," she said bitterly, "I'd have arranged a more convenient alibi."

"Let's get back to the Skylight," I said quietly. "He told you to name your price. Then?"

"We haggled—the Chinese love to haggle—and arrived at an acceptable sum. He had some business to attend to. Gave me the card to his room, told me to let myself in. I struck for the bar first and ordered a drink. Nic turned up. I explained the change of plan."

"How did she react?"

"She didn't mind. Business is business."

"She didn't seem scared or apprehensive?"

"No."

"You don't think she had any idea of what was coming?"

"Hardly."

"What happened next?"

"She went her way, I went mine."

"That was it?"

"Yes. I gave her the card to 812 before she left."

"She went straight up?"

"I presume so. I didn't leave with her—I'd slipped off my shoes, so I stayed a few seconds to put them back on."

"Did she tell you the name of her john?"

I could see Priscilla's withering smile in the panels of the glass. "We'd hardly be sitting here talking if she had. I wouldn't have let shame stop me from revealing the name of her killer if I knew it."

"You didn't see him? He wasn't in the lobby?"

"Nic had gone up by the time I came out of the bar."

"She didn't say anything about him? His nationality, job, if he was rich or poor, what he looked like?"

"Nothing." Her fingers stopped twirling the glass and she gripped it firmly. "My Chinaman was in poor form that night. I finished early—about half past eleven—and started for home. I was on the sixth floor. As I got into the elevator, I thought about joining Nic and her companion. I almost did."

"What stopped you?"

She sighed. "I was tired. Went home and got a good night's sleep instead, rare for a Friday. I rang Nic the next day. Didn't think anything of it when there was no answer. I didn't connect her absence with the trick in the Skylight until..."

She broke off and took several deep breaths. The tears had forced their way back and were rolling down her cheeks.

"From what I read, she was still alive at half past eleven," Priscilla moaned. "If I'd gone up, or if I'd gone with her earlier, when I was meant to..."

"You might have been killed too," I said, touching her hand briefly, wishing to be supportive without seeming forward.

"Or I might have saved her," she sobbed. "She was alone. The first time she pulled a trick, she begged me to go with her—she was afraid. I told her not to be silly and sent her off with him, laughing. I should have been there. I..."

Again she broke off, and this time I knew there'd be no recovery. Our interview was at a close. I covered her hands with mine—I felt confident enough to make real contact this time—and made soft, cooing noises, gently guiding her back to normal conversation.

She smiled weakly once the worst had passed. "Thank you," she said.

"For reducing you to tears? I should have kept my mouth shut."

"No." She took one of her hands from mine and wiped tears from her face, then tenderly laid her palm against my left cheek. It was cool from the glass. "It was good that you confronted me. I needed to confess. It was tearing me apart. This way it's out in the open. I can cry about it now and maybe start to forgive myself."

"There's nothing to forgive," I assured her. She made a face, then set about restoring her looks, wiping away the worst of the tears, applying makeup while I sat twiddling my thumbs, wishing I were holding her hands again.

Snapping her compact shut, she rose. I was getting up to walk her to her cab when she laid a hand on my forearm and smiled. "It's OK. Finish your drink. I'll settle the check on my way."

"Don't be stupid," I said, but she squeezed lightly and stopped me.

"Please, Al. I'd like to be alone. I'll give you a call soon, when I feel better."

"OK," I said. "But let me pay. I arranged this meeting, so it's only fair that—"

"I won't argue about it." She grinned, made a fast turn and scurried away, only to find her path blocked by another woman. They collided, clutched at each other to prevent a fall, then separated. "I'm sorry," Priscilla said. "I wasn't looking."

"Not at all," the other woman replied. "You had the right-of-way. I should have... What the hell are you doing in a suit?" This last part was addressed to me.

"You know each other?" Priscilla asked, politely standing aside so that Ellen—early for once in her life—had a clear view of me.

"Yes." I rose awkwardly, as if caught in a clandestine embrace—for a second I forgot we were divorced—and welcomed my second guest of the night. "Priscilla, I'd like you to meet Ellen Fraser. Ellen, Priscilla Perdue."

"Doubling up on dates, Al?" Ellen mocked me. "You're getting cheap in your old age."

"Please," Priscilla said quickly, "don't get the wrong idea. We weren't here on a date. It was merely a—"

Ellen laughed and raised her hands. "No need to apologize. I'm not dating the sap either."

Priscilla blinked and looked at me questioningly.

"Ellen and I used to be married," I muttered.

"*Oh.*" She opened her mouth to say something, thought better of it and made the sign for buttoning her lips. "I'll leave you two alone."

"You don't have to leave on my account," Ellen said.

"I was going anyway," Priscilla told her, then winked at me and said goodbye.

Ellen watched Priscilla march away in her skimpy top and skirt, a sly smile twitching the edges of her mouth. "New girl?" she asked casually.

"A friend of a friend," I answered truthfully.

She turned the full force of her gaze on me. "So that's what friends of friends are wearing these days."

"Skip it," I mumbled gruffly. "Let's order."

"Yes, Romeo," she said, hiding behind a menu to cover her smirk.

Ellen asked what the occasion was while we were waiting for the meal to arrive. She always came straight to the point.

"You heard about the girl who was murdered in the Skylight last Thursday?" That was the official public date of her death.

"Sure. The papers have been making a meal of it. They love taking jabs at The Cardinal. It's not often they get the chance."

"I knew her," I said.

Ellen frowned. "Socially?"

"We were lovers." I'd meant to present a condensed version of the facts—keeping The Cardinal and the extent of my involvement out of it—but I'd never been good at keeping secrets from Ellen. Soon the whole story was tumbling out. I told her about my fling with Nic, how I'd found her, when she'd been killed, what I'd learned of her since then, my meetings with The Cardinal, Priscilla, Ziegler and the rest. The only cards I played close to my chest were Paucar Wami, the vision I'd had and my father. Knowing about Wami might scare her off when I asked her for help. I would have been embarrassed talking about the vision. And Tom Jeery was my concern alone.

The tale took us through dinner and dessert, and on to coffee. She listened quietly, displaying no emotions other than an occasional raised eyebrow, and kept her questions to a minimum.

When I finished she shook her head, sipped at her coffee and said, "Wow." I held my tongue, knowing there'd be more once she'd thought on it some. "The Cardinal. After all these years. Is he as impressive as they say?"

"He's more imposing than anyone I've met, but there's something small-time about him, like he's this tough kid in the biggest sandbox in the city."

"You used to say you'd run for the hills if The Cardinal took a personal interest in you," she reminded me.

"I almost did. If not for Nic..."

"How close *were* you two?"

"Not very. I hadn't guessed how duplicitous she was. I knew she'd been around but I'd no idea she was a..." I didn't like to say it, so I didn't. "There was very little romance in it."

"So why get involved now that she's dead?" A blunt but fair query.

"Because she was a friend and I value friendship."

"Or because you like the idea of cracking the case and being king for an hour?" Ellen suggested, seeing inside my mind as she'd always been able to.

"Would it be so bad if I did? You always said I was meant for better things."

"Absolutely. I deplored the way you settled for so little. It helped drive me away from you. Ambition's good, Al. But there's a difference between standing tall and standing up to your neck in shit."

"You think I should ditch the case?" I loved the way she put it so plainly.

"Not necessarily. If this is what you want, go for it. But it's a messy business. I've had dealings at work with detectives. What those guys go through isn't pretty—hours spent following people, bugging phones, invading privacy. Detectives destroy relationships, people, lives. I'm not sure you're cut out for that."

"But this is different. It's personal. I won't hurt anybody."

"You can't make a pledge like that. You might have to."

I stared down at the table. "You think I should stop?"

Ellen sighed. "I'm not your wife now—what you do is none of my business. All I'm saying is, think before you act. Don't rush in halfhearted. Do it right and *know* what you're doing, or don't do it at all."

Ellen watched intently as I pretended to mull her words over, saw that I had no intention of letting matters drop, and tutted impatiently. "You should let me know when I'm wasting my breath. You don't have the slightest intention of quitting."

"Not really," I chuckled apologetically.

"So why drag me out and bare your soul if not for my sage-like advice?"

I smiled sheepishly and said, "For your help." Then I drew her back to Rudi Ziegler and explained my hunch, how I felt the murderer might be connected to him, how I needed to learn more about the mystic.

Ellen said nothing until I'd finished, then fixed me with one of her iciest stares and snapped, "You're insane."

"Is that a no?" I quipped.

"This guy could be a killer!"

"I doubt it. He's meek as they come."

"But he might send his clients to killers? Forget it! Look somewhere else for a stooge. I wouldn't touch something like this if you paid me. If that's a problem—if you think I owe you—tough. I don't."

"Of course you don't owe me," I snapped back. "I never—"

I broke off before I said something I'd regret. I began to wish I hadn't started this but it was too late to back out now.

"I've no right to ask this of you," I muttered, "but I'm asking anyway, because I have no one else to turn to. You wouldn't be in danger. I wouldn't ask if I thought there was any degree of risk involved."

Ellen sighed. "I know." A long pause. "But I've got work to consider. We're real busy. I couldn't—"

"It wouldn't interfere with work," I said quickly. "You could fit it around your office hours. It would be fun. A dibbling of divertissement." That was one of Ellen's favorite expressions—she'd made it up herself. She smiled and I knew I'd almost won her over.

She made a show of pondering my words, then finally let her head roll back and sighed wearily. "OK. I'll listen. But I'm promising nothing. Get it?"

"Got it."

"You better!"

I wet my throat before continuing. "You'd go along to a couple of sessions, have your palm read, your future told, that kind of thing. Get to know the guy, laugh at his jokes, flirt with him a bit. Then ask to sit in on a séance and express interest in going further, tell him you want to make meaningful contact with the other world and find a lover among the shades of the dead."

"*What?*" she squealed, delighted in spite of her misgivings.

"That's what Nic was after," I grinned. "A spirit lover, a ghost she could get hot and horny with."

Her eyes sparkled. "I bet you had some fun with *her* beneath the sheets."

"You don't know the half of it," I smiled. "Made certain other parties I've slept with look like dead fish."

"Watch it," she growled, tweaking my nose.

"Whatever your story, however crazy, act like you're serious and he'll treat you with respect. He deals with cranks all the time. If he thinks you believe, there'll be no problem. Say you want to delve into the secrets of past incarnations, mumbo jumbo like that. Mention Egyptians and Incas—he's got a passion for Incas—anything along those lines you can think of."

"That sounds harmless so far," she said. "What next?"

"If he says he doesn't do stuff like that and turns you away, you walk— thanks for the help, end of your involvement, *adios*. If he leads you on, play along, but push him toward a conclusion."

"What sort of conclusion?"

"Insist on results. If he can't provide them, ask him to send you to someone more in touch with the dead."

"If he does, what do I do? Go see them?"

"No. If he gives you a name, pass it along to me and leave it there. I'll check it out. The other guy will never know about you. See? Just as I said, no danger."

She weighed up the pros and cons, then grimaced. "What the hell. I've been meaning to visit one of those fakirs for years. Maybe he'll direct me toward the man of my dreams. I've tried every other approach."

"You're a peach." I leaned across and kissed her, a chaste kiss between two old lovers who were now mere friends.

"When do you want me to start?" she asked.

"As soon as possible."

"What if he draws a connection between the two of us?"

"How could he? If you don't mention Nic or me, he has no reason to be suspicious. Treat it like a joke at first. Don't start off serious. Let him *make* you believe. Let his act convince and propel you further along."

"All right. But you'll owe me big for this. I've got a birthday coming up and I won't settle for a box of chocolates. Understand?"

"It'll be diamond tiaras and slippers of gold," I vowed.

"It'd better be," she snorted, then raised her mug in a toast. "Here's to Fraser and Jeery, the Miss Marple and Hercule Poirot of the twenty-first century."

"Marple and Poirot," I repeated, and we grinned stupidly as we clinked mugs and downed the coffee as if it were champagne.

12

I spent Thursday morning checking for news of Wami. The streets were teeming with stories and unsubstantiated sightings but no real leads. I toyed with the idea of offering a reward for information leading to his whereabouts, but that would have brought the crazies out in full.

I stopped in at Party Central and looked for Frank. I wanted to ask him about the Troops guarding the Skylight the night of Nic's murder. His secretary paged him—he was in a meeting but would be free in a quarter of an hour. I said I'd be back and moseyed down to the canteen to catch up on the latest gossip.

I passed Richey Harney in the corridor on my way, the guy who'd originally been destined to haul Nic back from the Fridge with Vincent.

"How'd the party go?" I asked.

"Party?" His face was a blank.

"Your daughter's party."

"My...?" The lights came on and he chuckled edgily. "It was great. Thanks for letting me off the hook. If you ever need a favor..."

He hurried on and I wondered what he had to feel edgy about. Maybe he skipped the party for a rendezvous with a mistress, or simply went off for a beer.

No sign of Jerry or Mike in the canteen. A couple of guys I half knew saluted me. I waved but didn't go over—they were watching the horses and that's something I had no interest in. I sat and watched a different channel, then took myself back to Frank's office. He arrived soon after.

"Al. What's up?"

I asked if he had a list of the guards at the Skylight. He did. Could I have a copy? Normally, no, but since I was The Cardinal's current favorite…

Thirty-six names in all. "Any dirt on these guys?" I asked halfheartedly, not savoring the idea of investigating that many suspects.

"Every Troop's clean, Al, you know that."

I grinned. "Sure. Clean as angels. You know what I mean. Are there any you have doubts about, guys stuck at the Skylight because you don't want them getting in the way here?"

Frank took the list and examined it. "Nobody I'm at odds with," he declared. "Good soldiers, the lot. What are you looking for?"

I told him about Nic and how she hadn't been killed at the Skylight. It was the first he'd heard of it. His face darkened as I broke the news.

"That bastard," he snarled. "I can't believe I wasn't told. I'm the head of the goddamn Troops for Christ's sake! I should be the first he comes to with—"

"Frank." I whistled. "Calm down before your head explodes."

He glared at me, then relaxed. "He gets on my tits, Al. You've got no idea what it's like working close to that maniac."

I thought—from my brief experience of The Cardinal—that I had, but kept the opinion to myself.

"The sooner he moves me on and lets that prick Raimi take over, the better," Frank grumbled.

"What are you talking about?"

"I'm on my way out," Frank huffed. "He hasn't said as much, but we had a few conversations recently and I got the whiff. I'm not as dumb as he thinks. My days as head Troop are numbered, thank fuck."

The Cardinal had told me that at our first meeting, but I figured it would be better not to mention it to Frank. Instead I asked who "that prick Raimi" was.

"Capac Raimi. Theo Boratto's nephew. You know him?"

"Yeah. I heard he was being groomed for big things. Didn't realize he was up for your job, though. Vincent mentioned him the night we picked up Nic from the Fridge. He doesn't like Raimi either."

"Not surprised. Vincent always fancied himself as Ford's successor. The way Raimi's going, he's gonna leapfrog us all. The Cardinal's got the hots for him. He'll take my place, Ford's, even The Cardinal's in the end, you wait and see. Fucking golden boy." Frank muttered a few more curses, then shook thoughts of Capac Raimi from his head. "Anyway, the Skylight. If she wasn't killed there, what makes you think one of our guys might have been involved?"

I shrugged. "I know the Troops at the Skylight aren't the sharpest, but I can't picture them missing a guy dragging in a corpse."

"Only her back was cut up," Frank reminded me. "The killer could have draped a coat over her, pretended she was stoned, waltzed her through in front of everyone. You wouldn't get away with it here, but at the Skylight…"

"I'd like to check on them anyway. No objections?"

"It's your time—waste it as you see fit. But have a word with me before you hassle any of them. I can do without insurrection in the ranks, especially with that fucker Raimi snapping at my heels."

I decided to leave before he went off on another rant. I was on my way out with the list of names when I stopped on an impulse. "Do you know Richey Harney?"

Frank closed his eyes for a second, putting a face to the name, then nodded.

"He said he was at his daughter's birthday party last week. Could you check—"

"Richey Harney doesn't have a daughter."

I paused. "You're sure?"

"Absolutely."

"Is he married?"

"In the middle of a divorce. No children."

"Then I must have been mistaken. See you, Frank."

Richey had left the building when I went looking for him. I was about to get his address and track him down when I spotted Vincent Carell chatting up a secretary. I decided to have a word with him instead. He wasn't happy to be interrupted but came when I said it was important.

"What's bugging you?" he growled. "Couldn't you see the sparks zapping between us? I was this close to—"

"You recall our trip to the Fridge?" I cut in.

"Do I look like a goldfish? 'Course I fucking remember. What about it?"

"You asked Richey Harney to go with you first."

"Yeah?" Growing guarded now.

"He said he had to go to his daughter's birthday party. He told us he missed her First Communion and if he missed the party on top of that, he'd be in the doghouse with his wife."

"So?" Vincent said unhappily.

"Richey Harney doesn't have a daughter."

"He doesn't?"

"He's in the middle of a divorce."

"He is?"

I leaned in closer. "You can tell me what's going on, or I can worm it out of Richey. Either way, I *will* find out."

"Harney won't say anything. He's got more sense."

"But he's also got less to lose than you. If he talks in exchange for my oath that I'll swear everything came from *you*…"

Vincent's nostrils flared. "Don't fuck with me, Algiers."

"I won't. Not if you play ball. Tell me what that scene was about and I'll keep it to myself. Not a word to anyone. It'll be our little secret."

Vincent took a deep breath. "If you say anything…"

"I won't."

"Ford set me up to it."

"Up to what?"

"He said to wait until you came down, then go in after you. Harney would be there, waiting, ready to respond when I said what Ford told me to."

"*And?*" I pressed.

"Ford thought you'd take pity on the fool and offer to step in for him. If you didn't, we were to have an argument on the way out and I was to storm back in and tell you to take his place."

"Why?"

"Don't know."

"Vincent…"

"No shit, Algiers. Ford didn't know either. He was following The Cardinal's orders. Neither of us knew about your girlfriend."

"You didn't know it was Nicola Hornyak lying out there on the slab?" I snorted skeptically.

"I'd never heard of her before you ID'd her. Ford hadn't either."

"The Cardinal knew."

Vincent shrugged.

I stepped away and thanked Vincent for his cooperation. He made a face, warned me again not to tell anyone he'd told me, and went back after the secretary. I found a chair and sat down.

I knew The Cardinal had known about Nic from the start—the file was proof of that—but it never occurred to me that I'd been deliberately sent to discover the body, that he'd arranged things to make it look as if it were my choice.

I recalled card tricks I'd learned as a kid, and how important the *force* was. A good magician could force his chosen card on a member of an audience, making it seem as if that person had chosen for himself. My trip to the Fridge had been an elaborate force, arranged by The Cardinal to look like an incredible coincidence. Sap that I was, I bought it.

Now that I knew about Vincent and Richey, I got to wondering what other tricks Mr. Dorak may have been playing. I'd assumed Nic was the reason The Cardinal had taken an interest in me, but maybe it was the other way around. He'd confessed to having had his eye on me since I joined the Troops. Perhaps he'd decided it was time to wind me up and see how I jumped. Could Nic have been killed on his orders and planted for me to find? If so, I was on a fool's quest. There could be no justice for Nicola Hornyak if The Cardinal had signed her execution slip.

I spent the rest of Thursday and most of Friday stuck in Party Central, checking on the thirty-six Skylight Troops, scouring the files for incriminating evidence, of which there was plenty. Nineteen had chalked up at least one kill, twelve had served time, four were junkies, nine were being or had been rehabilitated. One had served as a covert agent in the Middle East, an authorized anarchist who suffered a moral crisis after bombing a school full of children. Three used to be rent boys. Two were fashioning alternate careers as pimps. Most gambled, drank a lot and screwed around outlandishly.

But there was nothing to link them to Nic, Rudi Ziegler or Paucar Wami. I devoted a lot of time to the rent boys and pimps, figuring they might have moved in the same circles as Nic, but if they had, it wasn't recorded. I made a note to have a few words with them in private, but there was no rush. I had other fish to fry in the meantime. Namely, Paucar Wami.

There'd been no confirmed sightings since he annihilated Johnny Grace, though several bodies had been discovered bearing some of his numerous trademarks. I made inquiries that Friday by phone, which wasn't the best way—people were always inclined to reveal more face-to-face. I planned to wrap up my investigation into the private lives of the Troops early Saturday and spend the rest of the day pounding the streets. If nothing turned up, I'd go see Fabio on Sunday.

I cycled home late, bleary-eyed, head pounding. I wasn't accustomed to all this paperwork and screen time. I felt drained. I dropped into Ali's and got a couple of bagels. I couldn't face a book, not even a magazine, so I just ate the bagels, brewed a hot lemon drink to soothe the throbbing in my head and went to bed. I was asleep within minutes.

The sound of dripping woke me. Soft and steady, too gentle to disturb an ordinary sleeping ear. But I'd been trained to spring awake at the faintest unfamiliar sound—footsteps, the creak of a door, an unexpected drip.

I knew it wasn't coming from my taps—I checked them every night, as water-conscious as every good citizen should be in these days of global warming. Besides, the position was wrong. My bathroom was on the other side of the wall at the head of my bed, the kitchen lay to the far right of the apartment, but the drips were coming from the center of the living room.

I swung my legs out smoothly. My fingers felt beneath the mattress and located the gun I kept there. I stood and started for the door, naked, moving stealthily, primed to open fire.

I pressed an ear to the door. The steady drip continued but I tuned it out and listened for other sounds, such as heavy breathing or the beat of an anxious heart.

Nothing.

Leaving the light off, I turned the handle and let the door swing open, stepping to the left in case there was someone on the other side waiting to barge through.

No movement.

I stepped out, left hand steadying my right as I led with my gun.

Nobody there. The room was full of shadows but I knew after a brief once-over that it was clean. Except for the object hanging from the lightbulb in the center of the room, the source of the drips.

I moved toward it swiftly, head flicking left and right, not letting my guard drop. As I closed on the object the sounds of the drips magnified. Again I focused to tune them out.

A foot from it, I stopped. I was staring at the back of a severed human head. It was hanging from a wire and revolving slowly.

As the face spun into view, I thought this was one of my nightmares come to life, Tom Jeery's ghost head. My breath caught in my throat and the nozzle of my gun lifted. I almost let the head have a full clip, but controlled myself before I fired. The head posed no threat and firing would be a waste of ammunition and a sign of blind panic.

I watched breathlessly as the face crept into view. I knew it couldn't be my dead father, but I couldn't shake the fear that this was his spirit come to chastise me for not taking care of his mortal remains.

Then I caught sight of two twisting snakes running down the sides of the face and all thoughts of supernatural specters fled. This was no phantom. It was the solid, disconnected head of the city's emperor of death— *Paucar Wami!*

13

Years of training evaporated. I froze, arms dropping, eyes widening. Wami's face filled my vision. The sound of his blood splattering onto the floor crowded the cavities of my ears and deafened me to all else. The city could have gone up in flames and I wouldn't have noticed. There was only the head, its eyes gouged out, the skin at the sides of the nose peeled away to create a pair of thumb-size holes, chin chipped in two (hammer and chisel? a drill?) where the heads of the snakes should have met.

I was so obsessed by the head, I didn't stop to ask how it got there, who hung it from my lamp and where he was now.

A hand slid over my right shoulder and fingers gripped my throat. Another hand darted around the left side of my face. On the middle finger was a ring, a four-inch spike protruding from it. It was one stroke away from making a gooey puddle of my left eye.

"Drop your weapon, relax, do nothing stupid." It was a soft but confident, cruel voice. I let the gun slip from my fingers and allowed my arms to hang by my sides.

"Sit," my captor said and I felt the edge of a chair—it must have been the one I kept by the window of my bedroom—bite into the backs of my legs. If the head in front of me hadn't been so distorted by pain, I would have sworn it was laughing.

The hand around my throat withdrew. Seconds later, so did the hand with the ring. A fool would have dived for the gun. I sat firm.

"Where were you?" I asked, sickened to be caught so cheaply.

"Under the bed," he chuckled. "Isn't that where all the bogeymen hang out?"

It must have taken more than the few seconds I was frozen for him to slide out, fetch the chair and cross the room after me. Why hadn't I sensed him? Even a ghost would have made some kind of noise.

"Who are you?" I asked. "What do you want?"

"In time," he replied, then reached forward and poked the head. "Know who this belongs to?"

I gulped. "Yes."

"Say his name. I want to hear it."

I licked my lips. I didn't know what was happening but I had to play along. Whoever this guy was, he'd killed the man many said couldn't be killed. He wasn't to be taken lightly.

"It's Paucar Wami," I croaked.

"Indeed?" He sounded amused. There was a long pause. I came close to bolting. Managed to stay in check, though it wasn't easy.

"Do you know why I am here?"

The question caught me by surprise. I couldn't answer. Then I felt something sharp scratch along the width of my bare back and the words tumbled out.

"No. I don't even know who you are. How could I—"

"Enough." He patted my right shoulder. "I am not here to kill you." His hand crept forward and he pointed at the head. "I have had enough killing for one night."

"Could I have that in writing?" My chattering teeth made a mockery of the show of bravado.

"I will write it for you in blood if you wish," he teased. Then, "Do not, at any stage, turn around. If you gaze upon my face, I will have to kill you."

"Who are you?" I asked, calmly this time. It was possible he was playing with me, and had no intention of letting me live, but things didn't seem as desperate as they had at first.

"Ask instead who I am not," he replied cryptically.

"OK. Who aren't you?"

"I am not *him*." The hand poked the head again. "And *he* is not Paucar Wami. His name is—was—Allegro Jinks."

I frowned and focused on the tattooed features hanging from the thin wire. The face was the image of how I'd pictured Wami. I began to mutter, "I don't follow. If he isn't—"

Then the penny dropped and I groaned.

Paucar Wami—as my assailant most surely was—laughed. "I see I have no need to introduce myself. Good. I hate formal introductions."

"Why are you here?" I asked. "What do you want?"

"I want nothing, Al. I come as an ally, bringing you this fine head as a goodwill token. I was going to send it by mail, but I thought you might appreciate the personal touch." I felt his breath on the back of my neck as he leaned in closer to whisper, "You were looking for me. Asking questions. Spreading rumors. You said I killed the Hornyak girl. I could not stand for such slander. Normally I would have put a quick end to the lies. But I could not understand why you were so sure of my involvement. I did some digging and discovered she had been seen with a Paucar Wami ringer."

"A *ringer*?" I almost looked over my shoulder, then remembered the warning. "It wasn't you with Nic?"

"I never met Nicola Hornyak or even heard of the girl until your queries drew my attention to her." I felt him pressing into my back. I didn't move, though the temptation to shy away from his touch was great. He stroked the dead man's cheeks, caressing the writhing snakes, one after the other.

"These beauties belong to me and no other. No one else has a right to wear the snakes. When I heard of the impostor, I made the rounds of various tattoo parlors, to find out who had copied them without my permission. A slim Chinaman called Ho Yun Fen was the guilty party. Quite an artist. A shame to kill him, but lessons must be taught. Ho Yun remembered the snakes, the customer's name and that a pretty white girl had been with him at the time."

"When was this?" I asked, curiosity getting the better of my fear.

"Five weeks before her death. Yes," he said as I opened my mouth to form the question, "the girl was Nicola Hornyak, though that only came out when I paid a call on Mr. Jinks. He protected her identity as vigorously as he could, given the circumstances, but in the end was forced to part with the secret, painful as it was."

I stared at the ruined face of Allegro Jinks and made up my mind to tell Wami anything he wanted to know, the second he asked.

"Did Jinks kill her?"

"No," Wami sighed. "She rang him earlier that night and told him to stay in, that she would come to see him. He fell asleep waiting for her. Heard nothing more of her until she made the papers the next week."

"That was his story?"

"That was the *truth*." I could feel Wami's smile. "Men don't lie when you scoop out their eyes, then start on their genitalia."

My testicles retreated at the thought.

"Did he know who killed her?" I asked, driving the picture of the dismembered Jinks from my mind.

"No. He was not acquainted with her ways. She picked him up a fortnight or so prior to his tattooing. Gave an alias. Never told him where she lived. Used him as she pleased."

"For sex?"

"And more. The tattoos were *her* idea. He did not want them. She performed acts of wanton abandon—which I blush to think about—to win him over. She also made him shave his scalp—he had a full head of curly locks when they met."

"Did she say why?"

"She told him it would make him look sexy." Wami chuckled. "Which, dare I say, is true enough."

Once again my eyes fixed on the snakes, but now I focused on the shaven head and noticed it was covered by a light layer of bristle. As I stared, trying to make sense of the craziness, Wami spoke again.

"So much for my story. How about yours? Any idea why your girlfriend would have kitted Allegro out like this?"

"She knew a medium called Rudi Ziegler," I answered, client confidentiality be damned. "She took Wami—Jinks—to see him. Said he was her demon lover. Maybe she'd heard about your exploits and thought this was how a demon would look."

"Interesting. Allegro mentioned her interest in the occult. Do you think I should pay a call to Mr. Ziegler?"

"No. He's a harmless old quack. He had nothing to do with her death."

"Then who had?"

"I don't know," I groaned. "I thought it was you until you turned up with that." Meaning the head.

"It was not *you*?" Wami asked casually.

"Me?" I blinked.

"Concern is a fine form of camouflage. Nobody is going to suspect a man so determined to bring her killer to justice, a hero who charges around, accusing all but himself."

"I didn't kill her."

"It makes no difference to me if you did or not. I will let you live either way. But confessing can do wonders for a man's soul."

"I didn't kill her." Stiffly this time.

"Very well," Wami sighed. "Just thought I would ask." There was the briefest of sounds as he stood. "I will be off then."

"That's it?" I asked, startled.

"Unless you want to share a beer and pretzels," he laughed.

"That's all you came for? To show me the head and tell me about Jinks?"

"And clear my name. I need not have. Many murders in this city are attributed to me, and usually I care not what people think. But I knew of your connection to The Cardinal and also…" He paused, then shrugged (I knew by the rustling of his jacket). "It was pride. I solved the mystery and wanted someone to share it with."

"You only solved part of the mystery," I reminded him. "You didn't find out who killed Nic."

"That is of no interest to me. I wanted to know who was impersonating me and why. If the Hornyak girl was alive, I would pay her a visit and ask why she demanded the makeover, but even *I* have never managed to pry secrets from the dead."

"How can I trust you?" I asked. "You might have ordered Jinks's tattoo yourself, to serve as a red herring."

"To what end?"

"To stop me sniffing around after you."

Wami laughed loudly. "I said you interested me, Al Jeery. You never irritated me. If you had, I would have sent you the same way as Allegro Jinks. You may inquire after me further, if you wish, but I would not recommend it."

"What about Jinks?" I asked, sensing—more than hearing—Wami begin to retreat. "Aren't you taking him with you?"

"Al," he chuckled, "*I* disposed of the body. It is only fair that *you* take care of the head."

"But if I'm caught with it..."

"You will not be." My bedroom window slid open and there was a slight creaking as Wami eased through. The fire escape at the rear had collapsed years before. He must have been clinging to the wall, like a bat. "Count to fifty," he said. "And Al?"

"Yes?"

"Count slow."

Then he was gone, leaving me to make the slowest count of my life.

I wanted to take Wami's revelations and run with them. What had Nic been up to with Allegro Jinks? Why the façade? Had it been a game, making her lover up to look like a famous serial killer for a thrill? Or had somebody put her up to it?

I pushed the thoughts aside and concentrated on the problem closest at hand—the head. I had to get rid of it quickly. Paucar Wami could whistle carelessly while carting heads around, but if I was found with this, I'd be screwed. There were people—Howard Kett for one—who'd love to send me down for a long stretch, and this would provide them with the perfect opportunity. For all I knew, that was what Wami was setting me up for.

I cut down the head—the knots in the wire would have taken too long to unravel—and stuck it in a plastic bag, wrapped that in a pillow case, then dumped the package in a black bag and tied it shut. Quickly wiped up the worst of the blood with a rag and squeezed it into the sink. I'd clean up properly later. Disposing of the head was my first priority.

I dressed in dark clothes, grabbed the bag and skulked down the stairs.

I had no basket on my bike so I rode one-handed, the other holding the bag above the knot, ready to toss it away at a moment's notice.

I arrived at the Fridge unimpeded. As I keyed in the security code, I was certain a posse of cops would spring out of nowhere, but they didn't. When the door slid closed behind me, I fell against a nearby wall and relaxed, feeling safe for the first time since I awoke to the sound of drips.

A male clerk helped me check in the head. He didn't raise an eyebrow when I dumped the bag on the counter and told him I wanted to make a deposit. "Will you be requiring a casket or a box?" he asked politely.

"Are you kidding me?" I growled.

"No, sir. The choice is yours."

I told him a box would be fine. When he asked for the corpse's details I said I'd rather not provide any. He keyed something into his computer, then swiveled the terminal around and handed me the keyboard. "Do you have a clearance code, sir?" I shook my head. "Then please type in your name and position, then press Enter."

"I don't want to give my name."

"I understand, sir. I won't see your name, only your status. I need that to ensure you have clearance."

I did as he asked and pressed Enter, not turning the screen back to him until I'd seen my name disappear to be replaced with a string of coded numbers. The clerk examined the data, nodded, then handed me a brief form and an envelope.

"Please fill in the name of the deceased and any details you care to include. Age, address, known relatives, et cetera."

"Do I have to?"

"I'm afraid so. You have blue clearance. That requires a form. It will be locked away unseen, and may only be retrieved by direct order of The Cardinal."

"And me."

He shook his head. "No, sir. Only The Cardinal."

"You mean, once I drop this off, I can't reclaim it or check on it?"

"You can do anything with the *bag*, sir, take or move it as you please. It's the form you can't touch. That remains the property of The Cardinal."

"Where does it go?"

"I can't say. But I assure you, only The Cardinal or someone with his express authorization can access it."

"I don't have to include my name?"

"No, sir."

"What if I made up a name for the…?" I shook the bag.

The clerk smiled. "You may lie to The Cardinal if you wish, sir."

I scowled, then scribbled the name of Allegro Jinks. Since I knew nothing about the man, I left the rest of the form blank, sealed it and passed it back to the clerk.

"I don't want the *object* taken out of the bag," I told him.

"Very good, sir."

"How would I retrieve it again if I wanted it?"

"I'll give you a slip when I'm finished processing it," he said. "The box's number will be on it."

"Will I be the only one who knows the number?"

He shrugged. "We'll have a record saying the box is occupied but that's all the information that will be in the system."

I was going to leave it at that when I had a brain wave. Only Wami and I knew what had happened to Jinks. If Nic had been encouraged by another to persuade Jinks to reinvent himself, that party might come looking for their missing puppet.

"Is there a way of tagging names?" I asked. "Of setting things up so, if someone asks about a certain name, I can be informed?"

The clerk nodded. "For those with clearance, yes."

"Do I have clearance?"

"Most certainly, sir."

"Let's do it."

He keyed up another screen and again handed control to me. "Type the corpse's name at the top. Tab down, then add your own and how you wish to be contacted. If anybody asks us to search for it on our system, you'll be notified."

"What if they don't give their name?"

"Then we will simply inform you of their interest."

"Is there any way, by doing this, that they can trace the corpse to me?"

"No, sir. Not unless The Cardinal authorizes the release of your details."

I typed in the two names and my number, pressed Enter and watched the information disappear with a beep. Seconds later it was finished. The clerk handed me a slip of paper while the bag was placed on a tray, soon to be removed and boxed. I let myself out, cycled home and began mopping up blood.

14

If Wami was telling the truth—and, as he said, it would be easier for him to kill me than lie—I'd have to look for a new prime suspect. It was a pain having to start over again, but at the same time a relief to know he wasn't involved. And it had done my confidence no end of good—if I could survive a confrontation with Paucar Wami, I figured I could survive just about anything.

I spent Saturday digging for connections between Allegro Jinks and the Troops at the Skylight. Jinks had a string of arrests and convictions stretching back to his childhood, four years as a juvenile detainee, a total of eight years behind bars since he turned eighteen. He was hooked on crack, did some dealing when he was low on cash. Affiliated with several gangs at different times, but none since he'd snitched on two of his *brothers* in exchange for leniency.

There was surprisingly little violence in his past. Jinks was a coward. Avoided fights whenever possible. Stole from his women—the few there'd been—but never beat them. Never killed anyone, though he'd boasted of it. Maybe Nic was taken in by the boasts. Perhaps the thought of bedding a killer had excited her and, when she discovered the truth, she'd made him over as Paucar Wami in the hope that some of the killer's dark passion would rub off on a look-alike.

I couldn't find any direct links to the Troops. One lived a couple of blocks from where Jinks had boarded since completing his last prison spell. Another six had grown up in the same neighborhood, so might have known him as kids. A further three—one of whom was a rent boy, which sounded promising—had served time in prison while he was there.

I cleared it with Frank before talking with the jailbirds. Two were on duty at the Skylight; the other was at home. Frank summoned all three to Party Central and I went one-on-one with them, quizzing them about their pasts, Nic Hornyak and Allegro Jinks.

None of the Troops had known Nic personally, though all were familiar with her name following the furor at the Skylight. The rent boy remembered Jinks from prison. He said he'd bought grass from Jinks a couple of times—Jinks managed to smuggle in a stash, and for a while made a tidy profit, until he smoked what he had left—but that was as far as their relationship stretched.

None of them knew what Jinks was doing these days, where he was staying or what had become of him. They seemed to be telling the truth, so I crossed them off my list and looked to pastures new.

Priscilla called late Saturday. A long conversation. She was more open now that I knew the truth about her. Talked freely about Nic and the tricks they'd pulled. I asked if she was prepared to provide me with a list of Nic's boyfriends. No, but she said she'd introduce me to friends, colleagues and customers of theirs. She also promised to get in contact with Nic's old beaux and ask them to talk to me. We agreed to make a start in the morning.

"Not too early," she giggled. "I spell Saturday night P-A-R-T-Y."

While Priscilla went to party, I returned to my mire of papers—they covered the floor like a plague—and panned through them for a clue that would place me on the track of the killer.

Nic's friends were understandably loath to discuss their private affairs, and if I'd been alone I'd have gotten nothing out of them. But Priscilla sweet-talked them and got most to open up. We didn't learn anything. A few had tricked with Nic in the past but none had seen or heard from her the night of the murder. They didn't know of any dangerous customers she'd been with. Nobody recognized the name of Allegro Jinks.

A few mentioned Nic's interest in the occult. A teenager with a line of holes up his arm like a seam had seen Nic crouched over a paper bag in an alley once. "Her face was painted like those Indians in the movies. Or the Africans. The ones with war paint or whatever the hell. Squiggly lines, circles, triangles, that sorta shit." She'd been naked, staggering around, muttering to herself, lifting the bag to her face and inhaling. After a while she dumped the bag in a trash bin and staggered away. The kid went for a peek.

"It was a dead rat!" he squeaked. "The paper was soaked through with its blood. That's what she'd been sniffing. I steered clear of her after that."

One of her friends said Nicola had tried interesting her in black magic. "She was always urging me to read weird books—*tomes*, she called them. I looked at a few. Ugly, horrible things. Photos of dead animals, lurid masks, incantations to raise the dead."

I asked if Nic had invited her to spiritual meetings.

"A couple of times."

With whom?

"Some Ziegler guy."

Rudi.

There were more like that, with similar stories. Nearly everyone who'd known her said she'd been mixed up in witchcraft, sorcery, dark magic, "shit like that." I decided maybe I should give the human sacrifice theory more thought.

I called Ellen on Tuesday and asked how she was getting on with Ziegler. She wasn't happy to hear from me.

"I said I'd call when I had something to report," she snapped.

"I know. I was just—"

"Don't pressure me."

"I'm not—"

"If you call again, the deal's off."

And that was that.

I enjoyed the couple of days I spent with Priscilla. She insisted on linking arms whenever we were walking and had a nice habit of resting her head on my shoulder and mumbling in a low voice that only I could hear. I never made a pass, but I spent a lot of time imagining the two of us getting it on, undressing her with my eyes when she wasn't watching.

Tuesday night, she said I'd have to do without her until the weekend. She'd been neglecting her job at the salon but couldn't call in sick indefinitely. She invited me out Friday, after work, to meet more of her friends. I said I'd think about it and get in touch. She favored me with a kiss as we parted, a sisterly peck. There was nothing romantic or promising in the kiss, but I spent most of the night dreaming about it.

I meant to dive back into the paperwork on Wednesday—looking for links between Ziegler, Jinks and the Troops—but when I stared around at the files and their bulging intestines, a switch clicked off inside my head. I'd been cramming my brain with profiles, theories, facts and figures for nearly two weeks. I needed a break. And, since I was my own boss, I took one.

I cycled to Shankar's for breakfast, a full meal to set me up for the day. I ate by myself, not wanting anything to distract me from my day of rest. Went for a long walk by the river afterward, two hours at medium stride. The scenery wasn't much but it was nice to watch the boats drift by. I'd always dreamed of owning a boat. If I cracked the case, maybe I'd ask The Cardinal for a small yacht by way of a reward, take a few months off and sail up and down the coast.

It was a sweltering day and I was soaked with sweat by the end of the walk. I was heading for home and a shower when I had a better idea, located a public pool and went for a swim. Did forty lengths, changing strokes at regular intervals. Felt like a fish by the time I got out.

I went to a bar called the Penguin's Craw later. A quiet drinking hole, no music, TV or gimmicks. Just alcohol, a bar and plenty of chairs. I ordered a cup of coffee and watched a couple of guys in their sixties playing darts. I got to chatting to them about their children, what they'd worked at before retiring and how they spent their time these days.

I cruised the city after that, walking aimlessly, mingling with the late-night crowds. I popped into a twenty-four-hour bookshop and picked up a James Ellroy page-turner. Wandered down to the river again and observed the boats, now lit up and filled with drunken revelers. Went for a late supper in a pirate-themed restaurant called Blackbeard's Galley. Got home about one and went to bed.

I enjoyed the break so much, I took Thursday off as well. Alas, my second day of rest was cut short when my cell phone buzzed as I was just starting the Ellroy book.

"What is it?" I snapped.

"Mr. Jeery?" A female voice. Unfamiliar.

"Yeah?"

"My name's Monica Hope. I work at the Fridge. You wished to be notified if we received any inquiries regarding Allegro Jinks?"

My heart beat fast. "Yes."

"There's been one."

I grabbed a pen. "Did he leave a name?"

"Yes, sir."

Touchdown!

His name was Breton Furst and he was one of the Troops who'd been guarding the Skylight the night of Nic's murder. One of the cleaner of the clan, never served time, no illegal habits, married since nineteen, three kids, trustworthy.

I didn't ask Frank for permission to interview him—I'd have had to tell him about Jinks if I did, and that was something I'd prefer to keep between myself and Furst. I checked his whereabouts with Party Central and learned he was at home on a day's leave. I got the address and shot across town.

He was on the street when I arrived, loading a basket into the back of his car, preparing for a picnic. His two oldest kids—a boy and a girl— were in the backseat, leaning on the headrests, watching their father. His wife emerged, youngest kid in tow, and asked if he had everything. He said he did and she shut the door and started for the car.

"Mr. Furst! Breton!" I yelled, propping my bike against a wall and hurrying over. He glanced at me suspiciously, right hand edging toward the pistol I could see strapped to his left side. I smiled and showed my empty palms. I recognized his face from photos in the file, but he didn't know me.

"Can I help you?" he asked. His wife had stopped on the pavement and was passing a bag to the kids in the backseat. The youngest had wandered toward his daddy.

"My name's Al Jeery. I have to—"

"I've heard of you. You work at Party Central, right?"

"Right. I have to talk to you."

He frowned and looked at his wife and children. "Can't it wait?"

"It's about Allegro Jinks." His face dropped and he glanced around. An elderly gentleman was on the sidewalk farther up, washing his car. A woman pushed a stroller along the opposite pavement, a second kid following behind.

"You're just here to talk?" He looked nervous.

"That's all."

He sighed. "I don't think I can help, but come on in. Just let me—"

He was turning to tell his wife about the delay when he staggered and took a few steps back. I thought he'd lost his footing, but then I spotted a red stain spreading down the front of his shirt. I realized the twitching in his hands was the start of a death rattle, not a feeble attempt to regain his balance.

"Breton?" his wife asked sharply. She moved toward him, to steady him on his feet, but he hit the ground before she cleared the car. "Breton!" she screamed, and darted forward. She opened her mouth to scream again. Before she could, a bullet made a fleshy rag of her throat. She collapsed to her knees, then crawled to her already-dead husband.

"Stay back!" I roared. Stunned as I was, my gun had leaped into my hand and I was covering the rows of houses across the road. But the assassin had struck too quickly. I hadn't managed to pinpoint his location. "Mrs. Furst! Don't come any—"

The top of her head fanned out in a cloud of blood and hair and she fell facedown. The two kids in the backseat began to scream their lungs out. The girl hammered at the window, yelling, "Mommy! Mommy!" The boy kicked wildly at his door, which must have been child locked.

"Stay down!" I shouted. "Get your heads the fuck down!"

They didn't hear me. The boy abandoned the lock and rolled down the window. He was halfway out when his chest erupted in a forest of red, bony splinters. His head flew back, connected hard with the roof—not that it mattered by this stage—then slumped forward.

I made the marksman—two houses to the left, second-story window—and fired. But I was on the ground with a handgun. He was in an elevated position with a rifle. I should have saved my ammunition.

The glass in the rear window of the car shattered over the girl. She shrieked with pain and covered her face with her hands. She fell out of sight and for a few seconds I thought she was going to stay there, out of harm's way. Then she sprang up like a jack-in-the-box, yelling about her eyes, pleading for help, calling for her mommy. There were two soft popping sounds—like damp lips peeling apart—and she cried no more.

I was on one knee now, gun braced, focused on my target. I hit the window—no small feat from where I was—and the sniper drew back. My eyes swiveled to the youngest of the Furst children, the sole survivor. He was by his father, tugging at the dead man's bloodied shirt, bawling, too young to understand what was happening but old enough to realize something was seriously amiss.

I should have held my position or ducked behind the car, but how could I leave a kid out in the open, at the mercy of a killer who had shown none?

Praying the sniper wasn't back in position, I dived toward the boy, grabbed him with my left arm, pulled him off his feet and spun around.

A bullet nicked the top of my right arm. Red spray arced up into my eyes. I held on to my gun, useless though it was now that I was temporarily blind. Stumbling, unaccustomed to the weight of the child, I fell on my ass, presenting a ridiculous target. I started to pull the boy into my chest, planning to turn over and shield him, so at least one of us might walk away from this, but before I could make the ultimate sacrifice his face disappeared in a howl of red and I found myself staring down into a nightmare of blood, bone and brains.

Cradling the boy in my arms, I let my gun drop and waited for the killer to finish the job. Seconds passed. I thought the sniper was reloading but eventually, as stunned neighbors crept from their houses, it dawned on me that he'd wrapped up for the day. I'd been spared.

As I gazed at the lifeless swath of bodies through blood-filmed eyes, I found little to be grateful for. In the face of so much tragedy it seemed that this must be the most cynical act of charity since God let Lot go but turned his wife into a pillar of salt, just for looking back.

I refused to surrender my hold on the boy until the ambulance arrived. I sat in a cooling pool of blood and rocked him lightly to and fro, unaware of the pain in my arm, heedless of the crowd forming around me, staring dead ahead at nothing.

The first cops on the scene approached me warily, eyeing the gun, shouting at me to kick it away. An old man—the one who'd been washing his car when the madness began—stepped into their path and told them what had happened, how I'd been injured trying to save the child. They relaxed after that and lowered their guns. One asked if I was OK. I nodded. Did I want to let go of the kid? I shook my head.

When I eventually handed over the boy—they put his tiny body on a gurney, covered it with a sheet and wheeled it away—a medic crouched beside me and attended to my arm. A light graze. Nothing a bandage and a few days rest wouldn't cure. The supervising officer checked to make sure I didn't require hospitalization, then had me loaded into the back of a squad car and escorted to the local precinct for questioning.

They went easy on me, allowing for shock, asking if I wanted anything, a drink, something to eat, a lawyer. I replied negatively to all offers and told them I just wanted to tell my side of the story and go home.

Three cops handled the interrogation (polite as they were, that's what it was). One was in uniform, one in a suit, the third in casuals. They gave their names but I found it easier to identify them by their clothes. The one in uniform was an asshole, and though he refrained from harassing me, he was the least sympathetic of the three. They noted my particulars, name, address, occupation. Their ears pricked up when they heard I was in the Troops. I saw Uniform's eyes narrowing.

"Do you have a license for that gun?" he asked, even though he could tell by the make that it was standard Troop issue.

"Yes."

"Breton Furst was in the Troops too, wasn't he?" Casual asked.

"Yes."

"Were you good friends?"

"I never saw him before today."

They glanced at one another, then Casual gave Uniform a nod. "So what were you doing at his house?" Uniform blurted out.

I had to think quickly to come up with a lie that would sound legitimate. It wasn't easy after what I'd been through.

"Breton works—worked—at the Skylight. My post's at Party Central but I was thinking of changing. I've been trying to find out whether switching to the Skylight is a good career move or not. One of my friends said to try Breton—he'd been at the Skylight nearly six years, so if anyone knew the setup, it was him. I called today. He said he was going on a picnic but I could tag along and we'd discuss work over a hot dog and a beer."

"Do you drink a lot?" Uniform asked.

"I'm teetotal these days but Furst didn't know. As I said, we hadn't met before."

"Go on," the cop in the suit encouraged me softly.

"There's not much more. I got there, walked over to greet him, next thing I knew…" I drummed my fingers on the table, putting sounds to the volley of bullets the marksman's silencer had muted.

"You didn't see the assassin?" Suit.

"I saw where he was but couldn't get a make on him."

"Any idea who had it in for the Fursts?" Uniform.

"No. I didn't know them."

"You don't think it was connected to your being there?" Suit.

"No." A bald-faced lie.

"No chance the sniper was after *you*?" Uniform asked, and even his colleagues looked embarrassed by the question.

"Yes," I said, smiling grimly. "But he was a lousy shot. An accidental ricochet accounted for the five others."

"Must have been the same rubber bullet that killed Kennedy," the casually dressed cop chuckled, then looked contrite when Uniform turned on him.

It went on in that vein for hours. When they made up their minds that I was unbreakable or innocent, they let me go. New clothes had been purchased for me during the interim and I was led to the showers to wash. I could hear reporters clamoring for news. The suited cop stepped into the locker room as I was slipping on my socks and asked if I wanted to confront the media. I said definitely not.

"What about my name?" I asked. "Was it released?"

"No, but it'll probably leak."

"Any way of holding it back?"

He shrugged. "We won't be able to keep the press quiet, but your guys might. The Cardinal's more accustomed to glossing over scandals than we are."

"What happens when I leave? Am I free to come and go as I please?"

"Sure. Stick around the next few weeks, in case we need to get in touch, but I doubt you'll hear from us again, not unless we catch the guy who did this."

"Think you will?" I asked.

He snorted.

When I was ready to leave, he told me there was someone waiting to escort me home. I'd been expecting one of the Troops but it was Bill. "Tasso called and told me," he said. "He thought you'd rather I came to pick you up than one of the party faithful."

I smiled weakly. "He was right. I guess I have you to thank for the clothes."

"I picked them up on the way. Want to go back to your place or mine?"

"Yours. I can't face home."

"Give me a moment to clear it." Bill told the officers on duty where he was taking me, gave them his number if they wanted to get in touch, and asked them to let him know if they turned up any evidence. A few of them knew him and he had to spend a couple of minutes chatting. He made his excuses as soon as was politely possible, led me out a side door, tucked me down in the backseat of his car and started for home. As we turned our third corner, I asked him to switch on the radio and I spent the rest of the journey listening to some MOR station, not saying a word, thinking about the boy and how light his lifeless body had felt in my arms.

Bill lived in a crumbling old house in the suburbs. A wreck of a place, but it was his family home and he loved it. I entered ahead of him while he parked the car. I ran my eyes over some of the many bookshelves in the hallway while I waited. Bill was a bibliophile. He owned thousands of books, rare first editions, some of them hundreds of years old, many signed by their authors. He spent a small fortune on his hobby. Had most of Dickens, Hemingway and Faulkner—his three favorite writers—and a fabulous collection of mystery novels.

Bill kept the books neatly stacked on innumerable shelves throughout the house. They were valuable but he didn't believe in locking them up. He kept them where he had ready access to them. He read and reread them all the time, even thumbed down the corners of pages to mark his place. Librarians and fellow bibliophiles would have shot him if they'd known of his irreverent handling but Bill didn't care. He collected for himself and didn't give a hoot what happened to the books when he passed on. "When I die and go to hell, the books can burn or rot," he often declared. "I'll have protected them as long as I've had a mind to."

"I got an Ellroy novel last night," I said as Bill entered.

"Ellroy's great," he said, trying to sound as if everything was fine, but failing.

We moved into the front room and I took my place in a large rocking chair opposite Bill's. My back was directly to the huge front window and I could feel a draft. This place should have been double glazed years ago but Bill wouldn't hear of it.

"Coffee?" he offered.

"Later."

Uneasy seconds ticked by.

"You had a lucky escape," Bill muttered.

"No," I sighed. "I was spared. He took them out one by one. Gave me this"—I tapped my wound—"when it looked like I might save the child. It would have been simpler to kill me, but he wanted me alive."

"Any idea why?"

I shook my head.

"Anything to do with Nicola Hornyak?" He spotted my wary look and shrugged. "I'm a cop. Part of my job's talking to people and keeping up with what's going on. I couldn't help but hear about what The Cardinal's set you up to."

"How long have you known?"

"A week. I hoped you'd come to me about it. When you didn't, I figured it was a deliberate snub and I should keep my nose out."

"It wasn't a slight, Bill. I just didn't want to bother you with it. If I find her killer, he won't be brought in for trial. Didn't think you'd want to get mixed up with shit like that."

Bill smiled drily. "Well, I'm involved now. So tell me, any link between Nic and the Fursts?"

"I think so," I said guardedly, not wanting to draw him in too deeply. "I went there to ask questions about her. I'm sure the executions were related."

"The killer didn't want Furst speaking to you?"

"Guess not."

Bill frowned. "But why take out the others, the wife and kids? Afraid he'd discussed it with them?"

"I guess. Husbands tell their wives things. Kids overhear."

"Would have been a lot simpler just to shoot *you*," Bill mused.

I nodded slowly.

"Any idea who it might be?" he asked.

"Wouldn't be here if I did. I'd be out nailing the bastard's balls to the clouds."

"I heard you were looking for Paucar Wami. Think he could have—"

"No," I interrupted. "Wami's clean."

"You reckon?"

"He told me he didn't kill Nic. I believe—"

"He *what*?" Bill almost leaped out of his chair. "You've met Paucar Wami?"

"He paid me a visit." I told him the story of my midnight encounter with the angel of death.

"Jesus Christ," Bill gasped. "If that was me, I'd have run for the hills, down the other side and into the ocean. What were you thinking? I know you don't mix with the fair and timid, but Paucar Wami!"

"Don't give me a hard time," I pleaded.

"I won't, but surely this implicates the son of a bitch. Whoever slaughtered those kids was a monster, and that's Paucar Wami to a tee. We should—"

"Bill, *please.*" I dropped my head to hide my tears.

"Al?" He came over and crouched by my side. "Are you OK?"

"I was holding him," I sobbed. "I saw his face explode and then he was dead."

I broke down. Bill paused a moment, then wrapped his arms around me and whispered, "It's OK. It's over, Al. You're all right. It's OK."

It took a long time for the fit to pass. An age of sobbing, cursing the unknown killer, then myself for not moving quicker. I tried explaining it step by step to Bill, so he'd know I wasn't to blame, so I could prove—to myself as much as him—that I'd done everything I could. But Bill only patted the back of my head and whispered softly, "Easy, now, easy," as if I were a shy horse in need of calming.

When, late into the night, I'd recovered and wiped the tears away, I told Bill I'd like that coffee now. He made some sandwiches and broke open a packet of cookies. We spent the next twenty minutes tucking in and didn't mention Nic or the Fursts again.

Later, Bill led the way downstairs to the cellar. It was a huge room, full of crates and boxes, packed with every kind of firework imaginable, barrels of gunpowder, even explosives he'd bartered with the bomb squad for. Bill had plenty of contacts on the force and could get almost anything he wanted.

Bill was a pyrotechnics expert. He'd been staging fireworks shows for decades. If he wasn't putting one on, he was acting as safety inspector for somebody else's. It was his only interest aside from his books and the occasional fishing trip.

He was getting ready for a big show, an annual event for orphans. There'd be film stars, the mayor, everybody who was anybody in attendance, so he wanted to make it a good one. He was buzzing with excitement.

We spent a few hours examining the boxes. They were brightly illustrated and Bill explained how they'd work, the shapes they'd make, the way he'd interweave them. I preferred his speeches to the actual displays. His face lit up when he spoke of the animals and caricatures he would build in the air. Timing was everything, he'd say. If you timed it right, you could make marvels out of a fistful of gunpowder, cheap cardboard, a child's chemistry set and a pocketful of tinsel. If you got it wrong, all the money and technology in the world wouldn't help.

I think Bill was wasted on the force. He should have been designing magical aerial shows somewhere exotic, like China or Japan, where he'd be appreciated and revered.

"Will you come to the show?" he asked.

"Maybe," I said, knowing I wouldn't. After my brush with disaster today, I'd be too busy to bother with fireworks. I'd decided, while sitting in the gutter with the remains of the youngest Furst boy in my lap, that I was going to get this killer. No matter what else happened to me, I was going to make that bastard pay.

"Come on, Al," he groaned. "It'll be great. I'm getting in a couple of big model planes and I'll fly them through the middle of a huge shower of rockets. There'll be explosions all around, inches to the left, inches to the right, above and below, but they won't even rock the planes."

"What about air turbulence?"

"Got it covered. Like I always tell you, with explosives you can account for everything. You wait and see. It's going to be like those old war movies, where the planes fly through seemingly impassable barrages." He tapped the lid of a box. "It'll be my best performance yet."

When we got back upstairs it was nearly two-thirty. I was tired but this was an ordinary time for Bill to be up and about—he was an insomniac and rarely went to bed before three or four. He offered to make more coffee. I refused and told him I should be getting home.

He blinked. "I thought you were staying here tonight."

"So did I. But now…" I smiled shakily. "I think I'll be better off by myself. It's been a long time since I cried that hard. I'm embarrassed."

"Don't be. After what you've been through, a few tears were the least anyone could expect. Stay, Al. The spare room's ready."

"I want to go."

"Well, let me drive you. I'll come in with you and—"

"No. Thanks, but no. The walk will do me good. I might cry some more on the way."

He didn't like it but knew better than to argue with me. "Give me a ring when you get there?"

"If it's not too late. Otherwise I'll call in the morning."

"Al?" he stopped me as I started for the door. His face was grave. "Be careful. You had a fortunate escape today. Next time—and we both know there'll be *some* kind of next time—you might not be so lucky."

"I know," I sighed.

"I'd hate to bury you, Al."

"Wouldn't be too keen on it myself." I grinned sickly, then let myself out. It was a long walk home but that didn't bother me. While I was walking, I couldn't dream about the boy and the gap where his face should have been.

15

I kept my head down the next day, in case reporters were on the prowl. As things turned out, I had nothing to fear. The Cardinal's people must have been hard at work because although the news bulletins on the radio made heavy mention of the Fursts throughout the day, my name never cropped up. They didn't even report that there'd been a survivor, and only a few of the papers commented on it.

A cop came by with my bike around ten—"Compliments of Bill Casey," he smiled—but apart from that I saw nobody until I ducked down to Ali's in the afternoon for bagels. I passed a beggar on my way, going from door to door, selling photos of one kind or another. Ali was discussing the Furst slaughter with a customer when I entered. It was a disgrace, in their opinion, and the man who killed so immorally deserved to be roasted alive without a trial. I didn't want to join the conversation—afraid my emotions might betray me—so I just paid for my bagels and made a hasty departure. Passed the beggar again on my way up. He was close to my apartment and would be calling on me soon. Inside, I got some change ready and stood by the door, waiting for him.

The beggar knocked twice. I opened the door and held out the coins. "Here you go," I started to say, but stopped when I saw his walking stick and dark glasses. I immediately thought of the blind men I'd seen at the funeral and building site, but this guy looked nothing like either of them. He was younger, shorter, dressed in ordinary clothes.

The beggar smiled and held out a small group of photos bound together by a rubber band. "Visions of the city," he intoned. "Can I interest you in visions of the city"—a moment's pause while he sniffed the air—"sir? Best snapshots money can buy. Swiss Square at night. Peacock Wharf. Pyramid Tombs. Very scenic postcards. Ideal for framing or sending to—"

"How much?"

"Donations are voluntary."

I dropped the coins into the tin hanging by a string around his neck. He listened, head cocked, judging their worth by the sound, then smiled and pressed the photos on me. I had no use for them but took them anyway, to humor him.

"May the gods bless you, kind sir," he said, bowed politely and moved along to the next door. I glanced at the top "vision"—a tacky shot of Pyramid Tombs, where wealthy fools paid to be buried in the manner of ancient Egyptians—then tossed the package to one side and tucked into my bagels.

I returned to the Ellroy book in the afternoon, radio on as I read. The pages flew by in a blur and I was soon caught up in his reconstruction of earlier times—supposedly more innocent, but, as he wrote it, just as deadly as today—and two hundred pages further along before I set it down and rested my eyes.

I listened to the six o'clock news and, satisfied that my name wasn't going to air, stuck a bookmark in the novel and went for a walk. At the end of the street I chose a direction at random. It was a surprisingly cool day and I was glad of the light jacket I'd brought. The exercise stimulated my appetite, so I bought some fruit and bread from a stall and chewed as I strolled.

Back home I spotted the postcards on the floor as I was shrugging off my jacket. I decided to take a closer look, picked them up and removed the rubber band. I studied the photo of Pyramid Tombs and read the blurb on the back, when the cemetery opened for business, who built it, how it was an exact scale replica of the Egyptian original, some of the famous names housed there.

The villas of Versailles were next. That was a part of the city I was unfamiliar with. It had been established by a band of fleeing French aristocrats shortly after their Revolution and to this day the language favored there was French. The ornate houses were walled off from the surrounding suburbs and many had been converted into hotels, even though the tourist trade here had never been brisk.

As I turned the card over to read about its history I spotted the third photo and let the first two flutter to the floor. I checked the final pair—Swiss Square and Conchita Gardens—before disposing of them and concentrating on the joker of the pack. Unlike the others, this was an ordinary photograph, not a card, and the setting and subject could have been of interest to nobody but me.

It was the lobby of the Skylight. Impossible to tell whether it was day or night—the photographer must have been standing with his back to the windows. A couple of people in the background, but they weren't important. It was the man at the center, caught unaware as he turned from the register, who mattered. He was heavily made up, wearing a veiled hat to obscure the finer details of his features. But the face was unmistakable—Nicholas Hornyak.

Turning the photo over, I discovered a short, printed, mocking message. "Guess the date, Clouseau, and win *Furst* prize!"

It was easy to confirm that the photo dated from the night of Nic's murder (which I assumed was what I was meant to deduce). I had a copy of the Skylight's register and there were many samples of Nick's handwriting in his file. It took less than five minutes to make a match. He'd booked in under a false name—Hans Zimmermuller—but the writing was unmistakably his. And the room number for "Mr. Zimmermuller"? Eight-one-four, the room next to Nic's.

I couldn't find Nick. I tried his home, the Red Throat, a string of gay pubs and clubs he was known to frequent, with no success. Lots of people I spoke to had seen him earlier in the day, but nobody had spotted him in the last few hours. A drag queen told me he often made early nights of the weekend, whisking a lover home or off to some hotel or other. He preferred to party late during the week.

I didn't sleep much—still wary of nightmares about the boy—and spent most of the night and following morning pawing through my files, trying to link Nick to Allegro Jinks and Breton Furst. I came up with squat. In the evening I hit the streets again, resuming my search.

The Red Throat first. No sign of him, but the barman said he might be in later—few Saturdays went by without his making an appearance. I swung around a few more of his favorite watering holes, then returned, determined to grab a table and wait.

I parked around back and nipped in by the fire escape when someone staggered out to be sick in the alley. The Red Throat was busy now. I was heading for one of the few vacant tables when I spotted Nick by the jukebox, looking immaculate in a kilt and matching tartan top, chatting to a pudgy man. I barged my way over and squeezed between the two. "Hi, Nick. How's tricks?"

He stared at me, then placed my face and broke out in a smile. "Al! You came back. How charming."

"Who is this man, Nicholas?" his companion asked, peering indignantly at me.

"Beat it," I said, nudging him aside.

"Nicholas?" he asked uncertainly.

"Run along, dear," Nick told him. His companion made a sour face and clacked away in a huff. "So," Nick purred, "what can I do you for, Mr. Detective?"

"I know you killed your sister."

"Really?" he drawled, unfazed. "How dreadful of me. It's so unpleasant when siblings turn on one another."

"You were at the Skylight the night of her murder, in the room next to hers."

His face blanched. "You can't prove that."

"I've a copy of the register. Your name's different but the handwriting's the same." I grinned. "Mr. Zimmermuller."

"I was with a date," he stammered. "I never saw Nic. I wasn't there when the murder took place."

"No?"

"I swear it wasn't me. I was with a guy called Charlie Grohl. He'll vouch for me. We left the Skylight about midnight, hours before Nic was killed."

"Hours before she *died*," I corrected him. "The attack took place earlier."

He shook his head vehemently. "It wasn't me."

"You know I work for The Cardinal. If I tell him it was you, he'll take my word for it, then…" I smiled tightly.

Nick took a deep breath. "All right. I *was* there, with Charlie, as I said. I ran into Nic in the lobby when she was checking in. We decided to get adjoining rooms for the hell of it. She said to rap on her door when I was leaving and if her date had left, she'd let me in."

"She was there with a date?"

"Obviously."

"Not a john?"

"John who?" he asked. I let it pass.

"I don't believe you."

"It's true."

"You're lying. Nic didn't check in."

His face caved. "What?"

"Her *date* signed for the room." I kept Priscilla's name out of it.

"But I thought…" He trailed off into silence.

I said nothing for a minute. Then, earnestly, "Why did you kill her, Nick?"

He looked confused and afraid. "I didn't!"

"You lied about meeting her in the lobby."

"No. I mean…yes. But only because it sounded more feasible. The truth is, it was an accident, us ending up in rooms beside each other. But I didn't think you'd buy that."

He was lying again. A child could have seen through him. But I thought he was telling the truth about not killing her.

"Maybe you helped," I suggested. "Set her up accidentally for the killer?"

"No! I had nothing to do with it. I didn't kill her. I don't know who did."

I considered pushing him for more details but there seemed little point—he was panicked but not hysterical. Better to let him wander away and think things over, then hit him again later, when I had more evidence.

"OK," I said. "I'll back off for now. But I know you were at the hotel. It's only a matter of time before I prove you were in her room. I'll be seeing you again soon."

I looked for the exit. Nick grabbed my shoulder and I glanced back at him. "I didn't kill her," he snarled. "She was my sister. I loved her."

"Tell me the truth—why you were there and how you ended up in the room next to hers—and I might believe you." He bit his lip and shook his head. I brushed his hand away. "Later, Nick." He didn't stop me this time.

The alley was deserted. I stood over my bike, thinking hard, head bowed, eyes closed. I didn't think Nick was the killer but he was implicated. The question was, how much? Was he covering for someone, maybe this Charlie Grohl he'd named, or was he afraid of—

An arm snaked round my neck, cutting off my air, throwing my thoughts into disarray. As my hands rose defensively, someone clutched my midriff and jerked me backward. I connected hard with the ground. My assailants were on me before the stars cleared from my eyes. One kicked me in the ribs. The other swung a club hard at my head.

I dodged the club but not the foot that scythed in at my face. It caught me clean on the chin. The one with the club dug it into my stomach. I struck back blindly, but met fresh air.

A second later, the club slammed down on my back. I writhed. One of them went for my face with a boot again, but he only scraped it this time. Then a barrage of blows followed and it became impossible to tell one strike from the next.

My body rocked between the kicks and punches. The men—laughing and panting like dogs—were clumsy and scuffed a lot of their shots. If I'd been in better shape, I could have dealt with them. But they'd hurt me already. I could only lie there, take it and pray they didn't do any serious damage.

Finally, one of them had a brain wave. Picking up a glass bottle, he smashed the top off and waved it under my nose. His partner yanked me to my knees and giggled.

"Gonna slice you, nigger," the one with the bottle whispered. "Cut you so bad, you won't have a face left."

"I want to cut him too," the other pleaded.

"You'll get your turn," came the promise.

I watched with sickened fascination as he drew the glass back. It wasn't the slicing I was worried about. What terrified me was the thought that he might go too far. I could live with ugly—as long as I lived.

There was movement to my right. A figure darted forward silently, swiftly, almost invisibly. There was a snap to my assailant's wrist and suddenly he wasn't waving a bottle any longer, but was backing off, screaming about a broken hand, cradling it to his chest.

The guy holding me didn't know what to do. He shoved me at the mystery man, but not hard enough to create a problem. The Good Samaritan leaped over me and went after his prey like a tiger.

My head was spinning. I felt consciousness slipping away. Rolling onto my back, I saw my savior disarming the one who'd been holding me, clubbing him to the floor, then turning to wrap things up with the disabled bottle-wielder.

My labored breath caught in my throat. Though it was dark, I could see the coiled snakes running down the sides of his face and knew it was Paucar Wami. But that wasn't what stunned me. It was the face itself that sent me spinning into shock before I blacked out, a face almost as recognizable as my own. It had been many years since I last looked upon it, there'd been no snakes back then, and a thick mane of hair had adorned the now-bare skull. But there was no mistaking the all-too-familiar features.

It was the face of *my father*.

part four

"the red fingerprints of death"

16

I could tell, as I returned to consciousness, that I'd been out a long time. I was in a pitch-black room, so I couldn't check, but according to my body clock it had been anywhere between twelve and eighteen hours.

I ran my fingers over my scalp, assessing the damage. Every touch produced a sting but nothing seemed to be broken. And although my bruised stomach flared agonizingly every time I breathed, I didn't think any of my ribs had snapped. All things considered, it could have been a lot worse.

Then I remembered Paucar Wami and his familiar face.

I might have called it wrong. I'd only glimpsed the face in the alley, I'd been thinking a lot about my missing father and I wasn't at my most coherent at the time. Maybe I'd just noticed a similarity and the rest was conjecture. But in my heart I knew that was bullshit.

I got to my feet and almost fell down again as geysers of pain erupted all over. I thrust out an arm, found a wall and propped myself against it, breathing hard, letting my head clear, groaning softly.

"Awake at last," came a voice from the darkness. "I thought you would sleep forever."

I stiffened. It was Paucar Wami's voice but I couldn't see him. Not even a vague outline.

"Where are you?" I asked.

"Around," he replied, and now the voice came from another spot. He was circling me, silent, unseen, a shark. "You saw my face in the alley, didn't you?" He sounded petulant.

I thought about lying but didn't see the point. "Yes."

"You know who I am? Who I *was*?"

Again I considered the lie but opted for the truth. "Yes."

"I thought so."

The light snapped on.

I had to close my eyes and shield them with a hand. I counted to twenty before opening them again. I was in a small, whitewashed room. Nothing in it apart from the mattress I'd been lying on, me and Paucar Wami.

Or Tom Jeery, as he used to be called.

Now that I saw him up close all doubt evaporated. The years had barely touched him and he was exactly as I remembered, except bald and tattooed. He said nothing while I ran my incredulous eyes over him, taking in the lean, muscular frame, the slender, hooked fingers, the jeans, T-shirt and leather jacket. Spreading his arms, he grinned. "Got a hug for your dear ol' pappy?"

"This is a nightmare," I groaned, sliding down the wall. "This has to be a fucking nightmare."

He tutted and squatted. "Your mother never approved of foul language. She even complained when I swore during sex."

I stared at him, appalled. How could I be related to this grinning monster? It was like discovering you were the offspring of Adolf Hitler.

"Did my mother know?" I gasped. "Did she know who you—"

"—Really were?" He nodded. "But not right away. I held that back for the first night of our honeymoon." He laughed with delight at my expression. "That was a joke. It was years before she found out, long after you came along. A neighborhood busybody spotted me without my makeup one night and recognized me from word-of-mouth descriptions. She wasted no time sharing the news with poor, befuddled Mrs. Jeery. Needless to say, I slapped the interfering old bitch's wrists afterward." He chuckled. "And some more besides."

"You wore makeup?"

"Face paint. A wig. Contact lenses to disguise my beautiful green eyes. This is my natural appearance."

"What did she do when she found out?" It was important to know my mother hadn't been involved with his crimes. Getting my head around this would be a long, unpleasant process, but far messier if my mother was also implicated.

"She kicked me out," he laughed, sounding almost human. "She knew what I could do to her but took no notice. Batted me around the head with a frying pan, tore the skin off my shins with her shoes, nearly gouged out an eye with a poker. She was a feisty woman, your mother."

"Yes," I said proudly. I stretched my legs and began rubbing the aching flesh around my middle. "Is that when you left us, when you *died*?"

He shook his head. "I kept Tom Jeery on the go for three more years, but stayed out of your way most of the time. I dropped by occasionally to see how you were progressing—as my firstborn, I have always had a soft spot for you—until my position became untenable. Your mother threatened to go into hiding if I did not stop visiting."

"Why didn't she do that as soon as she found out?" I asked.

"The same reason she never told anyone the truth about the man she married, not even her son—I vowed to track the pair of you down and kill you if she did."

"But you just said—"

"—That I had a soft spot for you, yes. But business is business."

"You'd really have killed me?"

"I never lie about the important things, as your mother knew. That is why, even if she had lived to be a senile old woman, given to spurting out her darkest secrets to all and sundry, she would never have told about me." He tapped the floor. "Fear is a great silencer, Al m'boy, especially if it is fear for one you love."

He got up and offered me his hand. I refused it and struggled to my feet by myself. He smiled, asked if I could walk, opened the door when I said I could and gestured me through to a long corridor.

"Where are we?" I asked, glancing up at the flickering tubes overhead.

"A building," he answered vaguely. "One of my many places of work. You do not need to know more."

As we walked, Wami in front, me struggling to keep up, something he'd said struck me and I stopped. Wami looked back.

"You said I was your firstborn."

His face split into an approving smile. "You are slow but not entirely witless."

"You have other children?"

"Many. By many different women."

"I have brothers? Sisters?"

"Forty-plus at the last count. Quite a few nephews and nieces too."

The news left me reeling. I'd always believed I was alone in the world.

"Where are they?" I asked. "Here in the city?"

"Some, yes, but I have also sown my oats in the ports of strange and distant lands. You even have an Eskimo sister." It was hard to tell if he was joking or not.

"Do you keep in contact with them?"

"I keep tabs on them. I do not have time for personal relationships."

"Is that why you were following me? Why you were outside the Red Throat when I was attacked?"

He pondered his answer, then turned and beckoned me to follow, deciding on silence.

"What happened to the pair who jumped me?" I asked, shuffling after him.

"They await our pleasure."

"They're *here*?"

"I told you this was a place of work."

We passed several doors before he stopped at one and entered. It was another dark room. He didn't turn on the light until the door was closed. When he did, I wished he'd left it off.

The two men from the alley hung by chains from the ceiling, one upside down, the other horizontally. The latter had been disemboweled and his guts trailed over his sides like some long, pink mess that had been dumped there. His eyes had been gouged out and nailed to his nipples so he looked like an obscene alien from a cheap sci-fi movie. Most of the other's face had been sliced away and a pin had been driven through his genitals, which stretched upwards tightly, suspended by a shorter chain, so that every time he moved he was in agony.

Both were still alive.

I turned aside and retched. Wami laughed and warned me not to vomit on his shoes. When I'd recovered, I asked who they were.

"That was my first question too," he replied. "Tell me, did you *really* escort a white woman to the Ku Klux Klub?"

I nodded warily. "Yeah. So?"

"*So* these two fine, Caucasian queers were there and took it as a personal insult. By chance they noticed you in the Red Throat yesterday and decided to—as one so poetically phrased it before I removed his tongue—'teach that fucking nigger some goddamn respect for his betters.' "

"They had nothing to do with Nic or the Fursts?" I asked, examining the face of the man who still had one.

"Nothing," Wami said, sounding as disappointed as I felt. "Still, I thought it too good to be true. Life is rarely that simple."

The man with no face groaned and twitched on his chains. Something—it may have been the remains of his nose—slipped from his forehead and landed in a pool of blood with a gentle plop.

"Will you for Christ's sake make an end of those two?" I moaned.

"I have grown rather fond of them. I was thinking of keeping them on."

"Just kill them!" I shouted.

Wami regarded me coolly. "Do not adopt such tones when addressing your father, Albert. You are not too old for a spanking."

"Please," I said sickly. "They can't tell us anything and I can't stand looking at them like that."

Wami produced a knife and held it out. "Care to do the honors?" I stared at the knife, then the men, and shook my head. "You have killed before. Why shy away from these two?"

"I killed when ordered, when there was a reason."

"You will be putting them out of their misery. Is that not reason enough?"

"They were a pair of fools but they didn't deserve to be—"

Wami spun the knife around and reholstered it in the twinkling of an eye. "Then make no further entreaties of me. If you are incapable of dealing the final blow, I shall do so in my own good time. One must never expect another to extend the hand of mercy on his behalf."

He strolled past the stricken pair—they sensed his presence and started groaning and writhing anew—toward a door set in the far wall of the room. I followed, steering as far clear of the anguished captives as I could. I found myself in a room with a mahogany desk and two leather chairs, one on either side. There was a computer in the corner and shelves filled with books behind the desk. I glanced over them, expecting tomes on torture and sadism, but they were mostly computer manuals, the odd thriller strewn among them.

"Sit," Wami instructed, taking his place on the far side of the desk. I was glad to rest, but my sense of relief vanished when Wami produced a gun and aimed it at me. "I *will* use this if provoked. I will not shoot to kill—it should be obvious by now that I have no wish to harm you—but I will disable you without a second's hesitation."

"I'll be still as a mouse," I promised, stomach clenching in anticipation.

"You asked why I was at the Red Throat. It was not because you are my son. I was there in search of answers, hoping to trace a client through you."

"What client?" I frowned.

He paused a second, then said, "The one who hired me to eliminate the Fursts."

I came dangerously close to disregarding his warning and going for his throat. If I'd had a weapon of my own, I might have.

"You bastard," I muttered, feeling tears prick my eyes as I thought of the boy I'd held in my arms. "He was a child. Little more than a baby. How could you—"

"Please," Wami yawned, "spare me the sermon. You have killed in the past. The men you murdered were also children once."

"It's not the same."

"Of course it is. Age is irrelevant."

"A man who'd kill a child…" I glared at him contemptuously, remembering my vow to murder the one responsible. Wami must have seen something of that in my eyes because his expression darkened.

"I am not the villain you want," he said. "If I had not killed them, somebody else would have. If you seek vengeance, seek the architect, not the hired gun. Do not waste your hatred on a mere messenger boy, which is all I was."

"Why them?" I snarled. "Why Breton Furst?"

He shrugged. "That is what I hope to find out. I had no direct contact with my employer. I received a cryptic message—to shadow the Fursts but only kill them when 'the one I would know' appeared. My curiosity was piqued, so I set up camp and waited. Then you turned up."

"Somebody knew I'd go after Breton?"

"It appears so."

"And they didn't want me talking to him."

"Apparently not."

"But they didn't want you to kill him before I met him."

"If you continue stating the obvious, I shall have to administer a slapping."

"They wanted me to witness the execution," I went on, ignoring him. "We were both set up." I stared at the killer. "Why?"

"If I knew, I would not have been trailing you around the city."

I thought about it in silence. Whoever it was must have known Wami and I had met, or else they couldn't be sure that Wami would recognize me. They knew that Breton Furst was connected to Allegro Jinks, and that I would find out and go after Furst. I didn't know how anybody could be that clued in to what was going on, but more worrying was what else the puller-of-strings might be arranging. Wami was right—he wasn't the man I wanted. Someone had to pay for the death of the boy, but it should be the one who ordered the hit, not the triggerman.

We discussed it further but neither of us could pinpoint a viable suspect. I told him what had been happening with my investigation, how Nick had been at the Skylight the night of his sister's death, but we both agreed that the Hornyak brother couldn't have set up something this elaborate. Wami was half-tempted to pay him a call and find out exactly how much he knew, but I convinced him that more might be gained by shadowing Nick than torturing him.

With night falling, Wami returned to the torture chamber and told me to wait in the corridor outside. He didn't spend long on the Red Throat pair, and when he came out he was dragging two black body bags, one of which he nudged across to me. We hauled them through the building to a parking lot. Wami disappeared into the neighboring streets, returning with a hot-wired car, into which we dumped the bodies. He then tied a blindfold over my eyes so I wouldn't know the location of his hideout and off we set for the Fridge.

Five minutes into the journey Wami stopped, removed my blindfold and swapped places with me. He said he didn't like driving. Motorcycles were his vehicle of choice. He commented wryly on how endearing it was that his son's favored mode of transport mirrored his own, but I saw nothing cute in that.

As we neared the morgue my mind turned to Tom Jeery's empty casket and I asked when he'd left the note. He didn't know what I was talking about.

"The 'Out To Lunch' note," I reminded him.

"I have no casket in the Fridge," he said.

"Sure you do. When you killed off Tom Jeery you hired a casket and pretended…" I trailed off. "Didn't you?"

He shook his head.

I slowed down and pulled over, despite the fact that we were within rifle range of the Fridge. "But it's there. I checked it. There was a note— 'Out To Lunch.'"

Wami sniffed. "A staff prank. The ghouls of the Fridge do many strange things with the bodies in their care."

"But there wasn't a body, only a name—*Tom Jeery.*"

He frowned. "Different person, same name?"

"No. The Car—" I stopped. An empty casket. Tom Jeery's name. Somebody eager to push father and son together.

"How many people know about you and me?" I asked.

He shook his head. "I have always been adept at keeping secrets. One or two from the old neighborhood might have linked Paucar Wami to Tom Jeery, as the gossiping biddy did, but if so, they have kept it to themselves. Otherwise the only one who knows is…" He made a face and groaned.

I waited for him to say the name. When he didn't, I did, to have it out in the open.

"It's The Cardinal, isn't it?"

"Yes," he sighed. "He knows of all my children."

"The Cardinal told me about the Tom Jeery casket," I said, and at that the killer turned to stare at me. For a short instant I saw the poise evaporate from his eyes, and realized that he was just as shaken by this as I was.

We agreed that I'd have to confront The Cardinal. He was a master at covering his tracks. If he had staged Nic's death, the execution of the Fursts and our meeting, the only way to reveal the truth would be to take our findings directly to the ogre and challenge him with them. I was less than thrilled by the thought.

"What if he doesn't take kindly to my accusations?"

"If this is one of his games, he will expect a confrontation, since he hired you to unmask the killer."

"And if he says it wasn't him?"

"We shall take it from there."

"You still think he might be innocent?"

"The game is certainly one The Cardinal might play," Wami said. "Were I not involved, I would be quick to point the finger. But we go back a long way. Hiring me to kill the Fursts was an act of contempt. I do not think The Cardinal would abuse me so openly."

Wami drove me home—once we'd dropped off the bodies and collected my bike from behind the Red Throat—and set me down outside Ali's. He kept the engine running while I got out and didn't linger once I closed the door, pausing only to roll down the window and say he'd call tomorrow for an update. Then he was gone.

I took my time climbing the stairs, wheezing painfully.

Somebody was waiting for me outside the door of my apartment. My first thought—trouble. I began to edge away quietly. Then I recognized the shapely legs of Priscilla Perdue.

"About time!" she snapped as I shuffled up the final steps. "I've been waiting for ages. Ten more minutes and I'd have...What on earth happened to you? You look like you fell through a shredder."

"I should be so lucky," I grimaced.

She hurried forward. "Give me the key," she commanded, then opened the door and guided me through. I wanted to collapse into bed and sleep but she was having none of it. She henpecked me into the bathroom and had me disrobed down to my boxers before I knew what was happening. She wet a sponge and wiped the worst of my cuts and bruises. It would have been highly erotic if each swipe hadn't elicited a stream of gasps, winces and curses.

"Why don't you just run a cheese grater over me!" I roared.

"Don't be such a baby," she replied calmly. "This has to be done. By rights you should see a doctor. There could be internal injuries."

"There aren't."

"You can't *know* that."

"I'll take a gamble. Shut up and rub."

Next came the antiseptic—my roars must have been heard in Zimbabwe—then the bandages. After that she wrapped a robe around me and led me through to the living room, where she left me on the couch while she brewed coffee.

"You should have been a nurse," I mumbled.

"That would have meant facing crybabies like you every day."

"If you'd taken the beating I have..."

"We can't all be big, brave boys who go around settling our differences with our fists, can we? Let me guess—somebody insulted your mother?"

"As a matter of fact, you're due the credit."

She laughed. "Don't tell me you were defending my honor."

"Not exactly. A couple of your friends from the Kool Kats Klub decided to teach me a lesson, to deter me from setting foot on their hallowed turf again."

"No!" she gasped, immediately contrite. "The dirty sons of...Give me their descriptions. I'll find out who they are and have them disbarred."

I coughed guiltily. "No need. They won't do it again."

"Was this why you skipped our date?" she asked.

I stared at her blankly.

"We were *supposed* to be stepping out together last night," she reminded me. "You *said* you'd call."

I smiled sheepishly. "Sorry. I forgot."

She slapped the back of my head. "You're a no-good son of a diseased mongrel, Al Jeery. I should have left you as you were. That's the last time I'll do a good deed for—"

"Please," I interrupted as she stormed for the door. "Don't go. I've had things on my mind."

"Such as?" she sneered.

I silently debated how much I should tell her and decided on a morsel of the truth. "You heard about the Fursts, those people who were killed?"

"Of course," she said, face softening. "That was awful. The poor children. Whoever did that should be taken out and..." Her lips shut slowly, then opened to form a fascinated O. "Some of the reports mentioned a survivor, a man who tried to save the boy." She looked at me questioningly and I nodded. She covered her mouth with a hand.

"Breton Furst was on duty at the Skylight the night of Nic's murder. I believe he was connected. I went there to question him. Before I could..."

Priscilla sank to the floor and took my hands as I briefly ran her through the horror of that nightmarish day. She said nothing and kept her head lowered. When I finished, she looked up and there were tears in her eyes.

"I'm sorry, Al."

"Don't be silly," I smiled. "You couldn't have known."

"But I should have guessed something was wrong. I assumed you just stood me up, thinking—as usual—that I was the center of the world and nothing happened that didn't revolve around me. God, it must have been awful. Then you get pulped by a pair of my *friends*. Then I turn up and..." She stood. I was amazed and rather flattered by how upset she was. "I'll leave and let you recuperate in peace."

"No," I said quickly, pulling her back. "I want you to stay."

She stared at me, then said in a voice as soft as velvet, "The night?"

My heart almost exploded, but I was in no shape—either physically or mentally—for sexual entanglement. "Well, a couple of hours at least," I muttered.

Priscilla sat on the couch, leaned forward and pressed her lips to mine, gently. "OK," she sighed. "I'll stay. For a while. And we'll see how things go."

"Sounds good," I agreed, then returned her kiss as gently as she'd kissed me.

17

I felt a lot better Monday than I'd feared. The worst of the bruising had subsided and although I was tender from top to toe it was nothing I couldn't live with. Some light exercise, a healthy breakfast, a brisk walk around the block and by eleven I was ready to take on God himself. Since the supreme being wasn't available, I caught a cab to Party Central to see The Cardinal.

I was in luck—his secretary could fit me in at two. I wandered the halls of Party Central, catching up on what had been happening during my absence. Breton Furst was the talk of the establishment, but hardly anyone knew of my involvement with him. I asked if Furst had any close friends in Party Central—I wanted to learn more about him—but nobody I spoke to had known him personally. Mike, who was on his lunch break, said Jerry and Furst were good buddies, but Jerry was on sick leave. Mike said he'd tell him to give me a call when he returned.

When it was time to meet The Cardinal, I turned up at his office, only to be led down the corridor and shown into a private gymnasium. The Cardinal was there alone, jogging on a treadmill, naked.

"Come in," he said amiably. I advanced halfway, cleared my throat and averted my eyes. The Cardinal laughed. "No need to be embarrassed. I'm not."

"Surely you can afford a tracksuit," I quipped.

"I can't spend half the day changing in and out of clothes. Besides, it's good for the penis. Poor fellow spends so much time locked away, he must feel like the Man in the Iron Mask."

"Will you be long?" I asked, staring at the floor.

"Yes," he said. "But we can talk while I work out. You're not afraid of a little prick, are you?"

My head automatically lifted and I stole a glance. The Cardinal howled with glee, pointed a bony finger and sung out like a schoolkid, "Made you look!"

I grinned at his childish antics, then straightened and nodded to let him see I was ready to talk.

"I heard about your unfortunate encounter with the Fursts," he said. "A nasty business. It had something to do with the Hornyak investigation?"

"You tell me," I replied evenly.

"A curious answer," The Cardinal grunted. "Why should I know anything?"

"You hired Paucar Wami to kill them."

The Cardinal trundled to a halt, sat down on the mat of the machine and gazed at me with interest. "I thought you didn't see the assassin."

"I didn't, but the two of us had an enlightening encounter yesterday."

The Cardinal mopped the back of his neck with a towel. "You've met him?"

"Yes."

"Then you know..."

"...That he's my father."

"I'm sorry I missed *that* family reunion." He squinted. "Surely he told you I wasn't the one who hired him."

"His employer preferred to remain anonymous."

"Ah. And you think it was me?"

"Yes."

"Let me see...I hired Allegro Jinks to masquerade as Paucar Wami, Breton Furst helped him murder Nicola Hornyak, and I sent Wami after the Furst family when you uncovered the link. Is that how you picture it?"

I smiled. "The fact you know about Allegro Jinks proves it."

He stood and started drying his groin. "Return to the waiting room. I'll be with you shortly."

I passed an anxious ten minutes waiting for him, not sure what he'd do now that the mystery had been "solved." When he appeared he was in his usual clothes. He cocked a finger at me and led the way to a room filled with TVs, computers and video equipment. He located a disc and inserted it into one of the many machines.

"I've been keeping an eye on you," he said, fiddling with the control as he talked. "One of my spies at the Fridge rang a while back and said he had something interesting to show me."

He hit play and one of the screens flickered into life. It was a recording of me the night I dropped off Jinks's head. The Cardinal turned up the sound and I heard myself asking the clerk about keeping tabs on the corpse.

"Enough?" The Cardinal said sweetly.

"Enough," I sighed.

He turned it off. "It was a simple matter to trace the head and make an ID, though I didn't connect Allegro Jinks to Breton Furst until Furst went looking for him."

"Is that when you hired Wami to kill Furst?"

"I didn't hire Paucar Wami. I *want* to know who killed Nicola Hornyak. The person who ordered Furst's death *already* knows."

"You didn't kill her?" I asked skeptically.

"No."

"So how come you had a file on her when supposedly nobody knew her name?"

"It only took a couple of hours to identify her body," he said. "I recognized her name as soon as I was informed. I've been observing your progress ever since you were a child. I follow the lives of all of Paucar Wami's children. I have a network of informers—friends, neighbors and colleagues of yours—who tell me how you're getting along. I knew of your involvement with Nicola Hornyak before she turned up dead in the Skylight. That's how I was able to put together a file on her so swiftly."

"Why not tell me? Why the subterfuge?"

"I wanted to clear your name first, in case you had killed her." I was

stung by the accusation. "Please, Al, don't be offended. You are the son of
Paucar Wami. I've been expecting your father's evil genes to bubble to the
surface for years."

"I'm nothing like him," I snarled.

"I know," he sighed. "That's a pity. Paucar Wami has served me loyally
but he is getting old and soon I'll be looking for a replacement. What better prospect than one of his own flesh and blood?"

"You thought…," I sputtered.

"I *hoped*," he corrected me. "If you had killed her, I didn't want to do
anything which might stunt your growth."

"And when you found out I hadn't killed her?" I growled, disgusted
that anyone could think so lowly of me.

"Disappointment. Then curiosity. I took an interest in the case. The
detectives I assigned were making progress—they knew about the Paucar
Wami look-alike for one thing—but I was forced to withdraw them."

"Forced?" I couldn't imagine anyone forcing The Cardinal's hand.

"Perhaps *invited* would be a more accurate term. Have a look at this. I
found it on my desk one morning." He handed me a postcard. There were
four lines of print on the back.

> *Howard Kett knows about Nicola Hornyak.*
> *He will be demanding her return.*
> *Remove your investigative teams.*
> *Install Al Jeery in their place.*

I flipped the postcard over and studied the front. A grotesque, three-
breasted statue stretched the length of the card. Underneath its breasts was
a tiny calendar, although the names of the months were in a language I
couldn't identify. At the bottom was a caption—EARLY INCAN FERTILITY
SYMBOL AND CALENDAR. The eleventh month—represented by the word
Ayuamarca—was highlighted in green.

"What's this about?" I asked.

"I am interested in our Incan past," The Cardinal said. "I suppose the
sender thought it would grab my attention. He was right."

"How did it get on your desk?"

"Somebody must have sneaked in while I was asleep. That's why I went along with the request—a man who can slip in and out of Party Central unseen is not to be taken lightly."

I turned it over and read the message again. "When did it come?"

"Two days before Kett came looking for the body."

"Then he knew about the murder before he claimed to?"

"It seems so."

"You've investigated Kett?"

"That's *your* area of expertise."

"Did you have the card analyzed for fingerprints and the like?"

"Naturally. It was clean."

"I received a similar card recently."

"Oh?" He leaned closer, intrigued.

"A blind beggar was selling cards in my apartment block. I purchased a pack. One was a picture of Nicholas Hornyak in the lobby of the Sky-light, the night of his sister's murder, with a note on the back inviting me to make the connection."

"A blind beggar." The Cardinal was troubled.

"I've spotted a few blind people since I started investigating."

"This city has its share," The Cardinal said.

"You think they might be behind the murders?"

"Unlikely. The man who made a mockery of Party Central's defenses could hardly have done so without the use of his eyes. And a blind man wouldn't know a photograph of Nicholas Hornyak, or an Incan fertility god, from a snapshot of my ass."

"Rudi Ziegler would know an Incan god if he saw one," I suggested.

"He would indeed," The Cardinal said. "That's something I thought myself while perusing your reports—which have been arriving rather slackly of late."

"I've been too busy to write everything down."

"Or you didn't trust me," he countered, a gleam in his eyes. "You didn't want me knowing that *you* knew things which you thought *I* did too. You believed I was setting you up."

I grinned guiltily. "A bit of that too."

"We must learn to trust one another, Al."

"I'll trust you when you start playing straight with me," I said.

"Are you suggesting I haven't been?"

"You let me think Nic was murdered at the Skylight when you knew she wasn't."

He smiled apologetically. "I was testing you. This game is not of my making but it's one I have attempted to profit by. As I told you at the start, I believe you have great potential. You now know the genesis of my faith in you. I guessed this investigation would turn nasty. I suspected you were being set up, though I didn't—and still don't—know why. I could have protected you.

"But I wanted to see how you'd react. This was a chance to watch you wriggle and grow. I found it impossible to resist. So I set you up to *find* the body, and I held back certain details—such as the Wami look-alike, and that she'd been murdered elsewhere—to make your work more of a challenge."

"And now?" I snapped. "Are there more secrets you're keeping from me?"

"Ah," he clucked, "that's for me to know and you to find out. I will say this—I don't know who killed your girlfriend or why they're interested in you."

"You wouldn't tell me if you did," I replied bitterly.

"Maybe. But you've been trained to tell a lie from the truth. I am, of course, the king of liars, but you should be able to make an educated guess. Judge for yourself, do I lie or not?"

From what I could read of him, he didn't. I decided to keep an open mind on the subject but—for the time being—take him at his word until I learned different.

"Where do we go from here?" I asked.

"Wherever you decide. I have full faith in your abilities."

"Maybe it would be best to let things lie. A lot of people have died. If we drop the investigation and I leave town for a while…"

The Cardinal frowned. "We call that chicken talk around here," he growled.

"Call it what you like—do you think it would work?"

"No. The only one who can change the rules in a game of this nature is the game's master. If you attempt to force their hand, they'll probably respond with a suitably harsh countermeasure."

I nodded slowly, then followed him out as he headed back for his office. He paused outside the door and took a sheaf of notes from his secretary. "Anything else?" he asked.

I thought a moment. "No."

"In that case..." He disappeared without a word of farewell. I caught the eye of his secretary and we shrugged at one another, then smiled. I tipped an imaginary hat to her and she waved back, then I caught the elevator down and went home to wait for *Pappy* to call.

He came in person, shortly after eleven, and we discussed my conversation with The Cardinal late into the night. Wami was satisfied that The Cardinal wasn't the one toying with us. Although I harbored doubts, I agreed that we should broaden our horizons.

He was fascinated by the postcard The Cardinal had received and the possibility that the blind beggar might be involved. He chastised me for not mentioning the beggar before but I told him I couldn't be expected to reel off every last detail at the drop of a hat. Besides, as The Cardinal had said, a blind man couldn't have penetrated Party Central's defenses or identified Nick Hornyak.

"I would not be so sure of that," he said. "I know of some blind enigmas. They haunt the streets. I never paid much attention to them—they do not interfere with me—but I have tortured a few over the years. Not one uttered a single word, even under the greatest duress."

"Well, this beggar had plenty to say, so he couldn't have been—"

I stopped, remembering the blind man at the building site. "These blind men... They don't dress in white robes, do they?"

"You know of them?"

I told him about the strange fall of rain and the vision.

"Most peculiar," he mused. "I would love to have a vision. Perhaps I should ask those eyeless Incan wonders to—"

"*Incan?*" I interrupted sharply.

"I believe they are of Incan extraction."

I told him about the front of the postcard. He became agitated when I spoke of the highlighted eleventh month.

"*Ayuamarca,*" he muttered, although I hadn't mentioned the name.

"It means something?"

"You know of The Cardinal's many files and dossiers." Wami spoke hesitantly. "One of his most secretive is titled *Ayuamarca*. It is a list of ghost names, people who have been written out of existence and memory."

"I don't understand."

"Nor do I, completely. But it is of great importance to The Cardinal. No wonder he jumped when our mystery killer snapped his fingers." I started to ask about the list, only to be silenced by a gesture. "Be quiet. I am thinking."

Moments later, Wami nodded unhappily. "A sacrifice. It must be."

"You're talking about Nic?"

"I am talking about *you*. The Cardinal said he withheld information in order to test you. I think that is a lie. He played dumb because he was afraid."

"Of what?"

"Being exposed or eliminated—I am not sure. He is fanatical about the Ayuamarca list. I believe he would sacrifice anyone to protect it."

"You're not making sense," I groaned.

He leaned in close and there was a cold fire burning in his eyes. "That note to The Cardinal was a warning. In effect it said, 'We want Al Jeery. Give him to us. We know about Ayuamarca, so help us, *or else.*'

"You are being sacrificed, Al m'boy. Somebody wants your head and The Cardinal is delivering it, no questions asked. He has no interest in testing you. He only wants to see the back of whoever it is that's threatening him. You have been cast aside like a pawn to protect a queen. That is the bad news. The good news is"—he grinned grimly—"you are not alone. I am part of this game too, and I will stick by you to the sweet or bitter end."

He clasped my neck and winked. I forced a smile, although in truth the thought of having a monster like Wami on my side depressed more than comforted me.

18

The more I thought about it over the next handful of days, the more it seemed like a paranoid delusion of my father's. It wasn't that I trusted The Cardinal more than his hired killer. I just found it impossible to believe he could have his arm twisted the way Wami believed. The Cardinal ran this city. Nobody could harm or scare him, certainly not a collection of blind men in robes.

Wami had an old copy of the Ayuamarca file, but when he presented it to me it failed to assuage my doubts. It was nothing more than a few sheets of paper bearing dozens of names, most crossed out. According to Wami, these were people he'd once known but no longer had any memory of, people who had vanished from the public psyche, who to all intents and purposes had never existed. I agreed it was most passing strange (as he put it), but behind his back I was starting to think that I was dealing with a schizophrenic psycho who'd murdered Nic and then forgotten he had killed her.

He was a strange man, my father. He must have been in his late sixties but he was in incredible shape, fitter than I'd ever been. The lethally assured grace with which he moved, the speed of his thoughts and his capacity for reading a situation in an instant made me feel as if my years with the Troops had been nothing more than kindergarten training.

No matter how warm a front he put on for my sake, he was at heart as cold and distant as the stars. His world was one of death. If I mentioned the weather, he'd sigh and remark, "It was on a night such as this that I killed my first nun." If I asked for his recollections of our time together when I was a child, he'd say, "I would bounce you up and down while your mother was out working, tuck you in for a nap, slip out to slit somebody's throat, return in time to feed and burp you."

I asked him for the names of some of my siblings one night but he refused to divulge any. None of his children knew of the others and he preferred it that way. I argued with him—what if I started an affair with a half sister?—but he laughed and teased me, "Maybe you already have."

We were focusing on Nicholas Hornyak. Ellen still hadn't gotten back to me about Ziegler, the blind Incas wouldn't say anything and there was nothing in Breton Furst's file of any use. Nick was our boy. Wami wanted to snoop after Priscilla too but I warned him to stay away. I said I'd keep my own tabs on her.

We dug up every clipping on Nick that we could find and scoured them for any hint of scandal. He was hardly clean, but his vices ran no further than sexual kinks, drugs and friends with dubious pasts. No hint that he was into murder.

So we shadowed him, followed him everywhere, Wami trailing after him on his motorcycle, keeping me informed of his position over a cell phone as I cycled along behind. He was easy to keep up with by day, since he spent most days in bed. When he got up, he'd mope along to the Red Throat or a similar establishment and pass the time drinking and playing pool.

Nights were trickier. He bounced from one club to another like a pinball. We lost him a few times, in cabs and when he ducked out unseen amid a crowd, but we usually managed to pick him up again. When he retired for the night—home or a hotel—one of us would leave to catch some sleep while the other stood watch.

We stopped taking notes and photos after the first night, as it became clear that there was no point—he moved in loose circles and met scores of people. Unless we saw him with somebody who looked especially dangerous, or someone we recognized, we took no notice.

He didn't go anywhere out of the ordinary. Just pubs and clubs, parties and orgies. After four days I knew it was hopeless—if he was in league with the killers, he was being kept at arm's length. Shadowing him would lead nowhere.

Wami was more philosophical about it. Time, he said, was a great provider. Trailing after Nick left our foes with time on their hands, time to plot, grow restless and reveal themselves.

Nevertheless, by the weekend he was leaving me alone more than he was partnering me. He said he was exploring alternative avenues of inquiry, but I think he was just tired of the lack of bloodshed and was using the time to do a bit of freelance killing, of which the less I knew the better.

I kept in touch with Priscilla by phone, even managed to drop in on her at work a couple of times. We didn't talk about that night in my apartment, when we could have easily become lovers, but we discussed all sorts of aspects of our lives—dreams, aspirations, past lovers. It was early days, but I had the feeling something was growing between Priscilla and me. I didn't know if that was good or bad—things were complicated enough as they were—but I couldn't control it, so I rolled with the flow and let the situation develop as it might.

Ellen invited me over to her place Sunday afternoon. I called Wami and told him I wouldn't be tracking Nick, and why.

"My ex-daughter-in-law," he chuckled. "I should come with you and introduce myself." I knew him well enough by now to know he was joking. I asked if he'd cover Nick for me. He said he would but I felt he was only saying it to appease me. I didn't care. I was starting to lose interest in the Hornyak heir.

Ellen looked divine, dressed in white, a blue ribbon through her hair. I used to love combing those fine, blond locks. If I had to say what I missed most about her, it would be waking up in the early hours of the morning to find her hair spread out on the pillow and gently combing through it with my fingers.

She'd cooked pasta, which we quickly devoured. Stuck the dishes in the washer, retired to the balcony—she had a nice apartment overlooking the river—and made the most of the weather. She noticed my faint bruises—a memento of my run-in with the KKK boys—and inquired about them. I made up a story.

"Now," she said when I finished. "Rudi Ziegler." She pulled a file out from beneath a chair. Licked the tips of her index and third fingers and flicked over the first page. "That's his real name, by the way, not an alias."

"I know."

She glared. "You might have told me. I spent days tracing his roots."

"Sorry."

"Well," she sniffed, "you probably know the rest as well. No police record, never in trouble. Fills out his tax forms, operates aboveboard. Worth a small fortune. He started out with very little, a meager inheritance when his father died, which he used to launch and advertise the business. A couple of office jobs when he was younger, but most of his life has been devoted to magic. I tried finding out who he studied under but he seems to have picked it up from a variety of sources, fairground fortune-tellers and the like. Never married. No children."

She zipped forward a few pages. "I attended four meetings. The first time, it was just the two of us. I told him I'd been having odd dreams and wanted to explore the spiritual plane to make sense of them. He read my palms, did the tarot, the usual rigmarole. I said I'd like to try a séance. He promised to phone when a place came up. Said it might take a few weeks—my karma had to be compatible with the group's, or some such hogwash. Called a couple of days later to say he'd found the perfect companions. I went along to three sessions."

"Anything happen?"

She chuckled scornfully. "Lots of fog, strobe lights, eerie noises and shaking of tables. He's got a crystal ball and he conjured up some images. Spoke in voices. I was disappointed—it was so fake. The others seemed to enjoy it but I'm not sure they believed it was real any more than I did."

"Nothing dark or magical?"

"No. I asked after the third séance if there was anywhere further to go. Said I wished to make meatier contact. Told him I wanted to dance with demons."

"You didn't!"

"*You* told me to say it." She couldn't hide an impish grin.

"How did he react?"

"He said he wasn't that way inclined—he was more involved with gods of light than demons of the dark—but he could pass me on to people who were. He gave me a couple of names."

"That sounds more like it." I rubbed my hands together. "I hope you didn't go visit these guys."

She shook her head. "I got your leads. The rest is up to you." She handed me a sheet of paper with two names and addresses. They meant nothing to me, so I laid the sheet aside, to investigate later.

We discussed the case and how I'd been progressing (I told her nothing about Paucar Wami or the Fursts), then talk turned to love. Ellen asked if I'd been seeing anyone. I told her I had. Was it serious? I thought of the way my heart leaped when Priscilla kissed me, and said it might be.

"How about you?" I asked, as you do when someone makes inquiries of that nature.

She smiled nervously. "Actually, I think I might be falling in love, Al." She awaited my reaction.

I stared out over the river. It was a surprise—there'd been nobody meaningful in Ellen's life since our marriage dissolved. A month ago the news might have sent me running back to the bottle, but after all that had happened these last few weeks, it didn't seem as earth-shattering as it once would have.

"Anybody I know?" I asked.

"Yes."

"You going to tell me the name or do I have to guess?"

She hesitated. "Not yet. I don't know how involved we're going to get. I'm not at the stage where I want to make a public commitment."

"So why mention it?"

"In case word leaks. So you don't feel like I've been going behind your back."

"We're divorced," I reminded her. "You can do what you like."

"I know. Still, if it was *you* and things were getting hot and you didn't tell me, I'd be hopping mad." I knew what she meant. As far apart as we'd drifted, there would always be a special bond between us.

"Well?" she asked when I said nothing. "What do you think?"

"Does it matter?"

"You know it does," she said softly.

"I don't know the guy," I protested. "How can I have an opinion?"

"Who says it's a guy?" she smirked.

"You don't swing that way," I laughed.

"Maybe I'll surprise you. But seriously, what do you think? Are you jealous?"

"No," I answered truthfully. "I'm delighted for you. It's great. I wish you all the best. I've only one question—can I give you away at the wedding?"

"There won't be a wedding. One was enough. Besides, it wouldn't be appropriate."

"Why not?"

"You'll see," she grinned and said no more about it.

She kissed my cheeks before I left and rubbed my nose with hers. In the old days, that would have been the sign for our lips to meet. Now it was simply a nice way for two close friends to say goodbye.

"Give me a ring if anything comes of the Ziegler tips," she said.

"I'll be sending over the finest bouquet of flowers if one of these names leads anywhere," I vowed.

"And be careful. I don't want the killer carving you up like that poor girl."

"I'll watch my back, kemosabe."

"See you 'round, Grasshopper."

Then I slipped away, to spend the rest of the day wondering about her new beau. Whoever he was, he'd better treat her well—better than *I* had—or I'd be after him. No matter how heavy things got between Priscilla and me, Ellen would remain the true love of my life. Nobody would do the dirty on her as long as I was on the scene.

The names of the two mystics led nowhere. No outstanding connections to any of the key players, though Priscilla had been a customer of one. I asked her about him. She said he was graver than Ziegler but no more genuine. Nic had never been to him.

Apart from the two names, there was nothing in Ellen's report of any use. I hadn't expected anything—it wasn't as if I thought Ziegler would talk openly of human sacrifice—but I was disappointed all the same. I'd agreed with Wami that if nothing happened with Nick over the next few days, we should shift our focus to Ziegler. Since Ellen had produced no dirt, that would mean more shadowing, more long hours of hanging around.

I felt glum on Tuesday when I rolled home shortly before midnight and hit the sack. I was sleeping soundly these times, too exhausted to dream. So when I jolted awake in the middle of the night, I thought something was wrong. For a few seconds I couldn't hear over the sound of my pounding heart. When my hearing returned, I realized it was only the buzzing of my cell phone that had disturbed me. I checked my watch—three a.m., for Christ's sake!—groaned and reached blindly for the phone.

"This had better be a matter of life or fucking death," I snarled, expecting the mocking tones of my father. But it wasn't.

"The public phone in front of the library. Be there, ten minutes from now."

"Who—," I began, but the caller had hung up. I sat on the edge of my bed trying to place the voice. When I couldn't, I rolled off and got dressed. I might be walking into trouble but I was too tired to care. I thought of calling Wami but there wasn't time for him to come over.

As I headed for the door, my eyes flicked to the mantelpiece and I slowed. The black, gold-streaked marble I'd found in the trout's mouth and placed there was missing. For a moment I was sure someone had stolen it. But that was crazy. More likely it had rolled onto the floor. I didn't have time to look for it, and anyway it wasn't important. I'd forgotten about it by the time I unchained my bike.

I arrived at the phone booth with a couple of minutes to spare. Stood in out of the cool night breeze, yawning. A patrol car passed, two officers giving me a suspicious once-over. I half-waved and they carried on without stopping. Then the phone rang and I answered immediately. "If this is a joke, I'll kick your—"

"There's a phone outside the post office in Marlin Street. You know where that is?"

"Yeah," I said cautiously.

"How long will it take you to cycle there?"

"Fifteen, twenty minutes."

"I'll call in twenty-five. If you're being tailed, pass it by and I'll get in contact another time."

"Who is this?" I snapped. "Why should I—"

He was gone again.

I hung up and considered my next move. It could be a trap but it would have been just as easy to strike at my home or outside the library as across town. This way I had time to call for assistance. Besides, the caller sounded scared.

With hardly any traffic to contend with, and jumping red lights, I made Marlin Street in seventeen minutes. As far as I could tell I wasn't being followed, though from my experience with Nick I knew how simple it was for a cautious hunter to track his prey undetected.

I'd been thinking hard about the voice and this time, when the phone rang, I spoke first. *"Jerry?"*

There was a nervous pause, then, "No names. There's an all-night diner at the top of this street. I'll be waiting."

I was sure when I hung up—it was Jerry Falstaff, from work. I'd seen virtually nothing of him since The Cardinal took me off regular duty. What was he doing, calling me in such a provocative fashion? Only one way to find out…

A handful of late-night souls were scattered around the diner, eating silently, reading or staring out the windows. Jerry was near the back. From the way he sat, I knew he cradled a gun under cover of the tablecloth. I glanced around at the other diners again, searching for danger, but they seemed oblivious.

I strolled across but didn't sit.

"That a gun in your lap or are you just pleased to see me?"

"Get something to eat," Jerry ordered, voice low and strained. "Make it look natural. Sit opposite me and cover the area to my back. First sign of trouble, open fire and make a break for the kitchen—there's a door, leads to a set of stairs running down to an alley."

"I'm sitting nowhere and doing nothing till you tell me what this is all about."

Jerry looked up briefly. "You trust me, Al?"

"I've never had reason not to," I answered indirectly.

"Then listen carefully and do what I say." He took a bite out of a large roll and, using it for cover, muttered out of the side of his mouth, "It's about Breton Furst."

I took my jacket off, draped it over the back of the chair and went to order a slice of pizza. When I returned, Jerry let me have it.

"I graduated from basic training with Breton. We kept in touch. He drew me aside at Party Central a few weeks ago and asked me to be his Tonto." That was a phrase we used in the Troops when one of us passed a message to another to be opened in the event of his disappearance or death. Sometimes the message was no more than a note to be handed to a loved one, but other times it was a way to gain revenge from beyond the grave.

Tontos were forbidden—if you were found holding a note that contained even a hint of classified information, you were dismissed without benefits, and that was the most lenient reprisal—but common. We looked out for one another in the Troops. It was a way of protecting ourselves from the whims of our masters. They never knew if a Troop had left behind a Tonto, so they tended not to sacrifice us lightly.

"I fled as soon as I heard about the execution," Jerry continued. "Called in sick and went on the lam. Been sleeping in my van. Sent my wife and kids into hiding."

"You think whoever killed Furst knows about you?"

"Probably not, but would *you* chance it?" One of the customers rose and Jerry's body tightened. I thought he was going to start firing, but then the guy tossed a tip down and ambled away. Jerry relaxed.

"Do you have the message on you?" I asked.

"I'm not crazy. I read it—figured I owed him that much—then burned the fucker. Laid low and let some time pass before getting in touch with you."

"I was mentioned in the message?"

"No. But I heard you were with him when he was killed and I figured you were as good a person to come to as any. I don't trust anybody else."

"What makes you think you can trust me?"

He shrugged. "It was your girlfriend he died for."

I swallowed a mouthful of pizza. "What was in the message?"

"Breton was on duty the night Nicola Hornyak was killed. Some guy bribed him to leave his post at ten o'clock—said he wanted to sneak in a friend. According to Breton, that sort of shit happens all the time at the Skylight."

"Did he know the guy?"

"Not straight off."

"But he found out?"

"I'm coming to that. There was more. He told Breton to come up to his room between two and three and let out the *friend*. Said he'd be chained to the bed and wearing a mask which Breton wasn't to remove."

"It was Nic's room?" I guessed.

"No. The room next door, 814."

"*Nicholas's* room," I sighed.

Jerry looked surprised. "You know already?"

"I've been digging around."

"Breton only found out when Hornyak's picture turned up in the papers. He shat himself."

"Why not tell Frank as soon as he heard about the murder in 812? He must have known it wasn't coincidence."

"He wasn't thinking clearly. See, he let the guy out in the middle of the night like he'd promised. He was masked, chained to the bed and naked, as Breton was expecting, but also mad as hell. He wanted to know where the bastard who'd tied him up was hiding, threatened to have both their heads. Breton told him to shut up or he'd remove his mask. That worked. He got dressed and left."

"Furst didn't see his face?"

"No. He'd no idea who he was."

But I did. Nick's lover of the night, Charlie Grohl. I hadn't gone looking for Grohl—he'd slipped my mind—and now I cursed myself for the oversight.

"Breton didn't hear anything in 812," Jerry went on, "but only a fool would think the two events weren't connected. The guy who bribed him probably killed the girl too. He thought about going to Frank, but that would have meant admitting to taking a bribe. Plus he'd untied and released the one person who could identify the killer. It would have cost him his job, maybe worse. So he kept his mouth shut."

"I can understand that," I grunted. "What happened next?"

"For a long time, nothing. When he saw Nicholas Hornyak's photo in the paper and realized it was the dead girl's brother who'd bribed him, he almost confessed—that was proof that the events of the two rooms were connected. But having kept quiet so long, he figured he'd be better off saying nothing.

"Nearly two weeks later, someone called Breton. The caller knew everything, how Nicholas Hornyak bribed him, that he'd been in the room next to the girl's, that he'd kept quiet. He said he needed a favor and arranged a meeting. Breton didn't want to go but he had no choice.

"They met in a movie theater. It was dark and the blackmailer tried not to show his face, but Breton made him and put it in his message."

"Who was it?" I snapped, certain it must be the mysterious Charlie Grohl.

"In a minute. I'm almost finished. The blackmailer said he was looking for the body of a guy called Allegro Jinks. He thought it was in the Fridge. He wanted Breton to go there and find it. If he cooperated, his secret would be safe.

"Back home, Breton wrote up his confession and passed it along to me. He said at the end that he was on his way to the Fridge. He didn't know what would happen but wanted to make sure—if something went wrong—that the guy who set him up didn't escape unpunished."

"The *name*," I snarled. I was afraid someone would burst in and pump a bullet through his head before he could spit it out. "Who the hell was it?"

Jerry smiled thinly, glanced around, then said, "Does *Howard Kett* ring any bells?"

19

It was a three-hour train ride to the lake resort. I grabbed a window seat and spent the journey reflecting.

I'd run Jerry through his tale a couple more times, in case he'd missed anything. I put the names of Charlie Grohl, Rudi Ziegler and Priscilla Perdue to him, none of which were familiar.

Jerry felt better by the end of the conversation. He'd dreaded making contact, afraid he'd be killed like Furst when he met me. Now that it was over, and he had my word that I wouldn't mention his name to anyone, he could relax. He'd lie low a few more days before reporting back to work, then try to drive all memories of Breton's message and our meeting from his thoughts.

He left before I did. I hadn't thanked him, as thanks were unnecessary. We both knew the risk he'd taken and the debt I owed. It went without saying that if he ever needed a favor, he had only to call.

I stayed on at the diner, thinking about Nick and Charlie Grohl. Nick had said he'd been with his lover the whole night, but according to Breton, Grohl had been trussed up and left alone. Where had Nick been? Busy slicing up his sister? Plotting with Howard Kett?

Howie...

Where did the cop fit in? Earlier he'd warned me away from Nick. Now I knew he'd sent Breton Furst to the Fridge in search of Allegro Jinks, which meant he knew about the Wami imitator. Had Kett killed Nic and set Wami on the Fursts?

The evidence was strong, but I wasn't convinced. Kett was a son of a bitch, and I was sure he had what it took to kill if needed, but he wasn't the kind of man who'd calmly toy with the likes of Paucar Wami and The Cardinal. He was involved, clearly, but I couldn't see him as a criminal mastermind.

I called his office the morning after my meeting with Jerry. He was on a week's vacation, not due back until the weekend. I hung up and phoned Bill. Pretended I was calling to say hello. Maneuvered the conversation around to Howie. Expressed surprise when Bill told me he was on vacation and asked where a guy like Kett went in his spare time. Once I was off the phone with Bill, I booked a return ticket and cycled to the train station.

It was early afternoon when I reached the hotel, only to learn Kett and family were out for the day. I positioned myself at a shaded table near the front of the building, pulled on a pair of dark glasses and spent the next few hours sipping nonalcoholic cocktails while keeping watch for the Ketts.

They turned up after seven. Howie, his wife, and five of their eight (or was it nine?) kids. Howie was in a pair of shorts, a flashy Hawaiian shirt and a cardboard ten-gallon hat. I grimaced and wished I'd bought a camera-phone the last time I upgraded my cell. The kids were arguing about what to do next. As they drew closer and entered the hotel, I heard Howie say they'd change clothes, then head down to the jetty to unwind.

A quarter of an hour later they reemerged, Howie in more somber attire. I let them get ahead, rose and slowly followed.

The kids started to pester an old guy on a yacht down at the jetty. I gathered he knew them by the way he didn't lose his temper when they clambered aboard. Mrs. Kett warned them to be careful and wandered over to keep an eye on them. Howie stood gazing out over the water at the setting sun, shirt rippling in the lake breeze.

I stepped up behind him and said, "Beautiful, isn't it?"

"Yes," he agreed, turning with a smile that disappeared when I raised my glasses and winked. "*Jeery?*" he gawped. "What the fuck are you doing here?"

"Came for the fresh lake air."

He stared at me suspiciously. "Bullshit."

"You're right. I came to ask you to connect the dots between Nicola and Nicholas Hornyak, Charlie Grohl, Breton Furst and Allegro Jinks."

He turned ghostly white. "You scum," he snarled. "I'm on vacation with my wife and children, and you have the fucking nerve to follow me here and—"

"If you want to create a scene, I'm game," I interrupted softly. "I don't mind having it out in front of your family."

I thought he was going to hit me but then his shoulders sagged. He yelled at his wife that he'd be back soon, jerked his head toward the far end of the jetty and struck out for it. He walked fast and I only caught up with him at the edge, where he stood rooted to the boards like a statue overlooking the lake.

"Make it quick, asshole," he snapped. "I'm only here for a week. I want to waste as little as possible of it on you."

"Tell me about Nicholas Hornyak. Why did you warn me away?"

"I told you, he's got friends who look out for him."

"Name them."

"No."

"OK. Let's forget about Nick for a while. What about Breton Furst? You sent him after Allegro Jinks. That inquiry led to his death. His wife and kids too. Care to tell me what they died for?"

"I had nothing to do with that," Kett said. "I was trying to locate a missing person. I had no idea it would end up the way it did."

"How did you know about him and Nicholas? Come to that, how'd you know about Jinks?" When he didn't respond I sat and hung my head out over the water, studying my reflection. "This is a lovely spot. Come here a lot?"

"Most years," he answered guardedly.

"Tell me what I want to know or it'll be a long time before you come again. How long do you think they'll send you down for if I go public? Nobody would have raised much of a fuss if it was just Nicola and Breton Furst. But the children…People are outraged, thirsty for blood. They want the killer ideally, but I'm sure an accomplice would do. You might even get the chair."

The grinding of Kett's teeth was louder than any motor on the lake and I was half-afraid he'd chew down to the gums. But, with great effort, he said, "It all goes back to Charlie Grohl."

I hid my smile and waved for him to continue.

"Grohl got in touch with me shortly after the press ran details of Nicola's death. He'd been in the room next to hers with her brother and was afraid his name would surface. He didn't know Nicholas Hornyak—he was in town a couple of days, they hooked up at some gay joint and went to the Skylight for sex. Hornyak took off during the night, leaving Grohl tied to the bed. A guard let him go. Grohl was furious, went looking for Nick, didn't find him, left the city and went home."

"He knew nothing about the murder?"

"No."

"What did he think when Nicola's name turned up in the papers?"

"At first, nothing—it was a week after the event, so he didn't connect it to the night he was there. Then he heard a rumor that she'd been murdered the week before and realized he might be implicated if Nicholas had been involved in her death. That's why he told me his story."

"Why come to *you*?" I asked.

"He made inquiries. Knew I was handling the case. Knew he could trust me to keep his name to myself."

That sounded dubious but I let it pass. "So he pointed the finger at Nicholas. Why didn't you go after him?"

"I did," Kett sighed. "That's when I was warned to keep my nose out. My kids were threatened. I didn't like it but I backed off. When you started sniffing, I was told to have a word with you. That's the bitch about these fuckers—give in to them once and you're giving in the rest of your life."

"We keep coming back to these so-called *friends* of Nick's. Names, Howie."

"And wind up like the Fursts?" He laughed bitterly. "If you put a gun to my children's heads like these guys did, and tell me to talk, I'll yap like a dog. Otherwise go fuck yourself."

I wasn't happy but I could see no room for leverage. As Kett guessed, I wasn't the sort of guy who'd kill a child.

"Tell me about Allegro Jinks," I moved on.

"I'll get to that," he said. "Grohl gave me a description of the Troop who freed him. It didn't take me long to case the Skylight and pinpoint Furst. Although I'd kept Nicholas Hornyak out of my investigations, I hadn't let the case die. I'd been pursuing other angles, asking questions about Nicola. I knew she'd been seen with a guy answering to Paucar Wami's description."

"You found that out?" I was surprised.

"I do know a *bit* about detective work," he sneered. "Then a woman turned up looking for her missing son. Sobbing her eyes out, begging for help. She said he'd had problems in the past but had seemed to be settling down. Then he shaved his head, tattooed his face with snakes, split from his friends and took up with some rich white girl."

"Allegro Jinks," I muttered.

"I searched for him but, as his mother had said, he'd vanished. Then I heard about a Chinese tattooist who'd been ripped to pieces shortly before Jinks went missing. I put two and two together and came up with the Fridge. I know Wami leaves a lot of bodies there—or so rumor has it— and I figured that was the only chance I had of finding Jinks.

"I couldn't just trot along to the Fridge and ask if they had Allegro Jinks on ice. It doesn't work that way. I had to go through someone who was part of the system, who wouldn't be questioned, someone like—"

"—Breton Furst," I finished.

"There were others I could have used, but I had recent dirt on Furst. I reckoned he'd still be shaky about not coming clean when he should have. He'd be easy to manipulate."

"You met him in person," I noted. "That was foolish."

"Couldn't discuss it over the phone," Kett countered. "Besides, we met in a dark theater. I didn't think he'd recognize me. Obviously—since you're here—I was wrong."

"Furst left a note," I said, quietly analyzing Kett's story. "So you sent him to ask about Jinks. What next?"

"Nothing. I heard about his murder. Figured it tied in and that if anyone knew I'd put him up to making inquiries about Jinks, I was fucked. Kept my head down and booked a vacation. Thought I'd left the mess behind till you turned up."

A neat story. I wasn't sure I believed it, but it was neat.

"You think Nick arranged Furst's murder?" I asked.

"I neither know nor give a shit," he answered. "I feel lousy about what happened to his wife and kids, but what can I do? Step forward and risk my own family? Nuh-uh. I've had my fill of killing. You investigate if you want. Me, when I'm finished here, I'm going back to less lethal detective work."

"You're a coward, Howie."

"So was Breton Furst. Difference is, I'm a *live* coward."

I stood, brushed the dust from the back of my pants and wondered how much of his story was true. It was easy to call Kett a coward—and easy for him to admit it—but we both knew he'd gone after tougher fish than Nick Hornyak, regardless of the risk to himself or his family. Bill had often told me—usually when I was belittling his boss—of the time Kett crawled out onto the top of a train to take on a couple of teenagers stoned out of their heads on PCP, how he'd kept after a gang boss till he nailed him, in spite of a mail bomb and an attempt on his oldest son's life.

"You'll save us both a shitload of trouble if you play straight with me," I said. "Nobody needs to know. Tell me the truth and I'll leave you be."

"I've told the truth," he insisted.

"Some of it, perhaps, but not all. I'm no fool, Howie."

"I think you are," he said softly. "A fool to come here. A fool to keep pressing. It looks to me like Paucar Wami killed Jinks and the Fursts. You keep on with this and next thing you know he'll be coming for *you*. What'll you do then, Jeery?"

I smiled as I thought of what he'd say if I told him about my relationship to Paucar Wami, but sweet as it would be to watch his face drop, that was information best not shared.

"See you in the city, Howie," I said, taking my leave.

"Not if Paucar Wami sees you first," he retorted, then scurried off to collect his family and shepherd them back to the hotel.

I could have caught the last train home, but this was a nice little town and I was due a night off, so I checked into a different hotel, had a meal in a quiet restaurant, bought some toiletries in a shop, then strolled back to my room to call Paucar Wami.

I hadn't forgotten about my father in my haste to catch up with Kett, but if I'd told him of my meeting with Jerry, he would have insisted on coming with me to *assist* in the interrogation, and though I bore no love for Howard Kett, I didn't want to see him winding up as bait on the end of a fishhook.

There was no answer when I called, so I went for a walk and tried his number again later.

"Al m'boy. Sorry I missed you earlier. Couldn't take the call. My hands were full." There was a groan in the background.

"What was that?" I asked.

"Our friend Nicholas. I tired of trailing him, so I—"

"No!" I shouted, gripping the phone furiously.

Wami chuckled. "Relax. Nicholas is safe. This is some nobody I picked up off the street. Would you care to share a few last words with him?"

"You're a sick son of a bitch."

"And you are the son of a son of a bitch. No matter. Where are you? You were supposed to be shadowing our target this afternoon."

"I've been busy. A lead fell into my lap."

"Do tell," he said eagerly.

"Not over the phone. Listen, I want you to try and find Charlie Grohl. He's one of Nick's lovers. He was with him in the Skylight. He lives out of town."

"Any idea where?"

"No."

"That might take some time."

"It'll be time well spent."

"Very well. I will wrap things up sooner than planned and apply myself to the tiresome task. Will you be joining me tonight?"

"Tomorrow."

"I will miss you. Good night, son."

"'Night," I threw back gruffly, hating him for his murderous ways, hating myself more for turning a blind eye to them. There were times, trailing Nick, when Wami was vulnerable. The opportunities to take a stab at him had been ample. Maybe I could have put him out of the city's misery by now.

But I needed him to find Nic's killer. I was putting my own selfish motives before the welfare of millions, any one of whom could be next on Wami's hit list, and it churned my stomach to think of it.

I tucked myself into the comfortable bed when I got back and stared out the window at the clear sky. Living in the city, it was easy to forget about the stars. I recalled the old myths that our destinies were written in the skies and fell asleep thinking, if everything were mapped out for us in advance, how much simpler life would be. I need feel no guilt if I believed I was an agent of fate. I could blame my complicity on destiny and sleep the sleep of the just.

I caught an early train back to the city and arrived home before ten. Bounced up the stairs brightly, only to find my key wouldn't turn. Taking it out, I got down on a knee and peered into the keyhole. Some clever bastard had filled it with glue. It was the third time this year. A bored kid, no doubt. One day I'd catch him and...

I got to my feet, took aim and kicked at the lock. It busted and the door burst open. I dumped my overnight bag on the sofa and croaked to the stale, gloomy room, "Welcome home!"

I brewed a mug of coffee and drank it slowly, then set out again, swinging the door closed behind me. I cycled to my friend Danny's hardware store. It was out of my way but Danny was an old pal. I'd met him through Bill, who used to work for him when he was a kid, many years ago.

Danny was behind the counter. After Fabio he was probably the oldest guy I knew. He was found more often in the back these days. He'd been threatening to retire for ages but everybody knew he wouldn't. He laughed when I walked in with a scowl. "Not the lock again!" he hooted.

"If I ever get my hands on the little bastard..."

"Maybe it's a locksmith," Danny grinned. "The guy who owned this place before me used to pull that trick when business was slow. Glued up locks and waited for the calls to flood in. He got busted a few times but that didn't stop him. He was a mad old buzzard."

"You never tried it yourself, of course," I smiled.

"Certainly not," he said indignantly, but I could see him reddening around the throat. "Same make as before?"

"Unless they've devised a glue-resistant model."

He asked about Bill as I was paying for the lock. I told him he was fine and mentioned the fishing trip we'd been on. Danny used to come with us before his health deteriorated. He sighed and asked me to let him know the next time we were going—he'd come along if his doctor OK'd it. I promised I would, waved away my change and wished him well.

Back home, two squad cars were parked outside the building and cops were in my apartment, talking softly. I hesitated in the hallway, wondering whether to proceed or beat a retreat. I decided to face them— maybe someone had noticed the busted lock and called them in to check on it.

I knocked loudly as I entered. I didn't recognize the three young officers but smiled as if they were friends. "Help you any?"

"Al Jeery?" one of them asked.

"Yes."

"Yes, *sir!*" another snapped.

I sighed inwardly—assholes everywhere. "Yes, sir," I mumbled.

"We'd like you to accompany us across town." It was the one who'd spoken first.

"What for?"

"I'd rather not say."

"Am I under arrest?"

"Not yet, punk," the asshole snarled.

"What if I don't want to go?"

"It would be better if you did." The first cop again.

I yawned to show I wasn't worried. "OK. I'll come quietly."

"Thanks," the first cop said.

"Jerk," the asshole added.

The third stayed silent.

I peered in the window of the bagel shop as I was passing. Two more cops were inside, talking with Ali, taking notes. Ali looked numb. He was shaking his head and appeared to be crying. A bad sign.

They ran me across town, sirens blaring, saying nothing. They avoided the roads to the station. I checked their uniforms in the glow of the street-lights. They looked real but I had a bad feeling. I was between two of them on the backseat but I wasn't cuffed. I could maybe grab a gun from one of them, force them to let me out.

I was finalizing the plan when we pulled up at the Skylight. I immediately let it drop. The uniforms were real, and I had a premonition of what lay in store. The dismayed faces of the staff in the lobby confirmed my worst suspicions. By the time I reached room 812 and saw a corpse draped over the bed, it was something of an anticlimax.

The ranking officer was called Vernon Ast. Bill had introduced us on a couple of occasions. He was grim when he stepped in front of me and asked if I could account for my whereabouts the previous night. I told him I'd been out of the city and could produce witnesses if required. (I grinned inwardly as I thought of Kett taking the stand in my defense.)

"I hope that's true," Vernon sighed, massaging the bridge of his nose. "I know Bill thinks highly of you."

"Who is it?" I asked, nodding at the naked female.

"You don't know?" I shook my head. "We found a credit card, sunglasses, a sock. Your name on the card. The rest of it's probably yours too."

"A thorough frame," I noted, smiling tightly. Was it Priscilla? Had the bastard who murdered Nic made an end of another of my girlfriends?

"You want to ID the body?" Vernon asked. "You don't have to. If you want to consult a lawyer…"

"The suspense would be the end of me."

I walked slowly to the corpse, feeling time contract, barely aware of the police clearing a path, drawing back from me as if I had the plague. She was lying facedown. The killer had been even more brutal this time. It looked as if they wouldn't be able to make an accurate count of the puncture wounds.

I stopped at the foot of the bed, noting something shining in the pools of blood. My right hand darted forward before anyone could stop me. My fingers brushed aside jagged, fleshy folds and closed around a hard, cool ball. Lifting it to the light, I examined a familiar black, gold-streaked marble.

"Recognize it?" Ast asked quietly.

"It's from my apartment. I don't know how it got here."

"You'd better put it back."

Replacing the marble—which had unnerved me more than the body—I rounded the bed, reaching a position where I could view the face. It was half-smothered by a pillow. I had to kneel down for a decent look.

I was expecting Priscilla, but as I knelt I realized the hair was wrong and the legs were too long. I smiled with relief. This woman was taller, broader, a beautiful head of long...blond...

My stomach dropped. I no longer had to see the face. I knew by the hair, strong yet soft to the touch. Hair I'd combed a thousand times with my fingers.

I tried not to think her name. I focused on the hair, driving all else from my thoughts, for fear the truth would madden me. Fanned out on the pillow the way I remembered so well, only now flecked with the red finger-prints of death.

I obsessed on her hair as they read me my rights and led me down the stairs. Her hair as I was bundled into a car and driven to the station. Her gleaming, blood-smeared hair as they processed my details, then locked me away.

When I was finally alone and the hair couldn't keep the name at bay any longer, I whispered it to myself, feeling my heart wither and my world burn.

"Ellen..."

part five

"the blood of dreams"

20

Isolation suited me. It was good to be cut off from the world. I could have hidden in the cell forever, undisturbed, thinking about nothing.

A cop entered and shattered the silence. "You want something to eat or drink?" I shook my head. "What about your phone call?" A careless shrug. He hesitated. "I know you and Bill Casey are friends. We're trying to contact him. If you need anything…"

"Thank you," I said softly, since my response was obviously the only thing that would shift him.

He smiled. "No problem. We all know this is so much shit in a sack. Killers don't leave their fucking socks behind!"

Then he was gone and I was alone again. But the interruption had jolted me. My thoughts churned. I was dragged back to the world of memories against my will.

When I first met Ellen she was a friend of my then-girlfriend. Ellen didn't like me—she'd heard I'd been cheating. Came to my apartment and grilled me. I listened calmly, watching the bob of her hair, then asked if she'd like to make the beast with two backs. She slapped my face, stormed off, rang her friend and I was single again.

A park, some years later. Relaxing by a pond, wondering what to do with my life. A weeping woman sat down close by. I studied her out of the corner of my eye. I thought I recognized her and asked if we knew each other.

She lashed out blindly and I remembered her. She apologized moments later, then proceeded to tell me about the man she'd loved for two years, who'd just walked out. Her father had died a couple of months before and she was still aching from that as well. She was lonely and frightened and didn't know where she was going to end up.

I said I was lonely too, not sure where I was heading. Told her life was hard, there were no smooth rides, we had to do the best we could and hope we didn't get screwed over too often.

We spoke for ages. I told her loads of stuff about myself, even the last time I cried, many years earlier. By the end of our chat she was smiling and we both knew something special might blossom between us, given time. Then she looked at me clearly and frowned. "You're that bastard Al Jeery!"

The door opened and shut. A large man sat opposite me and said nothing for a while. When he finally spoke, his voice was hoarse. "I don't know what to say."

I saw a pair of fists clench on the table.

"All these years comforting the bereaved and I can't think of a single fucking thing to say to you."

I concentrated on the fists, tracing the angry, red knuckle lines, noting the quiver in the fingers.

"I thought it was a sick joke when they called. Refused to believe it until I saw the body."

"A piece of work, wasn't it?" I looked up into Bill's sad eyes. I hadn't cried yet. Couldn't.

"Who did it, Al? Do you know?"

"What would you do if I did?"

"I'd find the bastard and…" He gripped the edge of the table, tears falling, shoulders hunched painfully.

"I don't know who did it," I said, "but if I did, I wouldn't tell. She was *my* wife. I'll deal with it."

Bill nodded, wiped his eyes, then produced a bottle of whisky, set it in the middle of the table and cleared his throat. I stared at the bottle, then Bill.

"Take it," he said somberly.

"No." The word was barely a sigh on my lips.

"Don't fight it, Al. This isn't the time."

"You know what that does to me."

He nodded slowly. "I weaned you off it, remember? I said I'd kill you if I saw you touch it again." He leaned forward and gripped my hands. "But things change. All I care about now is getting you through the next few days, and if you have to be steaming drunk to do that, so be it."

"And after?"

"Fuck after!" Bill roared. "We'll deal with that when it comes. Drink."

He let go and sat back, looking ashamed. I knew this offer was tearing him apart. He must think I was close to the edge of madness if he was willing to resort to such desperate measures. Maybe I was.

I reached out to caress the bottle. Unscrewed the top, bent over and inhaled. He was right—I did need it. More than anything else. A couple of swallows and all would be right. I'd cry for Ellen and drink myself to sleep. Hide until all the pain and guilt went away. So tempting. So easy.

I sat back.

"No. The pain's bad but it keeps me going. I'll find her killer but only if I stay sober. There'll be time for drinking later."

"Al, you mustn't—"

"No!" I stopped him. "There's nothing without her. It's not just that she was killed—she was killed because of *me*. I'm the reason she's dead."

"You can't be sure of that."

I stared at him coldly until he dropped his gaze.

He pocketed the bottle. "I can't tell you what to do. But if you change your mind, don't be afraid. No man should have to face something like this alone. I pulled you back from the brink before. I can do it again if I have to."

We sat listening to the silence. I kept thinking about the bottle in his jacket. I wanted him to take it out and offer it again.

"What about the evidence against me?" I asked, trying to focus.

"It's bullshit. All the same, I called Ford Tasso and he'll send along a lawyer to bail you out with the minimum of fuss."

"Anybody contact Kett yet?"

"No. He'll hear about it sooner or later. If I have my way, it'll be later."

Kett could have cleared me instantly but if I called him as a witness, I'd have to explain what I was doing down there. It might complicate matters.

"When did it happen?" I asked.

"Early hours of this morning."

"Was she killed in the hotel?"

"I assume so." He glanced at me. "Any reason to think otherwise?"

I didn't reply. I could find that out later.

"Anybody see anything?"

"No."

"Who was the room checked out to?"

"Nobody. It hadn't been used since..." He coughed.

We talked some more, then he had to go. I was alone again, just me, the silence, the whisky fumes and the memories. There was no escaping the memories.

Ford Tasso stormed into the station within an hour, Emeric Hinds and a posse of lawyers in tow. Shell-shocked as I was, I couldn't help being impressed. Hinds was The Cardinal's sharpest legal mind, usually reserved for the elite. If this had been serious, I would have thanked the gods. But he wasn't really needed. As Bill had said, the evidence against me was risible, more an insult than anything.

I asked Hinds if he could get the marble. It had set me thinking and I wanted it back, so I could gaze into its dark heart and think some more. He said he could get it for me later, not right away. I had to settle for that.

Tasso said The Cardinal sent his regards and would receive me any time I chose to drop by. He'd also said that I could proceed with the Nic Hornyak investigation or drop it as I wished. As if I could quit *now*.

I moved in with Bill until the funeral. He was going to take time off work but I told him not to—I preferred being alone. I sat in his big old house, staring out the huge front window. It wasn't as quiet as the cell but it was quiet enough. I thought about Ellen and Nic, and what I'd do with the killer when I caught up. I also thought about the marble, its black sheen and golden streaks, the smears of Ellen's blood.

The days blurred into one another. I didn't take much notice. Didn't stop to think about Nick, Kett, the blind priests. Didn't call my father or hear from him. All that could wait. This was a period of mourning. A time for Ellen.

The liquor cabinet in the living room mesmerized me. It was full of familiar friends. They sang to me and made seductive promises. If I hit the bottle I'd forget about Ellen and escape to the blessed sanctuary of drunken oblivion.

Finally, when it seemed I must burst or give in to temptation, I took to the streets on my bike—Bill had brought it over—and spent hours cycling, losing myself in a maze of alleys, stilling the memories, the demons, the needs.

I was for some reason drawn to the Manco Capac statue. I passed it several times without stopping, but finally drew up at the building site and staggered in. I wasn't sure what had brought me here but it seemed like the right place to be. The site was teeming with workers but none paid attention to me. The giant statue was in much the same shape as before. If they'd made progress, it wasn't visible.

The shadow of a crane passed overhead. I followed the arm of the machine as it rotated from one side to the other. A dim part of my mind wondered again how they got these monsters up, but I wasn't in the mood for riddles and the question rapidly slipped from my thoughts.

When my gaze returned to the ground, a tall man in white robes was standing opposite me. His eyes were round and blank. He was smiling. By the mole on the left side of his chin I recognized him. I wasn't surprised. Part of me had been anticipating something like this from the moment I decided to stop.

I started across to confront him. I didn't know what I'd say—I was playing this by ear. As I closed on the blind man he extended his arms, said something in a language I couldn't understand, turned and darted behind a shed. I sped after him, only to find the area deserted. I spotted a flash of white near the base of the statue. Not pausing to wonder how he'd crossed so much ground so quickly, I raced after him.

No sign of the blind man when I reached the statue. I circled it twice before noticing a ladder up the calf of one huge leg. I climbed, taking the rungs two at a time. Emerged onto a platform dotted with the protruding ends of thick steel girders. In the center a trapdoor had been flung open. I caught a glimpse of the blind man's head as he disappeared.

When I reached the opening I discovered a narrow ladder inside. For the briefest moment I hesitated—the Troop in me screaming, "Not a good idea!"—then let caution go to hell and started down.

After twelve feet I'd almost caught up with my prey, when all of a sudden he let go of the ladder and vanished into darkness. I scuttled down a few more rungs, only to learn he hadn't let go on a whim. The ladder ended here. I peered down, not sure if I dared proceed, when the trapdoor overhead slammed shut.

My heart leaped wildly. I reprimanded myself—I was too old to be afraid of the dark—and focused on my options. I could ascend the ladder and try the door or I could follow the blind man. Since I saw no reward in retreating, I explored with my feet and hands, realized the shaft was narrow enough to wedge myself in and proceeded to do so. Back jammed against one wall, knees and hands braced against the other, I shuffled down.

It was stuffy, the air was poor, the darkness was oppressive, but I went on. When I appeared to be getting nowhere, I extracted a coin and dropped it. It rolled and clanged for an age before trickling to a stop. Taking a deep breath, I did what had to be done if I was to stand any reasonable chance of catching up—pulled in my legs, lay back and slid.

At first it was almost a straight drop and I thought I was falling to my death. Then the tunnel angled and I gradually slowed, until I came to a stop in what seemed from the echoing sounds to be an enormous cavern. I put my hands out but couldn't see them. Got to my feet and took a few steps, testing each new section of ground with my toes before settling my weight on it.

The sound of swishing robes pierced the silence. I froze, alert, relying on my ears. Drew my pistol but held it by my side until I had something to aim at.

"Welcome, Albert Jeery, Flesh of Dreams."

The voice could have originated anywhere in the room—echoes came from all directions.

"Where are you?" I snapped, only to have my own words bounce back at me. *Are you? Are you?* "Show yourself," I shouted. *Self. Self. Self.*

"You seek answers, Flesh of Dreams. You seek truth. Death stalks your every move and you wish to know why." The speaker paused between sentences.

"What's with the Flesh of Dreams shit?" I retorted, but my query was ignored.

"Only through us may you access the truth. We know all that occurs in this city. Accept us and we shall share our knowledge. Deny us and you shall be denied."

"Get to the point," I growled, at which a match flared in the distance and a torch was lit. I trained my gun on the torch but there was nobody in sight.

I edged toward the light. When I reached it I discovered the torch was set in a wall and couldn't be moved. Underneath it hung a pouch. I glanced around the cavern—rough-hewn walls, gothic shadows, no sign of life.

"We are of Dreams," came the voice, filling the cavern, appearing to come from everywhere at once. "You are Flesh of Dreams, but currently more of Flesh than Dreams. To move beyond these walls, you must move beyond Flesh. There is dust in the pouch. Inhale it. Place the mouth of the pouch to one nostril and squeeze sharply. Repeat the procedure on the other side." With the pauses, the instructions seemed to take forever.

"The hell I will," I laughed.

"You must."

"What's in it?"

"Seeds of Dreams."

"What if I refuse to play along?"

There was no answer, which was answer enough.

If I'd been in full command of myself I'd have scouted around for tunnels, or tried making my way back up to the surface the way I had come, long and painful as the climb might be. But I hadn't been in control since I found Ellen's body in the Skylight. It was easiest to surrender completely, to hell with reservations.

The first inhalation nearly blew me away. I don't know what was in the pouch, but it was as strong as any shit you'd find on the streets. Rockets went off and the light from the torch intensified a thousand times. Of their own accord, my hands raised the pouch again, located my left nostril and I inhaled more dust. The walls of the cavern dissolved. I lost all sense of body and time, and became part of a sphere of light that was brighter than all the torches of the world put together. I swam in that light, deliriously, and all else was forgotten.

Minutes—hours—later, the effects of the dust diminished, and though the light persisted, it wasn't absolute. I flickered in and out of reality, one moment aware, the next immersed in the dreamy vision. In my more lucid moments I realized I was being led down a staircase, dark as a mine, that seemed to burrow to the very bowels of the Earth. When we hit bottom there was a long walk through a maze. Some time later I found myself in a dimly lit room. The walls were draped in curtains the color of blood and skeletons dangled from the ceiling, low enough to touch in places.

"Pretty," I murmured.

"They are the remains of the lower servants of Dreams." Looking around I saw two men, both in white robes, both blind. I started to ask where we were and who they were, but before I could I was swept away by another wave of light.

The next I knew, we were in an antechamber and they were removing my clothes. There was nothing sexual in their actions and I didn't resist as they stripped me naked and daubed my body with painted symbols.

"Your eyes," I said dreamily to one of them. "There are clouds. And yours"—to the other—"mountains. I've seen them before. And rivers. Rivers of blood." It was only later that I remembered where I'd seen them, in the rain-induced vision the first time I came to the Manco Capac site.

The blind men smiled. "That is good," one commended me. I beamed proudly, then slipped down another corridor of light inside my head.

I was brought back to the real world sharply. One of the men blew something up my nose that made me vomit and jolted me back to semi-consciousness.

"We must present you now," I was told. "Try to stay with us."

I nodded wordlessly and concentrated on my feet as I was guided through a door and into an immense cavern that made the first seem like a cranny. Thick candles dotted the walls and ceiling. Dripping wax had formed random sculptures on the floor. The cavern receded into the distance as far as I could see. Symbols—similar to those I'd been painted with—adorned the walls. Many of them were of the sun. I thought they were beautiful.

Directly in front of me lay a circular stone platform, roughly two feet high, maybe forty in diameter. A huge golden sun medallion hung suspended overhead. The platform was dotted with the stiff remains of preserved corpses. They sat upright in plain chairs around the edge, facing inward, mummified. Three ornate thrones stood at the center of the circle, set about three feet apart from each other.

The robed, white-eyed man with the mole occupied the middle throne. Similarly blind men stood behind the other two, faces just visible over the tops of the high backs. They looked almost identical, except the one in the middle had the mole and a few years' march on the others.

In front of the trio a young man sat on his haunches, crouched at the feet of the seated man like a dog. He had long, silver hair and brown eyes, and was naked, his body covered like mine with intricate designs. He was the one who addressed me throughout.

"Welcome, Flesh of Dreams," he greeted me. I blinked nervously, lost for words. The man on the throne said something in a language I couldn't place. The younger man nodded. "Don't be afraid. You have nothing to fear. We shall not harm you."

"Thank you," I replied, then fixed my eyes on the huge sun ornament. One of the men who'd accompanied me from the first cavern gently redirected my head so that I faced the platform again.

"We are villacs, the priests of the sun," the young man intoned. "We are the builders of this city, the architects of its future. You are a spirit of destiny, of our planning and making. Great things will come of our union."

"That's nice," I giggled.

"We would tell you of our plans but it is not time. First you must be cleansed. You cannot join us as you are. Only the pure may serve."

The man on the throne spoke again. The young man listened. I staggered on my feet and tuned into the sound of dripping water. This made no sense to me but I was happy enough to go along with it in my drugged, spaced-out state.

"Unclean as you are," the naked man resumed, "it is time to draw your blood. This city was built on a chakana of blood and is sustained by it."

"What's a chakana?" I asked.

"A three-stepped cross. Chakanas are sacred to us. We have always operated on three levels, three different realms of existence. In this city we have forged a chakana of blood streams. The blood of man, of the sun, and of dreams. For centuries the streams have run separately. Soon they will merge and there will be one stream—a chakana—which will feed this city eternally.

"You are here because you are a son of Dreams made Flesh. You will form one-third of our new chakana. We bring you here to prepare you for the day of union, to make you aware of the glorious destiny to which you were born.

"*Blood,*" he hissed. "All revolves around the sap of the living. You thirst for blood. Your women have been murdered and you live to avenge their deaths, yes?"

My eyes narrowed. "Ellen," I sighed.

"She was killed for the chakana. Your other lover too. Sacrificed for *your* destiny. Slain, that *you* may grow in spirit and move toward—"

"You killed her!" I screamed, surging forward, only to find my way blocked by the two men who'd been my guides.

"We did not kill your women," the man on the platform vowed. "The murderer resides elsewhere."

"Who killed them?" I shouted. "Tell me or—"

"That is for you to discover," he interrupted. "Answers must be earned. Blood must find its own way."

"Fuck blood!" I screamed. "Tell me who killed Ellen or I'll—"

The blind man on the throne barked an order. It was commanding enough to silence me. He got to his feet and walked to the edge of the platform, passing the naked man, who averted his eyes. The blind priest continued speaking, empty eyes fixed on my form.

"My master says you must show respect," came the translation.

I was afraid of this sinister man but the memory of Ellen drove me to snarl, "Fuck respect."

The blind man stiffened, then chuckled and mumbled something to his servant.

"My master says your blood is hot and that is good. Respect will come later. He can wait. For now you must lend us your hands."

I stared down at them. The blind priest reached into his robes and produced a curved dagger. I took a nervous step back. "You're not taking my hands," I moaned.

"We don't intend to," the young man laughed. "We need only your blood, and little of that. Step forward." I shook my head and jammed my hands behind my back. The priest with the mole began to chant, then made a beckoning motion with his knife. Suddenly I was stumbling toward him involuntarily.

I stopped at the platform. I wanted to flee but was under the blind priest's spell. He leaned forward, took my left hand, laid it on his head, said something under his breath, lowered my hand and kissed the palm. Next he made a quick slice with the knife across the soft flesh. Maybe because of the dust, I felt no pain.

I thought he was going to lick the blood off but he didn't. He let it drip to the platform, where it disappeared as though absorbed by the stone, then repeated the ceremony with my right hand. Finished, he stepped back, handed the dagger to one of the priests behind the empty thrones and resumed his central position.

"It is done," the naked man said. "The blood of Flesh of Dreams is diminished. To replenish it you must take blood in anger. By doing so, the way for the union will be open. Take him back now," he said to my guides. As they stepped forward to escort me away, he addressed me a final time. "When next we bring you here, it will be to celebrate the union of the blood streams. On that day every question will be answered."

"No," I mumbled, shaking my head. "I want to know *now*. You're going to tell me. I won't leave until you do. I'll tear you apart if I have to, but I won't—"

As I was making the threat, I stepped onto the platform, only for a shock to course through my body like a flood of electric eels. It was as if

I'd rammed my fingers into a live socket. I was hurled through the air. The world went white, then red, and I knew nothing except dreams.

Bill was standing over me when I returned to the land of the living, slapping my face lightly. "Al?" he asked softly. "Are you OK?"

"Where am I?" I groaned, sitting up.

"My place," he said. "You've been asleep for two whole days. I thought you'd never wake."

"The cavern," I sighed, remembering parts of my underworld adventure, though full recollection wouldn't come until later.

"What?"

"The cavern. The platform. I was…" I bent forward and examined the soles of my feet, expecting to find burnt patches, but they were unmarked. "Where was I found?" I asked, wriggling my toes.

Bill frowned. "You've been here, sleeping."

"Not two days ago. I was out cycling."

Bill shrugged. "You were here when I got back, dead to the world."

"That can't be. The cavern. The priests. They took my blood. They told me—"

"You've been dreaming," Bill chuckled.

"No! It was real. I was—"

"OK," he said, taking a step back. "You were cycling in a cavern. I believe you. Now, are you gonna get up and dress or do you want to cycle some more?"

"Later," I muttered, scratching my head, trying to remember everything. "I'm starving. I'll have breakfast, then…" I stopped. My suit was hanging from the back of the door. "What's that for?"

Bill took my hands and squeezed tightly. "It's Thursday." When that didn't register, he added sorrowfully, "Ellen's being buried today."

21

The funeral was devastating. Ellen's mother was a vibrant, forceful woman, in the normal run of things capable of taking anything life threw at her. She lost her first child to crib death—came to terms with it. Cancer drove her husband to an early grave—she survived that too. But Ellen's death was one blow too many. Hysteria descended. She wept throughout the service, keening like a professional wailer, pounding her knees with bunched fists.

Ellen was buried on Glade Hill, a carefully tended cemetery perched above the city like a bird's nest. The cost of burial was outrageous—nearly everyone I knew went for cremation—but Ellen feared fire and had often expressed her desire to be buried.

None of her family knew about Nic Hornyak, or that Ellen was dead because I'd drawn her into my sordid little world. I had that much to be grateful for—I couldn't have attended otherwise. But being blameless in their eyes did nothing to ease my conscience. If anything it made matters worse. There I was, mixing with the innocent, accepting their condolences with a wan smile, a sad shrug. I felt lousy. Hypocritical. Guilty.

The service came to an end and cars began pulling out of the drive. I'd have been happy to stay by the grave but I was expected at the house for the wake.

As I hunted for a lift—Bill had driven me here, but kept to the back of the crowd and slipped away before anyone else—a fleet of five black Cadillacs wound their way up Glade Hill and came to a halt not far from the gates. A tall, bony figure stepped out of the middle car. I had to double-check to make sure I wasn't imagining things.

It was The Cardinal.

He blew into his cupped hands, as if there were a chill in the air, then nodded at me and got back into the limo. I went to see what was going on.

I stood by the open door of the Cadillac and stared in at The Cardinal, who was rubbing his arms and gazing out the side window uneasily.

"Get in," he snapped. "I hate the great outdoors." I got in without a word. "Take you anywhere?"

"You know where the wake's being held?"

He nodded and the chauffeur passed word on to the other cars. He said nothing until we were off the hill and shadowed by ugly gray buildings.

"The city looks prettier from the fifteenth floor of Party Central," he noted, nose crinkling. "I'd forgotten how seedy it is up close."

"It's home," I said softly.

"Hmm." He opened a mini-refrigerator and produced two bottles of mineral water. "If you have to travel, this is the only way."

"What are you doing here?" I asked, dispensing with the chitchat.

"You didn't come to see me. I wanted to check that everything was good between us."

"I've just buried my ex-wife. How could everything be *good*?"

"I said between *us*. I'm aware of your grief. I share some of it—though I didn't know the woman, I know how much she meant to you and I feel partly responsible for what happened."

"So you should," I snarled. "You as good as murdered her."

"No," The Cardinal sighed. "I had nothing to do with Ellen Fraser's death. I know you've teamed up with your father behind my back—that was hardly likely to go unnoticed by my network of spies—and I suppose you're suspicious of me, given the degree of secrecy you've sunk to. But I don't know why your ex-wife was killed, nor Nicola Hornyak, and I certainly don't know who did it."

"Wami thinks you allowed us to be set up," I said. "He thinks you were spooked by that Incan card and played along because you were afraid."

"He's not far off the mark." The Cardinal sipped his drink. "I've never run from a challenge or retreated out of fear. It's not in me to back down. But I've learned to play my cards right and sometimes it suits my purposes better to lay low rather than attack. This is one such instance.

"When the postcard came, I was furious. If I'd been twenty years younger, I'd have torn the city apart till I found the prick who thought he could fuck with me, and taught him a valuable lesson. But my blood doesn't run as recklessly as it did. I had other problems to deal with. Though it galled me to play along, it was the right thing to do. So, yes, I threw you in at the deep end. But I'd no idea it would end like this."

"Would it have made a difference if you had?" I asked.

"It might. I know the pain of losing a wife. I would wish it on no one."

"That's right," I murmured. "You were married once. Drove her crazy. Walled her up in the Skylight."

"You're treading on thin ice, Al," he growled.

"Do I look like I'm worried?"

"You should be. I could have you…" He stopped with a curse. "I didn't come to make threats. I came to clear my name before you did something stupid. I'm not your enemy and you'll only waste your time treating me as one."

That was debatable, but it was big of him to come, so I didn't want to provoke him. "The blind priests say they know who killed her," I told him instead.

"You've had contact with them?"

"Yes."

"They spoke to you in English?" The news startled him. "I didn't know they were capable of common speech. Tell me what they said."

I gave him an abbreviated version of my encounter with the *villacs*. "Of course they could have been lying," I concluded. "About not killing Nic and Ellen."

"Doubtful," he replied. "I don't see why they should drag you all the way down there just to lie to you." He stroked his chin with his twisted little finger and glanced away. "Did they explain why they referred to you as Flesh of Dreams?" Though he phrased the question casually, I could tell it had significance for him.

"No. They babbled on about blood and something called a chakana, but none of it made sense."

"Did they mention the word *Ayuamarca* at any point?"

"No." But I didn't tell him that Paucar Wami had.

"Curious," he muttered, then made a dismissive gesture. "Enough about the blind fools. The investigation—do you wish to continue?"

"It's too late to stop," I responded.

"Nonsense. I can remove you from the case and set another team on it. Fuck my blackmailers. If you like, you can leave the city and not return until everything's been cleared."

"I'm not running," I told him. "And I don't want you interfering. Ellen's killers are mine. If anyone gets in my way…"

The Cardinal chuckled. "I was right about you, Al. You *were* wasted in the Troops. Very well, the case is still yours. Good luck."

"I won't need luck. I have this." I opened my jacket to flash my .45.

"As persuasive a tool as any," The Cardinal noted drily, and said nothing further during the remainder of the journey.

The wake was held in a large house belonging to one of Ellen's cousins. Family and friends milled around, talking in low voices, drinking heavily, smoking as if the tobacco industry were about to go out of business.

There was a huge grate for an open fire in the main room. Somebody lit it in the afternoon, despite the glorious weather, and I retreated to its side when I couldn't take one more comforting pat on the back. I would have left but that wouldn't have been polite, and for once in my life I wanted to do the decent thing. For Ellen's sake.

I sat by the hearth, watching the flames, cold as I'd ever been. After a slow, lonely half hour, Deborah—Ellen's elder sister—approached. "Holding up?" she asked, dabbing at her eyes with a handkerchief. I nodded numbly. "Mom's taking this badly. We're worried sick about her."

"Some people take things like this worse than others. She'll come to terms with it eventually. You just have to make sure you're there for her when she needs you." The platitudes came naturally. "You seem to be bearing up OK," I noted.

She glanced around to make sure we were alone, then spoke quietly. "Remember Donny, my son?"

"Sure. He was a real terror. Must be thirteen, fourteen now?"

"Fourteen," she confirmed.

"Is he here?"

"No. He's in the hospital."

"Oh?"

"It's cancer." A confidential whisper. "Just like Dad." I stared at her. I hadn't cried since finding Ellen dead at the Skylight, but I came close to it then.

"Is it serious?" I asked stupidly.

"He's dying. They've operated twice without success. He's there again today. We didn't tell him about Ellen. He's going to die. In a few months we'll be back here mourning again. That's how I'm so calm. I've been preparing for a funeral."

"Is that why your Mom's so shattered?" I asked.

"Mom doesn't know. We wanted to keep it from her. We've kept it quiet from most of the family. We live outside the city, so we don't see them much. We were going to tell them after this operation, if it fails. Now though..." She looked over at her weeping mother. "Excuse me," she sobbed, voice cracking, and hurried away, shaking helplessly.

I sat there, thinking of Ellen, her mother, Donny. Everyone was drifting around like zombies, drinking too much, talking about the past, their jobs, their kids, but not about Ellen. They didn't want to discuss the dead, not like at most funerals. Ellen's corpse was lying peacefully up on Glade Hill, but might as well have been here, in the middle of the room, the way people were acting.

And it was all my fault.

I thought about the coffin being lowered. The words of the priest, trying to comfort the mourners. The sound of the earth as it hit the lid. She'd looked so healthy laid out before. The killer hadn't touched her face. She could have been sleeping, except I knew that Ellen slept with her mouth open and was never still. She was forever moving, wriggling her toes, snoring, scrunching up her face. But not anymore.

I had to do something. The hunt for the killer would come later, but I couldn't wait that long. Rising slowly, I tracked down Bob—Ellen's brother—and asked if there was a pack of cards somewhere. He looked bemused by the request but fetched one. I located a spare room and asked Bob to guard the door for me.

"What's going on, Al?" he grumbled.

"Trust me," I said. "I want to help."

Then I went to find Ellen's mother. One of Ellen's aunts was trying to console her. I pushed the aunt aside as politely as I could and took the distraught woman by the arm. "Mrs. Fraser, I'm so sorry," I said.

She wept still, not resisting as I led her away.

"I've got something to show you, something Ellen would have wanted you to see."

"Ellen?" There was painful hope in her voice, as if she believed I could bring her daughter back from the dead.

"Yes. This way, please. It won't take long." At the door of the room I told Bob to let no one in. There was doubt in his eyes but he did as I said, not wishing to create a scene.

I sat Ellen's mother on the bed and turned on the light. Took the cards out and shuffled them. "I want you to watch the cards, Mrs. Jeery. I'm going to show you a trick."

"A trick?" she echoed uncertainly.

I smiled and slapped four cards down, faces up. "Don't worry. It's a good trick. Now, pick a card, but don't tell me what it is…"

She was eager for consolation and didn't fight as I created a world of colors, followed by the connecting tunnel. There was so much unhappiness inside her, I knew I couldn't relieve her of all her pain, but sometimes a little is enough. If she could get through the next few days, she'd hopefully find the strength in herself to continue after that.

She wasn't quite so haggard-looking when I led her from the room, and she began circulating, thanking people for coming, offering to help make sandwiches. Bob was bursting with curiosity but didn't push me for an answer, just slapped me on the back and let his eyes express his thanks.

After that it was back to the fire and thoughts of Ellen. I'd been able to forget her while helping her mother, but now the memories returned with a vengeance and for the longest time I sat there, slumped in the chair, staring at the flames.

Finally, mercifully, the wake drew to a close. I bid Bob and a couple of others farewell. Ellen's mother hugged me and told me Ellen had loved me. Then I was clear, free to get down to the only thing that mattered anymore, the business of bloody, final, uncompromising revenge.

22

Bill was sitting in his excuse for a garden when I returned, drinking a can of beer, several empties scattered around him. I packed my bag, wandered outside and told him I was going back to my apartment. He wasn't happy, but I said I couldn't stay with him forever. He'd been great, I couldn't have pulled through without his help, but it was time to stand on my own two feet and get on with life. He told me to take advantage of his hospitality anytime, no matter what the circumstances.

Ali spotted me pulling up and rushed out to commiserate. I thanked him for his kind words but didn't stay to chat. He told me to call in if there was anything I needed. I said I would, then hurried up the stairs, eager to make a start.

Somebody had fixed my door. Probably Bill. Also, the fridge and freezer were stocked, the bed had been made and all the notes that had been strewn around the place were in boxes, tidied away. I threw my bag down and started pulling out the notes. I hadn't gotten through two of the boxes when the door to the bathroom opened and Paucar Wami stepped out.

"Al m'boy," he croaked, "you've come back to your dear ol' pappy."

I laid the box down. "How long have you been in there?"

"Most of the day." He flopped into a chair. "I had a feeling you would return after the funeral. I was expecting you earlier. What delayed you?"

"The wake."

"You stayed for that? I detest wakes. Everybody speaks so well of the dead. Nobody mentions the infidelities, the scams they pulled, the people they betrayed. I worry that somebody will throw a wake for me when I pass on."

"I don't think there's much chance of that," I replied icily.

"You might be surprised," he grinned. "Enough beating about the bush. You have had your time of mourning. On to business. Have you learned anything new?"

I thought of the marble and sat down opposite him. "There's something I have to ask. You won't like it but I'm going to ask anyway."

"Go ahead." He looked interested.

"Did you kill Ellen?"

He frowned. "You suspect me?"

I told him about the marble, black with golden streaks, how I'd discovered it, how it had gone missing and turned up in my locker, how it had been found on Ellen.

"You think I left it on her?" he asked. "That I rolled the marble your way in the first place, meaning I've been fucking with you from the very start?"

"Maybe."

Wami stared at me in cold silence, then slid a dagger out of a pocket. He pressed it into my right hand and placed the blade against his bare, unprotected throat, offering himself to me.

"If you doubt, destroy," he hissed.

I stared at the blade and the hairless flesh of his throat. I took a deep breath. As agile and powerful as he was, he couldn't stop me if I decided to kill him. One flick of my wrist and he was a dead man.

I started to lower the knife. Wami grabbed my hand and pressed the blade back against his throat. "Be sure," he snarled. "I have never volunteered my life before. I will not do so again. Be sure of me or kill me."

I withdrew the knife. He didn't stop me this time.

"I had to ask," I muttered.

"No. But you did, and it is perhaps just as well. Now we know where we stand." He pocketed his knife. "With the dramatics out of the way, I will ask again—anything new?"

"You first. What's happened since Ellen was...?" I didn't want to say it.

"Nothing much. Nobody knows who killed her. The room at the

Skylight was officially vacant. The police do not know whether it was a copycat killer or the original."

"The original," I snapped.

"Of course. No luck on the Charlie Grohl front. I have been following young Nicholas, without joy. I tracked down the two leads of Ellen's—I found them by going through your notes—but they knew nothing of her or Nicola Hornyak."

"Did you kill them?" I asked quietly.

"One of them. The other was a crook with political connections. I let him live in case I have use for him in future."

"How come you didn't hit on Ziegler?"

"I was saving him for when you returned. We will go after him together, father and son, a proper team. Now, what news with you?"

For the second time I related the story of my underground sojourn. Wami sat through it uncommonly slack-jawed.

"I know of the tunnels and caverns," he noted at the end. "I have explored them. But I never came across anything like that."

"Can you make sense of what the *villacs* said?" I asked.

"No."

"*Flesh of Dreams* means nothing to you?"

"Should it?"

"It did to The Cardinal." His eyebrows rose, so I told him about our meeting.

"It grows more incredible by the minute," he sighed. "The Cardinal leaving his fortress to declare his innocence. I never heard the like."

"The Cardinal knows about the *villacs* and their plans," I said.

"That does not surprise me."

"I thought their rantings about blood streams, Flesh and Dreams were gibberish, but if The Cardinal takes them seriously, so should we."

"Absolutely," Wami agreed.

"So find out," I told him.

"How?"

"Torture a few blind men. Take The Cardinal out back of Party Central and beat the truth out of him. I don't care. That's your concern. My hands will be full with Nick and Ziegler."

"Why divide? Let us pursue Nicholas and Rudi together, then—"

"No," I cut him short. "If either was responsible for the murders—or knows who was—he's mine. Same if you find the killer—leave him for me."

"You grow greedy, Al m'boy," Wami murmured. "You want all the fun."

"To hell with fun!" I shouted. "This isn't a game anymore. I *loved* Ellen. Can you understand that, you black-hearted son of a bitch? Do you know what love is?"

"Please," Wami winced. "Spare me the pop lyrics."

"Don't joke," I growled. "I'm serious."

"How can you be serious about a little thing like murder?" he protested. "We all die in the end. She is dead—accept it and forget her. It is not like the two of you were still an item."

"That doesn't matter. I loved her."

"*Love*," he sneered. "It is the basest of emotions. Love owns the weak—owns, cripples and destroys."

"You don't know what you're talking about. You've never loved. You can't understand it unless—"

"But I have!" he exclaimed. "I do. I love *death*."

"Hardly the same thing as loving a human," I noted.

"It is better," he insisted. "Death is the only mistress worth love because she owns us already. Loving one of your own is a form of slavery. Only by learning to love death can one taste freedom. By acknowledging the bonds of our mortality, we are freed to explore the loops that form the chains of life."

"I'm not going to get philosophical with you," I said. "Love whatever the hell you want. *I* loved Ellen and I'm gonna find her killer and murder him. Alone. If you've got a problem with that…"

"Al," he tutted. "Sons should not pit themselves against their fathers. It runs contrary to the laws of nature."

"Will you leave the killer to me?" I asked.

"If I do not? Will you raise your hand in anger?"

"If I have to."

"And if I raise mine in return?"

I didn't answer. Wami studied me, then shook his head with disgust. "So be it. The killer is yours."

"Thank you," I responded coolly.

"You know," Wami smiled, "I almost envy you. It has been many years since I took a life in anger. Nothing compares with that first drawing of blood, the thrill of…" He stopped when he saw a shadow pass across my face. "Did I say something amiss?"

"Just something similar to what the blind priests told me."

I thought about what the naked man on the platform had said. *"You must take blood in anger."* Perhaps it was wrong of me to go it alone. Maybe that was what they wanted, and I was playing into their hands.

"You are having second thoughts," Wami noted.

"Some," I admitted.

"You want to change your mind?"

I considered it thoroughly. "No. I don't like the idea of flying solo but this is the way it must be."

"As you wish." He started for the door. "If you require assistance, you know how to find me."

"You'll remember your promise?" I called him back. "You won't act without contacting me?"

"Unless it is unavoidable."

"Wait." I stopped him as his hand was on the knob. "You said you only loved death, that nothing else was worth loving. Does that mean you don't love *me*?"

He squinted as if I were kidding him. "You interest me as few other humans do. I have certain fatherly feelings for you."

"But not love?"

"Perhaps if you were dead," he chuckled drily, and let himself out.

The Red Throat was almost deserted when I got there, shortly after it had opened for the day. There was no sign of Nick, but I hadn't expected him this early. I ordered a mineral water and found a corner where I could sit back and observe.

Nick turned up a couple of hours later. He looked rough, as if he hadn't had a lot of sleep, and was dressed in a T-shirt and jeans. He stumbled to the bar, ordered a drink and looked around. Frowned when he saw me, then came over.

"My old friend Al," he commented, running the cool surface of the glass across his forehead as he sat down. "More questions?"

"Feel up to them?"

"Not really. I went on a bender last night. Still, if you ask nicely..."

I stood and nodded toward the toilets. "Want to do it in there?"

"Don't tell me you've come over queer," he snorted suspiciously.

I forced a smile. "Afraid not. I just want to talk in private. It won't take long. Will you come?"

He laughed. "Be careful with your words, Al." He set off ahead of me, hips swaying, smirking over his shoulder. I grinned bleakly in return.

The room was brightly lit and empty. "You know," he said as I closed the door, "this isn't the first time I've been in here with a friend, but the management really doesn't like—"

I was on him. I jammed his mouth shut, grabbed his left arm and jerked it behind his back until he screamed into my palm. I stopped short of snapping the bone, rested the arm, then jerked it up again, harder, not releasing the pressure until I heard it break. I held him in place, muffling his screams, then swung him around and unleashed a flurry of punches to the walls of his stomach. As he doubled over, I grabbed the back of his head and slammed him face-first down onto the floor, not hard enough to knock him out, but with force enough to smash a few teeth.

He slumped when I let go, groaning pitifully. I let him get his breath back, then kicked him cruelly, stomach, thighs, the soft parts of the arms. I steered clear of the groin, saving it for later.

When he was whimpering softly I took a break. I washed my hands in one of the basins, studying my face in the mirror, barely recognizing the vicious, hateful image. I didn't like what I was doing and what I had yet to do, but a quick mental fix on Ellen as she lay in the coffin set me up for round two.

Nick was sobbing, trying to stanch the flow of blood from his mouth with his unbroken arm, building up his breath to scream for help. I took out my gun and tapped it against the side of the basin. His breath caught. I dried my hands and turned to face him.

"If you scream, I'll have to shoot you."

"What is this?" he asked through a mouthful of blood and broken teeth. "Taken up gay-bashing?"

"Gay's got nothing to do with it."

"Then what?" He spat out a couple of teeth and began crying. "Christ, Al, what the fuck—"

"I want to know about Ellen."

He stared, bewildered. "Who?"

"Ellen Fraser. My ex-wife."

"Don't know her."

"You heard about the copycat killing at the Skylight?"

He stared. "No," he whispered.

"I want to know who killed her." I pointed the gun at him.

His eyes were wide with terror. "I don't know anything about it," he spluttered.

"I'll shoot you in the leg first," I said. "Your left. Then the right. People will rush to investigate when I open fire, so I'll have to work quickly. That means moving straight to your groin. Ever seen someone shot through the balls? Not a pretty sight."

"It wasn't me," he moaned.

"I don't believe you," I said, crouching to give him a better view of the gun. "Tell me what you were doing in the Skylight when your sister was killed. Lie once and I shoot."

Nick stared at the gun, gathered his wits and began painfully. "It was meant to be a joke. We'd done it before."

"Done what?"

"Swapped partners." He wiped his mouth with his good hand. "Nic arranged for rooms with interconnecting doors. Both our guys were into bondage. The plan was to tie them up, then swap places and..."

"You mean you'd screw Nic's guy and she'd get off with yours?" He nodded. "Seems like hers was getting the worst of the bargain."

He showed his broken teeth, all bloody. It might have been a grin. "She had a dildo..."

"Cute. Go on."

"I got there before Nic and went into action. About half past ten, I looked in her room. She wasn't there. I kept my guy going another hour, then I put the mask on him and went to see if Nic had turned up."

"Why the mask?" I asked.

"To protect his identity. I left him tied to the bed, slipped into 812 and..."

I waited for him to continue. He didn't. *"And?"* I snapped.

"I saw the state of her back. How still she was. I thought she was dead. So I ran."

"She was still alive then," I roared. "You might have been able to save her."

"Thanks for reminding me," he replied bitterly. He was crying, but not from the pain. "I should have checked. I should have gotten help. But I panicked, fled for the stairs. I stopped on the third floor, ducked into a bathroom and cried till I was dry. Then I went back—the longest fucking climb of my life—and got my clothes. I should have let my guy go, but I just left him there—I wasn't thinking straight. I took an elevator down and slipped out. Nobody noticed. That was it." He looked at me with scared, small eyes, awaiting my verdict.

"Who was the man with Nic?" I asked.

"I don't know. And she didn't know who I'd be with. That's how we always did it."

"Did you see anyone or hear anything?"

"No."

"Any chance the guy you were with—Charlie Grohl—knows more than you do?"

"He was tied up," Nick said quickly. "Gagged."

"Maybe later, after you left," I suggested.

"No," he insisted, but there was something in his denial which jarred. For the first time I got the feeling that he wasn't playing straight.

"Remember what I said I'd do if I caught you lying?"

"I haven't lied!" he yelped, scrabbling backward.

"Did Charlie Grohl say something to make you suspicious?"

"No. I swear. He knows no more about it than me."

"I don't believe you." I pointed the gun at his groin. "Three seconds, Nick. Spill the beans or kiss goodbye to your greens."

"Al, don't do this. You—"

"One."

"People will hear. They know your face here. They'll—"

"Two."

"I swear, I don't know who it was, I haven't—"

"Three."

"No!" he screamed before I fired. "There was no Charlie Grohl!"

My eyebrows creased. "Come again?"

"It's a name I made up. But I only did it to protect his identity. He said he'd kill me if anyone—"

"It's an alias?" I shouted.

"One of my first lovers was called Charles Grohl. His name sprang into my—"

"Forget that," I silenced him. "Who was in the room with you?"

Nick hesitated the briefest of moments. Then, shoulders slumping, he said, "I was with a cop called Howard Kett."

I helped Nick clean himself up and called for an ambulance. He said he wouldn't press charges because he knew how upset I was, but added that he never wanted to see me again, not even if I found out who murdered Nic. I felt ashamed, but for Ellen I'd face all the shame in the world. I left Nick cradling his arm and waiting for the medics, then tracked down Howie.

He was on the phone in his office when I walked in, brushing past the startled officers outside. I yanked the cord from the wall, cutting him off in mid-sentence.

"What the fuck!" he yelled, stumbling to his feet.

"I know about you and Nicholas Hornyak," I said, sitting down.

The rage drained from his face and he fell back into his chair. One of his colleagues came to the door and asked if everything was OK. Kett nodded and told him to close the door. For a long time he sat staring at me, saying nothing. Finally, "We met a couple of years ago. Bill and I busted him one night. I got chatting to him. A few months later we ran into each other and—"

"I'm not interested in ancient history," I snapped.

"I don't make a habit of it. But sometimes I just—"

"The Skylight, Howie," I growled.

"My wife has no idea. She guessed I was having an affair, but thinks it's with a woman. You mustn't tell her. My life's over if she finds out."

"Tell me what happened at the Skylight or I'll phone her now," I threatened. That brought him out of his daze.

"How much do you know?" he asked.

"Nick paid Breton Furst to turn a blind eye so you could slip in unseen. He tied you to the bed and masked you. Furst freed you later."

"I went home," he said. "I rang Nick to chew him a new asshole but he couldn't be reached. I spent most of the week trying to contact him. A couple of days before I learned about the murder, a photo turned up on my desk, of me and Nick, in the room. Naked. No note. Just the photo. I stormed over to Nick's. I thought the photo was another of his sick jokes, like chaining me to the bed and vanishing, but he swore he knew nothing about it. He told me how he found his sister."

"That's when you turned up at the Skylight, looking for her body?"

"Was it, fuck!" he snorted. "If I interfered, someone might've found out about me and Nick. I kept the news to myself. But the next day I got a call at home, a man's voice. He asked if my wife would like a framed print of the photo. I asked what he was after. He told me about Nicola and said I was to pick up her body after I called The Cardinal and invented a story about a snitch."

"What did he tell you to do once you'd recovered the body?"

"Keep the news that the corpse was a week old to myself, and treat it like any normal homicide victim. Which is what I did. A few days later I got another call. This time I was told to go around to your place and tell you to keep away from Nick. I knew it'd make you suspicious but my hands were tied."

"I wondered what you were up to," I grunted. "It made no sense."

"That's because they were setting us up. I could see that from the start. Broke my fucking balls to play into their hands."

"And Allegro Jinks—you were told to send Furst to look for him? That story about his mother was a crock of shit?"

Howie nodded. "I found a message in the pocket of my pants one morning."

"Any more messages since?"

He shook his head. "When I got back from holiday and heard about your ex, I thought they'd be in touch, but so far, nothing."

"If they contact you again, I want to know."

"I can't make any guarantees."

"I'll tell your wife about you and Nick if you don't."

He laughed bitterly. "And the others will tell her about us if I do. Screwed however I turn. Look, Jeery, much as I hate you, these are scum of a different order. I'll do anything to help you fuck them up. But I have to blow with the wind. They scare me more than you do."

"You're not much of a man to have in my corner, Howie."

"Never claimed I was," he retorted. He nodded at the door, inviting me to leave.

"One last question. Ellen—any leads?"

His face softened. "It's not my case. I've steered clear of it. I'm not even listening to office gossip. Bill can probably tell you more about it than me."

"If you learn anything, will you let me know?"

"If I'm able," he replied.

I left. The last thing I saw as I let myself out was Kett lowering his head into his hands, groaning quietly. Another time and place, I could almost have felt sorry for the bastard.

Rudi Ziegler wasn't surprised to see me. "Come in," he said glumly and took me through to the parlor. He sat at the table and played with his crystal ball, head bowed over it. I gave the room a quick once-over before sitting. I'd made up my mind to start softly—more softly than I had on Nick—but if I had to get vicious, I would.

"You know why I'm here?" I asked.

"I heard about Ellen. I'm sorry."

"Did you know she was my ex when she came to see you?"

"No. She never mentioned Nicola or you. I wouldn't have known the two of you were related if your name hadn't been mentioned in the news."

"That's *your* story."

He looked up. "You think I'm lying?"

"Two of your clients go under the knife, exactly the same way, exactly the same place. Coincidence?"

"Maybe," he muttered.

I placed my gun on the table. "You're in deep shit, Rudi. Talk."

He put his face in his hands and breathed deeply. His eyes were raw with tears when he looked at me again. "I never knew it would go this far," he sobbed.

My fingers slid away from the gun.

"I knew nothing about Ellen, but Nicola...It was *her* idea. She wanted to be carved. It was meant to be a symbolic sacrifice. There was a ceremony, by the base of the Manco Capac statue. It concluded with the symbol being cut into her back. There was pain but she welcomed it, offering it up to the god of the sun. I said rites before, during and after the carving. That was it. We cleaned up, bandaged Nicola, said our farewells, and I headed home."

"Nic stayed?"

"I thought she'd left too, but she must have doubled back, or met her killer elsewhere."

"You didn't kill her?"

"No!" he yelped. "I worship the sun, life, the positive aspects of the universe. I would never—"

"So who did?" I challenged him.

He chewed his lower lip nervously. "I don't know," he lied.

"Who arranged the *sacrifice*?"

"Nicola. I organized the ceremony but she initiated it."

"She didn't plan on being killed?"

"Hardly."

"What about the carving? You did the praying. Did you handle the knife as well?"

"Yes," he said quickly. Too quickly.

"You're lying."

"No." Sweating now.

"Who was it?" I pressed. "Who sliced her?"

"Nobody! We were the only—"

His eyes flicked to a spot behind me. My training kicked in and I threw myself to the left, not even pausing to grab my weapon.

A gun exploded. A bullet screamed past the spot where I should have been and hit Ziegler in the chest. He went down silently. Blood and splinters of bone arced from his breast, spraying the table and floor. He might not have been dead before hitting the floor, but there wouldn't have been much in it either way.

"Shit!" the assassin cursed. Feet shuffled. A silver barrel glinted. I lunged as the second shot was fired, feeling it tear through the heel of my shoe, somehow missing my flesh. Then I was on my assailant.

I drove my head into his stomach, my fist into his face. He grunted, gave a couple of inches, then rooted his feet to the floor and struck at my head with the gun. I took the blow on my shoulder and punched again. He stumbled. Blood was flowing from his nose or mouth. I grabbed his legs and pulled. He fell heavily.

I scrambled up his body to pound his face. When I got there, I paused with shock. It wasn't a man—it was a large, mean, bullheaded woman. I knew her, but before I could place her name, she went for my eyes with her nails.

I rolled away just in time, though she scratched my cheeks pretty badly. With a growl she pushed after me, scuttling across the floor in a grotesque, arachnid fashion, teeth gnashing at my flesh, hands scrabbling for a hold.

I backpedaled swiftly, trying to make space for a counterattack. I struck at her face with both feet. She took the blow on her giant breasts. It slowed her but didn't put her down, and she was on me again moments later, saliva spraying, teeth seeking my nose.

I hooked my fingers under her gums and pried her away. I tried kneeing her groin but only caught a meaty thigh. She slammed her own knee forward and fared better, driving much of the wind from my sails.

We thrashed about and crashed into the table, her hands around my throat. Something heavy rolled off and thumped to the floor. My mind put a shape to the sound. I jerked one hand back and punched the side of her head a few times without any effect, so I grabbed an ear and tugged. She screamed and drew away.

I let go of the ear and hit both sides of her neck with the inner edges of my hands. She screamed breathlessly and sank down, gasping for air. I slid across the floor and grabbed the crystal ball, which was what had toppled from the table moments before. It was cracked but intact. I got to my knees, raised my hands and slammed the glass globe down over her head.

There was no swift recovery from a blow like that. I had plenty of time to truss her up, tend to my wounds and check Ziegler's corpse before she came to.

I studied her as she groaned and returned to life. I had her name now—Valerie Thomas, the maid-with-attitude from the Skylight.

When her eyes opened, she found herself staring down the barrel of my .45. She looked up at my scratched, bloody, determined face. And she laughed.

"Men!" she snorted. "Always resorting to guns to settle battles."

"You drew first," I reminded her.

"That was business. An execution. Once the fight began, I wouldn't have used it, no matter what. Only a coward goes for a gun in a fight."

"You killed Ziegler," I said.

She tried hunching her shoulders but I had her tied too tight to move. "So?" she smiled. "He was a puppet. Ziegler was a fool who couldn't tell the difference between fantasy and reality. He dug his own grave."

"Did you kill Nic too? And Ellen?"

"Your lovely ex-wife," she cooed.

"You killed her?" My finger tightened on the trigger.

"Eligible Ellen. So sweet. So naïve."

"Did you kill her?" I screamed, jabbing the gun into her mouth, giving her a taste of the pain to come if she didn't talk.

She spat the gun out. "No," she coughed. "I didn't kill your precious Ellen. But I saw her die. I watched her lips widen in a silent scream and her back arch. I saw the terror in her eyes as the blade bit into her soft flesh." She laughed again, cruel as an eagle's cry. "So beautiful. So helpless. So terrified. She called for you. 'Al!' After all you got her into, she didn't blame you. People that stupid deserve to die."

Finally, after so much time, tears came. I cried pitifully, thinking of Ellen in this vile creature's grasp, crying out for me, dying with my name on her lips. My legs went numb and I collapsed and wept.

"Poor Al," she crooned. "Poor Ellen, poor Nic, poor Rudi. So many victims. I feel like spilling a few tears myself."

"Shut up!" I screamed, then trained the gun on her again. "Who killed them?"

"My lover," she replied. "My wily, sensual, murderous lover."

"The same one Ellen said she was in love with?" I guessed.

"What a fool. It's easy to love one so strong and imaginative, but to miss their dark heart, the evil at their core...Ellen was doomed from their first kiss."

"Tell me his name," I snarled.

"Love knows no names," she laughed.

"Tell me the fucking name or I'll kill you!"

"Go ahead," she said. "I have no fear. There's nothing in dying that scares me. Kill me, little man. Send me to my sun god and damn yourself in the process."

I took that in and blinked slowly. "Are you in league with the *villacs*?"

"Who?" she deadpanned.

"The blind priests." She smirked knowingly and didn't answer. "OK. Just tell me who killed Ellen."

"I told you—my lover."

"His name, bitch. His name!"

"What's in a name?" she chuckled. Then, seriously, "Find out for yourself. Embrace the sun, worship its god, and you will learn."

"Don't waste my time with talk of gods," I warned her. "Tell me who killed Ellen or so help me..."

"What? You'll torture me? Try, little man. I'm a hard nut to crack. I *know* pain. Do your worst. I'm up to anything you can throw at me."

"We'll see about that," I said grimly, then twisted her over and ripped her shirt open. I'm not sure what I was planning. I'd learned all sorts of terrible techniques during my time with the Troops. I knew the places that hurt most, the everyday instruments I could use to heighten the pain, how to prolong it. I'd sworn never to put that knowledge to use, but in that room my resolve crumbled and good intentions went up in wreaths of bloodstained smoke.

However, upon my removal of her shirt, the option of torture was removed. I discovered a grotesque map of pain beneath the cloth. Her flesh was burned, cut, whipped beyond recognition. Pins were stuck in her, the heads glinting like tiny silver stars. Bandages covered fresh, deep lacerations and scars. Acid burns, wounds with salt rubbed into them, sores that were pustulant and seeping. She was a walking advert for sick masochism.

I threw the shirt back over her, nauseated. There was nothing I could do to this woman that hadn't already been done.

"You see?" she whispered proudly. "My god fed me pain, thus placing me beyond it. He is gracious, generous, wise. If only more knew the beauty of being in service to one so powerful, they'd..."

I left the woman babbling about gods and the like. I could listen to no more. I thought about pleading with her, trading her life for answers, but I knew she'd laugh at such offers. Perhaps I should have tried to trick the truth out of her but I was in no state for intrigue. I was weeping like a baby.

I called Bill before leaving. Told him what I'd learned, where to pick up Valerie, what had happened with Ziegler. He told me to stay where I was, but I couldn't. I said I'd be in my apartment. He started to say that wasn't good enough, I had to remain at the scene, but I hung up and walked away, into a world more awash with pain and grief than I'd ever thought possible.

23

Valerie confessed to all three murders—Nic, Ellen, Ziegler. Told the police I had nothing to do with any of them. Made no mention of an accomplice or lover. I didn't contradict her story. They thought they had their killer, the case was closed. Why piss on their parade?

An eager reporter uncovered the connections between myself and the female victims. For a while I was an outstanding news story, a determined lover who exposed the murderer and handed her over for trial. A public hero, a role model for children everywhere. I was chased by news crews around the city. Bill and Kett kept them off my back, Bill because he cared, Kett for fear I'd implicate him.

Valerie was dead a couple of days after her confession. Hanged herself in her cell. Nobody knew how she got the rope, but the police didn't care. She'd have gone to the chair in any case—this saved the city time and money.

The media went into a feeding frenzy when Valerie killed herself. It was the perfect end to the story and all they needed to cap it was an interview with me. They hounded me mercilessly till Bill called in a favor from the mayor and he got their editors to call them off.

The days blurred into one another as I sat in my apartment, staring at the walls, thinking about Nic, Ellen, Valerie. I should have been chasing the mystery lover, the man who lured Nic and Ellen to their deaths and inspired Valerie to lie herself to ruin. But I was too tired. A great depression had settled over me. I just wanted to sit in darkness and weep.

Wami and The Cardinal rang to congratulate me. I accepted their praise with barely a murmur, telling neither the truth. They'd have dragged me out of myself if they had known the case was still live.

I stopped washing and shaving. Wore the same clothes day after day. I ate rarely and unhealthily. Lost myself in memories of Ellen. The world made no sense any longer. All that seemed real was Ellen.

Bill and Ali tried to help. They brought fresh food and cleared away the trash. Some mornings I awoke to find one of them had slipped my clothes off while I slept and laundered them. They held one-sided conversations with me, chattering on, pretending all was well. I tried responding—I appreciated the effort they were making—but hadn't the strength. I was like a lobotomized half-wit who could only stare, drool and nod my head occasionally.

I stayed away from the bottle. Even during my lowest moments, I resisted the temptation. I was a pathetic wreck, but part of me knew I could haul myself out of this wretchedness in time. If I drank, there'd be no coming back. This mess of a life would be for keeps.

In the midst of my sorrow, Priscilla Perdue breezed back into my life. She turned up one day, demurely dressed and smiling uncertainly. "I tried calling," she said, "but you didn't answer. I had to come. I'll leave again if you want me to."

I said nothing, only ushered her in.

Her nose crinkled when she saw the state of the apartment. Neither Ali nor Bill had been up for a few days and I'd really let things slide. Dirty dinner trays, filthy clothes, overflowing garbage cans.

"Is it the cleaner's year off?" she quipped.

"If you don't like it, piss off," I snarled.

She started for the door.

"Wait," I called her back. "I'm sorry. I don't know what I'm saying or thinking half the time. Don't go. Please. Sit."

She looked around. "I'd rather stand if it's all the same."

I managed a thin smile. "So. Here you are."

"Here I am," she agreed.

There was a long silence.

"Anything in particular you wanted to talk about?" I asked.

"Oh, Al." She threw herself into my arms. I toppled backward onto one of the socks-and-underwear-strewn chairs, dragging her down with me. "What that woman did to your wife was awful. I don't know how you didn't rip her throat open. If it was me, I'd have..." She started to cry.

"It's OK," I said, stroking her hair, thinking about Ellen's. "It's over. She's dead. There's no need for tears."

She wept a while, then looked at me hopefully. "It *is* over, isn't it? She did kill them?"

"She confessed, didn't she?"

"I know, but..." She gulped and sat up straighter. "I can't stop thinking about that night I went to the Skylight to meet Nic. She definitely said she was bringing a man. I've been reading the papers daily. According to them, Valerie acted by herself. The reporters say she was mad."

"They got that much right."

"And the rest of it?"

I knew why she cared. If Valerie had been a lone crazy, and the guy Nic brought to the hotel wasn't involved, it absolved Priscilla. She needn't feel guilty if it had been a random attack rather than a client of Nic's who might not have killed her if Priscilla had been there.

I wanted to lie, as I'd lied to the others, so she could sleep easier, free of the demonic imps of guilt that plagued my every moment. But as I stared into her eyes I found myself telling her the worst of all things—the truth. She listened silently, clutching my hands. At the end she said nothing for a while, then finally stuttered, "She could have been lying."

"She wasn't."

"She was an evil, crazy she-devil. She knew the game was up. It might have been one last sly twist of the knife, to leave you wracked with doubt."

"No," I sighed. "It wasn't a trick. I was face-to-face with her. I know."

"But——," she began.

"I *know!*"

"Then the killer's still out there," she whispered, shivering.

"Yes."

"I'm scared, Al."

"Me too."

"*Really* scared. Ellen was your wife and Nic was your lover. What if this guy's working his way through every woman you've been close to?"

"There are a few old girlfriends whose numbers I wouldn't mind giving him," I laughed, but she refused to see the funny side.

"I could be next," she said.

"Why? There's been nothing between us."

"Not yet." She leaned forward and kissed me. I pushed her away.

"What are you doing?" I snapped. "You just got through telling me I'm a jinx and now you—"

"That's why I'm scared," she interrupted, silencing me with a second kiss. "If we'd had something in the past, I could run. But what we've got is now and in the future. I can't run from that." She kissed me again.

"This shouldn't be happening," I sighed, returning her kisses. I felt one of her hands slide into my lap. I ran my fingers through her hair, then down to her breasts. "It's madness."

"I don't care," she gasped as my fingers tightened on her breasts. "I've been so frightened since Nic died, terrified every time a door swings open. When I read about your wife, do you know what my first reaction was? Thank God it wasn't me."

She shifted her weight. Undressing and caressing each other, we rolled, so I was underneath and she was on top.

"You could be signing your death warrant," I said, mouth dry as she peeled off her underwear.

"At least I won't die alone," she replied, lowering herself onto me, guiding me with one hand, digging into the flesh of my neck with the fingernails of the other.

There was no more talking for a long time after that.

She moved into my cramped apartment the next day. I wasn't sure I wanted this—there was something unhealthy about a love affair forged courtesy of a brace of murders—but found myself powerless to resist. As much as Priscilla needed me, I needed her more. I'd been going mad on my own, and without someone to cling to, I was most certainly doomed.

Ali found us together that afternoon. He walked in unannounced, as he usually did, and stopped when he spotted the beautiful naked woman by my side. He exited rapidly, ears burning, apologizing profusely. Just before he left, his head poked round the door for a sneak look at Priscilla. That produced my first genuine smile in a long time. I squeezed her tightly and cuddled up close, burying my face in her hair, trying not to compare it with Ellen's.

She didn't bring much with her—a small bag of clothes, underwear, shoes, cosmetics—but enough to make it clear this was more than a one-night stand. She also brought spirits and liqueurs. I didn't like having them in the apartment, or the way she left the tops open so they filled the rooms with their sickly-sweet scent, but I didn't say anything. She needed the drink, and I understood that. I'd just have to be stronger while she was around.

She slipped out to work every morning and returned as early as she could. We'd make love or talk or simply hold one another. Cook a late dinner, eat slowly, make love again. Most nights we didn't get to bed before two.

Bill was delighted. He thought Priscilla was the best thing that could have happened to me. He had dinner with us in the apartment a couple of times and we sat around talking, none of us making mention of Ellen or Nic.

One night, when conversation did turn to the murdered women, Priscilla blurted out the truth about Valerie Thomas. She'd been drinking a lot. Bill said something about being glad Valerie was dead. Priscilla snorted and said, "One down. Now we just have that fucking boyfriend to—"

She caught herself. Tried to backtrack. But it was too late. She caught me glaring at her, burst into tears and fled to the bathroom. A stunned Bill prevented me from going after her.

"Something you want to share with me, Al?"

Since there was no point trying to hide it any longer, I told him the truth about Valerie, her *god*, the boyfriend.

"Why didn't you tell me before?" He sounded more pained than outraged.

"It would have been my word against her confession."

"You know only too damn well which *I* would have believed," he growled.

I nodded. "I should have told you, even if I kept it quiet from the others. But…" I wasn't sure I could explain. "I want out of this, Bill. I'm sick of suspects, clues, twists, death. I want to drop the whole sorry sack of shit and pretend it never happened."

"Do you think you'll be allowed to?" he asked softly. "Do you think the bastard who killed Nic and Ellen will stop? Whatever his motives, he'll come after you, or Priscilla, or somebody else. I wish to God you'd never gotten involved in this mess, but you're in it now. The time to quit passed long ago. Drawing in on yourself like this serves no purpose. It only leaves you—and those close to you—open to attack."

"I don't care." I locked gazes with him and said it again for added effect. "I don't care. That's why I didn't tell you about Valerie, why I holed up. I don't have the energy to worry anymore. I can't fight any longer." Tears were rolling down my cheeks. "When they took Ellen, I went crazy. I was capable of anything. But then I confronted Valerie and saw the hate in her. Something snapped. I was ready to fight to the very end. Now it seems useless. So I'm walking away from it."

"But this isn't the right time to throw in the towel. You're vulnerable."

"Fuck it. If they want to kick me while I'm down, or kill me, let them."

"This isn't you speaking," he said sadly.

"It's me, Bill," I assured him. "What's left of me."

When he went, it was with a vow to carry on the investigation. He swore he wouldn't rest until the real culprit was brought to justice. He'd even bend the law if he had to. Snap it in two if that was required. It was the first time I'd heard him speak like that. I didn't like it, but if he wanted to waste his time chasing ghosts, let him. I was through trying to sort out other people's problems for them.

Priscilla apologized when she emerged. I told her not to worry, took her in my arms and we made love. And for the first time I realized how mechanical our lovemaking was.

I started going for walks while Priscilla was at work, long, punishing walks, during which I strove to clear my mind, concentrating on my lungs and leg muscles, oblivious to everything else.

Bill called a couple of times to say he was following leads. I lent him my notes and files, even material that was for Troop eyes only. I neither encouraged his investigation nor tried to dissuade him. As far as I was concerned, it was his life and he could do what he liked with it.

Frank got in touch, sounding me out. I said I was considering a return to work, but wanted more time to think about it. He never mentioned Ellen, Valerie or any of that, though I knew he must be frothing with questions.

I studied a calendar one morning and realized it had been almost two months since Nic met with her end, three and a half weeks since Ellen went the same way, and only—I had to count three times before I'd believe it— ten days since Priscilla moved in. Ten days! It felt like months. I wondered if time was moving as slowly for her as it was for me.

I returned from a walk to discover Priscilla sitting in the living room, look- ing troubled. She was tapping a small parcel on the table in front of her. I sensed danger. I almost turned tail and ran. But where would I go?

"Buy something?" I asked, closing the door.

"No. I mean, yes, I had a half day and I was shopping, which is why I'm home early. But my bags are in the bedroom. I got…" She stopped and pushed the parcel away. "Nice walk?"

"Lovely." I sat beside her and gave her a quick squeeze, eyes fixed on the box, which was wrapped in brown paper, something scrawled across the top.

"I ran into a blind beggar on my way back," she said, and the ice in my stomach spread. "He gave me that." She pointed at the box. "I thought it was a religious book. I started to tear it open. Then I saw the name and decided to leave it."

I studied the name. Block letters. AL JEERY. No address, just my name.

"Do you think it's a bomb?" Priscilla asked.

I smiled grimly. "I doubt it."

"Maybe we should call the bomb squad anyway, or take it to someone who knows about these things."

"*I* know. I learned about explosives in the Troops." A lie, but it calmed Priscilla. I picked up the box and shook it gently, listening intently, as if I could tell from the noise whether it was safe.

"It's not a bomb," I said, faking confidence.

"Thank God," she sighed, relaxing. She glanced at me and licked her lips. "Are you going to open it?"

I nodded. "But you'd better go to the bedroom and lock the door before I do."

"But you said—"

"I know. But it's as easy to be safe as sorry."

She half-rose, hesitated, then sat again in spite of her fear. "No. If you stay, I stay too."

I unwrapped the paper. It peeled away, revealing an unremarkable cardboard box. I handed the paper to Priscilla, who crumpled it up and held it in front of her lower face, as if it would protect her from the blast if there was one.

I ran my fingers around the join between the lid and the box—no trace of a wire. I thumbed up the section of the lid closest to me, lifted the other end a few inches, shifted the lid clear of the box and laid it on the table. Inside was a cloud of pink tissue.

"What is it?" Priscilla asked.

"Tissue," I told her, rubbing part of it between my thumb and index finger.

"Nothing more?" she frowned.

I studied the rosy stain on my finger, put it to my mouth and tasted blood. "There's more," I said quietly.

Parting the folds patiently, I burrowed through the layers of tissue, noting the way the pink hue darkened the deeper I went. Near the bottom, on a tiny silver tray, I uncovered the source of the blood—a severed human finger.

Priscilla moaned but I was less disturbed. When you've found a head hanging from your ceiling in the middle of the night, a lone finger isn't that much of a deal.

"Don't touch it," she pleaded as I leaned forward. I ignored her and picked it up by the tip. It was a white male's, wrinkled and blotched. Sliced clean through, just above where the first knuckle would have been. Still warm, so it had been amputated sometime that morning, maybe early afternoon.

There was a note on the tray, almost unreadable because of all the blood that had soaked into the paper. I had to hold it up and squint to decipher the words, and it fell apart as I was laying it back into the box.

"What did it say?" Priscilla asked.

"'Guess whose, Al m'boy.'" I turned the finger around on my palm, closed my own fingers over it and squeezed softly. The sly motherfuckers. I had thought that nothing could make me care or draw me back in. But as Bill had predicted, I was wrong. My tormentors knew exactly which strings to pull.

"What does that mean?" Priscilla asked.

I shook my head and lied. "I don't know."

"Who do you think it belongs to?" When I didn't answer, she pinched me and snapped, *Who?*"

I relaxed my grip and revealed the finger. My hand was stained with blood. In all the red, it could have been anybody's. But I had no doubts. I propped the finger on the table so it was standing vertically, then said sickly, "It's Bill's."

part six

"we could all be dead by then"

24

Guess whose, Al m'boy.

     The killer's insight puzzled and troubled me. How did he know of my father's ironic term of endearment? Nobody had heard him call me that. For the briefest of moments I thought Wami had sent the finger, that he'd been toying with me all along. Then I recalled the blade at his throat. Offering himself to me could have been a deadly bluff, but I didn't think so. Paucar Wami was many dreadful things but he wasn't my enemy.

The killer's identity would come later. Right now there was the finger to ID. I knew it was Bill's, but the Troop in me needed to be convinced. If Allegro Jinks could be passed off as Paucar Wami, a detached digit could easily be substituted for one of Bill Casey's. There was no answer when I called him, and nobody at the station had seen him in a couple of days, but that hardly constituted proof.

I could have gone to Party Central with the finger, but I didn't want to involve The Cardinal. Instead I rang the Fridge and asked for Dr. Sines's home address.

Sines was watching TV with his wife when I arrived. His wife answered the door and scowled when I asked to see her husband. "Is this to do with work?"

"Yes, ma'am."

"You people never give him a break," she muttered, calling him to the door. He looked even less happy to see me than his wife had been.

"This better be important," he growled, not inviting me in.

"It's personal, Dr. Sines," I said, remembering to address him formally. "May I come in?"

"Can't it wait?"

"No, sir."

He grumbled some curses, then beckoned me in, but didn't lead me beyond the front hall. "Make it quick," he snapped and I produced the finger, still on its silver tray, though now transferred from the box to a small plastic bag. He studied it in silence, then said drily, "I think it's a finger."

I chuckled obligingly. "I was hoping you could tell me whose."

"Offhand, I couldn't." He cracked up.

I grinned, finding it harder to shape my mouth into a smile this time. "Good one."

He wiped a few tears of mirth from his eyes. "Gallows humor. You need it to get by in a job like mine." He got serious. "Any idea who the owner is?"

"Yes, but I'd rather not say."

"It would be quicker if you did."

"Regardless…"

"As you wish. Care to tell me why you brought it here, tonight, instead of down to the Fridge tomorrow?"

"I don't want anyone connecting it to me."

"I smell espionage. May I have the finger?" I handed it over. "You realize I must note where it came from? I can't waltz in and pretend I found it on my way to work."

"Why not?"

"You've got gold clearance—congratulations on the promotion—but a report must be filed, for The Cardinal. It would mean my job if I took your side against his and was subsequently discovered."

I nodded understandingly, then asked if he'd heard about my wife. He said he had and offered his condolences.

"I'd appreciate your assistance more."

"You don't understand," he retorted. "There are rules and procedures. I can't—"

"You can," I interrupted. "You guys are a law unto yourselves, don't try telling me otherwise. You take bodies as you please, do with them as you wish, and everyone turns a blind eye."

"That's different. Our superiors grant us a certain amount of leeway to get the best out of us. But that doesn't run to bucking the chain of command, to falsifying reports or sneaking in body parts."

"You could do it if you wanted," I pressed.

"Probably, but that's not the—"

"You won't get into trouble," I said quickly. "All I want you to do is identify who the finger comes from."

He shook his head. "Why should I put my neck on the line for you?"

It was a fair question, for which I had no ready answer.

"If your wife had been killed—," I began.

"—I'd be mad as hell, just like you. But my wife's alive and well, in no kind of danger whatsoever. I'd like to keep her that way."

I thought about threatening him but he'd have gone to The Cardinal if I did.

"Sorry for disturbing you," I said and started for the door.

"That's it?" he asked, startled. "You're not going to twist my arm?"

"No."

"Wait." He held out the bagged finger. "You forgot this." I reached for the bag but he didn't hand it over. Instead he turned it around and examined the base. "A clean cut. Either an extremely sharp blade or an electrical implement." I'd figured as much myself, but said nothing. "The smallest finger of the left hand. This ties in with your wife's death?" I nodded. "How?"

"I'd rather not say."

He hesitated. I could see fear in his eyes but also professional pride. The human side of him wanted nothing to do with this, but his medical half was fascinated. It became a question of which would win out—self-preservation or curiosity.

"Can you tell me anything about where you think it came from?" he asked.

"I think it comes from a cop."

"That should be simple enough to check. Assuming one was inclined to…" He tossed it about in silence, then said, "A man in his mid-forties was dropped off with us last night, unidentified. I could take a print of his little finger, swap it for this one and run some tests. I don't make a habit of turning up for work on my day off but it's not unheard of."

He was nervous but excited. "OK. Here's what I'll do. I'll run the print of your finger against the police personnel database. If I make a match, fine. If I don't, I go no further. Is that acceptable?"

"Great," I smiled.

"But if somebody challenges me, I'll 'fess up."

I frowned—that wasn't so great.

"It's my best offer," Sines warned. "Nobody will inquire unless they're already suspicious, so if I have to tell the truth, it will be to someone who's onto you anyway."

"That's reasonable," I agreed.

"I'll go now," Sines said, pocketing the finger. "You know the abandoned car plant three blocks west of the Fridge? Wait for me in the showroom there. You can get in by the side door. I shouldn't be more than a couple of hours, unless I get detained. If I'm not there by"—he checked his watch—"eleven, go home and I'll be in contact in the morning."

"I can't tell you how much—," I started to thank him, but he cut in.

"Stuff it. I need my head examined, getting mixed up in something like this. If you say anything else, you might snap me around to my senses."

I let myself out without a murmur.

I faced a long wait at the car plant. It was nearly ten past eleven when he turned up. I was getting ready to leave.

"Caught you," he gasped. There was no light inside the room, but it was illuminated by the streetlamps. Sines pulled a pristine camp bed out from under a litter of papers and sat.

"A lot of guys at work use this place for making out," he explained when I looked at him curiously. "I was here a few times myself in my courting days."

"You're late," I noted. "Any trouble?"

"No. Just didn't want to appear too anxious to leave."

"Did you make a match?"

He nodded and came straight out with it. "Bill Casey." I lowered my head and sighed. "It's what you expected?"

"Yes."

"You don't look happy."

"I hoped I was wrong."

"Sorry." He handed the finger back. It was stained with ink.

"You didn't get rid of it?" I asked.

"You didn't ask me to."

He'd ditched the tray. I tossed Bill's finger into the air and caught it. "Is it any good now? I mean, could it be sewn back on?"

"No."

"You're sure?"

He didn't bother to repeat himself. "I think I got away with it. Nobody asked any questions. But if The Cardinal or one of his men calls tomorrow and starts quizzing me…"

"Fine." I started for the door.

"If it's any consolation," he called after me, "he was alive when the finger was amputated."

I halted in the doorway. "No," I said softly. "That doesn't console me at all." Then I went home to tell Priscilla.

We were awake most of the night. Priscilla thought Bill was dead and sobbed for him at regular intervals, but I was sure he hadn't been killed. My tormentors hadn't hesitated to mock me with the bodies of my dearly beloved before, so why stop now? It suited them to keep Bill alive, otherwise they'd have sent more than his finger. Perhaps they thought Bill's death would drive me deeper into depression, whereas the possibility of being able to rescue him might draw me back into the game. If that *was* their plan, they knew me at least as well as I knew myself.

At one stage Priscilla pleaded with me to flee the city with her. She was afraid to be parted from me, sure the killers would come after *her*. She clung to me, wept and said I couldn't leave her on her own. I stroked her softly and said I had no choice. She started to argue. Looked into my eyes. Fell silent.

In the early hours of the morning she asked how I was going to track Bill.

"By going after Ellen's killer, like I should have when I finished with Valerie. When I find that bastard, I'll find Bill."

"You sound confident," she remarked.

"His kidnapper *wants* me to find him. Bill would have been killed if the plan was just to hurt me. I'm being lured into a trap."

"Then you can't go after him!"

"I have to. Bill will be killed for certain if I don't. At least this way he has a chance."

When it was time to leave, she again begged me to stay. I told her gently but firmly that I couldn't. When she persisted and said she was scared, I said, "Do you know how to use a gun?" She sobered up and nodded. I passed her my .45. "Stay here. Don't go out. If anybody comes to the door, start firing."

"I've only shot targets before," she said, handling the gun nervously. "I don't know if I could shoot a person."

"You'd better hope that you can, or you'll end up like Nic and Ellen," I answered grimly, then left her and went hunting.

The lover was the link. One person connected Nic, Ziegler, Valerie and Ellen. When I found him, I'd have my killer. I could forget about Jinks, Breton Furst and the rest. All I needed was the lover.

I'd already failed to get to him through Nic. And I didn't think anything would come of investigating Valerie's or Ziegler's backgrounds—since they'd been in league with the bastard, they'd have covered their tracks, sly snakes that they were.

Ellen was the key. She was the only innocent. She'd been coy about revealing her lover's name, but the chances were that *somebody* knew who she'd been seeing, a friend she'd spoken to, a colleague who'd overheard her talking on the phone, a waiter who'd seen her with her beau in tow. That person might take a lot of finding, but I had time on my hands and hate in my heart. I'd root them out in the end.

I began with her family. Called Bob, Deborah and a few others. Discussed the funeral and wake, gradually working the conversation around to

Ellen's last few weeks. I mentioned to each that I thought she'd been seeing someone. A couple said that she'd dropped hints about a new lover, but none knew anything about him. Ellen had been as tight-lipped with her family as she'd been with me.

Before moving on to her friends, I rang Party Central and asked if I could meet The Cardinal. I thought it would be good to utilize his army of informants. Maybe one of them had seen Bill or knew of his whereabouts. If they didn't, they could be told to keep their eyes and ears open for signs of him. But The Cardinal couldn't be reached. His secretary promised to arrange a meeting as soon as possible, but it wouldn't be today. Possibly tomorrow. I had no choice but to settle for that.

I called as many of Ellen's friends as I could think of. Most were no friends of mine—many thought Ellen had married beneath herself when she hitched up with me, and they were right—and normally they wouldn't have taken my call. But, given the grisly circumstances, they put aside their dislike and spared me a few minutes of their time.

As with her family, a few were aware that she'd been dating, but nobody knew a thing about him. The phone conversations weren't an entire washout—her older friends passed on the names of newer acquaintances—but I found no leads of substance.

The last of her friends to see her alive was a woman called Ama Situwa. I'd never met her—she was somebody Ellen had befriended recently—and I only got her name through one of the others. She sounded nice on the phone. Turned out she was the daughter of the guy who ran Cafran's restaurant. Small world.

Ama had run into Ellen in the lounge of the Skylight the night before her murder. She was there for a birthday party, saw Ellen at the bar with another woman and went to say hello. Ellen greeted her warmly and said they were waiting for dates. Ama made a joke about men always being late and invited them to Cafran's later if they were at a loose end—the birthday gang was moving back there after the Skylight. Ellen said they'd drop by if the men failed to show, and that had been that.

"Any idea who the other lady was?" I asked.

"No. I didn't know many of Ellen's friends."

I'd have to try and find her companion—she might know the name of the guy Ellen was supposed to meet. "Can I come around sometime and discuss this with you?" I asked.

"Sure," Ama said. "I'd be happy to help. It was terrible, what happened. Ellen was a lovely person."

"Yes," I said hollowly. "She was."

I dropped by the Skylight and questioned the staff, asking if they'd noticed Ellen in the bar that night. Negative answers all around. I paid special attention to the Troops—since the room hadn't been signed for, Ellen might have been sneaked in, perhaps past a bribed guard—but they swore they knew nothing. More than one told me that they'd been more alert since the Nicola Hornyak fuckup. Frank was coming down hard on shirkers and several soldiers had already been replaced.

While I was there I asked after Valerie Thomas, on the off chance that I might stumble across a lead. Nobody knew much about her. She'd worked at the Skylight a long time but had never gone out with the girls or attended a staff event.

"She was creepy," one workmate opined. "Like Bette Davis in that movie, the one where she feeds her sister a rat?"

"She worked hard," an assistant manager assured me. "I was sorry to see her go. Never took anything, not even a sugar cube. Honest, loyal, trustworthy. An ideal employee if you exclude the two dead customers."

"Men in her life? She didn't mention any."

"Valerie never seemed keen on men. She hadn't much time for them. Wouldn't surprise me if she'd been a lesbo."

"*Valerie*? With a *man*? I don't think so!"

It was late when I finished at the Skylight. I decided to give Ellen's circle of friends a rest. I still had plenty of names to work through, and more would probably crop up in the course of my inquiries, but they could wait till morning. I called Priscilla to check that she was all right— as I had several times throughout the day—and told her I'd be a while, to go to bed and get some sleep. She agreed, but only if I promised to wake her when I got home.

Next I rang Paucar Wami.

My father was surprised to hear from me but agreed to meet, even though I wouldn't tell him what it was about. He wanted to come to my place but I quickly put paid to that suggestion—I didn't want him any-where near Priscilla. I asked if he could meet me at the site of the Manco Capac statue instead. We fixed an hour, I nipped into a burger bar for a bite, then it was rendezvous time.

The site was deserted apart from a few guards who were easy to dodge. I looked for blind men but there weren't any on parade. I stopped by the foot of the statue and waited for Wami. I'd been there a few minutes when a small pebble dropped on my head. I scratched my crown and moved aside, but moments later another fell. I glanced up and there was the tat-tooed face, grinning down at me.

"You should choose your ground more carefully, Al m'boy. What if I had meant you mischief?"

I climbed up to join him. I looked for the trapdoor when I made the platform but the foundations had been built upon since I was last here. The entrance to the underworld was now sealed off.

"The builders have been busy," Wami noted. He was dressed in black from head to toe. Except for the snakes, he appeared invisible against the dark backdrop of the night sky.

"They're not the only ones," I said, then told him about Valerie's con-fession and what had happened since. The snakes on his face appeared to flicker angrily when I mentioned the note with the finger, but he said nothing.

"And now they have Bill," I concluded.

Wami scowled. "I agree with you—they have kept him alive to tempt you back into the game. But can you save him or is he doomed whatever you do?"

"Probably doomed," I sighed, "but I have to try. I'm dancing to their tune, but what else can I do? If I give up on Bill, he's finished. I'll be getting fingers, toes and other parts in the mail from here till doomsday."

"A despicable ploy," Wami chuckled. "I too have sent a few men home to their loved ones in such a manner. It never fails to elicit mad screams and illogical behavior. You should write off Bill Casey."

"I can't do that," I said flatly.

"No," he agreed with a wry smile. "You lack the detached killer's in-stinct which would make life much simpler. So, what *can* you do?"

"Go on looking for Ellen's lover. Keep asking questions. Scour the streets. Raid every den in town."

"You will be an old man by the time you are finished."

"You know a better way?"

"Go after the blind men," he suggested. "Drop your search for your friend and call their bluff. Put out word that if he is not returned immediately, you will quit this city."

"You think the *villacs* have him?"

"If not, they can get him."

I thought about it, then shook my head. "They wouldn't buy it."

"They might. They value you highly, judging by your previous encounter. If you threaten to walk, they might cave in and deliver, if not the answers you seek, at least the friend you wish to save."

"And if they don't? I just leave?" He nodded. "No. I won't gamble with Bill's life."

"It is your best hope of saving him."

"I don't agree."

"Very well," he sniffed. "I have offered my advice. If you ignore it, you must continue as you are, ineffective as your methods have so far proved."

He slipped toward the ladder.

"I need your help," I said quietly as he was about to drop out of sight. He stared at me curiously. "You know more about this city's dark heart than anyone. You can go places no other can go. If I fail to get a fix on Ellen's lover, I'll have to track down Bill the hard way. I'll need you for that."

"Asking your pappy for help, Al m'boy?" he chortled.

"I need you," I said again.

"But you do not *want* me." He shrugged. "Not that it matters. Filial love was never high on my list of priorities."

"You'll help?"

"I know Bill Casey," he muttered and his face creased. "There is...history between us."

I stared incomprehensively. "He never said he knew you."

"It is not the sort of history one readily shares." His expression cleared. "I would save him if I could. Call me if all else fails and I will help. In the meantime I will keep my ear to the ground and let you know if I hear of anything."

"Thanks." I tried to sound grateful.

"I hope you realize my aid does not come free," he said. "My time is precious. I have gone out of my way to assist you. When the day comes for you to repay the debt, I hope you remember."

"What do you want?" I asked, an icy chill snaking down my spine.

"I always dreamed of one of my sons following in my footsteps..."

"Bullshit," I laughed.

"What ungrateful creatures the young can be," he moaned, but the shine of his grinning teeth betrayed him. "You are right, of course—your actions once I flee this mortal shell matter as much to me as those of a slug. However, it would amuse me to think of you devoting your life to the cause espoused by your demon of a pappy."

"Forget it," I snapped. "I've been an executioner, but I was following orders. I could never kill for kicks or profit."

"Not even to save Bill Casey?"

I shook my head uncertainly. "I couldn't."

"You killed for The Cardinal. Why not for Bill?"

"That was different. It was business. I'm not a killer."

"Perhaps," Wami smiled. "Or perhaps you are, but have not yet realized it."

He left me with that thought, vanishing down the ladder like a spider, back to his web of a city.

I woke Priscilla when I got home and told her about my day (omitting the encounter with Wami). I didn't think I'd be able to sleep—on top of my other worries, I now had my debt to Wami to consider—but I was exhausted. I passed out while telling Priscilla about my conversation with Ama Situwa and didn't wake till the sun was high in the sky.

Priscilla cooked a huge breakfast. By the end of it I felt like sitting in a chair all day to vegetate. But there was work to be done, people to be interviewed, and though Priscilla again pleaded with me not to leave her, I was soon back on the streets.

I called several of those I'd talked to yesterday, in light of my conversation with Ama, and asked if they'd been in the Skylight with Ellen the night before her murder. Nobody had been, though a few had seen her earlier that day. I thanked them for taking my call, then started on fresh contacts.

I concentrated on work colleagues. I didn't know many people from Preston's, the company she worked for, and those I spoke to weren't as forthcoming as her friends. Some questioned my identity and wanted to know how they could be sure I was who I claimed to be. I offered to drop by and conduct my inquiries in person but the manager who dealt with me was set against that—yes, Miss Fraser had been a valued employee and they regretted her demise, but life went on and they didn't want strangers turning up at will, interrupting their routines.

Ellen had always said she worked for the most uptight employers in the city. Now I knew she hadn't been kidding. I convinced some of her less icy colleagues to meet me that night for drinks, and a few more said they might fit me into their schedules later in the week, but all claimed to know nothing of Ellen's personal life or the men she'd dated.

During one of the breaks I allowed myself between calls, my cell phone rang. One of The Cardinal's secretaries. The Great One was willing to meet me if I got over there in a hurry, but it would have to be brief.

Party Central was a hive of frenzied activity when I arrived. Teams of Troops were gathering in the yard, three or four per group, then setting out armed to the armpits. Frank was coordinating things. During a quiet moment I asked what was going on.

"Manhunt," he snapped, clutching a clipboard as if his life depended on it. "That bastard Capac Raimi."

"The Cardinal's golden boy?" I recalled Frank's previous outburst about the young pretender to the throne.

"They got into a fight last night. We could have taken care of him then, but The Cardinal—in that glorious, fucked-up way of his—let him go. Vincent Carell and a few others ran into him later. He took them out."

"Vincent's dead?" The news didn't disturb me—we weren't friends—but I was startled. Close confidantes of The Cardinal and Ford Tasso hardly ever met with sticky ends, unless they ran afoul of their masters.

"Dead as disco," Frank said without humor.

"On the off chance that I see him, what are the orders? Shoot on sight or bring him in?"

"Officially, bring him in. Off the record, blow the fucker away. There'll be shit to face if you do, but I'll back you up, even if it means my job."

Checking in my shoes and socks downstairs, I proceeded to the fifteenth floor. The halls were buzzing with Troops and other underlings. It took a while to shove through them and make it to The Cardinal's inner sanctuary. His secretary held me up until he was free. About twenty minutes later, a posse of soldiers spilled out of his room and I was ushered in.

The Cardinal was sitting at his desk, fiddling with a puppet. As I got closer I realized Frank hadn't been kidding when he said the boss had been in a fight—his face was a mess.

"You look like hell," I noted, taking a seat.

He managed a weak smile. "You should see the other guy," he chuckled, then grimaced and clutched his sides. "It hurts when I laugh but that's nothing to what it's like when I piss. I'm getting old, Al. Time was, I'd have taken a beating like this in my stride. Now I feel like a lump of shit that's been simmering on low for a couple of hours." He let the puppet flop to the floor and massaged the back of his neck.

"Enough of my complaints," he boomed. "You didn't come here to listen to an old fart moaning about himself. What can I do for you?"

I told him about Bill, Valerie, the *villacs*. I didn't run him through the entire story—time was short—but I filled him in on the key facts.

"It doesn't surprise me," he grunted when I'd finished. "About the woman lying to protect another, I mean, or those blind priests being involved. So, what can I do to help?"

"Set your people after him. Maybe one of your informants knows who kidnapped him, or can find out. Spread the word that you don't want him harmed. Demand his safe return."

"What makes you think his abductors will pay attention to me?"

"It's worth a try."

"Perhaps. But I'm too busy to deploy my agents. I'll need a day or two, perhaps a week. My business with Mr. Raimi should have reached a conclusion by then. Once that's done and dusted, I and mine are at your service."

"A week's too long. He could be dead by then."

"We could all be dead by then," The Cardinal replied. "My hands are tied. I cannot…" He hesitated. "You have heard the rumors that I've been grooming Mr. Raimi to succeed me?"

"Yes."

"What I tell you now stays between us. You don't tell *anyone*. Understand?"

I nodded wordlessly.

He took a deep breath, then locked gazes with me. "I'm dying. A brain tumor. I learned of it a year ago. By rights I should be dead already, but I fought like a tiger and earned an extra few months. I've three or four weeks to go, but any day now I'll start to slide. My vision will fade first. I'll lose my mental faculties soon after. I'll spend the last week or two in a coma."

He smiled bitterly and waited for me to respond. I couldn't. I'd always thought The Cardinal would go on forever. It never occurred to me that he was mortal like the rest of us, subject to the same random laws of life and death.

"Say something," he snarled.

"I don't know what to say. I…Are you certain?"

"Sure as shit. You're the only person who knows, bar my doctors. I've even kept Mr. Tasso in the dark. If word had spread, this last year would have been hell. I'd have spent it struggling to hold things together. You know what vultures are like when they scent death."

"Why are you telling me?" I asked, bewildered.

"I want you to understand." He leaned forward. "I've lived a life of sin and corruption. I suffer from no illusions—if there's a hell, I'm heading there by express train. I have nothing to look forward to. I never had, not since killing my first man when I was still a child. All I have is this empire. I've devoted myself to it, and if it dies with me, my entire existence will have been for nothing.

"I've groomed heirs in the past, to little avail. Capac Raimi is my last throw of the dice. If he fails, my life is a failure. That's why I didn't kill him for doing this to me." He tapped his face. "Why I'm still feeding him rope and praying that he doesn't hang himself with it. Why I'm clinging to hope rather than giving myself over to despair."

"But what does any of that have to do with *me*?"

The Cardinal covered his eyes with the middle three fingers of both hands.

"The *villacs*?" I frowned.

"If Capac Raimi survives the next seventy-two hours and proves himself worthy of filling my shoes, he'll need those meddlers. They're more influential than you can imagine, and without their assistance, no man can run this city. I can't afford to piss them off at this delicate stage.

"In a few days, matters will have been resolved. Capac Raimi will have made his stand or fallen. Either way, I'll be free to act, and then—assuming my tumor doesn't kick in and turn me into a fruitcake—I'll do all I can for you. We'll go after your tormentors, find your friend, put everything right that can be put right. Until then, I must be neutral."

I wasn't sure what to make of The Cardinal's extraordinary pledge, but there was no mistaking his earnestness. If he'd been playing with me before, he wasn't any longer.

"And in the meantime?" I asked quietly.

"Go about your business. If you find the killer, do with him as you wish. If not, I'll get in touch and we'll make plans."

His secretary paged him and said Ford Tasso was on his way up. He thanked her and said she should send him straight in when he arrived.

"I have to bid you farewell. Mr. Tasso has not taken his son's death well. If I can't calm him down, he might do something silly when and if young Raimi turns up again."

"His son?" I asked.

"Vincent Carell. Ford Tasso was his father. You didn't know?"

"No."

"I didn't realize the secret had been so well kept. That's why we went out of our way to overlook his deficiencies. In all honesty," he said in a tone of strictest confidence, "his death isn't too much of a blow. I'm only surprised the fool survived this long. He won't be missed. Mr. Tasso will realize that once he's had time to think about it. He'd better—if Raimi comes through, he'll be the new boss. Wouldn't do to have bad blood between them."

"You really think Tasso would serve under the man who killed his son?"

"Ford Tasso was born to serve," The Cardinal said, then led me to the door.

I would see him once more from afar, two nights later, after he fell to his death, but this was our last encounter. As I made my way downstairs to collect my shoes, I brooded on how healthy he looked for a man on his last legs, and found myself wondering if hell was big enough to accommodate both Ferdinand Dorak and the First of the Fallen, and if it wasn't, which of the two would be forced out. Old Nick was a mighty foe, but I couldn't see The Cardinal playing second fiddle to anyone. The Devil might be about to get his ass kicked. I almost wished I could be there to see it.

25

I ended up exploring more blind alleys on Tuesday night and Wednesday morning. Ellen's workmates proved as clueless as I'd suspected. None knew anything of her love life. I showed them photographs of Valerie, Ziegler and Nick, along with pictures of everyone else associated with the investigation, in case one would jog somebody's memory, but although several recognized the now infamous Miss Thomas, nobody could connect any of the suspects to Ellen.

Wednesday afternoon, following an uninformative interview with one of Ellen's friends, I realized I was close to Cafran's and called in to have a few words with Ama Situwa, to see if she could tell me anything about Ellen's dinner companion. I guessed it had been Valerie in the Skylight bar with Ellen, but figured I should confirm it.

It was quiet when I arrived and a bored-looking waiter pointed to Ama. She was laying cutlery on one of the tables. The silverware jangled loudly in her hands, which shook nervously. This impression was reinforced when I tapped her on the shoulder and she jumped.

"Easy," I said as she turned, brandishing one of the knives. "I come in peace."

"Then why are you sneaking up on people?" she snapped.

"Didn't mean to." I stuck out a hand. "I'm Al Jeery. I called about Ellen?"

Her face relaxed into a warm grin. "Sorry for biting." She laid the cutlery down in a bundle. "Shall we go through to the kitchen? We can talk in private there."

I followed her into the back. Ama found a quiet spot and pulled up a couple of stools. She asked if I'd like anything to eat. I said I didn't want to impose.

"So," she smiled. "What would you like to know?"

"You saw Ellen in the Skylight the night before her murder?"

"Yes."

"Any idea of the time?"

"After nine, maybe a quarter past."

"She was with another woman?"

"Yes. They were waiting for dates."

"Do you know if they were going on together from there or if they were planning to separate?"

"I've no idea. The bar was noisy, I'd had a few drinks. We didn't say much."

"The other woman—could you describe her?"

"White. Pretty. Well dressed." She shrugged. "I wasn't paying attention. I might recognize her if I saw her again, but..."

"No problem." I forced the smile I'd been making good use of recently. "If you can spare the time, I'd like you to look at some photos."

"Sure."

I took out the envelope, shook a few snapshots onto the table and shifted through the pile, lining them up. "If you see anyone you know, please let me..."

She wasn't listening. Her eyes had focused on a picture and her lips were pursed. She leaned her head sideways, reached for the photo, stopped. "May I?"

"By all means," I told her, heart starting to pound.

I watched with sick fascination as she picked up the photo and studied it. She sorted through the rest of the pile until she found another.

"This woman...I can't say for sure—it was dark and I didn't get that good a look—but I think this is the woman I saw with Ellen."

"It can't be," I said shakily. "You're mistaken."

"Maybe, but it sure looks like her."

I stared at the photos in her hand and suddenly, terribly, it made sense.

"Thank you," I muttered, sliding off the stool, almost tumbling to the floor.

"Are you all right?" she asked, reaching out to steady me.

"I'll be fine. Thanks. I have to leave now. You've been very helpful. Thank—"

I started for the door.

"Mr. Jeery—your photographs."

"Keep them. I don't...Goodbye."

I rushed out of the restaurant and fell to the pavement, panting, forcing back bile. I raised a hand and watched it shake like crazy. Gradually, as minutes passed, the shaking subsided and I breathed normally. When I felt steady, I stood, fetched my bike and pushed it along for a while, collecting my thoughts.

I knew who the link was. The lover. The pieces fell into place neatly in retrospect. Ellen saying she might surprise me. The porter in the Skylight who said Valerie Thomas could be a lesbo. Priscilla and Nic tricking together, closer than ordinary friends. Ellen laughing—a wedding wouldn't be appropriate.

So obvious. Hard to believe it had taken me this long to figure it out. I didn't know the motive, but that would come. One short ride and all the answers would be at my fingertips. I wouldn't even have to search. I knew exactly where to find the monster.

I climbed on my bike and started pedaling, slowly at first, then faster, furiously, till I was flying, a hurricane on two wheels, destination— home.

Ali was bagging bagels as I started up the stairs. I retraced my steps. He burst into a smile when I entered. "Hello, my friend!" he greeted me, emerging from behind the counter to pump my hand. "Back on your feet and hungry again? I can guess what you are after. Salmon and cream cheese, yes?"

"No," I said softly.

"The new lady in your life has changed you," he chuckled. "An occupational hazard of love, yes?"

I cleared my throat. "You should shut up shop for a while."

He frowned. "Is this a joke, my friend?"

I shook my head. "Go for a walk and don't come back for a couple of hours."

Ali stared at me. "You know I cannot desert my post."

"You're not a soldier, Ali."

"Still…"

"Trust me." I grasped his shoulder and squeezed softly. "You don't want to be here. You don't want to get involved."

His eyes swiveled upward, as if he could see through the ceiling. When he looked back at me, he wasn't any the wiser, but he nodded. He didn't know what I was going to do, but he knew I wouldn't ask him to leave unless it was bad.

"I will go for a walk," he decided. "I could do with the exercise, yes?"

I clapped his back and helped him lock up the store.

"I will be seeing you soon?" he asked as I resumed my climb.

"Maybe," I lied.

As I turned the key, I remembered I had left my gun with Priscilla. I glanced at my feet, collected my wits, opened the door. "I'm back!" I called out.

"You're home early," she welcomed me, stepping through from the kitchen. She stood on her tiptoes for a kiss. I took her in my arms and obliged. She squinted at me, puzzled, when I let go abruptly.

"You look very enigmatic," she remarked. "What's up?"

"I've got a lead." I gazed around the apartment, searching for the gun. "I have to go out again. Can I have my gun back? I might need it."

"You think you've found the killer?" she asked, a slight tremor to her voice.

"No, just a lead. I probably won't need the gun, but if you don't mind letting me have it for a while…"

"Of course not. It's in the kitchen. Wait here and I'll fetch it." She trotted off like a lamb. Good enough to eat. She came back moments later and pressed the pistol into my hand.

"Thanks," I said, holding it by the barrel.

"So, where are you——?" she began.

I slammed the butt of the gun into her face, smashing her nose. She reeled away, stunned. I followed after her and clubbed the back of her head. She fell to the floor, where I pinned her and cuffed her wrists behind her waist. Then I turned her over.

I'd been expecting a torrent of abuse but she only laughed at me, spitting blood out the side of her mouth.

"You found out!" she howled gleefully.

"Bitch!" I slapped her face with the gun. "Murdering whore!" Grabbed her hair and yanked her head forward, ramming the gun up under her chin. *"Why?"*

"Why not?" she giggled, then added as I started to shake, "Get a grip. You'll topple over from a heart attack if you carry on like this. Deep breaths, lover."

I sat back and regarded her contemptuously. "You killed Nic and Ellen?"

"Guilty. Valerie finished off Nic, but I did most of the damage. I handled Ellen on my own. She was easier. Weaker."

"You were their lover. Valerie, Nic, Ellen. You fucked them and killed them."

"It wasn't hard. Even Ellen. She'd never been with a woman before, but once I set my tongue in action, she lapped it up." A wicked chuckle. "So to speak."

I grinned in spite of myself, the grin of a lion with a keeper trapped in its cage. "You played me for a fool," I whispered. "I was suspicious of you at the start, but you convinced me of your innocence. I cut you out of the investigation. Took you into my life, my bed, my apartment, and never guessed, not once."

She smirked. "Don't be too hard on yourself. I did a bit of acting in my earlier days. Could have gone into the movies if Daddy hadn't been so set against it. But I never gave a performance this good. This was my *pièce de résistance.*"

"Why waste it on me?" I asked.

"Why not?" she replied again.

"It's as simple as that? You picked my name out of a book?"

"Not quite. I was following orders."

"Whose?"

"The sun god's."

I cocked the gun. "Don't fuck with me," I growled.

"I'm through fucking," she said. "Nic was a sacrifice. She knew what was up. She didn't know *she* was to be killed, but once things got under way she played along, making the most of a bad lot. She always was a good sport."

"Ziegler said he didn't know she was going to be murdered."

"He didn't. We brought Rudi along to read the necessary passages. When he went home, Jinks and I carved her up and carted her to the Skylight. I thought she was dead, but she was still alive when Valerie checked later. Not for long though." She sang the last line.

"You killed Nic to appease a fucking sun god," I muttered, thinking quickly. "But why leave the body at the Skylight?"

"Orders."

"The sun god's?"

"Yes."

"Did he tell you to fuck up my life as well?"

"Sure did."

"You've got a direct line to him?" I sneered.

"He spoke to me through his earthly agent. Told me to spin a web and draw you in. I don't know why he bothered with a sap like you, but you don't question the god of the sun. You obey his word or burn."

"Did he tell you to kill Ellen?"

"Yes. But through his priests this time. I ran into Ellen a couple of days after our encounter in Cafran's. An impartial observer might say it was coincidence, but I'm sure it was destiny. I saw she was attracted to me and lured her on. I told my agent and suggested killing her but he vetoed the idea. Then the *villacs* said to proceed. I'm not sure how they knew about us, but I was glad they did. I got a real buzz out of killing her."

The priests had told a half-truth when I met them in the underground cavern—they hadn't murdered Ellen directly, but they had sanctioned it. I'd make the bastards pay if I could.

"Why kill Ellen?" I asked.

"To destroy you. The *villacs* said it was important. I don't know why. I just followed orders and used my initiative when the opportunity arose." She started humming.

"You're crazy as a coyote," I muttered.

"Who are you to judge?" she retorted. "What do you think you look like to the god of the sun? Have you any idea how insignificant you are? How tiny? How——"

I gagged her. I'd heard all I needed to hear. There was still Bill to ask about but that could come later, when I'd loosened her lips. Right now I wanted to focus on the payback. I thought of all the tools in the apartment that I could use. I had a small Bunsen burner. A hacksaw. Pliers. A hammer. A drill. Lots of knives.

Once I'd gathered my implements, I laid them on the floor where she could see them. There was fear in her eyes, which excited me. Unlike Valerie, she hadn't inured herself to pain. She could be hurt.

I took the smallest finger of her left hand—the same digit she'd cut off Bill—and wedged it between the pliers. I gave a gentle squeeze and her body stiffened as she yelped into the gag. I stood there a moment and thought about what I was doing. Could I justify this? Revenge was one thing, but torture? Could I inflict pain on a woman I'd thought I might be in love with less than an hour ago?

I thought about Paucar Wami and the tainted blood running through my veins. Ellen in the Skylight, cut to ribbons, short life cruelly ended, hair plastered across the pillows.

My hands tightened. I saw the flesh of her finger start to whiten. A thin stream of blood trickled from the cut. She was made of weak stuff. One good wrench and the finger would be off. One sudden burst of energy and…

I let the pliers drop. Seconds later I dropped beside them. Tears rolled down my cheeks and my chest heaved with sobs.

I couldn't do it. I had every reason to, but something held me back and wouldn't let me take the last, damning step that would separate me from all that had once defined my humanity.

I removed the gag from Priscilla's mouth.

"Coward," she laughed.

"Yes," I agreed sadly. "I am."

"I thought you meant business. I should have known better. You're a waste of flesh. What sort of man are you, that you can't take it upon yourself to avenge the murdered love of your life?"

"Who said I won't avenge her?" I tapped the barrel of the gun. "I might not be able to torture, but I can kill."

"Any fool can kill. You might as well leave me for the chair if that's all you're going to do. If you were a real man, you'd torment me the way I tormented Ellen. You should have seen the way she jerked and—"

"I don't want to hear it. I took the gag off so you could make your peace with your god. I don't know if an afterlife awaits, if you believe in one or not—"

"I do," she assured me. "I do."

"—But if you want to depart this world with as clear a conscience as possible, tell me what happened to Bill, where I can find him, who your sun god's *agent* is."

"Al," she tutted. "You don't go looking for one with the power of the sun—*he* finds *you*."

"Even so. Humor me."

"You won't like it," she mocked. "Ignorance is bliss. You'll hate it if you make me tell."

"Leave me to worry about that. Who is he?"

She let out a fake sigh. "Lean close and I'll whisper his name in your ear."

I expected her to spit or bite my lobe, but she had something far more effective in mind—the truth.

"Here's a clue. His first name rhymes with *kill*."

Then she kissed the side of my face, threw her head back and cackled hysterically until I fired a bullet through the middle of her eyes and sent her twisted soul screaming on its way to hell.

I left the gun by the corpse and went to the bathroom to wash. The water was cold, fast, fresh. I ducked my head under the tap to wet my neck and head. I needed the cold shock to the system. Things had been hot in that room. Hot as

(rhymes with *kill*)

hell.

My mind was stuck in low gear, reeling from her final blow. Maybe it had been a vicious final tease. I knew it wasn't, but I prayed to whatever gods there might be that it

(rhymes with *kill*)

was.

I saw a couple of Priscilla's vodka bottles lying around. I picked one up and sniffed from its open top. I could have done with a drink. More than ever before. One for the road, to gear me up for the confrontation to come. One wouldn't hurt. Just one little…

I put it down.

Not yet. Not until this was over and there was nothing left but the drink and the grave. When the last hand was played, I'd toast my damnation and let the alcohol have its wicked way. But not before. Not while there was still a round

(rhymes with *kill*)

to go.

I changed clothes, grabbed the few articles I needed, stepped over the body and exited. There were facts to be checked. Deductions to be drawn. I knew what rhymed with *kill* but I didn't know how he tied in with Priscilla, Nic and the rest. I wouldn't face him till I'd pieced at least part of the jigsaw together.

One of the blind *villacs* was outside. His white eyes were fixed to my window and he was chanting in the strange language of theirs, his face a picture of rapture. I didn't stop to question him. Priests, Incas and sun gods didn't matter anymore. I got on my bike, turned a blind eye to the blind priest, and set off for Party Central.

It was quieter than it had been the day before. From what I gathered, the search for Capac Raimi had been called off, though nobody knew why. I wasn't bothered. The Cardinal's games meant nothing to me any longer.

With the aid of several secretaries, I took to the floors above the fifteenth and waded through the masses of paperwork. I was there all night—the secretaries called for replacements when it became too much for them—and well into the next day, becoming one with the records, picking apart the woven webs of deceit, layer by heartrending layer.

I started with Howard Kett because he was the easiest to connect to Bill. The pair had been colleagues for fifteen years. Though they were never close, it would have been a simple matter for Bill to keep tabs on his superior. Kett himself told me Bill had been with him when he first busted Nick. Bill must have known about them before he moved on Nicola. Known of the brother's and sister's penchant for playing tricks. Told Nick to set Kett up, so he could be used to lead me on.

I tried finding further insidious links between Bill and Nick, couldn't, so moved on to Nic. There was no hard evidence that they'd ever met, but I didn't need any. I could connect the dots using a little imagination. For starters there was the lie she'd spun about her reasons for joining AA. She had said her brother forced her to seek help. I'd thought nothing of the lie when it surfaced but now I reconsidered. If she'd set out to ensnare me, she must have known I was a member. I'd kept my membership secret from everyone except Ellen and Bill. Someone else could have found out and put her up to it, but I saw no reason to ignore the obvious—Bill sent her.

Allegro Jinks had been arrested several times, but it was only when I checked his files more thoroughly that I noted the name of his last arresting officer—the good Bill Casey. Jinks had been a perpetual offender, yet his record since being paroled (he got out early on the recommendation of Officer Casey) was spotless. Had he seen the light and mended his ways?

Had he, fuck! According to the files, he'd been as active these last few years as ever, but recently he'd had a guardian angel looking out for him, somebody who'd persuaded cops to change statements and drop charges, convinced informers to forget Allegro Jinks, kept things quiet. The records didn't state the name of this upright citizen, but I had no difficulty supplying it.

Valerie Thomas was a tricky customer. Not much on her. Nobody knew where she came from, what her background was, how old she was, or even if that was her real name. She'd never been arrested or cautioned. She would have been entirely unconnectable to the case, except for a copy of the form she'd filled out years earlier when applying for a job at the Skylight. The two references she listed were a certain Rudi Ziegler and William Casey.

There were no copies of the references they'd submitted, but I'm sure they had nothing but praise for the hardworking Miss Thomas.

Apart from their names appearing together on Valerie's form, it took me a long time to find anything linking Ziegler to Bill. There was nothing in their immediate files to connect them, and it was only when I asked the secretaries to check for mentions of anything Incan that results rose like dead fish after an underwater explosion.

Over the years, there had been many public meetings of those interested in the city's Incan history, and the names of Bill and Rudi cropped up regularly, usually as audience members, though in a couple of instances Rudi had given lectures. There was no proof that the two had met at the meetings, but I took it for granted that they had.

My inquiries were exhaustive. I even managed to link Bill to Ho Yun Fen, the unfortunate tattooist who created Allegro Jinks's serpent design, only to run afoul of the original lord of the snakes. He used to return home to mainland China every few years and had brought back small parcels of valuable fireworks on a couple of occasions, for use by his friend Bill Casey.

Pinning down evidence of a partnership between Bill and Priscilla proved damn near impossible but I was determined to do so, not wanting to believe the very worst of my oldest friend until my nose was rubbed in it. Priscilla was the key link in the chain. She introduced Nic to Ziegler and dragged her into the world of sun gods and human sacrifices. Manipulated Valerie and Rudi, acting as the main line of communication between Bill and his team of puppets. I refused to leave Party Central till I'd tied her to him.

It took laborious hours and countless dead ends, but eventually I found it. A photograph in Bill's file that I'd previously passed over, an innocuous group shot taken at one of his fireworks displays several years earlier. He was pictured with a group of girls in pirate costumes, young actresses who'd performed a short play as part of the show. He had his arm around one of the fresh-faced beauties, a cute waif of a girl, recognizable on closer scrutiny as a younger version of the viperous Priscilla Perdue.

Tucking the photo away, I took a break, shoveled food down and showered. While drying myself, I wondered how I was going to locate Bill and if he was aware that I knew about him. I was sure he did and, after more thought, figured I knew where I'd be able to find him.

Returning to the upper floors of Party Central, I set about cross-referencing the players, connecting Priscilla to Jinks, Nic to Valerie, and so on, just for the hell of it. I'd barely made a start when my cell phone rang. It was Paucar Wami.

"Events are coming to a head," he told me, sounding unusually agitated. "The secrets of the Ayuamarca file are about to be revealed, and you, lucky boy, are invited to the grand unveiling."

"What are you talking about?"

"The Cardinal is laying his cards on the table and I have a fly on the wall. It promises to be an invigorating experience."

"I don't have time for this," I sighed, then said, "I know who set us up."

I expected a gasp of surprise and a hundred questions, but all he said was, "Good for you. Now get your ass over here."

"Don't you want to know who it is?" I asked, taken aback.

"Tell me later. This is far more important."

"Not to me."

"Oh, but it is," he disagreed. "I was *told* to invite you to the grand unraveling. Can you guess by whom?"

I only needed a second. "The *villacs*?"

"Ten out of ten. Interested now?"

I didn't want to get sidetracked at this stage of the game, but glancing down at the reams of paperwork, I suddenly lost the heart to dig any further. I asked Wami where he was and learned he was holed up in an empty office on the sixth floor of Party Central. I said I'd be with him presently, asked the secretaries to tidy away the files, checked to make sure I was leaving nothing of any importance behind and headed down for what would prove to be the most surreal few hours of my life.

The room stood next to a doorway by the stairs. Wami was within, perched on a bare desk, half a headset plugged into one ear. I started to speak, only to be shushed, directed to a chair and offered the second earpiece. Fitting it into my left ear I found myself eavesdropping on a conversation between

The Cardinal and a man whose voice I didn't recognize. I listened while he regaled The Cardinal with the story of a strange trip he'd taken and a woman who claimed he had died years before.

"What's going on?" I whispered to Wami. "Who is this?"

"Capac Raimi. He is an Ayuamarcan. He fled the city when The Cardinal put a death warrant out on him and retreated to the town he seems to have come from. I will tell you more later. For now, listen."

And I did, as Raimi spun a grave-robbing yarn of sneaking into a cemetery late at night with his "wife" and digging up the coffin in which he had allegedly been laid to rest. Inside he found a corpse, which the woman identified as her late husband. The pair got into an argument, which ended with his caving her head in with a shovel and burying her along with the corpse.

"Nice fellow," I muttered drily. "Any relation?"

"Shh!" Wami snapped, in no mood for levity.

It was The Cardinal's turn next, and his tale made Raimi's sound halfway believable. He started with his past, a fascinating history of a grubby street urchin who mutated into The Cardinal. Then he went off on a fantastical tangent and made far-fetched claims that would have landed any other man an instant spot in the nearest lunatic asylum.

According to him, he had the ability to make people, to actually *create* human beings. As a teenager he'd imagined the face of Leonora Shankar and thought how wonderful it would be if she were real. The next day he wandered into a puppet shop and met a couple of blind priests (I paid special attention to this part) who ran him through a bizarre ceremony that involved taking blood from his hands and daubing a puppet with it. The day after, Leonora Shankar turned up and took him under her wing.

He found he could keep eight or nine of his Ayuamarcans—the name he'd coined—on the go at the same time. His bent finger was a result of his fiddling with the laws of reality—every time he made somebody new, it bent a little more. To unmake someone, he pierced the heart of that person's puppet (each had a look-alike puppet, which explained the marionettes of the fifteenth floor) and the blind priests summoned a magical fog—our famous green fog—that spread through the city and wiped out people's memories of the dead.

Raimi didn't believe him—he could smell bullshit and wasn't afraid to say so. He asked where the blind priests were. The Cardinal told him they were in the basement of Party Central and the pair descended for a powwow. Something odd happened—I couldn't tell for sure, but Raimi seemed to have some sort of vision—at the end of which the would-be successor stood as a convert, a firm believer in every crazy lie the madman had fed him.

The pair headed for the roof, where The Cardinal talked about "one-week pockets"—Ayuamarcans couldn't survive more than a week away from the city. He said Paucar Wami was an exception to the rules, who could not only make it on his own in the big bad world, but was fertile to boot—the others were sterile.

"Hear that?" I remarked, nudging my father. "You're one of a kind."

He shushed me again. He was taking this seriously. I thought better of irritating him and tuned back into the weirdest conversation of the century.

The Cardinal spoke of his inability to create a worthy successor. He told Raimi—as he'd told me a couple of days before—that his empire meant everything to him, and he wanted it to survive. No human could safely steer his empire in the long run, so he'd set about making a leader of his own, capable of overcoming the sturdiest of obstacles, even death itself. He'd made Raimi resistant to physical damage—if injured, his body would heal quickly—and, if killed, he would be reincarnated and could continue where he'd left off. In a nutshell, he was immortal.

A lengthy silence followed, in which the only things to be heard were the howls of the wind and the beating of Capac Raimi's understandably agitated heart.

"You don't believe any of this, do you?" I asked.

"Every word," Wami responded quietly.

"But it's madness!"

"Yes," he agreed, "but the mad can also be true. Fifty-five million people died during the six-year jamboree of World War II. Madness? Certainly. True?"

"Hardly the same thing," I noted stiffly.

"Hitler tried to create a master race. The Cardinal set out to create a single superman. Which sounds more plausible?"

"Don't throw immature intellectual arguments like that at me," I retorted. "The Cardinal's a grade-A loon. Anyone who believes that yarn of his is crazy too."

Wami nodded. "Were I in any other's shoes, I would be inclined to agree. But I have spent the better part of my life trying to unravel a mystery that defies the laws of logic. I have observed people come into existence and pop out of it as quickly as they appeared, all traces of their lives vanishing with their bodies, failing to register even in the memories of those who knew them. In the absence of any other explanation, I must accept The Cardinal's."

"You're as crazy as they are," I sighed. "You, Dorak, Capac Raimi... nuts."

"And *you* are the only sane person," Wami smirked. "How fortunate you are."

"Look, you can't really believe—"

"Flesh of Dreams," he interrupted. "The *villacs* called you Flesh of Dreams."

"So?"

"You can be incredibly dense," he chided me. "Think, boy. If what The Cardinal says is true, Ayuamarcans are creatures of the dreamworld. *Dreams made Flesh*, if you will. And you are the son of a dream person and a human. One could say you are of Flesh *and* of Dreams. Plain *Flesh of Dreams* if you want something that rolls off the tongue."

I decided not to argue. Partly because you can't argue with a madman, partly because a small section of me believed the tissue of lunatic lies. The more we discussed it, the more I seemed to be sucked into the madly intricate mire.

"How did you get here?" I asked instead, returning to more practical matters.

"The *villacs* contacted me through a messenger last Monday, not long after you and I had parted. They knew The Cardinal had put out word for Capac Raimi's execution and they knew where the fugitive was heading. They said, if I helped him escape, it would lead to the solving of the mystery. So I did.

"They sent another messenger two days later. This one bade me make haste to the train station, to meet Raimi on his way back. He told me to plant a bug on him, then call you when they were in conference, for both of us to listen in on his conversation with The Cardinal."

"Any idea why they told you to include me?"

"This must tie in with the murder of your bedmates but I cannot see how. Perhaps we will learn more when the pair on the roof resume their talks. I have a feeling there are a few twists left to the tale."

He got *that* right.

Capac Raimi started up again. "It's a trap," he muttered, and they discussed the downside of immortality and The Cardinal's insane plan. Raimi didn't believe the Ayuamarcans could survive their creator's death. The Cardinal admitted he couldn't guarantee Raimi's survival but had made provisions to hopefully ensure it. Raimi mulled this over, then delivered the bombshell that changed the course of the evening. He told The Cardinal he'd replace him, run his empire from here to doomsday, *but* he wanted an immediate transfer of power. He wasn't prepared to sit around waiting for The Cardinal to die, worrying about what would happen. Either all would be handed over now, or The Cardinal could go screw himself and cast his nets for a successor again.

I knew that wasn't an option—The Cardinal was dying—and I expected him to accept the condition instantly, but he acted cautiously, advising against such a move. He encouraged Raimi to make use of his years of experience, to keep him around and exploit him. But Raimi was having none of it. He told The Cardinal to go take a jump. Literally. Off the roof of Party Central.

Wami stiffened when he heard that and the snakes on his cheeks seemed to shimmer nervously.

"What's wrong?" I asked.

"He cannot jump," Wami replied, though he seemed to be talking to himself. "He mustn't."

"Do you like the old bastard so much?"

"I care nothing for him. But if what he says is true—if I am one of his creations—then his death means my own."

"Oh, come on," I groaned, "don't tell me you buy into any of—"

"Quiet!" he hissed.

The Cardinal was in the process of throwing Raimi a curveball. Ford

Tasso was on the roof with them—he'd been hiding—and now emerged, a bound woman in tow, none other than Ama Situwa. The woman who'd helped me tie Priscilla to Ellen seemed to be the love of Raimi's life. I was sure this wasn't mere coincidence, but there was no time to puzzle over it.

Once again The Cardinal acted as if he had years left and tried talking his successor out of calling for his instant death, urging Raimi to keep him around for Ama's sake. She was also an Ayuamarcan, but without special powers, and would perish when he did.

Raimi hesitated. He asked The Cardinal to remake her, this time granting her the ability to transcend her maker's death and live forever. The Cardinal said he couldn't and started to explain why, which was when Wami tore the headphone from his ear.

"What are you doing?" I asked as he launched for the door.

"The fucker's going to jump!" he shouted. "I have to stop him. I won't die, not like this."

"You can't stop him."

"I can try," he growled.

"But he's going to die anyway. He—" I started to tell him about The Cardinal's brain tumor, but he was gone, up the stairs like a squirrel, acting rashly for the first and only time of his otherwise lethally precise life.

Picking up his discarded earpiece, I tuned back into the soap opera, now with the benefit of stereo, and placed bets with myself on how it would end.

Raimi betrayed Ama Situwa and told The Cardinal to jump. I heard the sound of the old goat's footsteps as he walked toward the edge of the roof, his voice coming faintly now. He was preparing for his leap when Wami burst onto the roof, roaring at him to stop. "Wami knows?" I heard The Cardinal ask, and Raimi explained about the bug.

I felt sorry for my father, listening to him issue threats that were worthless. As a merchant of death, he had power only over those who wished to cling to life. A man who'd surrendered himself to fate was beyond the killer's reach.

The Cardinal disarmed Paucar Wami with a few withering words. Wami vowed to kill Capac Raimi if he survived the kingpin's death. Then The Cardinal made his final ever speech, wrapped matters up with a hearty "Farewell!"

And jumped.

Tearing off the headphones, I rushed to the window but wasn't in time to catch the downfall of the city's legendary leader. But I was in a good position to study his corpse, smashed to pieces on the concrete, arms stretched as if he'd attempted to fly. A crowd of startled Troops was forming around the crumpled mess. Within minutes the place would be black with those wishing to associate themselves with this moment of bloody history.

I wanted to return to the headphones and listen for signs of life on the roof but two thoughts stopped me. One was practical—when word of The Cardinal's death spread, a cordon would be thrown around Party Central, setting my date with Bill back by hours or even days. The second consideration was more mystically rooted. I didn't believe The Cardinal's outlandish story, but part of me couldn't help speculating on what it would mean if it *was* true. If it wasn't bullshit, then a green fog would soon be spreading and minds would be washed clean. People would forget about Ama Situwa, Paucar Wami and Leonora Shankar. The Ayuamarcans would become ghost figures, like those in my father's file.

What if Bill was one of them?

A crazy notion, but the fear of losing him to the realm of dreams, forgetting about him and what he'd done, would have been enough to galvanize me into action even if I hadn't already set off running for the stairs.

I raced to ground level and rushed into the yard, not pausing to collect my socks or shoes. I grabbed my bike and was wheeling it clear of the building when I glanced up and noticed—to my horror—banks of thick green fog billowing down from the roof like a giant's clammy fingers.

I stared at the fog, thinking everything The Cardinal had said was true, rooted to the spot with superstitious fear. Then I snapped out of it, decided to give the fog a run for its money, and struck for the gate as fast as I could.

The Troops on guard were already beginning to restrict access in and out of the complex. If not for my gold clearance, I'd have been turned back like the others who were trying to leave. As it was they let me through without argument, though I'm sure they'd have been stricter had I been five or ten minutes later, when word came down from Tasso or Frank not to let anybody out.

As I took a right turn away from Party Central, I noted a familiar motorcycle—Wami's. I braked, jumped off my bike and ran to check for keys. Wami wasn't a man to leave his keys in the open, but this had been a special occasion and in his rush to learn the truth of the Ayuamarcans he may have acted uncommonly. To my delight, I found he had. The keys were in the ignition, a fob—a tiny shrunken head—dangling gently from them in the brisk wind.

I jumped on and tore ahead of the banks of creeping fog, trying not to think about how awfully fitting it was for the son to follow in the saddle of his father.

26

It had been a long couple of days and I was all but dead on my feet. If Bill wasn't waiting for me at his house, I wouldn't know where to turn next. Thankfully the light was on when I pulled up outside. I rapped loudly on the window as I passed and he was at the door when I got there. He nodded somberly and ushered me in without saying a word. I sat in the guest chair in the living room, the huge window to my rear, Bill directly opposite. Our usual positions.

"I've been waiting for you." He sounded weary.

"How did you know I was coming?"

"I had your apartment bugged long before you moved in. I recommended it to you and introduced you to Ali, remember?"

Then he'd been eavesdropping on me for years.

"Did Ali have anything to do with this?" I asked.

"No," he answered to my relief.

"You heard me kill Priscilla?"

"Yes. That's when I came back. I expected you last night. Where'd you get to?"

"Party Central. I wanted to make sure."

"You didn't believe her?"

"I didn't want to."

He smiled sadly, then said softly, "The house is wired. The explosives in the cellar are ready to blow." He showed me a detonator in his left hand (which was wrapped in bandages and short a finger). "When we're done talking, it's over."

"We're dead men?"

"Yes."

"So we can speak the truth?"

"That's the idea. No more lies."

I took a deep breath and said the words that tore me apart. "Why did you kill Ellen?"

"It was Priscilla's doing. She belonged to the blind priests. I recruited her, and I was her superior, but her first loyalty was to the *villacs*. When she suggested killing Ellen, I rejected the idea, but the priests contacted her behind my back. I wasn't told. I'd have stopped them if I knew. I never meant to involve Ellen. I loved her like a daughter."

"I don't believe you," I sneered.

"It's true," he insisted. "I loved Ellen. I love *you*."

"Then why destroy my life?" I screamed.

"The usual motive," he said casually. "Revenge."

"What the fuck did I ever do to you?"

"I've been planning this longer than you can imagine," he said by way of reply. "I've had my sights set on you since you were a snotty-nosed kid who chased girls around the schoolyard and pulled their panties down. You were a real monster."

I ignored his attempt to lighten the atmosphere. "What have I done to you, Bill? What did I do to make you hate me?"

"I don't."

"So why fuck with me like this?"

"I didn't mean for it to go this far. It was the *villacs*. They were determined to ruin you. I had to go along with them. They wouldn't have helped me otherwise."

"I don't understand," I moaned. "Just tell me, Bill. Why did you do it?"

"Revenge," he repeated, then added, "Not revenge for anything you did. I was after..." He reached into a pocket with his right hand, pulled something out, leaned down and rolled it across the floor to me.

My fingers snatched for it. A black marble with golden squiggles down the sides. Now I knew how the marble had gotten into the trout's mouth.

"Wami!" I gasped, and the fury drained out of me. I stared at Bill, horrified. He looked so small, timid, harmless. He wasn't enjoying this.

"I've known you were his son all your life. I've been shadowing you since you were a kid, observing you, plotting around you. That's how I teamed up with the priests. They were also interested in you, and feared I intended you harm. They wormed my scheme out of me, then struck a deal. If I gave them you, they'd give me Wami. If I'd turned them down, they'd have killed me."

"Wami," I said again. He'd told me he knew Bill. I tried recalling exactly what he'd said but couldn't.

"The *villacs* have plans for you," Bill went on. "They destroyed your old life in order to build a new one, to mold you the way they want you. I don't know why—all these years, I was never able to work them out. But I helped them. As your friend, I showed them how to hurt you. If I hadn't, they'd have eliminated me. That would have meant I couldn't go after Wami."

"Wami," I said for the third time, then leaned forward. "Tell me about *him*."

"He did something terrible to me a long time ago."

"What?"

Bill shook his head. "I can't tell you."

"He killed someone close to you? Your mother? A brother? A lover?"

"Don't ask, Al. Don't push me there. My hand might slip if you do."

I didn't like it but I was in no position to argue. "OK," I growled. "He fucked up your life. *And?*"

"I've spent the past few decades plotting to get even." Bill's eyes were dark. "At first I meant to kill him. Plain, simple revenge. Track him down, put a gun to his head, blow his brains out the back of his skull."

"Why didn't you?"

He shrugged. "It wouldn't have been enough. I wanted..." His Adam's apple bobbed up and down. "You could say *poetic justice*, but that doesn't really explain it. I wanted *you* to kill him, you or one of his other sons. I didn't want him looking into my eyes when he died—that would have been too easy. I wanted him to stare into the eyes of one he gave life to, one he brought into the world. I don't expect you to understand, but there it is. That was my plan."

"You're crazy," I whispered.

"No!" he snapped. "Vicious, yes. Crazy, no. I knew what I was doing and why. I spent years preparing. I used Nicola and Jinks to pitch the two of you together. I thought you'd hate him when you found out he was your father. I fingered him for Nic's death, then had him kill the Fursts.

"When I learned of Ellen's murder, I put my horror on hold, rushed to your apartment, found the marble and planted it.

"And when I sent you my finger, I thought, 'Surely *now* he'll react and strike the monster down.' I never thought you would unite, that you'd side with him and believe him when he denied involvement with the murders or my kidnapping."

He was crying hoarsely. "Why did you trust him, Al? Why didn't you kill the bastard when you had the chance?"

"He was my father," I answered.

"All the more reason!" Bill yelled. "If I was related to a beast like that, I'd move as swiftly as I could to rid the world of him. Ellen would be alive today if you'd—"

"Don't!" I snarled. "Don't blame me, you hypocritical son of a bitch. Ellen's dead because of *you*. Not Wami, me or the blind fucking priests. You could have warned me, told me they were after me. You were my friend. I trusted you, loved you, took you into my confidence, and you did nothing but betray me. This is *your* fault. I don't care what Wami did to you. Hurting me to get back at him is the act of a sick, unholy motherfucker."

"Maybe you're right." He grinned through his tears. "But it wasn't just Wami I was after. There were the priests and The Cardinal. They could have stopped him. All those years ago, they knew what he was up to. They could have shielded me. But they sat back and let him destroy me. I wanted to hurt those demons as well.

"The *villacs* would have destroyed your life anyway. I couldn't have protected you from them. They'd have swatted me aside and spun their own devious webs. I could have used one of Wami's other children—I've discovered several—but, by using you, I could hit the *villacs* and The Cardinal too.

"So I worked with them. I handed your head to them on a plate. And you know something? It would have been worth it." He nodded madly. "Your life, Ellen's, Nicola's, my own. If you'd killed Wami, I could have gone to my grave happy. I'd have sacrificed this whole stinking city if I had to."

I shook my head uncomprehendingly. "You were like a father to me. Didn't it ever bother you, the way you manipulated me?"

"Why should it?" he replied weakly. "I was willing to sell my soul in return for a slice of revenge. A man who surrenders himself totally will hesitate at nothing. I'm not saying it was easy—my love for you was true— but if I had it to do over again, I wouldn't do any different."

He tapped his chest. "I'm empty here. Wami tore my heart out and devoured it. I'd have killed myself years ago, but hate kept me alive. I couldn't die before I made him pay."

We were going in circles. It was time to pin him down to facts.

"Tell me more about your plan," I encouraged him, wiping tears from my cheeks. "You set me up with Nic, then used Jinks to pit me against Wami?"

"Yes." A hint of pride invaded his tone. "I noticed Allegro's resemblance to Wami when I busted him and had been keeping him in reserve. Nicola wasn't part of the *villac* organization—she was one of Priscilla's puppets—but she knew a bit about them and was a willing accessory."

"OK," I moved on. "Manipulating Nicholas, the Fursts, Kett…I follow most of that. What about Ellen and Priscilla? Did you plan to toss them together?"

"I already told you I didn't. Priscilla didn't know about Ellen until she ran into her in Cafran's. The plan was for you to fall in love with Priscilla, then for *her* to be killed. You'd have found evidence linking her murder to Wami, and that should have been enough to prompt you into action." He paused. "Priscilla wasn't aware of that element of the plan. She thought *you* were being set up for a fall. The *villacs* told her you were to be sacrificed to the god of the sun."

"What did you plan to do if I didn't kill Wami?" I asked.

Bill frowned. "I hadn't considered it. I was so sure…" He petered out. "After Ellen it would have been redundant to kill Priscilla. Since Ellen's death failed to turn you against him, it was unlikely that Priscilla's would. So I faked my kidnapping, hoping my disappearance might push you over the edge."

"You didn't arrange for Ama Situwa to see Priscilla and Ellen together?"

"No. That was either a stroke of misfortune or set up by the *villacs*. You found out the truth far swifter than I imagined. I was working on ways to convince you that Wami had kidnapped me. Now…" He sighed miserably.

I leaned back in the chair. A lot was clear, but there was much I still couldn't get my head around. "What I don't understand is why you assumed I'd be able to kill Wami. He's an elite assassin. What made you think I stood a chance?"

"You're his son," Bill said.

I raised an eyebrow. "You thought paternal instinct would stay his hand?" Bill nodded. "That's ridiculous!"

"I know Wami better than you do," he disagreed. "He isn't as emotionally lacking as he seems. I wouldn't say he's capable of love, but his children mean something to him and he's never harmed any of them. If anyone was capable of getting close enough to him to strike, it was you or one of your siblings."

"What about Valerie at Ziegler's?" I asked. "She almost killed me. What would have become of your plans then?"

"They'd have evaporated." He shrugged. "That's life. There are no guarantees."

"Who chopped off your finger?"

"I did it myself," he said, caressing the bandaged stub. "Hurts like the Devil. It would have been simpler to send hair samples or toenail clippings, but I wanted to be dramatic."

Bill reached behind his chair, produced a bottle of vodka and tossed it to me. I caught it in midair. "A toast to our success?"

"Later," I said. "When we're through." I put it aside. "How many people have you killed over the years?"

"Do numbers matter?" he sighed. "We've both killed. Once you murder, your soul is damned. The ones that come after are inconsequential. The first is all that really counts."

"Tell me what Wami did to you, Bill." It seemed a good time to ask again, but he shook his head mutely.

"Have a drink," he said instead. "We'll get roaring drunk together and maybe I'll tell you then."

It sounded like a good idea. I'd be dead soon—why not enjoy one last tipple? The bottle had slipped down the side of the chair. I retrieved it and unscrewed the top. The fumes were intoxicating. I pressed the tip to my mouth.

I stopped and fixed the top back in place.

"Why do you keep pressing alcohol on me?"

Bill frowned. "What?"

"This isn't the first time you've invited me to drown my sorrows. Why are you so anxious to get me back onto the bottle?"

Bill stared at me in silence, then at the vodka. He smiled, then laughed. "Jesus Christ! You know what I was up to?"

I shook my head. "Tell me."

"I was trying to save you!" His face had lit up. "All those years of planning, manipulating people, working with the priests, secretly plotting against them, The Cardinal and Wami. I devoted my life to it. Yet there I was, closing on my goal, but at the same time unconsciously trying to screw myself over."

"I don't follow," I said.

"If you fell off the wagon, you wouldn't have been of any use to me. It would have been a waste sending a drunken sop against Paucar Wami. But part of me must have wanted to spare you the trap I'd set. If you hit the bottle again, I'd have had to turn to one of his other sons."

"You were subconsciously offering me a helping hand?" I asked dubiously.

"Crazy, I know, but I guess I wasn't as hell-bent on revenge as I believed. Not as big a bastard as I thought." He winked at me as if it were a big joke. I couldn't help smiling in response, though I saw nothing funny in it.

The sound of the front door opening wiped the smile from Bill's face. He sat up and buried the detonator down between his thigh and the arm of this chair. "More company," he noted. "How delightful." He was trying to make light of it, but there was a strain to his voice.

Moments later the old priest with the mole, and the translator—clad in a rough brown cape—entered. They kept to Bill's rear but he could see their reflections in the dark glass of the front window.

"Gentlemen," he greeted them. "You're late."

"You were supposed to bring him to us," the translator said harshly.

"Change of plan," Bill said easily. "It's a cold night. I have a weak chest. I decided to stay in. You don't mind, do you?"

The young man grunted. "It makes no difference. As long as he is safe, we are content."

"Oh, he's perfectly safe. Aren't you, Al?"

"Perfectly," I echoed quietly. Then, to Bill, "You were meant to take me to them?"

"Learning the truth about me was supposed to be the end of your hardships. They wanted to reel you in when Priscilla broke the news. I told them to leave you to me. I said I'd be able to calm you down."

"They went along with that?"

He smiled. "I'm the Al Jeery expert. They bow to my knowledge of you."

"Where do they want to take me?" I asked.

"Underground, I'd imagine."

My eyes narrowed. "Do they know about…?" My gaze flicked to the concealed detonator. Bill's spreading smile was answer enough.

I looked up at the two modern-day Incas and gloated inside as I realized I was a step ahead of them for once. They'd been pulling the strings from the start, but it seemed Bill was playing a game of his own, whose rules they weren't privy to. Life was about to get very interesting.

"Good to see you, boys," I said smugly, buoyed by the dark sword of Damocles dangling over their heads.

"It is good to see you also, Flesh of Dreams," the translator replied stiffly.

"You know what happened with Priscilla?" I asked.

"We do."

"And at Party Central? The Cardinal and—"

"We are fully aware," he interrupted.

"What's this about The Cardinal?" Bill asked.

"Tell you later," I teased, then focused on the genial monsters. "Bill's been telling me his side of things. Time for *your* story."

The younger man looked for guidance to the blind *villac*, who shook his head. "This is not the place, Flesh of Dreams. Our brothers are preparing for your arrival. Come with us, assume your rightful position, and all will be revealed."

"Where might that be?"

"On the *inti watana*. The underground platform," he added when I looked blank. "It is the hitching post of the sun, the source of our power, our link to the gods. When the bloodlines merge and flow as one, we shall raise the giant stone from where it lies and the city will be ours."

"That's my 'rightful position'?"

"It is the heart of the city," he said earnestly, "where all blood mingles. The thrones you saw are thrones of power, thrones of blood. One is yours, Flesh of Dreams, by right of birth, right of will, right of blood."

"Hear that, Bill? They've got a throne for me."

"Very nice," he chuckled. "Is there a crown as well?"

"*Is* there a crown?" I asked politely.

"This is not a joking matter," the translator growled.

"Murder never is."

"Forget the murder. That was necessary but is in the past. We need dwell on it no longer."

"Oh, I think we should," I disagreed. "In fact I insist on it. I'm going nowhere till you tell me what it was all about."

The young man looked again to his mentor. The blind priest thought on it a moment, stroking the mole on his chin, then gave the shortest of nods.

"You had to come to us cleansed," the translator said. "To grasp your future, you had to abandon your past. That meant severing all ties to your old life. It was harsh of us to strip you bare of all you cherished, but we had to push you to the point where you had nothing but us, no family, no friends, nothing to come between you and your destiny, your blood and ours.

"You must join with us, Flesh of Dreams, because only we remain. Without us you are a shell of a man doomed to lonely suffering and death. Those you loved have died or betrayed you. There is no returning to the life you once enjoyed. None but we of the sun will accept you. Embrace your fate and we'll make a king of you, a leader of men. This city will be yours and your sons will rule when you are gone, theirs after them, and so on."

"You had Bill destroy me so you could give me a leg up?" I asked incredulously. The translator nodded. "*Why?* Of all the people in the city, why pick on me?"

"Because you are the son of Dreams made Flesh. You are the union of the physical and mental, the product of—"

"—An Ayuamarcan and a human," I finished, shaking my head with disgust. "You believe that shit of The Cardinal's?"

"We empowered him. We provided the means for him to take control of this city. He was a nobody until we granted him the powers of a *Watana*. After that he had the ability to seize the fabric of dreams and mold it into flesh. With our help he created the Ayuamarcans, ghostly individuals capable of responding to the community's needs and desires.

"That is why you were invited to Party Central," he went on. "We knew this was the day of The Cardinal's fall and wanted you there to hear the testimony from his own lips, to make it easier for you to understand and accept."

"You're saying he told the truth?"

"As much of it as he knew."

"Capac Raimi is immortal?"

"Yes."

"Who's immortal?" Bill asked, perplexed, but I ignored him.

"In that case, what do you want me for? From what I gathered, The Cardinal's left Raimi to run things, a successor who can rule the world alone."

"No man can rule alone," the translator said, "not even one as powerful and enduring as Capac Raimi. There must be three, a chakana of blood, as we explained before. Human, inhuman, and a mix of the twain.

"The *inti watana* has been fashioned with three thrones. One for Capac Raimi, whose blood is the blood of Dreams. One for a member of our ranks, a representative of the world of Flesh. And one for you, Al Jeery, son of Flesh and Dreams.

"Our three streams, united in one powerful chakana of blood, will ensure the longevity and majesty of our city. Inti—the god of the sun—will look upon our trinity and bless us. As long as the sun burns brightly, our city will prosper. Though all else crumbles, we will endure."

"You're loco," I said softly.

The translator smiled and pointed to the window behind me. Looking over my shoulder, I noticed clouds of green fog rolling by the panes of glass.

"That's supposed to convince me?" I scoffed, as if the fog and their power to summon it didn't perturb me.

"We do not expect you to believe at the beginning," the translator said. "In time you will learn to accept the truth. Under the folds of this earth you'll see wonders that will convince you. For now believe only this—however little faith you place in our spiritual power, our earthly power is undeniably real. We control this city. The Cardinal was our puppet. Capac Raimi will bow to our will. Nothing happens here which we do not control. Is this not true, Bill Casey?"

"True as mutton," Bill said. They were still to his rear and he hadn't turned to look at them. His eyes were trained on mine.

"We offer a third of all we rule," the translator said. "If you join with us, this city's joys are yours. You can have money and women. Politicians will obey you. Businessmen will pay homage. You need not believe in our gods, but believe this—we can fill your remaining time with every imaginable luxury and pleasure."

"And all you ask in return is my soul," I said quietly.

"No. We ask only that you accept us as allies, let your blood flow with ours, and be part of our chakana. Later, you may nominate one of your line to replace you, and free yourself of all responsibility if you so desire."

"A tempting offer," I mused aloud. And it was.

"A man could do a lot of good with that kind of clout," Bill remarked. "Build hospitals. House the homeless." He winked at me. "Rehabilitate the addicted."

"That's true," I nodded thoughtfully.

"Of course they do say power corrupts."

"You think it might turn my head?"

He shrugged. "I've never heard of a tyrant ruling with a kind hand. You need a heart of stone to run a city. I can't see you operating on a par with The Cardinal. You're too human."

"Would you take it?" I asked.

"Not for anything," he answered bluntly. "I've only ruined a handful of lives, yet the guilt is unbearable. I'd be lost within a week if I controlled the destinies of millions."

"Of course it doesn't matter what I decide, does it? With things poised the way they are"—I nodded at his clenched hand—"it's purely academic."

"No," he said. "If you choose to go with them, I won't stop you."

"You mean that?"

"I was never in this to destroy you. It was always and only Wami. I like the idea of hitting the heavens with you. It would be nice, in spite of all I've done, if you made up your mind to die with me, as my friend. But if you want to go with them, I won't stand in your way."

"Maybe we could both stick around. I could give Wami to you."

He smiled sadly. "You wouldn't. He's a monster but you won't bring him down. I don't know why. Maybe it's true what they say, and blood is thicker than water."

"It looks to me like Wami's going to come out of this considerably better off," I noted. "An enemy dead, his son in control of the city. He'll laugh at you, Bill."

Bill's face twitched. "He won't be laughing long," he muttered, then chuckled. "Death can't keep a good man down. Maybe I'll get even with him yet."

I faced the translator. "What if I reject you?"

"We will turn to one of Paucar Wami's other sons if we must," he sighed. "We hope to avoid such complications. You are the firstborn, and have been blessed by Inti—your healing powers are a sign that he has a high regard for you. But alternative measures exist should we have need of them. We cannot force you."

"Isn't that what you've been doing these last few months? Forcing my hand?"

"No. We have been cleansing you of your past, leading you to a point where you had to choose. But your cooperation must be volunteered, not commandeered. That is not to say we'll accept a refusal—we'll keep after you, harry you, destroy those who come close to you, interfere in your affairs, deprive you of happiness. But we won't—can't—openly force you to pledge yourself to our cause."

"Thank heavens for small mercies," I commented drily, then considered what it would be like to have the *villacs* on my back for the rest of my life. Suddenly my choice was clear. Welcome, even, since I had nothing to lose and no life to go back to. If they'd come to me before Priscilla and Nicola, before killing Ellen, I might have accepted their offer of power. But by pushing so hard, they'd taken all that I would have wanted power *for*. They'd misjudged me entirely, or had been led to misjudge me by Bill. They thought they had me in the palm of their hand, but Bill was calling the shots, and he had a card up his sleeve that would wipe the smiles off their faces and place me beyond their reach forever.

I sat back and gripped the arms of the chair. "It would've been an interesting life," I said to Bill.

"It sure would," he agreed, reading my intentions.

"Do you think I'd have made a good leader?"

"No," he laughed.

"Don't make any hasty decisions," the translator warned, sensing something amiss. "It does not pay to—"

But I wasn't interested in his words any longer and cut him short with a curt command. "Let's blow this joint."

Bill's fist unclenched. There was a tiny click. The face of the *villac* with the mole creased and he started talking rapidly, blind eyes filling with doubt. The translator darted forward, looking for the concealed object in Bill's palm. He tried to shout a question. But before he could say anything, the world exploded. There was a roar of undiluted rage. Bill, the *villac* and his translator were lost to jagged shards of red and white. I flew into black.

epilogue

"to catch the dead"

27

I awoke in the hospital, suffering from pain the like of which I'd never
dreamed of. I was on a drip for weeks, bedridden much longer. It was
almost three months before I was fit to release myself, and even then it was
against the advice of the doctors.

I caught the force of the explosion straight on, but rather than obliter-
ate me, it sent me flying, chair and all, through the huge front window. The
neighbors found me spread-eagled on the lawn, a burned chunk of flesh,
barely alive.

Later, the investigators discovered three corpses among the ashes and
debris, too charred for definitive identification, teeth melted, flesh burned
away to nothing, bones shattered and scattered. When I was able to respond to their questions, I told them about Bill and the Incan descendants,
and that cleared up the mystery of the bodies.

Bill left a note for Howard Kett, clearing my name and confessing to
his part in the murders of Nic Hornyak, Ellen Fraser and Valerie Thomas,
to whom he'd slipped the rope she'd hanged herself with. He even took
credit for Priscilla's death, swearing that he'd shot her. Kett knew better—
he'd been to my apartment while I was recovering in the hospital and found
the gun with my prints all over it—but he went along with the lie and
"lost" the evidence.

If I wished to be ungracious, I could say it was because he feared my dragging him into the public arena if I was put on trial. But that would be doing him a disservice. I think he did it because he felt sorry for me. He called in to see me when I was able to accept visitors. Told me he was quitting the city. Warned me to keep my mouth shut about his relationship with Nick, then wished me well.

While I recuperated, paranoid inner voices mocked me. "Bill isn't dead," they whispered. "He could have gotten his hands on a corpse as easily as a bottle of milk. He was an explosives expert who could have arranged it so you'd go out the window and the Incas to hell, while he walked away untouched." And so on, day and night without pause.

I didn't believe the voices but I couldn't rid myself of them. I knew I was only torturing myself, that I'd grown accustomed to betrayal and was seeing it where it didn't exist, but part of me was convinced that Bill was out there, waiting to finish me off, and I often woke screaming from nightmares of him.

When I could think straight, I spent days and nights wondering about Bill and my father. What did Wami *do* to him? What could drive a man to seek revenge on his tormentor through his own loved ones? Wami must have killed somebody close to Bill, but that only accounted for Bill's motive. It didn't shed light on why he was so intent on working through me, why he devoted his life to manipulating mine. No matter how I looked at it, it didn't make sense. I had a horrible feeling it never would.

As for the *villacs*, my father and his fellow Ayuamarcans...

They'd disappeared. The priests, I presumed, were keeping their heads down, but the Ayuamarcans had vanished from the face of the Earth, as predicted by The Cardinal. Nobody—myself excluded—recognized Leonora Shankar's name or Ama Situwa's, or that of any of the others on the list. They'd been erased from records and the minds of the city's populace. Nobody remembered them, not even Ama's supposed father, Cafran Reed, who swore when I interrogated him that he had no daughter of that name or description.

There was one exception—Paucar Wami. *His* name lived on. People's memories of him were sketchy—when I questioned Fabio, he recalled a vague rumor about a killer—but some small part of his legend had survived.

Could true evil never be eradicated? Did horror live on in the collective unconscious? Or had the *villacs* just failed to deal adequately with those who'd known of Paucar Wami? I still wasn't convinced they were as powerful as The Cardinal claimed. The green fog that covered the city for ten days following The Cardinal's death went a long way toward backing their extraordinary claims, but the ability to summon a fog doesn't mean you're able to create life at will. The Ayuamarcans could have been ordinary people under the control of the priests. Having served their purpose, they were then exterminated, and those who'd known them were subjected to brainwashing, which accounted for the lost memories.

Far-fetched? Absolutely. But that made more sense to me than the alternative.

Of course, if the Ayuamarcans were ethereal creations—and I was only saying *if*—Wami had been unique. The rest were sterile and city-bound, but the assassin was capable of reproducing and exploring the outside world. Had *that* something to do with his lingering presence? Through me and his other children, he had a toehold in reality. Were we sustaining his legend, by our very existence keeping part of him alive? And was that the reason I could clearly remember him and the other Ayuamarcans?

I thought of confronting The Cardinal's successor, Capac Raimi. As the man I'd been destined to share the city with, perhaps he remembered the Ayuamarcans too. It would have been interesting to discuss the situation with him. But that would have been playing into the hands of the *villacs*, and I'd no intention of doing anything that might favor those meddling bastards.

I kept expecting the blind priests to turn up, but they appeared to have been put off by the deaths of their envoys. There were no late-night visits, no sign that they were following me, no threats or evidence that they were conspiring against me. They might have given up on me and gone after one of Wami's other sons, or they could be biding their time, letting me recover and build a new life, so they could step back in and wreck it all over again.

Tough luck if that was their game. I was through building. It was isolation for me from now on. I would never leave myself open to personal annihilation again.

I cycled out to the Manco Capac statue one afternoon, drawn to it as I had been before. The statue was coming along nicely. It was a long way from completion, but the skeleton of the upper body had been maneuvered into place. It was a pity Ziegler hadn't lived to see it. He'd have appreciated it more than I could.

While there, I thought about the decision I had made back at Bill's. I'd never been a dreamer. I'd believed I'd been born to a life of drudgery and had brushed aside any nobler aspirations as idle fantasies. But in light of the *villacs'* offer...

Was I crazy to turn it down? I didn't regret my choice—Bill was right, I'd have made a lousy leader—but I couldn't help thinking what life might have been like if I'd accepted. Al Jeery, lord of the city.

Heh.

I never returned to my apartment. I couldn't face it after what I'd done there. I steered clear of Ali and the other well-wishers who tried bringing some light into my dark hell of a life. I couldn't risk getting close to anyone. I had to be by myself from here on in. No lovers, friends, associates— nothing. I rented a tiny apartment in a cheap sector of the city, into which I pretty much cemented myself, cutting off the external world.

After a while I bought a bottle of vile vodka and laid it on a shelf over the foot of my bed. I'd lie for hours on end, gazing into its clear depths, seeing hell, Bill reaching out to me from its fiery pits. I often reached back and, though we never touched, our fingers were getting closer every day. It was only a matter of time before I surrendered to its charms and sought the sanctuary of drunken oblivion.

While waiting for my resolve to crumble and the vodka to take me, I walked to Bill's house during one of my few outdoor sojourns, to face the ghosts of my past. Nobody had cleared the debris and the rain had turned the mess to ashy mud. It was filthy, stinking, offensive. I walked among the ruins, stepping over broken bricks, scorched scraps of wood, bits of vases and even a few soggy fireworks.

I didn't notice the discrepancy until I was about to leave, though it was in the back of my mind the whole time. I think that's why I went. Part of me suspected all along.

I retraced my steps and checked the rubble again, this time with purpose. They weren't there. Not a trace of them.

I went home, washed and shaved for the first time since getting out of the hospital, then popped across to Bill's station. His ex-colleagues were sympathetic and let me study the photos of the site that had been taken back when the ashes were smoldering. There were photos from every conceivable angle. I went through each with a magnifying glass. It took hours but I was patient. Eventually I returned the file, said nothing, thanked the curious officers for their assistance and left.

There were no books.

Amid the rubble, the bits and pieces from Bill's past, ragged strips of clothes and blankets, splinters of porcelain and wood, there wasn't a single page from any of Bill's thousands of precious books. He'd cherished, loved and adored them. He'd spent so much time and money on them, but had often said he didn't care what happened to them once he was dead.

Bill's books—which only mattered to him as long as he was alive— had been removed. He'd known things were reaching a head, yet even with so much else to do, the *villacs* to cross, bombs to wire, his speech to compose, he'd taken the time to spirit the books away.

Why? So some other bibliophile could profit from his years of collecting? Nuh-uh. I didn't buy it. Bill shifted those books for one reason and one reason only—he wanted to take them with him.

I stayed locked in my apartment for months on end once I realized the voices were right, that Bill was still alive, out there somewhere, waiting, planning. I lay on my bed, stared at the vodka and reviewed my ruined life. I thought about Nic, Ellen, Wami, the Incas, and marveled at how much I'd lost. Mostly I'd think of the bottle and its demons, how easy it would be to let them have me, forget everything and place myself beyond Bill's reach, and the *villacs'*, and anyone else's who might have an interest in me.

Each day I grew closer to the bottle. I took it down and clutched it to my chest, slept with it, lived with it, unscrewed the top a hundred times a day, never sure if I'd replace it or down the liquid damnation. I was nearing my limit and couldn't have lasted much longer—a week, maybe two, and I'd have succumbed. I'd have lost all control, direction and purpose. I'd have been ruined, but free.

But things changed. A thought sneaked through the barriers of pain and grief and altered everything. I was recalling Bill and our conversation, as I'd been doing every day, when suddenly I flashed on his expression near the end, when I referred to Wami's triumph. I said the killer would come out of this laughing. Bill sneered and said he wouldn't laugh long, then muttered something about rising from the dead and getting even with him.

Rise from the dead my ass! Bill's not dead and Bill's not finished. He plans to return, but not from the grave. He's out there, alive, scheming. I wasn't Paucar Wami's only son. I'm sure Bill's sights are fixed on one of my half brothers, that he's intent on using him as he used me. I was a fool to think he'd give up, that he'd stop with me. There are others to do his dirty work. His hatred for Wami is so strong, and his thirst for *poetic justice* so overwhelming, that he won't be able to rest till one of Wami's children lays low their father.

The problem is, Paucar Wami doesn't exist anymore. He's fled these waters for seas beyond the confines of reality. Whether he snapped out of existence when The Cardinal jumped to his doom, or was disposed of by the *villacs*, he's gone and he ain't coming back. There's no one for Bill to set his hounds after.

I was willing to forgive Bill when I thought he was dead. Someone who'd blow himself up was to be pitied, not hated. But the thought of him faking his death, continuing the game, putting one of my half brothers through the crazed hell he had inflicted on me...

That pisses me off. It's drawn me away from self-pity, apathy, the vodka and its promise of release. I won't let the bastard get away with it. For what he did to me, Ellen and the others, death's the least he deserves. And I'm going to make sure the son of a bitch pays his dues.

But how to track him down? With no Paucar Wami to strike against, there's no reason for Bill to show his face, nothing to tempt him out of hiding. He went to a lot of trouble to make people think he was dead. He's unlikely to risk blowing his cover, not without Wami to tempt him. How can you entice a man out of hiding when the bait he hungers for no longer exists?

The answer struck me in the middle of a long dark night, as I lay staring at the bottle of vodka—send the dead to catch the dead! Paucar Wami must return to haunt the streets of the city. If the killer can be brought back to life, I'm sure Bill will seek him out like a knight of King Arthur's upon hearing a rumor of the Holy Grail. Bill won't have forgotten Wami. His hatred will have kept his memories of the killer alive. I can't resurrect Wami physically, but his spirit can be rekindled, and when it is…

There's not much of a view from this apartment. A filthy avenue and the backs of a couple of buildings. But it's great for studying the sky come evening. I sit by the window and watch the sun fade on the horizon. I let my eyes linger on its jagged shadows, stretched out like so many blood-stained fingers across the sky. I stare into the red flames of horizoned hell, and empathize with the tortured edge of the Earth's rim.

When the sun drops out of sight and the glass turns reflective, I study my face. I shaved my head two nights ago, with an electric razor. It was hard to adapt to—bald, I realized how closely I resembled my father—but I'm getting used to it. I no longer jump nervously when I spot my reflection.

The left side of my face is the same as before, but when I rotate my neck a twisting snake comes into view. The tattooing will take longer than I thought. The design I asked for is tricky to create, and will require time and patience to get right. But I can wait. A week or two won't matter. When it's finished, I'll have the tattoos and the smooth skull, as well as the motorcycle. The clothes will be easy to replicate. Then I'll take his name, hit the streets and spread the word—*Wami's back!*

That should draw Bill out. He'll have to investigate. Even if he senses a trap, he won't be able to stay away. His hatred will drag him out of his pit and back into the playpen of the city. When it does, and he shows himself, I'll capture him, put a knife to his throat, kiss him once on the forehead, then make a swift end of him. Mere murder wasn't revenge enough for Bill Casey, but it will do for me.

But what if he doesn't show? What if the charade isn't enough to lure him out of hiding?

I spin away from the window and study the photo hanging next to the bottle of vodka, the snapshot of Bill and a young Priscilla Perdue. My eyes turn to the trinket hanging from a chain around my neck—Bill's little finger, varnished so it will last. I stroke it from tip to base, as I have many times since I conceived the ruse to tempt Bill out into the open.

The look might not be enough. Bill's no fool. Maybe he won't fall for rumors alone. I may have to do more than re-create my father's image. Wami's body of work might also have to be duplicated.

I think I'll have to kill.